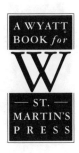

A WYATT
BOOK *for*

W

— ST. —
MARTIN'S
PRESS

THE CUSTODIANS

· NICHOLAS JOSE ·

A Wyatt Book *for* St. Martin's Press

New York

ISBN 0-312-18073-X

First published in Australia by Pan Macmillan Australia Pty Limited

First U.S. Edition: January 1998

10 9 8 7 6 5 4 3 2 1

for Rosemary Creswell

Many countries, many stories, many lies.

Aboriginal cameleer Tom Ljonga
in conversation with anthropologist
T.G.H. Strehlow, 1932

Contents

PART ONE

· ECLIPSE ·

1

THE children found it strange that the sun went dark, and stranger still that the round silver moon could turn into a flat black disc, giving off no light of its own. In the pinhole camera a cartoon image of the moon was passing in slow motion across the sun. The schoolyard had descended into gloom, as if the sky were filled with dirty smoke from a great burning-off. Only Alex, when the teachers were not looking, stared directly at the real thing with his naked eye, until the moon let the sun erupt again from the other side with a paring of light so bright it would brand the retina forever. Jane and Wendy and Elspeth and Ziggy checked that Alex's gaze did not flinch from the celestial beings in the dance of their orbits. But when he turned to his friends, blinking wide, he could not see them at all. He saw only a fingernail of light burning against the sphere of total blackness.

'Are you blind?' asked Ziggy.

'No, no, I'm not. Only wait –'

'Tell us what you see,' demanded Jane. There was something strange about Alex. He covered his eyes with his hands while the others looked on in horror.

Then he peeped out through his fingers. 'I can see you,' he said.

'He's lying,' said Wendy.

'Alex, are you sure?' asked Elspeth.

'Of course I'm sure. You're Elspeth, aren't you? Ziggy. Wendy. Jane.' Alex laughed with relief. What the teachers had said was wrong. He had proved that you could look directly at a total eclipse of the sun if you wanted, if you believed no harm would come to you.

'You're the winner then,' said Jane. 'What's your prize?'

'You can push me on the wheel as fast as it will go.'

So they spun him and spun him until he was dizzy and screaming for them to stop, and Mrs Hazlitt the school principal came over and told the children to behave.

When the wheel stopped turning, Alex fell to his knees in the dirt and put his head between his thighs to stop it spinning. The others stood in a circle around him. He looked up at them, then scraped the ground and held up a handful of the red playground dirt.

'There's another thing,' he bragged. 'You can eat dirt.'

'You can't,' laughed Jane.

'You can so,' insisted Alex. 'Dirt's no different from food.'

'Do it then,' said Wendy.

'Yuk!' groaned Elspeth. Alex was always so disgusting. He sat behind her in class and tied her plaits together. She had called him a bloody bugger.

'I will if you will,' bargained Alex.

'Certainly not,' said Elspeth. 'You're mad!'

'I will if Alex does,' offered Ziggy.

'You'll get sick,' squealed Elspeth.

'You don't believe me,' said Alex. 'Well, here goes.'

'Dogs eat dirt when they get ill. When their noses go dry. To make themselves vomit,' said Wendy.

The capacity of all things to be turned upside down was palpable while the dirty brown light filled the sky: sun and moon, light and dark, poison and food, right and wrong. That was the dare Alex Mack had taken. That was the bet. He had a palm full of dirt from the circle where the wheel was turning. Sifting a little through his fingers, he held the dirt up so they could see. He picked out the stones. Then bending his head, he clapped his hand to his mouth. The dry dirt coated his tongue. He tried to swallow, but it clogged his throat. He kept his mouth closed, his palm empty save for a dusting where the dirt stuck to his skin. The others were shocked and impressed.

'Say Ah!' ordered Jane.

When Alex opened his mouth, they saw how the dirt had been swallowed down that pulsating red hole. He had tears in his eyes from the distaste of it. Like a comedian, he turned to walk away, only rolling back to say: 'Your turn, Ziggy.'

'Don't you dare, Ziggy!' protested Elspeth.

'You'll get foot-and-mouth disease,' said Jane.

'Very funny,' answered Alex. 'Go on, Ziggy,' he coaxed, scared suddenly by what he had done. He wanted someone else to join him.

'I won't let you,' said Elspeth.

Ziggy bent down and scooped up a small handful of dirt as gracefully as if he were picking a strawberry. He looked at what he held and screwed up his nose, then he tossed his red hair out of his eyes and bowed his head to his hand in silence.

'I won't look,' said Elspeth.

Ziggy put out his wet pink tongue and licked the dirt. Then he retched. He ran to the seat of the carousel and spewed, barking and spitting until every last grain of dirt was removed from his mouth.

'That's where dirt belongs,' announced Jane.

'It won't go down,' said Wendy.

Ziggy looked back at them over his shoulder as his body disgorged the same substance that Alex's had taken in. The girls were giggling. Ziggy laughed back.

Elspeth turned to Alex like a cross mother. 'Go and wash your mouth out, Alex Mack!'

Then the bell was ringing to end the day. The eclipse had swallowed up the afternoon.

The dogs in the suburban yards were barking more than usual as Alex walked home. He was not in a mood to be pestered. If he detoured to avoid the barking dogs, he could loop down the hill through the park and cross the railway line to the street of close-together houses of white stone and red brick, where people sat on their front porches watching the passers-by over low fences – and Josie Ryan lived.

Josie was so white she could not go out in the sun. On the day of the total eclipse, that summer of 1958, she stayed in the scented rooms of her house. There were too many children for the teachers at the Catholic school to manage. When she was outside, Josie had to cover up from top to toe in a long dress with floppy sleeves, long white socks and patent-leather shoes, gloves and a straw hat with a band of blue flowers. She lived with her fat freckled mother, Mrs Ryan, and another Mrs Ryan, her mother's mother, whose skin looked like it had been scribbled on and who, despite her white stick, knew everything that went on. After school, while Mrs Ryan Senior rocked on the porch with a cup of tea in her lap, the younger Mrs Ryan, whose name was Audrey, did her bets from the paper with a brown bottle of beer on a table beside her and Josie, running beads through her fingers, watched the street through the pruned crepe myrtle. Josie had two black spots on her white skin. No one knew what would happen if the sun did get her. One day she told Alex Mack that if she took her hat off in the sun, the spots would spread to cover her whole face.

Alex got the giggles as he walked past the house. The interior was dark, the lace curtains drawn, but you could look right through to the statue of the Virgin Mary that glowed against the fiery sunset.

Josie's grandmother asked who it was and Josie, giving a cross glance, said it was no one.

When Alex reached the railway crossing the boom gate was down. He listened for the train's roar. At the last moment he ducked under the bar and ran across the tracks and up the hill before the stationmaster could yell at him. Then he was home, slamming the back door shut.

His mother appeared in a white tennis dress, her face hot and pink with a blue band holding down her curly fair hair.

'Darling, your mouth's all green.'

'It's only snakes,' Alex said, pulling the sweet snake out of his mouth to watch it curl. At the corner shop he had bought three snakes – a green snake for himself, a red one to keep for Josie, and a yellow one to spare.

'I'll butter you a finger bun,' his mother said. 'Elspeth Gillingham says you were silly at school today. She says you ignored the warning not to look at the eclipse.'

'I heard what they said.'

'And you ignored it. You looked straight into the sun with your naked eye.'

'You don't have to believe Elspeth. Anyway nothing happened to me, Mum, did it?'

'Don't be a know-all, Alex. It's not nice.' She grinned at her smart little devil, then looked out the window at the lacy leaves and splendid blue daubs of the jacaranda across the lawn. She had made Barb Gillingham, Elspeth's mother, run to return her serve that afternoon. It was her way of welcoming her friend home – back in Adelaide from overseas, from Italy. Sometimes Clarice Mack's life seemed hollow in comparison with Barb's. But after beating Barb Gillingham at tennis, Clarice always felt good. 'Elspeth had some hits with us, Alex, when she got home from school. Where have you been? You should've come over. You could practise with her. Elspeth's a lovely girl.' His mother flashed him a complicit smile.

'She's a bossy-boots,' retorted Alex, swinging his legs under the chair.

'She's *such* a lovely girl,' cooed his mother. The Gillinghams had a tennis court and a swimming pool hemmed by petunias. No object inside their grand two-storey colonial box of a house failed to make a public statement. The Macks' rambling bungalow was more of an accumulation; the rooms faded when people left them. The Macks had to keep their own world going by themselves, and so it was that Clarice Mack imagined Barb Gillingham's daughter Elspeth with her hair ruffled by the wind leaning from the balcony to young Alex, who stood on the steps below with his hair combed and his know-all look on his face. 'You and Elspeth will make a lovely couple one day.'

'Yuk, Mum. She's taller than me. She's like a giraffe.'

'Pigs play with their food, you two,' Clarice scolded, taking a sip of her gin and tonic. Her husband Tim had not come home yet and the kids were eating so slowly that the rainbow icecream had melted into grey soup. She pulled off her sweaty head band and tossed out her curls, sighing at her daughter and son. 'Bedtime, children! Bedtime, Susan! Bedtime, Alex!'

By Alex's bedside his mother teased: 'Shall I go on with the story of the bride and groom? Elspeth and Alex? Mr and Mrs Mack Junior!'

'Stop it, Mum.'

He shuffled his head along the pillow until, pressing against her, he could smell her perfume and feel the rise and fall of her body's breathing. On the ceiling the cracks and shadows formed a giant spider.

'I spy with my little eye something beginning with E,' his mother was murmuring.

'I give up,' he said. He let himself float on the secure rhythm of her heartbeat.

'E for Eclipse,' she replied, circling his eyes with her index finger. 'We'll have to get Dr Gillingham to test your eyes. But we won't tell Dad when he gets home, will we?'

~

Josie bent over her bed, her chin in the chenille bedspread. In her prayers she pictured herself serving a beautiful baked dinner at a table where her mother and her grandmother sat up like ladies and her father, Tom, back from the dead in a white suit and black bowtie, carved the meat with a silver knife. Her father was never mentioned except in prayers. There were no photos of him in the house. He had no name but Tom. When her mother was inflamed with emotion, tears rolling down her cheeks at the sad bits of a bed-time story, Josie would cry too. 'What's Tom doing now, do you think, up in heaven?' she would ask.

Then Audrey would grab her with a noisy convulsion, half sob, half pitying laughter. 'If only he was in heaven, my love.'

Josie had seen the man lying on his back across the step in the morning and the sun moving him from shadow to glare as she passed by with her schoolcase in her hand. The man's arms and legs were splayed, his face ruddy, with a purple-grey undercolour, his thick hair flaring around his head where he lay, and she could hear his heavy breath. The night before, her mother had announced that Tom the Father was back and waiting down in the pub. Never a word of explanation had been said to Tom about the child, and after discovering Audrey Ryan's situation, he had never once said that he loved the woman and wanted to be with her for the rest of his life. Tom was not interested in sacraments. So Audrey told the bastard to piss off, back to the hinterland and the rodeo circuit, where he came from. Only once in a blue moon he came sniffing round just to make sure that the proud Ryan women still needed him, and Audrey would put on her flowery dress and curl her hair sweet and lovely and go out to show that no one needed him. That brought the frown to his brow – the furrow that Josie had inherited.

The key fumbled in the lock, the door slammed, the kitchen light went on. There was the shrilling of the kettle for a cup of tea. Josie heard her mother's restless steps. Her grandmother was up too. It was the next morning as Audrey took Josie to school that they found Tom lying on the step outside the pub. The publican was hosing down the front tiles, letting the man lie there for all the world to see. Josie bent over the man's plum-red lips and the glistening stubble on his brick-red skin and smelled his breath, dog's breath, and touched him, as heavy and unmoving as the sofa in their front room.

In imitation of her mother, Josie walked on, decisively, continuing her way to school. 'Pray for my dad,' she whispered that night to the chenille bedspread, beseeching the image of a drunken man sleeping off his sorrow in the morning, spreadeagled across the half-shaded step outside the pub that was called The Crow.

Audrey Ryan had a basket of ironing to do before she could call it a day. The iron hissed when she tested it with her finger. Five shillings a load, supplement to the child endowment and her mother's invalid pension. She pounded the iron down on Mrs Gillingham's ruffled pillow slip, flattening it against the patched ironing cloth on the kitchen table. Finding her rhythm, she began to hum in company with the volley of dialogue from the radio play. She could never keep a tune.

'Girlie-girlie-girLEES!' chortled Mrs Woodruff, stalking outside the door of her daughter's room. 'Henry the Eighth had six wives. When he wanted a new one, he had the old one BEHEADED, and when he couldn't chop off *her* head, he got a DIVORCE, only the Pope won't let Catholics get divorced, so Henry the Eighth said he was a Catholic no longer, he was King of the Church of England. Know your history, girls!'

Wendy Sunner and Jane Woodruff squeezed their thighs to stop themselves from bursting. They had barricaded the door and turned out all the lights except one that was wrapped in a beaded shawl to work their transformation into fairy princesses.

Jane cut out the cardboard crowns and coloured them in. Wendy went through the dress-up trunk.

'The women were chattels of men's POWER, girls, until Elizabeth came along,' called Mrs Woodruff, 'the VIRGIN Queen!'

That brought on a renewed surge of giggles. Wendy found a satin slip and a scarlet chiffon scarf with golden threads. She brushed her hair to make it stand on end and when she did the hula in the mirror she looked *bee-you-tee-ful*. Placing the circle of cardboard delicately on Wendy's head, careful not to let the wet glue come apart, Jane rolled her eyes at her own leering reflection in the mirror – a vixenish handmaiden to Wendy, who put on a princess's swept-up look to match her crown.

'But the person Queen Elizabeth feared most was not any man but another woman, her own COUSIN Mary.' Mrs Woodruff pronounced it Meery with a rolling Scots grrh.

Jane put on the crimson Chinese dressing gown, covered with sprays of gold chrysanthemum, which her mother had brought back from Hong Kong. Then she put on the coloured plumage of her crown. She felt proud and tarty as the independent second fairy princess. Wendy licked Jane's pencil and rubbed carmine hard on her lips and cheeks. She did her eyebrows cobalt blue.

Mrs Woodruff's history lesson had disappeared down the corridor to the living-room, where the girls' homework was spread out on the table, and the girls came spinning in a fairy dance, chanting their high music. Jane's mother removed her glasses and opened her mouth wide in a show of amazement.

'Oh clever girls! Did you make the crowns yourselves?'

As they danced, Dr Woodruff came in the front door. The girls ran to him like dragonflies and escorted him to his seat. Jane slipped in between his thighs and threw her arms round his neck. Wendy pirouetted, eyes cast upwards, in a circle just beyond his knees.

Wendy did not understand why she had to go away and stay with Jane when her younger sister Sandy had stayed with their father, or why her mother went into hospital to get their new little brother and came home with nothing. Her father had dropped his voice, and her mother was weeping, when he talked to Jane's mother on the phone.

'Jane made the crowns,' reported Mrs Woodruff.

Jane had stopped her act, but Wendy continued her charged vibrations, her arms shuddering like insect wings. Through thick black-rimmed glasses, Dr Woodruff's scientist's eyes ogled his seven-year-old-daughter's little friend. She made his bushy eyebrows twitch, tempting him to reach out and grab her. She was like an electron passing through concentric rings of particles to the hypothetical central mass of his soul.

'We were able to watch the eclipse through our new telescope,' Dr Woodruff reported with satisfaction. 'With adjustments to the intensity of light we were able to see the shadows extending over the face of the moon.'

His wife nodded, affirming the achievements of the Weapons Research Establishment where her husband worked.

'Where's John?' Dr Woodruff asked, wanting to share the information with his son.

'You know,' said Mrs Woodruff. 'He's staying over with Garry Adams while Wendy's with us.'

'We only saw it through the pinhole camera,' grumbled Jane. 'Except for Alex Mack.'

Dr Woodruff said that the Japanese children who saw the atom bomb explode were blinded by the blast. The same could happen during a total eclipse. That was why his institute gave blindfolds to the Aborigines in the desert when they conducted their atomic tests.

Wendy saw a man's face, black and round as the eclipsing moon, coming for her with shining eyes and mouth. He rustled the bushes. His body was the night that filled the window behind the drawn-down blind. She let out a cry.

Jane snuffled, rolling over in the other bed.

'Jane?' called Alison Woodruff, alert in an instant to the empty space beside her.

'Wendy's had a bad dream,' Jane called back. 'It's all right, Mum. I'll look after her.'

Wendy was gasping. Something had pounced on her in the darkness – inexplicable, terrible.

'I saw him,' she whispered to Jane, climbing into her friend's bed and clinging to her, as if they were butterflies in love. 'He wanted to get me.'

'What would you do if there really was someone?' asked Jane.

Footsteps crunched on the gravel outside and a shadow crossed the blind.

Wendy hissed, digging her fingers into Jane. 'There *is* someone. He's coming in.'

Dr Woodruff had come into the garden to renew his wonder at what had been achieved by the precise calculations of science to pinpoint the eclipse within the infinity of time and space that day. In pyjamas and slippers, he gazed at the moon, captivated, holding the abstract laws of the universe in balance with a world that smelled of complex esters of jasmine and eucalyptus.

Then the girl screamed and a kerfuffle erupted inside. Not his daughter, the other girl. 'All *quiet*, girls,' he commanded in a low voice as his nightwatchman's shadow passed close to their door.

Jane squeezed Wendy, cuddling her to make her feel there was nothing to fear. Then she turned on the light under the beaded shawl and found her coloured pencils and block. While Wendy slept beside her, Jane drew, creating the great round spotted mask of the monster man. A clown. A bearded king. Her father. Deep into the night she rubbed her pencils, so hard that the colours shone.

~

The mining company in the north dug silver, lead and zinc from holes in the round red hills and sent the ore south to Adelaide by train, hundreds of miles. From the top of the hill the excavating machines at the bottom of the cut looked like toys. On the other side was a weed-covered pile of leavings where stunted trees shimmered in the pungent haze. Scrambling over the great mound, caked in mud, Alex used to find the stones that his father identified as silver, zinc or fool's gold – fists of ore in the web of his father's rough palm, then warm in the boy's pocket.

Now he displayed his collection on the windowsill of his bedroom where shafts of light made the stones shine like jewels. Since they had moved to the city, his father wore a pale shirt and a tie to work each day and in the piles of paper he carried back and forth he monitored the company's costs and projections, connected to the hacked-open hills of the mining town, but also now to faraway places, markets overseas, to what was in the news, wages, taxes, commodity prices, everything that made the world run. Sometimes a calendar of Japanese scenes or a copy of *Fortune* magazine found its way home, and once a bamboo cigarette case with a panda on it. Otherwise there was always the light, striking his samples of ore, to remind Alex of three-dimensional geometry and the stint in the mining town that his mother had detested.

It was in his second year at primary school after the Macks' move to Adelaide that Ziggy Vincaitis came along. The first time Alex brought him home after school Ziggy glided around the house like such a lordling that Mrs Mack asked who the strange little boy's parents were. He had come from somewhere so strange and faraway that it did not even connect with the world of Tim Mack's work, from a place that did not exist any more called Lithuania. Clarice Mack said Ziggy was a Balt, a reffo. Having learned English from an elocution teacher in the migrant camp, he spoke like a radio announcer. At school he was proudly claimed as a New Australian. But Dr Gillingham, Elspeth's father, said that the boy was a poor bloody refugee.

After putting dirt in his mouth on the day of the eclipse, Ziggy was allowed to join their gang.

'Ziggy!' Jane called, waiting in her Brownie uniform by the opening to the stormwater drain that was silted up and overgrown with weeds. 'Ready!'

Wendy tied her scarf with its yellow Good Work badges over Ziggy's eyes and led him forward. Alex lit a candle and stood it up in an old paint tin. Jane and Elspeth pushed Ziggy down into a kneeling position.

'The ground is wet,' Ziggy whined.

Alex took Ziggy's hand and held it over the candle until the heat of the flame began to burn his skin. He held it for another thirty seconds. Ziggy tried to decipher the smells of wax and paint fumes. He was squirming but he did not cry out or even screw up his face. With an expression of calm nobility, he slowly withdrew his hand when Alex released it.

'That's guts,' acknowledged Jane with a click of her tongue.

Wendy undid the blindfold. Then she pulled out a packet of cigarettes from her skirt pocket and passed one to each person in celebration. Jane picked up the candle and offered round the flame. Liquid wax scalded her hand, but she did not flinch either. They puffed – first Alex, then Ziggy. They were coughing. Only Wendy knew how to inhale. She could make smoke rings pop from her lips.

Alex was hot all over from the thrill of Ziggy's submission. Henceforward and forever Ziggy was initiated into the gang. He was eight then and Alex was seven, and they became best friends.

Mrs Titzoff Hazlitt, as the kids called her, wore prickly suits of dark wool to encase a splendid bosom that heaved in harmony with her rousing address to the school. Ziggy told Alex about a magician at the Lithuanian club who released a family of white doves from his mother's bra. One day at assembly when Mrs Titzoff was invoking Goodness, with her wide white lapel folded crisply back against her green serge jacket, a blowfly commenced a journey down among the white doves of her cleavage and the boys could not control themselves.

'There are some people who find the notion of Goodness funny,' said Mrs Hazlitt, pausing in her speech as the spluttering grew louder. 'Vincaitis. Mack. Wipe that insolence off your faces.' She moved in like a sheepdog through the whispering grass and bobbing flowers of the assembly, cuffing the boys round the shoulders and sending them to her office.

Whish! Whish! Whish! Each boy held his palm out for a caning, screwing up his eyes to hold back the tears.

Afterwards Ziggy said to Alex he wondered whatever happened to the fly and they started giggling all over again.

Alex's mother heard about the boys eating dirt in the playground and hanging round the stormwater drain. When she heard about the caning, she wrote a letter to Mrs Vincaitis to complain about Ziggy's bad influence over her son. She wanted Alex and Ziggy separated. Ziggy read the letter out loud to his mother. In bloodcurdling stage Lithuanian Vida Vincaitis cursed the stinking meddling Australian cows that dropped their dung all over the place. The letter went straight into the bin.

Clarice Mack was waiting in her car outside the school gates when the woman came out. She looked like a foreign movie star, elegant, poised, a little nervous, with every accessory matching.

'Mrs Vincaitis? Excuse me, I'm Alex's mother. I think you received my letter.'

Vida Vincaitis refused to take her glasses off to acknowledge Mrs Mack. 'Because of you I take my son away from this school. Because of this we move to another place. Better school, better place,' said Mrs Vincaitis with a smile of continental movie-star charm. She called to her son in Lithuanian. Recognising his duty, Ziggy took his mother's hand and turned away with her down the street, giving Mrs Mack a flick of his golden eyes just to make sure that she appreciated the dramatic resolution of the scene.

Mrs Vincaitis and her son were still standing at the bus stop further down the street when Mrs Mack drove past. She had picked up her kids. Susan sat beside her in the front seat of the car and Alex in the back. Alex waved, but Ziggy pretended not to see.

Later the other mothers said that the Vincaitis boy was taken away because the used car business had failed and his father could no longer afford the school fees. The Vincaitises moved down the hill, to the other side of the parklands, to live behind a shop. People said it was a shame that Ziggy had to go to a state school when he showed such promise.

~

In his last year at the primary school Alex played Jesus in the Christmas play. Not Baby Jesus in the manger with the shepherds and the three wise men – a younger class did that, the girl with developed breasts playing Mary, all in blue, nursing a doll while the choir sang and a dried-out cow and a bad-tempered Shetland pony stood in the straw giving off odours of humility – but Jesus the precocious boy-child running away from his earthly father's carpentry shop to visit the temple. Tall Elspeth played Joseph, who discovers his child Jesus astonishing the elders with his wisdom. The elders were Wendy and Jane, costumed in their fathers' tartan dressing gowns, with beach towels for turbans. As Jesus, Alex – he was eleven now – wore a striped blanket with a hole cut for his neck and Roman sandals on his feet. He spoke with exaggerated Biblical simplicity before the audience of family and friends that gathered on rugs and picnic chairs on the grass. The sports stand, turned into a stage for the occasion, was strung with fairy lights and glowed with a yellow spot that could swivel round to strafe the surrounding bushes if anyone got up to mischief.

'Don't you know I am about my father's business?' asked Alex, centre-stage, holding his finger in the air as he made his pronouncements, raising his eyebrows to hint at a mysterious power. Jesus's real father was God.

Then in the darkness he caught sight of Josie Ryan watching him.

Josie and her mother had come out for a stroll on this clear evening and, passing the gates of the school, saw a sign announcing the Christmas play. The sports stand, lit up beside the playing field, beckoned them. 'Go on, Mum,' said Josie, 'let's see what the Proddies are up to.'

'For a lark,' grinned Audrey Ryan.

The fathers stood at the back discussing politics in gruff voices. Mr Mack and Dr Gillingham were amused by the education on which they spent so much money. Mr Mack said it was wrong that Protestant private schools should be denied the government subsidy that went to the state schools and that the run-down Catholic schools were claiming too. But Dr Woodruff said they were paying for a better quality product.

Mrs Ryan lit up a cigarette, aware of sidelong glances from the men, while Josie slipped forward through the herd of adult bodies to where she could see Alex Mack prancing about as if he were coated in honey.

'*O Come All Ye Faithful*' everyone droned together to end the play. Voices rolled bravely from the sports stand, discordant and gradually diminished, carrying the tribal anthem up to the starry night.

Alex stood between his happy parents to receive congratulations from the elders in the audience and good wishes for the future. He would be going on to a different school now, where the boys were separated from the girls.

Then Josie crept up to him. Waiting for her, exultant in the moment, he kissed her pale cheek. 'Happy Christmas, Josie,' he said, blushing with surprise at himself.

Josie rubbed her branded cheek and pulled away. She was embarrassed – a stranger among these big laughing people. 'Stop acting, will you! Beware the sin of pride, Alex Mack.' Her eyes sparkled and she gave a throaty chuckle. 'Acting Jesus indeed! It's blasphemy!'

'It's only a play,' he retorted.

But Josie Ryan bent away from him like a slender reed in the wind. He stopped himself from reaching out to grab her, and she was gone.

~

The times when Alex and Josie could meet after that, as they grew up, were always a secret.

'If I married you, it would be a public service,' Josie joked to him. He had waited for her at the railway crossing. She was as pale as could be under her wide floppy hat, with her fringe cut like Cleopatra's, and fiercely logical. 'Not to save your soul, though that would be worth doing, since you'd have to become a Catholic to marry me – but for the sake of making amends. There are all those orphan kids we could rear as our own. Your parents' house would have room for all of them.'

It was not the naughty elopement that he imagined, with Josie white under her hat in a frilly dress as in the First Communion photograph she showed him, and himself in the robe of an oriental prince, escaping through a secret door to a world beyond. But he quite liked the sound of conversion.

'I don't believe in God,' said Alex.

'Same difference,' Josie replied. 'He believes in you. One of the drops in the ocean of God's tears because your heart is closed to Him.'

The train clanked past, the boom gates lifted. They crossed the tracks and followed the path behind the brewery where the air smelled richly of malt.

Josie imagined Tom her lost father as God the Father now, his face like Our Lord's on the Shroud, and her own birth as an Immaculate Conception. She did not doubt that she was chosen.

'Can we hold hands?' asked Alex.

Holding hands was the second rung of the numerical ladder by which the boys at his new school measured their progress with girls.

Josie's cheeks burned rose. She was solemn. 'No, I'm not ready yet.'

Alex did not altogether understand the wickedness of his suggestion. He smarted with desire to put his hand out and touch Josie's shining Elizabeth Taylor hair, to kiss her curling lips and the two black spots on her cheeks, to check whether her skin was the same white all over. Stopping outside her gate he responded to the daring she read in his darting eyes. She wanted him to be perfect for her before she would ever let him touch her. Her condition was a quest for perfection – nothing less. She understood that he crossed a line to come to her, singling her out among women – and she was ambitious to move in the direction he came from, to achieve a social power to match her spiritual standing and make redress – but she saw that she and Alex Mack could do no more than walk a stretch of the road together. Class and clan, distrust and contempt would divide them more forcefully than their mutual recognition confirmed them to each other.

'Forgive me, Alex, and forget me,' Josie said, opening the gate just wide enough to slip herself inside. Ducking her head, aware of his presence at the edges of her vision, she strode up the path without turning back, leaving him standing in the street as she went inside her front door, with nothing but his eyes scalding and a blaze of anger in his heart.

2

THE Vincaitises' mixed business had a smoked smell. They sold tea, sugar, butter, bacon bones, wrinkled apples, tired lettuce, pickles, dried mushrooms and continental sausage. When Ziggy draped himself in the coloured plastic strips that hung in the doorway to keep the flies out, the little interior was as seductive as a nightclub. Milk bottles, black babies, ripe raspberries, freckles and snakes. Icecreams and assorted lollies. On days when Ziggy worked in the shop after school, Mrs Vincaitis, in a gold knitted top and dark glasses to accentuate her Eva Marie Saint bone structure, waited on the street corner for a man to take her away in his car. She would be back by five o'clock, when Mr Vincaitis got home from his job. An aristocrat in Lithuania, Karolis Vincaitis had never worked in a factory before coming to this so-called New Australia, this Englishman's garbage dump, this arsehole of the earth. *Pasaulio šiknaskyle.*

The chocolate factory where he worked was owned by Wilbert Sunner, who was Wendy Sunner's grandfather. Wilbert's father had come from Germany to Christianise the Aborigines of the Central

Australian desert, and Wilbert had inherited the knowledge of running a God-fearing enterprise, combining labour and capital to produce profit and godliness, from that stern Lutheran. It was Mr Vincaitis's job to introduce refinements of European taste to the confectionary range for a more complex modern market.

'Why don't we go down the chocolate factory?' asked Alex, calling into the shop after school. It was insinuation as much as request.

Ziggy, in position behind the counter when Alex entered, tossed his red fringe out of his eyes. 'I don't know if Mum can mind the shop,' he croaked, fluttering his eyelashes.

'Do they pay you for this work?' sneered Alex.

'All the liverwurst I can eat.'

'Poo!'

'*Siegfriedeli! Siegfriedeli!*' sang a woman's voice from the inner room.

'She's sick today,' Ziggy mouthed, putting on a face of disappointment.

Mrs Vincaitis appeared in a satin housecoat of forget-me-not blue. She had pompom slippers on her feet. Alex wanted to touch her face, the lips glossy with Cha-cha red, the hair sprayed in place like a helmet.

'*Kas čia per vaikas?*' She looked through her dark glasses at the skinny figure of Ziggy's friend, putting a languorous hand to her brow and running a Cha-cha fingernail along her hairline. Then she sighed, turning to the shelf where the medicines were on display. 'Next time, boys,' she smiled solicitously, selecting a painkiller and withdrawing again to the bedroom.

Ziggy rolled his eyes at Alex, who laughed. 'What can I offer you instead?' he growled, lifting the glass tray of the sweets counter. 'Get your mitts into that, mate.'

Ziggy and Alex had the same piano teacher in the city. They would meet on the stairs behind the church that led to the piano teacher's little room. It was a zone their parents could not police, the time in between, between buses, a no-man's-land that was free for the boys. They sneaked off to see *A Hard Day's Night* at the specially built My Fair Lady theatre one afternoon. They were separated, attending different schools, living in different suburbs, and Ziggy, at thirteen now, was a teenager. But they stayed friends.

Solomon T. Cross had a scalp that looked like one of the eggs Ziggy's mother rubbed with cochineal and bacon fat for Lithuanian Easter. His scant silver hair produced snow that mixed with ash from his perpetual cigarette as it drifted down to his olive-green cardigan and his pupils' shoulders. His fingers were dyed a deep nicotine yellow, and from those extremities the colour spread to his flaky face, his teeth, his lips, even to the piano keys, as if it were a distillation of music. It was an adventure to enter that yellowed cave where the smoke eddied upwards through the sunlight to the small open window and the worn Persian rug rumpled every time the piano stool was adjusted. There was a small library, a desk cluttered with correspondence of a mostly financial nature, an armchair with a mulga wood ashtray stand and a black upright piano with keys kept loose by playing. Framed on the wall beside the qualifications of Solomon T. Cross was a print of Chopin – forever young.

Mr Cross would bring his weight to bear on his young pupils' bodies. He would press the shoulders, rearrange the spine, lift the hands and lower the elbows until another creature took over, a new pianistic young person. He knew where in the spectrum of possibilities he could work on each one. Alex Mack would never be a true performer, but he was in awe of Solomon T. Cross's own compositions and would urge the old teacher to play his great unfinished work *Fantasia on the Inland Sea*, or the *Ode to Albert Namatjira* that had won the Eisteddfod at Broken Hill, where Solomon had once met the noble Aboriginal painter. In his early years, before his talent made itself heard, Mr Cross had worked as a miner. His hands and arms worked the protesting piano as if he were hewing ore from a lifetime's passion and frustration, a crash and bang that had a personal fervour even the great Chopin could not elicit from the old man. The cigarette would burn down to the fag-end and Mr Cross would sweep the fallen ashes off the keys in a trill, then flop his watch out of his pocket, half turning to the door with a slight groan. Next!

He knew to win Ziggy with something less obdurate. This young Siegfried loved melody and, although he cheated on practice, he played with grace and charm. He had a good voice too. Often when he was working in the shop he would sing with stagey projection and his mother would join in with *Roses from Tyrol* or *Barcarole* or sometimes she would sing the Moon Maiden's part in the love duet from *Kęstutis ir Birute*, the national opera of Lithuania, and he would do the Knight of the Sun. Ziggy loved it when their singing made the neighbour's dog bark and kept the customers out of the shop.

Solomon T. Cross developed a repartee with Ziggy about great opera houses and enchanted soirees, tragic Chopin again, and he trained the boy in rhythm and dynamics, the use of the pedal to boom, the ripple of the hand to wring the heart. At the climax, in that warm close chamber, after the *Dream of Love* by Liszt (simplified for four hands), there would be tears in Ziggy's eyes, and Mr Cross, moaning a vocal refrain, would knot the boy's hands together on his thighs and mouth with smoky breath through yellow teeth, '*Bravo,* Siegfried!' *Sotto voce.* '*Bravo caro!*'

Alex waited for Ziggy at the bus stop. Ziggy had not done his practice and would be pleased to skip the music lesson for once. But he was anxious about visiting the chocolate factory without his father's permission.

'Come on,' goaded Alex, 'your old man won't mind.' Easter was approaching, which meant chocolate eggs and rabbits.

The two boys walked along the wide street past the solid colonial buildings, the old fire station, the courthouse, the library for the blind and the Freemasons' Lodge. To reach the chocolate factory, which had stood for a hundred years, they had to cross the square, where the yellow and red leaves fallen from grandly disposed

European trees made overlapping circles all over the civic lawns. At the centre of the square people were lying among the leaves, and two women were standing, gesticulating, kicking the leaves up – acting as if they owned the place. With their bags and rugs and bottles, they looked as though they were preparing to camp the night. Then, as Alex and Ziggy strolled by, a bus pulled up to the stop by the square and a boy got off, about their own age, wearing the braided blazer of St Joeys, with his grey trouser legs at half mast. He was bigger than Ziggy or Alex, and stronger-looking, with his dark hair and brown skin. He skipped behind the bus, swinging his satchel, and strode through the carpet of leaves. When he reached the group, one of the two standing women threw her arms in the air in greeting and called out his name. 'Cleve!' she shouted. That was what it sounded like. Alex nudged Ziggy. They could not hear it exactly. Cleve?

Sheets of dried fruit were cut into cubes, dusted with drying powder and placed in a copper, then chocolate was added, made from cocoa butter and sugar mixed with cocoa beans from South America that had been roasted and pulverised in Wilbert Sunner's antique wooden machine. The cocoa husks went to fertilise the garden. Several batches a day of the famous apricot cubes were produced, except when each year, as Easter approached, the cool basement was turned over to making chocolate eggs, chickens, rabbits and coins from complicated German moulds. The chocolate was poured by hand into a hinged metal mould, then the mould was closed and spun in a wire basket until its sides were evenly coated. But there was a fair proportion of failure, particularly in the large standing hares, which meant a pile of rejected ears and paws to be feasted on.

The chocolate was mixed in a rectangular bath kept at an exact temperature that allowed molecules to align and the chocolate to set shiny. Old Wilbert's policy had always been to employ his own people. He would never employ the blacks from the mission that his evangelising parents used to receive in the drawing room among the silver. But two anti-German wars had pressured Wilbert Sunner to make clear whose side he was on. The first refugee he employed was a Jewish professor of chemistry from Austria, a fellow called Orgel who made significant improvements to the manufacturing technique. Then Wilbert's son Peter, who saw himself as an innovator, insisted on hiring Italians and Greeks and other migrants. It was Peter Sunner who suggested employing Karolis Vincaitis as an adjunct to the foreman, to work on quality control. The best chocolates were made by the women, enrobed by hand and decorated by finger. The women wore gloves when handling the chocolates to minimise variations in temperature. Those who were menstruating had to be taken off the job because their blood temperature might be different. It was Mr Vincaitis's job to monitor temperature, hygiene and other such niceties.

Ziggy normally took the old lift up to the management floor when he came to visit his father, but today he led Alex straight to the basement. The boys were excited by the magic of industrial process, the workers in their long aprons, the high brick walls and the heavy posts and rafters, the sparkling sugar and fine brown dust, the smell of oil and fat, and a whiff of fermenting fruit from the machine that cut up the famous apricot cubes. The chocolate worked on them like a drug. As they ran around without being stopped or questioned, their pulses raced. The women in gloves nodded at Ziggy, Mr Vincaitis's pretty red-haired lad.

The boys lifted the lid of the chocolate mixing bath and gazed at the arm moving slowly back and forth, folding liquid chocolate in wide lengths, as if it were a bolt of brown satin-velvet unrolled endlessly to meet an insatiable demand. They bowed their heads to the expanse of chocolate, drawn into the replenishing rhythm of the mechanical arm. Then Alex reached in with his index finger, holding it in mid-air as he waited for the wave of chocolate to break, feeling nothing but blood-warmth as a fold of chocolate washed over his fingertip. He grinned at the shiny chocolate cap, then popped his finger in his mouth to suck it clean.

'You do it,' he dared Ziggy.

Ziggy unbuttoned his cuff, rolled up his sleeve and inserted his finger with the precision of a scientist making a test.

Alex laughed as the brown wave ploughed effortlessly over the length of Ziggy's finger. 'Hold it up,' he said.

Proudly Ziggy stuck his finger in the air, waving it as the chocolate hardened. He delicately removed the drips and rings until his finger was smooth. Then he sucked it clean.

Alex tried again. He was scared of getting his hand caught by the machine's implacable arm. You had to go in and out in time.

'Put your whole hand in,' Alex whispered to Ziggy. 'I dare you.'

With a cheeky smile Ziggy concentrated on the movement of the mixing arm, noting the space it allowed, feeling its regularity in his body. He thrust his arm down into the vat and, as if responding to his move, the machine arm propelled a crest of liquid chocolate that broke over his forearm up to his elbow.

Ziggy squealed. He pulled back his arm and held up a fist clenched in a victorious gauntlet of dark glistening chocolate, hot still, cooling to a sleek skin.

Alex was breathless with excitement. 'How are you going to get it off?'

'You eat it,' commanded Ziggy in triumph. He held his fist to Alex's mouth and slowly uncurled his fingers. His chocolate palm was a craze of paler lines. He thrust out his fingers in a challenge. 'Go on, else I'll smear your face.'

They were like cannibals, eater and eaten, in an ecstasy of appetite as they fell to the floor.

A voice boomed from above. 'Where did these kids come from?'

Alex looked up the creased navy trousers. It was Wendy Sunner's father.

'Ditch that vat, Vincaitis. Germs!'

Behind Mr Sunner stood Ziggy's father in grey overalls, wringing his hands. His eyes rolled angrily as he recognised one of the sticky urchins as his son.

'We can't afford to lose it, sir. These boys are not dirty.'

'We have no option,' retorted Mr Sunner. 'We're a family company. We have our responsibilities to the public. We must maintain our standards. What if word got out? All our Easter sales would be ruined.'

Peter Sunner liked to reiterate mottoes. Then he could turn his back on a problem and hurry back behind the management door. He scribbled a note and attached it to the bulldog clip on a string that ran up and down the pipe between the management and the workers in the basement. There was a security problem. These kids should not have been able to get in.

Then Mr Vincaitis lunged at Ziggy, grabbing his son's besmirched arm. Oily with saliva, Ziggy's skin slipped from the man's grasp.

'Dad, don't!'

The man seized a hank of his son's lank hair and hauled him to his feet. 'Outside! Wait for me outside!'

Out of shame Karolis Vincaitis was prepared to disown his son. That was fine with Ziggy. 'You're not my father anyway,' Ziggy shouted, throwing his head back as his mother would have done and striding across the factory floor to the employees' exit in his practised nobility and calm. Alex disappeared. *He* did not want to be recognised.

But no bus came before the whistle blew to end the working day. That left Ziggy standing beside his father at the factory bus stop like the good son he was not. Across the road was a red-brick terrace leased from the chocolate factory by a brothel. Beside it was the city morgue. His father was fuming.

When they got home, Karolis shouted at his wife that Ziggy had humiliated him in front of young Mr Sunner and all the other employees. His own son, the shameless creature this country had made him, writhing on the floor with an Australian boy like a filthy animal. She was supposed to look after the boy. He was her son too. Ziggy was meant to mind the shop after school, not roam the streets. So Vida began to scream that it was the day the boy was supposed to go to his piano lesson after school and *she* was stuck at home minding the shop. She was sacrificing the best years of her life for her precious son's musical talent so he would grow up a civilised human being and not a savage little Australian, and what did Ziggy do to thank her, he played truant from his lesson. He let down the honourable teacher, Mr Solomon T. Cross, who did not take on every little boy that came his way. He schemed to meet his ruffian friend, to go with him and play their stupid tricks together. She always knew that Alex Mack was a bad influence on her son.

'The lesson was cancelled,' blurted Ziggy. 'Mr Cross was sick.'

'Then Mr Cross must make it up or we won't pay the bill. I want a letter from him,' said his mother with a dazzling smile.

It was always like this. Ziggy stood before his accusing parents with a desperate sense of wanting to escape. He cocked an eyebrow at his mother. 'I'm usually home in the afternoon.'

'Don't answer back,' she shrieked.

His mother was the one who went out in the afternoons, leaving her son alone with the shop. It was an arrangement they kept secret from Karolis. Vida became agitated and cross if she was ever delayed or prevented for some reason. Her afternoons were openings in her life that she could not afford to jeopardise, when she went window shopping, or strolled in a park, pretending to be somewhere else, where one day she might meet a prince. The woman met her son's golden eyes, understanding his threat to expose her, and with an open palm she slapped his face, warning him not to take any more risks. She depended on him, but she wanted to punish him too, because if he did not exist, none of them would be in this cruel place.

Vida Vincaitis admired the beautiful things of life so much that she had not grasped until too late how they could become worthless overnight. Like the splendid, beautiful woman she had been back in Vilnius, the lustrous performer in charity galas, the hope for the splendid, beautiful cultural life of her people, courted by a handsome young man from an aristocratic family who was a patriot, an intellectual – why should she not marry him? When the Germans came with their greater power, why should not she and her young husband salute them? There was no point in suffering. But the Germans had turned into monsters in Lithuania, making it preferable for those who could to move while it was still possible.

In one camp after another, as the war raged, Vida was invited to cocktails and dances until, when the war ended, she and her husband believed at last they would make the journey home. But their country had been swallowed up by the Russian Communists in the meantime. They travelled from one transit camp to another, ending up in Dachau, which had been turned from a death camp into a way station, and one last time Vida went to cocktails with the man in charge, an Italian American officer called Vittorio, and in that season of rapture she fell pregnant. But not, as was thought, to Vittorio, who arranged a transfer to a castle near Salzburg that the Americans had taken over, where Ziggy was born. She named him Victor, after Vittorio, as she had promised, and it was there that black-eyed American Vittorio presented his namesake with the Red Cross parcel of fleecy pyjamas, a little fur coat and the carved wooden bear, rearing on hind legs, which the child became obsessed by. After two more years of waiting, they were able to board a ship from Naples for Vladivostock, and from Vladivostock by the first ship out to Australia, to a migrant camp in Roma, Queensland. Vida never forgave Vittorio for not sending them to America, so she changed her son's name to Siegfried after the commandant of an earlier camp, who knew her worth – the one she read about later in the war crimes trials.

Karolis Vincaitis periodically drank himself blind. He owed his wife too much ever to let her go. He came from hunting stock in the old country. As a youth he had gone out in parties to slay wolves and bears. He had a frustrated hunter's nature and when his blood was up he knew he did not really possess his wife. After saving his skin she made a beast of him by refusing to act out further pleasure for his sake. She had acted too much with others. When he laid his hands on her, she bleated like a rabbit having its neck wrung.

'Help me, help me, little man,' Vida would plead, making Ziggy learn to intrude himself.

She sat on the sofa in front of the television doing her Cha-cha nails. Karolis went to the cupboard and poured himself half a glass of schnapps. He drank it down, then crooned with mocking charm, 'We're here because of you, dear one. Because of all you've done for us. How can we ever thank you, except perhaps with a little kiss on the mouth?' He came right up to her red lips.

'Where's my cold cream?' she asked, getting out of his way.

He poured himself another glass of schnapps and belched as he lowered himself into his armchair.

Vida covered her face with cream, rubbing off her lipstick, to make it impossible for Karolis to kiss her.

'I don't want you to touch me,' she said in a husky stage voice. 'Leave me alone. Do what you want, but don't touch me.'

When she stood up, he grabbed her thigh and she hopped three steps backwards.

'I'm a man,' he moaned. 'You're my wife. You humiliate me in front of the boy. I wish I was riding my horse through the forests of Suwalkya in the light of the moon instead of going to bed with an alarm clock so I don't lose my job.'

'I wish it too,' she replied. 'Please, Karolis, I can no longer help with your dreams as you demand.'

He laughed roundly as he rose to his feet. 'To bed then.'

'Goodnight,' she said. 'Rest yourself.'

'I order you to come to bed with me. You are my wife. I beg it, Vida.'

She smirked. 'Please, not tonight.'

'Tonight. I beg it.'

'No, Karolis.'

When she heard her husband snoring, she would send the boy in to him and she would sleep undisturbed in Ziggy's bed.

'He snores like a pig,' Ziggy joked.

'I know,' she smiled. 'Put your head under the pillow. He loves you.'

She brushed her son's flame-red hair and kissed him goodnight. Ziggy wanted to sleep by his mother's side in his own bed. But he was too old for that now. He had to go in with his father.

The room at the back of the shop was curtained and dark. A glow of light came in from the other room where his mother kept a lamp on. His father was a hoarsely breathing mountain under the heavy bedding. Ziggy carefully folded back an opening for himself and put his pillow in place. He was familiar with the ritual. His parents would hack themselves to pieces without him. He curled up and closed his eyes. Dream visions of huge chocolate rabbits hopping across the greenest lawns and magnificent hunters on high white horses filled his mind. He and Alex were rabbits jumping from side to side beneath the horses' hooves. His father's boozy breath was close to him, hot under the bedclothes. Stirring and rustling, the man's body emitted heat like a furnace. The green lawn gave way to a rippling landscape of valleys and cleft mountains where the rabbits were jumping and the horses, spurred by hunters, were leaping high in the air, their iron hooves shaking and threatening. Then came the black bear, sharp and hard, bristles prickling. Breath roared in and out. In his dream Ziggy saw the ferocious animal seize a young hunter in its arms and tear at his flesh. His father's arm reached out and Ziggy turned away in a tight bundle under the blankets. He felt his father's weight against him and squirmed to the side of the bed as if he were an animal being edged towards a precipice. The breathing was loud in his ear.

'*Taip!* Snow witch,' Karolis growled. '*Mano sniego karaliene!* Snow queen. Yes!' Chaste as ice, clean as snow.

'No, Papa! *Teveli!*' Ziggy cried through clenched teeth. He buried his face in the bedclothes and kicked the man's weight away. His father was drunk and oblivious. Ziggy pretended to be asleep. Karolis grappled, as if he wanted to wrestle. Ziggy kept up his act, as he had learned to do, without making a sound, until his father fell back face down against the mattress and a throbbing moan came from his throat.

3

Cleve Gordon couldn't help but get himself noticed. He was a spirited kid. That was why his foster parents had chosen him from the orphanage when he was three years old. By the time he was twelve, he was an altar boy, wearing the dress and hanging round with the old priest in the country town where they lived. That was how he got the scholarship to St Joeys. Cleve knew how things worked. The Adamses, who had taken Cleve in as an act of thanks to God when their daughter's leukemia was cured, were proud to send him off to boarding school with the Brothers in the city, feeling they had done their duty. The scholarship provided sports gear and hand-me-down clothes, plus food and board – but no cash to call your own. It was that sort of scholarship.

The best time at school was training, when you could show how good you were. Cleve could fight his way out of most situations, but when sometimes he ended up moping in corners for a couple of days and the boys caught him having a cry, no one said anything. If it had been one of them, they would have jeered without mercy. Only if Cleve missed a moment during training would they taunt him. 'Gone walkabout, Choco,' they yelled. Cleve laughed. They were not his own people. Everyone knew that, but no one ever said anything.

The school emptied on weekends. On Saturdays, after the match, the place went quiet. Most boarders had relatives in the city and money to go out by themselves. That was when Cleve invited the mob from the square to come and visit him. They had picked him straightaway. An uncle who came into town from the riverland drove them all out to the school in his old car. They got lost on the way and lost again inside the school grounds, driving round and round looking for someone to ask. The highest spot Cleve could find to keep lookout for them was up the fire ladder at the top of the chapel spire from where the city of Adelaide looked like a patterned green carpet. Squatting dizzily on the raked tiles, the boy could see across to the flat shiny sea. Then he saw the car turning in a loop around the lawn below. He hollered out three times until the mob heard him. Sticking their heads out the car windows, they cast their eyes up in astonishment.

Brother Gavin was waiting for Cleve at the bottom of the fire ladder, ready to lead the gaggle of visitors to the staffroom for a pot of tea.

'The boy's doing all right, eh Brother?' asked one of the aunties, speaking on behalf of all Cleve's friends from the square. They were making sure he was all right. But after they had gone, Brother Gavin gave Cleve a thrashing. He should think about the consequences of what he did. He might have fallen off the chapel roof. He should not invite strangers to the school. He should not take the law into his own hands.

The people never visited Cleve again after that. If he was going to have a proper education, he was better off obeying all the rules anyway. He was better off left the way he was going.

As a sports star, Cleve had privileged status at St Joeys. On weekends, when he was hanging around school by himself, the Brothers would kick a ball with him, or play serious cricket. In return Cleve was expected to put in the full complement of appearances at Mass. They talked of the day when Cleve would be a holy man like them.

One time Garry Adams, the class captain, invited Cleve home to his birthday party in the suburbs. Cleve borrowed a set of good clothes for the occasion. Garry's father, a pharmacist, had organised a barbecue. The Adamses, country people originally, had worked with the Mastermans, the big pastoralists, in the old days. Elspeth Gillingham's mother had been a Masterman, so Elspeth was at the party too, and Sophie and Robbie Masterman, Elspeth's country cousins. The Adamses were Catholic and the Mastermans Protestant but despite the sectarian divide, and the political differences that went with it, the families kept up the association because of old land ties. Cleve was part of that too. It was other Adamses, Garry's uncle and aunt, who had fostered him. That made him a sort of cousin, although no one thought of Cleve in that way.

They were playing cricket in the backyard. Garry had told Robbie that Cleve was a top sportsman and Robbie was determined to test him. Cleve bowled and Robbie puffed up his cheeks and frowned, prepared to smash. Cleve gave him some easy balls to hit to start off with, although hard to score runs from. Then when Robbie was starting to feel confident, Cleve delivered a ball that bowled him clean through the middle stump and Robbie was out for a duck.

'Good one, Choco,' said Garry, embarrassed for Robbie, who was the oldest boy there.

'Shit, I didn't even see it coming,' said Robbie, unable to look Cleve in the eye. 'Who's he training with?'

'Under 15s.' Cleve answered for himself.

'Fuck that for a joke,' swore Robbie. 'I bet they lost the birth certificate.'

Elspeth, who was wicketkeeper, found the ball in the back of the garden and came loping back with it. She was pleased to see her uncouth cousin cut down to size. She tossed the ball neatly back to Cleve, who plucked it from the air, bowing his head as he returned to his mark.

When the food was ready, they sat around on the grass eating their grilled chops and sausages in their fingers. Garry's mother passed Cleve extra helpings, saying he needed feeding up. Even the birthday cake, after the coloured candles were picked off, was cut so as to allow one extra piece for Cleve.

'It's not fair,' declared Elspeth. 'Why should he be treated differently?'

'Don't forget who's a visitor,' warned Mrs Adams. 'Family hold back.'

'I'm not family either,' said Elspeth. She passed the last piece to Cleve.

'I'll halve it with you,' Cleve grinned to her. 'I'm family too, Mrs Adams. Don't forget.'

Mrs Adams laughed. 'That's right, Cleve dear. You're family too.'

While they sat on the grass, the kids compared their smallpox vaccination marks. Mr Adams explained that the size of the mark depended on the age at which a child was inoculated. Mr Adams talked about the way immunisation programs were organised across the country and around the world, like a net, to catch everyone, until in the end contagious diseases would disappear from the earth. As a pharmacist, he looked forward to that day, even if it would be bad for his business. But that did not explain why Cleve had a whole string of vaccination marks down his arm.

'What happened to you, Cleve?' asked Mr Adams.

Cleve said that according to his foster mother all the vaccines were trialled on him in the orphanage. Elspeth shuddered when she looked at the five rings of pale stretched skin on Cleve's arm. Mr Adams said how wonderful it would be if Cleve could become a doctor one day himself

Cleve shook his head. 'Too much study.'

'He's going to be a football champion,' said Garry. 'That's what he's got to be.'

'I wouldn't mind being an astronaut, actually,' said Cleve and they all laughed.

Elspeth was picked up from the birthday party by her father. Dr Gillingham sat outside and watched the kids come out. Once his daughter was in the car, he asked who the dark boy was.

'He's a scholarship kid from St Joeys,' said Elspeth. 'He's an Aborigine,' she clarified.

'They must have brought him down from the river to be in their football team,' commented her father.

Angus Gillingham mentioned it to his wife later. 'There was an Abo at the kids' party. Do you think it's a good idea? For Elspeth, I mean. She gets funny ideas. Micks and Abos,' he snorted. 'There's a limit, isn't there? Did you have any idea?'

'It's good for her,' Barb Gillingham replied. 'Why does it bother you?'

'I think the Adamses should have warned us, that's all. You can carry mixing too far. Elspeth's only a girl.'

'Nothing's going to rub off on Elspeth, darling,' his wife laughed. 'Her lasting friendships will be with her own kind.'

Barb Gillingham squinted at her husband as he said that, wondering whether he, after all, was *her* own kind. That was the Masterman in her. Angus came from a wine family. Barb had met him at a school dance. Good-looking, racy, brainy in a way, he had been on the move then. But he stopped at General Practice. It was Barb's money from the family pastoral company that gave the Gillinghams the best house in the neighbourhood.

Cleve would never be one of them. He could do too many things that they couldn't do. He knew too much that they would never know. He gave his light releasing laugh as he walked down the school corridor, turning sideways to squeeze past Brother Gavin. He sat down at his desk and opened the mathematics book. History was easier. He could remember the people and the stories and the battles, long ago or today, it was all the same. He had a good sense of time. He was good with language and could put the words down. Yet for him there was no relationship between what he wrote down in the examinations and the future that lay ahead. The other boys would grow up to be doctors or pharmacists or accountants. The priesthood was within Cleve's grasp. All the school families produced a priest if they could. No, he would prefer to be a footballer first. Did he love Christ? Christ healed the sick and fed the hungry. Christ brought the dead back to the living. Christ was the mightiest of the invisible powers. If he did not love Christ, Christ would not love him, and that thought was terrible, he might as well be in a box in the ground. But could Christ, who loved mankind, love *him*?

Cleve wondered.

The only place to go at night, when you got a cramp in the leg and needed to walk, where no one would question you, was the chapel. There, if anyone approached, you could cover your face and pray. Cleve would sit in the empty chapel and look at the coloured glass, the cut lilies, the gold candlesticks and eagle-shaped stand from which the priest recited holy words. He would look at the scuffed, scratched wood in front of him, carved with furtive, durable initials, feeling completely alone, except for Christ, hanging up there on His cross, who had suffered more than Cleve had ever suffered, they said. If he spoke, Christ would hear him. But he felt like an intruder. That suffering of Christ's was not something you could share, although Cleve could guess what it was like to be nailed up on two bits of wood. He had been pushed against the turnstile, a turning tree of iron, at the public swimming pool in the country town where he grew up. He knew what that bloke up there with the long blond curls and the droopy blue eyes and the wispy whiskers had gone through. If only He would come down off the cross and open His arms wide and walk across the floor on those bare bleeding feet of His. Put it on equal terms.

One night, alone in the chapel, Cleve raised his voice: 'Why don't you come down once in a while and show us all your Love and Hope and that, as it behoves you? Tell you something. No way a bloke like me can enter your Kingdom of Heaven except I come in as a slave on hands and knees.' He was holding the pew in front of him to steady himself as he shouted. The words reverberated in the hollow mock-gothic vault. 'Your arms don't reach that far, Jesus Christ. No matter how high I jump, and I can jump pretty bloody high, I can't jump up to you, mate. You're prominent. I know that. Not like me. Maybe I don't need your LOVE!'

'Gordon, what's all this noise about?' asked Brother Gavin, catching the tail-end of Cleve's outburst as he entered the chapel.

Cleve turned and stared at Brother Gavin. He hung his head. His tongue, from which words had been whipping, was tied. 'Just having my say, Brother.'

'You were shouting in anger. What's the matter? That's not the way to behave in God's presence.'

'I was praying to myself. There was no one else around, Brother.'

'You defile the things we hold sacred. All of us, Gordon. Including you.'

Cleve looked at the Brother, wrapped up in hocus-pocus – not a man.

'Yes, Brother.'

'Go to your dorm, Gordon. It's late. See me in the morning.'

'Yes, Brother. Goodnight, Brother.'

Josie thrilled to wild fancies. Solitary and reckless, she would sneak out of her room at night and cut across the park, retracing the route she took to Mass in the boys' school chapel on Sundays. The Virgin would protect her from the hissing possums and sighing gum trees, the rattling grass and howling dogs. When she reached the street-lamp on the other side, holding herself pure, she was elated. She was safe walking in the eerie, spooky grounds of St Joeys where scattered lights burned in the buildings as the day's tasks were completed and the thoughts of those who lived there turned towards bedtime. Her mother would die if she knew.

A solitary light shone in the chapel, making the shell-shaped building float in the darkness, like a ship, beckoning her. Then she stopped and listened. Coming from inside the chapel she heard the deep voice of a young man, rising in waves to a pitch, almost a shriek, of questioning intensity. She could not hear who he was arguing with. There was only the one pounding voice.

The side door to the chapel was left ajar. Josie came close and stood in the doorway. Then she crept inside where she could hear everything and watched from behind the door as he shouted and shook his open hands at the unresponsive crucifix. Her heartbeat was racing. He was the football champion. He was the swimming star. She had seen him presented with ribbons at the combined schools sports competition. He was the dark boy she had seen in his white smock singing in the choir at Mass. She nearly called out his name. She could not bear the thought of spying on him, or worse of being caught. She was about to step forward and declare herself when the voice of the Brother made her shrink back through the arched doorway to a place where she might still hear something without being caught.

She did not imagine that the boy would choose the side door to make his exit, in retreat from Brother Gavin, who was locking the main door. Josie kept herself still as Cleve came down the step, pulling the heavy door behind him. Glancing over his shoulder as he did so, he was suddenly aware of the girl pressing herself back against the stone wall. Her face was a white moon.

Nervous as a bush rat, she held her breath and sucked in her mouth. She was scared of being found out by the Brother, who would tell her mother and grandmother.

Cleve put his finger to his lips. All at once his righteous anger was converted into tickling bubbles of air. He smiled at her in conspiratorial silence. They could hear Brother Gavin walking away, satisfied that the side door was securely closed. The footsteps disappeared on the other side of the chapel. Then Cleve let out a hiss of mirth.

'What you doing?'

'Roaming. You won the freestyle and something else at the swimming carnival,' she said. 'Wasn't that you?'

'I won the diving. And the medley.'

'You're Cleve Gordon, aren't you? You're –' But she would not say it. She felt one with him, not different.

'Where did *you* come from?'

'I live down the hill.'

He looked at her askance. 'Running round at night like this – aren't you frightened?'

'Why should I be frightened?'

'What's your name?'

'Josie. My Mum doesn't care. And my grandma's blind. Anyway, I heard you. You must not take Jesus's name in vain. You're in the bosom of the Mother of God just like all the rest of us.'

'That's bullshit,' he said without a ripple in his voice.

Josie felt the stones of the wall, rough behind her. She laughed at him.

'You want me to walk you home?' he offered.

'No thanks. I'll be right. Don't tell anyone, will you?'

'Don't you tell either,' he replied, flashing his teeth at the joke of it. She puzzled him. 'Or you'll be sorry.'

Cleve could hear the snuffling, steady breathing of the boys in the dormitory, and the occasional muffled bleat or whimper. He was alone, the only one awake, wide awake, his senses alert and lucid, as if an irresistible energy filled and recharged him. He was able to look down on himself from the sky, as if he were in two places at once, from outer space, from a star, and connect himself to its shining power. He got out of bed and crept in silence to the window to watch the embryo of dawn. He was warm inside his pyjamas, but his feet were cold, and he just stood there, looking up at the morning-star, cold and beautiful and alone in the sky, as the bright shining point of the morning-star looked back at him, a single eye, fixing him from behind the indigo curtain of the night, making him indivisible from what he saw.

4

BROKEN trees bent limp parasols of silky leaves to the current. The high riverside cliffs were great shadowless red curtains. The houseboat churned the brown riverwater to a coffee-cream wake. Then a crow punctuated the emptiness with its mordant cawing. Jane sat on the deck with her block and pen recording the relativities of vast sky, dissolving cliffs, running river and outsized black bird. She saw only the landscape and heard, apart from the boat's low engine and the crackle of Wendy's transistor radio, only the crow. Covered with suntan oil, Wendy was stretched out on a towel reading *L'Etranger* by Albert Camus, marking the corners of the pages with her oily fingers. Mrs Schumann was searching through her binoculars for the waterbirds that nested in the reeds around fallen tree stumps. When she found one, she would pass the binoculars to Elspeth. But Elspeth searched with different eyes, following the contours of the cliffs for paths that might lead up from the river's edge. One of the Masterman properties was up there on the top.

Towards evening Mrs Schumann moored the houseboat to a tree on the bank and the school girls jumped ashore to gather firewood. They made a bonfire on the sand and after they had eaten their sausages and bread, Miss Jocelyn-Jones, the language mistress, good-naturedly continued her reminiscences. 'I was mistress of my own destiny as always, but Europe was to give me a larger canvas – of art, music, ideas. I had seen my first Bonnard –' (pronounced with Parisian aplomb) '– in our art gallery, Jane, and I was hungry for more of those pinks!' Joke – their nickname for Miss Jocelyn-Jones – handpicked the girls for the annual excursion. Tall straight Elspeth, with her flaxen hair pulled back behind her ears and her neck twisted like a Chinese figurine's as she posed a question; bubbling, drowsy Wendy, with her honey plumage and her ridicule; dark-curled, dark-eyed Jane, who claimed whatever she saw for her ink and paints. She went on, 'The voyage itself – well, the ship had every service – and on entering the Mediterranean, I felt as if the Graces of the Ancient World were there to greet us. Ah, arriving! In Naples I bought a scarf from a local young woman who rowed out to us in a little boat, singing as she plied her oars –'

'See Naples and die,' giggled Elspeth, who had heard about it from her mother.

The firelight danced, high as girls' dancing bodies. When a girl passed between, her shadow became a black giant that swept the cliffs behind. Flame mixed on the dark river with the silvering of the moon. Then a fish would jump, adding its plop to the tales Joke was telling, the girls' heads lolling as the fire died.

'Look at that,' shouted Brice Masterman, who had made his property available for an excursion by the masters and boys of his old school, as a mob of grey kangaroos bounded across the skyline towards the uncleared scrub. The roos sailed over the fence, bowing the slack wires with their tails, easily outstripping the dogs. 'Can't keep the bastards in or out.'

'You want the gun, Dad,' said Robbie, who was driving the ute although he was only fifteen.

'We could do a bit of spotlighting later on tonight,' called Masterman through the open car window. 'A spin around the bunny paddock before bed, eh fellas? If it's okay with the boss.'

'Wonderful!' replied Corin Pearson, the headmaster, who considered himself a hunter of the mind. His skill was breaking silly boys into fine beasts. Halting the mare that Masterman had saddled up for him – a reminder of riding the veldt in his youth – Pearson stretched a finger at the patch of russet, turning to gold in the sunset, that was racing across the rise. 'Fox!' he announced. The dogs were off again.

Carl Benjamin, a young master who was chief of the school corps, sat beside Alex on a hay bale in the back of the ute. He pointed out a flock of pink galahs, rising in their hundreds above the bush, like ash blown upwards from a fire. Then the dogs, outchased by the fox, climbed back on board, slobbering and panting.

The flat ground where they stopped, high above the river, was stubbled with limestone and balls of bluebush. Here and there the stones had been gathered into cairns or rough white walls. It was marginal country, in the rainshadow of the ranges, which Mastermans were gradually buying up from the single family farms that could not afford to irrigate. One day, with water pumped up from the river, there would be orchards and vineyards flourishing in the soil here. The track was a faint set of pumpkin-coloured lines, dipping down to a lower ledge, as the sun disappeared. It was difficult to sense the river below, out of sight – the scarlet cliffs opposite seemed to press forwards. The headmaster's mare chafed to go ahead down the snaky gulleys and rocky outcrops towards the sheer drop.

Brice Masterman got out of the ute and led the horse away from the cliff-face. They had descended into a hidden groin now, where there was a space as big as a playing field with a low mound at its centre, and within it a bare ring, the diameter of a cricket pitch, formed from an aggregate of stone and shell and charred wood. The farmer squatted down to feel it with his own hands. 'It's the burial ground I was telling you about,' he said.

'How old is it?' asked the headmaster, taking responsibility for the discovery.

'Dunno. They bury them sitting up, legs crossed, arms crossed. Like this.' Masterman bent up his body in mimicry.

Pearson tapped a bit of the black wood, hard as fossil, that was embedded in the orange clay. 'What's the circle?'

'They surround them with a ring of fire. The wood has petrified.'

'Wow! Is it that old?' Alex asked, following Mr Benjamin over.

'It must be a few thousand years at least,' guessed the teacher.

'Could be,' drawled Emmy Lawrence, the Latin master. '*Crimine ab uno, Disce omnes.*'

'What's that?' snapped the head.

'*From one crime you know them all.* To paraphrase Virgil.'

'Have you excavated at all?' Pearson asked the farmer.

'There'd only be a few skeletons,' Masterman replied cautiously.

'Let's dig them up,' said Johnny Woodruff in excitement.

'The ground is that hard,' Masterman added by way of excuse. He had never thought but to leave the place alone.

'We can help you,' declared the headmaster. 'Would you be in favour of that, boys?'

Andrew Findlay was already scratching at the ground with a stick. The clay was as hard as any rock that ever sealed a tomb.

'Great,' said Johnny.

'We need a plan,' insisted the headmaster. 'That's step one, for the morning.'

Masterman's wife had set up the trestle table by the roasting spit, where the hogget turned, pissing fat over the hot coals. The dogs started to whine as soon as they smelled the meat. Men and boys were sent to wash. The dogs were fed and chained up. Rosie Masterman considered that her social graces were rusting on the farm. Her daughter Sophie and son Robbie, when he was home from school, kept her company, and the rouseabouts, and Brice was a good husband: but this visit was something special. She couldn't help mothering her guests. The perfume of citronella, burning to keep the mosquitoes away, was in the air. The meat was tasty with her mint sauce. The schoolboys sat at the table to eat. The men took up standing positions. Her husband took charge of the hogget and kept on carving to feed the demand.

Talk turned to Masterman's younger brother, another old boy of the school, who was in the first group of Australian troops to go off to Vietnam.

'We've got to take the first step in defending ourselves,' said Masterman, mouthing the government line, 'before it's too late and we have to call in someone else who'll call the tune. We have to be prepared but. Vietnam's only a stepping stone. The Chinese will be next.' He realised that this line of argument might cost his younger brother's life. His brother was a boy of middling performance who had found his niche in the school corps, learning to repeat the tasks required until he was perfect at them. In Vietnam he was likely to make something of himself.

'It's the Yanks' adventure,' quipped Lawrence, dripping wine from his moustache. 'What's a civil war in Vietnam got to do with *us*?'

'Readiness is all,' Pearson interpolated, 'but that does not mean going out and looking for trouble. The country we should defend,' he said, 'is this one.' He was conscious of speaking as an expatriate South African. 'We should be creating a new society which is capable of absorbing threats. In that sense Australia can be the continuation of the British Empire into the next century.'

The Latin master laughed as the head rode his hobby horse.

Masterman threw his scraps to the dogs that ran to the end of their chains for them. 'Well, are we on for spotlighting, fellas?'

Rosie Masterman sighed. 'The boys are tired, Brice.'

'You've been more than hospitable enough already,' protested the headmaster.

'You boys on?' demanded the farmer.

'Too right,' declared Johnny Woodruff.

'Oh lucky man,' said Lawrence sardonically. 'Count me out.'

'I'll stay and help Mrs Masterman clean up,' said Carl Benjamin. At twenty-four, with slicked-back hair, obtrusive eyebrows and full lips, he was young enough for the boys to hero-worship. He played the bagpipes in the school corps. But detecting something unmanly in Benjie's reluctance to go rabbit-shooting, the boys were confused, and became all the more determined to go themselves.

Masterman unchained the dogs. They scrambled up onto the ute with the boys. The headmaster sat in front with the twenty-two. No one could tell them what was right and wrong out there.

Mrs Schumann heaved up from the bunk and found her slippers. The first shot, and the second, might have been some weirdness of the land. By the third it was time to investigate. Until then the night had been a miracle of velvety starry silence, with only the water's lapping, no louder than a cat, and the muted oboe of owls. *Boo-boo, boo-boo!* She stood at the rail, looking up. Men, shooters – but where? The sound splintered and sprayed along the water from the reverberating chasm of the cliffs. The girls, all awake now, joined her in a huddle against the rail as if they were witnessing the outbreak of war. Only Miss Jocelyn-Jones, sound sleeper, grumpy waker, failed to leave her bed.

'It's a massacre,' said Wendy.

'Rabbiters,' pronounced Mrs Schumann, 'or roo shooters.'

'No!' Jane was disgusted.

'Or just hoons,' groaned Elspeth.

'They never stop to think there might be other people around,' said Mrs Schumann. 'Senseless activity causing unnecessary danger. They think they own the place.'

'What if one ricocheted?' worried Wendy.

'Wendy,' scoffed Jane, 'what chance is there of that?'

'We should turn on the lights,' suggested Wendy, 'so they know we're here.'

'Next thing we'll be inviting them in to rape and pillage!' said a shocked Mrs Schumann.

Then Elspeth confessed that it was her cousin's place up there. This declaration of the girls' connections came as a disagreeable surprise.

'What are they like?' asked Wendy, fancying an adventure.

'They're pretty boring,' said Elspeth. 'Anyway, we'd have to get up the cliff first. It looks pretty crumbly.'

'We could take torches,' said Jane.

Through the cabin window Joke's voice boomed out. 'We are *not* on safari!' The aim of the excursion was to focus on themselves and their higher pursuits, not to go after the first sign of activity out of vulgar curiosity. 'I dare say Masterman Holdings have properties everywhere,' she opined. She did not approve.

'We could wave a white flag,' suggested Wendy.

'That's my last word, Schumann,' added Joke.

Mrs Schumann concluded pragmatically. 'If anyone dares to attack us, girls, we slip moorings and sail on.'

Carl Benjamin hung his bagpipes from a hook on the wall. The polished black pipes jutted from their lifeless bladder like the legs and neck of a gamebird on a meathook. He lay his folded kilt and sporran at the foot of his bunk and combed his Brylcreemed hair for bed. He liked the idea of piping out in the empty bush where no one could object. But not tonight, when only Rosie Masterman and Emmy Lawrence would hear. He went to clean his teeth and the rouseabout duo who were sitting on the step by the door of the hut introduced themselves as Alf and Kevin. Benjamin accepted a cigarette from Alf, the older man, and, leaning in the doorframe, smoked as he listened to the story of Alf's wife Pinkie, deceased, who had looked after Brice Masterman as a baby boy. She had nursed Kevin too, making him a kind of son to Alf. If things were different, Alf said, Kevin could have been a sort of brother to the young boss.

Later as he lay on the prickly bunk in his underpants, waiting for the others to return, Benjamin listened to the two men's low intermittent exchange continuing. He heard the roar of the ute's exhaust, and the dogs barking for home, doors slamming and Rosie Masterman chiding. Then the boys came running over to the shearers' huts looking for their places. They were exhilarated by the surge of lawlessness that had overtaken them out there, shooting at rabbits down tunnels of light that barrelled the darkness. Doors flew open and shut over in the washroom. He knew those boys' voices. 'You're sleeping here, Alex,' he called.

'Sh, Benjie's in bed in there!'

'You can smell that gunk on his hair,' said Andrew.

'Fucking poofter!' groaned Johnny.

'Watch your language, Woodruff. Get to bed all of you!' shouted the Latin master. 'At once!'

'Turn off the light, John,' said Benjamin, lying in bed with his lizard eyes slit.

Bumping against each other from tiredness, the boys found their places. Then there was the thud of a boy stubbing his toe against the bedpost. It was Johnny. 'Faarck! How'm I supposed to see where I'm going?'

The boys took a salt tablet at breakfast to stop them fainting in the heat. The headmaster had a map and compass, pencils and a swag of butcher's paper. The rousies helped load forty-gallon drums of water onto the back of the vehicles, with hoses, picks, crowbars, spades, forks and a straw broom, then Alf made himself scarce. Masterman moved over to let Johnny Woodruff have a turn at the wheel of the ute. Kevin sat between them up front, in the role of native guide. Even if nothing of substance could be discovered in this chewed-down land, it was a question of method. The boys must be taught the scientific basis of the great story of Man that stretched from the caves of Lascaux to Aristotle in Athens and Cicero in Rome, to Shakespeare, Faraday and Einstein, from London to New York, and on from there to the barely grasped potentiality of Australia. 'Mark anything that may be of significance. Take its bearings,' instructed Pearson. 'Our first task is to produce a detailed map of the site. We start digging only when we know what we are looking for.'

The brightness of the day conspired with the featureless terrain to hide any signs as they reconnoitred. Pearson brushed the orange dust away with a straw broom to expose bone here and there beneath the surface. The ring of stone and wood resembled his protruding brow, thought Masterman as he watched the man mark a possible half-dozen skeletons on a diagram, as well as fire spots and middens. Benjamin picked over the middens to distinguish stone tools and food relics from other bits of stone. He had studied palaeontology. The rest of the group set to work to recover any human bones.

'If they were human at all,' quipped Lawrence, keeping alive the possibility of finding a hominid precursor to *Homo sapiens sapiens*. In his opinion there was no limit to how far back in time the site might go.

Pearson remembered the time in Egypt when he had left the ship en route to Australia. In the Valley of the Kings, he had gone down a black burrow into the earth – hatless, sunstruck – paying an Arab boy in a grubby robe to shine a torch at the red, green and blue murals that were as brilliant as when they were first painted for the Pharaoh. Journeying to an educator's future in a resentful ex-colony, Pearson had felt like a Pharaoh himself. 'I'm reminded of King Tut's tomb,' he chuckled. Obliging the pink-faced chap with a laugh, Masterman stuck a black hose into the drum of bore water they had rolled over together. He sucked the other end of the hose, making a siphon, until water trickled out that would gradually soften the soil around the bones.

Kevin helped the boys fill their cans and buckets. Alf had not wanted a bar of the business when the boss asked about the burial site. But Kevin, new to the place, and needing to make some money to take back to his girlfriend at Swan Reach, who was having a child, wanted to make a good impression on the cocky. Anyway, the olden times meant nothing to him. Alf said that there could have been a big fight out there once. Their people were the Rufus River mob in the old days, the tributary not far away where the overlanders, massacring the blacks, made the water run red with blood. Rufus the Red River named for the bloodnut first mate of Captain Sturt, the first gubba to come down that way.

Now he was out there himself, Kevin felt uneasy, and when they asked him questions, he would not answer. When they asked if the dead might belong to his people, he shook his head. What they didn't understand was that *all* these people were his people.

'Of course they're generations older than any living person,' said the headmaster, dismissing whatever the rouseabout might say. It was a sense of inquiry that built the cathedral of civilisation, as far as Pearson was concerned.

Rust-coloured bore water flowed from the hose that Kevin held. A patch of bone no bigger than a coin showed in the ground. As the water soaked in, they could see that the bone was curved like the side of an egg. Kevin stared at the ground. Alex looked up at Kevin for clues in his X-ray eyes, but they were blank when he met the boy's gaze, as if a shadow of fear had passed over him. Kevin tossed his cigarette on the ground and moved away without saying a word, leaving the hose dribbling from the drum. Alex knelt on the ground and rubbed at the dirt with his fingers until he could feel the smooth bone. Unearthing a tibia or a tooth, the others shouted exultantly, but no one took any notice of what Alex found. It was his secret. He carted bucket after bucket of water, then when he was ready he got the crowbar and gently chipped the earth loose.

They stopped at lunchtime to unwrap sandwiches under the stunted mallee trees. The flies soon found them. Rosie Masterman arrived with cold drinks. 'Must be strange for you,' she said, taking a mutton sandwich over to Kevin, who kept his distance.

'Old Alf's the one with the spooks,' Kevin replied. A fly was swimming in the orange cordial she had given him. She saved them both from further embarrassment by offering him a piece of cake. Under the trees Benjamin was explaining that the Aborigines of the area were buried in a westward-facing position, where the setting sun would lead them to the land of their ancestors, their other-world, their Dreaming, where the creation begins and ends.

'Is Kevin all right?' Rosie's husband asked when she returned. He cocked his head in the direction of the clifftop where the rouse-about was wandering.

'He's looking for a nice spot over there,' Rosie replied drolly.

'Burial in the sitting position must surely predate the mission-aries,' commented the headmaster.

'If they're sitting in a circle, how can they all be facing west?' Lawrence wondered, twiddling his moustache.

'The newly dead bodies were placed in forks of trees and smoked dry before they were interred,' Benjamin went on. 'They were moved only when there was no spirit left. Where the bones went then was a matter of no great consequence.'

'What's true in one place is not necessarily true in another,' con-cluded Pearson. 'We are here with open minds and will reach our own conclusions, eh boys?'

'Then it doesn't matter if we dig them up?' asked Alex.

'It is our duty and our privilege to do so,' proclaimed the head-master. With that blessing the lunch break was over. 'Let's hop to.'

'Finders keepers,' quipped the Latin master.

By mid-afternoon they had excavated an assortment of bones and placed them, labelled with place, date and a guess at anatomy, in wooden fruit crates lined with newspaper. There was not yet a whole skeleton; the few skulls they had found were fragments. Pearson had unearthed a jawbone which he held up against Benjamin's chin to illustrate the difference. 'Carl might be closer to the apes than most of us, but there is still a long way to go,' he jibed.

Alex felt his way through the sloppy mud in his hole to find hard pieces of bone. He might have been playing mud pies. He could feel the vertebrae of the spine. The person was sitting with crossed arms and crossed legs, as Benjie said, facing westward beneath the earth. Alex washed the little bones that floated free in the red water and laid them on a sack to dry. Then, inching his fingers upward, he was able to take the skull in his hands.

Jane screwed up her face. 'Is it true that the Emperor of the Bush rounded up a truckload of Aborigines from his land and dumped them over a cliff?'

Elspeth scowled. Photos showed an indomitable old man with snow-white hair and sparky eyes. She wondered how the sins of her great-grandfather would be visited on her.

'It could have happened here,' whispered Jane grimly as her eyes surveyed the looming ramparts.

'They shoot them these days,' added Wendy, 'as we heard last night.'

Elspeth looked up at the cliffs and groaned. It was unthinkable, surely – but she could not resist the challenge of finding a way up the cliff to the Masterman property.

'What does it matter whose place it is anyway?' Jane wanted to know. 'You can't *own* it.'

'Come on,' said Elspeth.

'Back before dark, girls,' ordered Miss Jocelyn-Jones, retiring with a new book by Simone de Beauvoir.

Kevin sat on the brink of the cliff like a sentinel, brooding over the drop to the brown river that, trailing willow fronds and reeds as it flowed, pulled at the fringes of the land. His eye followed a solitary crow that descended to a perch on a dead forked rivergum. Then his gaze alighted on the heads of the girls bobbing up the eroded pink humps of the cliff face in front of him. A grin spread across his face at the sound of their high sharp voices. Quickly he got to his feet and backed away. Looking down on them in the hot, empty landscape, the rouseabout was the first thing the girls saw when they came over the top and found the whole strange scene.

Brice Masterman, not recognising Elspeth at first, yelled at the dogs to shut up. The girl stepped forward and said hallo. Johnny Woodruff stuck his head out of the hole he was digging and groaned at the sight of his sister Jane. 'Oh no, not you!' Then the headmaster came over. 'What's going on?' he asked.

'We're on the houseboat down below,' said Elspeth. 'What are you doing?'

Pearson conveyed in ringing tones the significance of their excavation of the site.

'Was that you shooting that woke us up last night?' asked Wendy with a tone of ridicule.

Jane sidled up to Alex. 'Are you real?' she sniggered. Bits of bones were spread out on the sack beside him to dry in the sun. With the crowbar he probed the sludge in the hole. She was curious, but she rejected what she saw. 'How can you do this?' she exclaimed, spitting out her judgement.

He hated to look so dumb in front of her, but his motives were private, different from the others. He could never explain to her the bond he felt growing between himself and the bones, even in the act of defiling them.

It was stupid boys' stuff, the girls decided. Even Elspeth agreed, with her spirit of cool inquiry, feeling a special responsibility since it was Masterman land. The discoveries should have been reported to the Museum. But the headmaster laughed down the girls' reactions. It was far better that they should dig scientifically than if some vandals had stumbled upon the site.

Robbie Masterman smiled at Wendy and whispered did she want a smoke. She went off with him to sit in the shade of a mallee tree. She told him to come down to the houseboat for a swim. She wanted to show off her all-over tan. 'We're prisoners down there,' she said, blowing a smoke ring.

Alex kept working until the end, patiently emptying buckets of water and kneading the soil with his fingers. He manoeuvred the crowbar deep into the hole to dislodge the compacted earth. When he was ready, he dragged the sack over and opened its mouth. Making sure that no one was looking, he lifted out the skull he had found, jaw and all, and transferred it to the sack. It might have been a lump of red clay. He was shovelling earth back into the hole in a hurry when the girls came over to say goodbye.

'What's in your sack, Alex Mack?'

The shadows of Jane and Elspeth fell over him, as if they were spies. Jane put her foot on the sack.

'Don't,' he grunted, scrambling round on his hands and knees in the dirt. 'It's mine.'

'I wouldn't want it anyway. Stinking thing!'

'It's private property, Alex,' smirked Elspeth, pushing through from behind. 'It can't be *yours*.'

He glowered at the girls, his skin burning with shame as he clutched the neck of the sack.

'Graverobber,' said Elspeth. 'Let's go.' Alex was not worth bothering with.

Johnny blared on the car horn as the girls disappeared over the lip of the cliff. Their departure made the headmaster hasten to call a halt to the day's proceedings. The bones lay labelled in pools of sand in the fruit crates. There was the problem of whether to fill in the half-dug holes or leave them. A good bushman covered his tracks, but to refill the holes seemed only to confirm the furtiveness of the exercise. The headmaster brandished his maps and diagrams in an attempt to recover a triumphal mode, reading aloud from Benjamin's inventory of finds from the middens. Then Kevin swung up onto the back of the ute, eager to be going, and the dogs jumped up after him. Pearson made a last minute check to see that nothing was left behind but the disturbed ground. Alex sat on his hay bale and stuffed his sack out of sight behind his knees. Through the sackcloth he could feel the hard mass of the skull.

Robbie was impatient to go in search of the girls on the riverboat but by the time they finished eating it was dark and no one wanted to go with him. His mother insisted on second helpings of food and refilled people's glasses in an attempt to lift the pensiveness that had settled over the gathering. They were back at the same trestle table, by the same fire as the previous evening, their mission accomplished, but there was an air of dissatisfaction. Something strange had passed during the day. Rosie Masterman would not have the bones anywhere in her house or her garden. They were stacked in their crates in the tractor shed. The headmaster intended to take them back to school. The kids took a few bones inside to the shearers' quarters and put them with their things as souvenirs, feeling audacious in doing so. Then in long, laughing, farting showers they rubbed the red grit from their skin that was their way of washing the day off. Robbie, towelling himself with elaborate tenderness as he thought of Wendy down by the river, was especially edgy. Then Johnny lashed at his stiffy with a wet towel, cacking himself.

'Don't be juvenile,' Robbie threatened him.

As he listened to their shouts in the showers, Carl Benjamin wondered what these boys would grow into. They would grow up like their fathers. He gazed across at Masterman. But you could always be surprised. His own bagpipe playing and science teaching were not what his smallgoods manufacturer father had anticipated.

'How come you're a Presbyterian?' the head asked suddenly.

'My mother was Presbyterian,' Benjamin answered unconvincingly.

'A Scot, was she? You don't look Scottish.'

'It was more of an accident,' Benjamin smiled. 'My father was German. Bavarian Catholic from the Barossa Valley. But Mum's religion took over and anyway Dad was happy to be certified Presbyterian when the war was on. Germans weren't too popular then.'

'But it's a Jewish name, isn't it?' asked Pearson. From Jew to German, from German to kilt wearer – there was a double shuffle in Benjamin's background. With his sleek black hair, pallid face and swelling jowls, he looked like no kind of highland Scot. Pearson looked from Benjamin to brick-faced Masterman, who was certainly the real thing. It was a distasteful matter, in any case. The genius of civilisation was a question of cultures, not the mix of individual genes. So he changed the subject. 'We should at least notify the Museum of our finds today, Benjamin,' he said.

After their showers the boys came back and sat around the fire within earshot of the adults' stumbling talk.

'It must be black down on the river,' said Robbie. 'They've only got gas lamps and torches on the boat.'

'The moon's pretty full,' his mother replied.

'Is the moon up yet?' asked Benjamin, looking around until he found it, low on the horizon.

'Looks like a skull,' said Alex, thinking of what he had under his bunk.

'What it really looks like,' smirked the Latin master, 'is buttocks. Do you see that?'

Rosie Masterman smiled. 'Peaches and cream.'

Emmy Lawrence was easily disgruntled by the conservatism of the country types who were the backbone of the school. 'Don't you go crazy living out here? I would,' he murmured conspiratorially to the farmer's wife.

'I love it,' she replied loyally.

'It must be uplifting sometimes,' said Benjamin. The more red wine he drank, the whiter his face became.

'Bedtime for this mob,' yawned Masterman. 'I'll leave you two the flagon.'

'Goodnight, Emmy. Goodnight, Carl,' said his wife, rising to her feet.

'Uplifting! Reckon it would give me the droops in no time,' said Lawrence. The others had gone inside. 'Banging away at the same old thing all your life.' The homestead lights went off as he spoke, except for the window of the guest room where the headmaster slept. 'Burning the midnight oil. Some people never stop. Well, I'm for the sack too,' sighed Lawrence, staggering to his feet. 'Hope these bloody kids don't keep me awake like last night.'

The fire had died down to the embers and the trestle table was strewn with glasses, bottles and dirty plates. Left alone with the remains of the feast, Benjamin poured himself a last glass of red

wine and gazed again at the swelling luminous moon in the big
black sky. Glass and flagon in hand, he crossed the yard and lurched
into the tractor shed where he hit his feet against the stacked crates
of bones. They rattled as if they would rise up and invite him to
dance. That was what the moon could make you do. He skipped
backwards out into the stockyards to escape those spirits. Daisy
bushes, growing along the yard rails, glowed in the moonlight. He
breathed their sharp smell, mixed with dung, dryness and the cooling night. Then he headed towards another doorway. He jumped
when he came upon the two rousies sitting on the step.

'Easy does it, mate,' murmured Kevin. He had noticed during
the day that this young bloke was a bit of an oddball.

'Sorry. I thought everyone was asleep. Do you want a drink?'
Benjamin settled down on the step and passed the flagon for the
men to take a swig.

'We wasn't invited,' grumbled Alf.

'Be my guest,' Benjamin said, draining his glass and getting to
his feet again. 'I'm restless.'

There was a strange violet illumination along the horizon that
enchanted him. He crossed to the shearers' hut and, as quietly as he
could, crept inside. The boys' breathing was heavy. He reached
across the bunk for the items of his kit and without saying a word
he changed into his kilt and sporran. Then he stepped out into the
yard and began to play.

A low harsh drone came from the bagpipes, a weird noise, loud
as could be, that haunted the sheepyards as the piper stepped out
the long dignified paces of a parade. He squeezed the bag under
his arm as he blew and the rumble of the bladder was heard in the
night with the pipe notes above in mordant harmony. He was
playing for the moon, summoning up the bones of today's act of
desecration and of all warriors fallen in ancient battles, all the
mothers and lovers wasted in grieving, the lament of the border
country, transported to this land, that sounded like cats groaning
on heat.

O wha is this has done this deed,
This ill deed done to me,
To send me out this time o' the year,
To sail upon the sea!

In the homestead lights came on. The boys turned in their bunks. The two rouseabouts laughed appreciatively. The lone piper pacing the flat earth in lines as straight as the yardrails, through daisies and sheep shit, piped the plaint of remorse for all of them, a pibroch under the moon, as they slept, letting them draw deep from life's renewing springs so they would live again in the morning.

'Not bloody now!' roared Emmy Lawrence. '*Procul este, profani!*'

A slow handclapping came from the homestead.

'That's enough, Benjamin. Thank you very much,' called the headmaster, sticking his head out the window.

There was laughter as the piper walked into the distance, his tune fading on the ears of the sleepers in the homestead and the huts. He tucked his beloved bagpipes under his arm and returned in silence. His pale face was burning with exultation, his hair and eyebrows bristled like sooty fur.

There was already the sound of running water coming from the washroom when he went in to splash himself with cold water and sober up. He turned on the light and squinted in the electric glare. Alex was there, standing at the sink in his pyjamas with a crumpled sack on the floor at his feet and the water gushing at full bore. He was washing something Benjamin could not see, rubbing red mud away.

'Why don't you turn the light on?'

'You woke me up, sir. Your noise. I didn't want anyone else to see me.'

'It's all right, Alex.'

A single light bulb projected from the wall. The cement floor was covered in water. The sink had a chipped mirror above it and there was a tongue of soap on the stainless steel tray. In the opposite corner, above a drain, a shower hose was rigged up. The boy stayed bent over the sink, cradling the precious object as Benjamin closed the washroom door and came inside. Alex peered at the man over his shoulder. He took a step forward, smiling at the boy's pink-striped pyjamas. Benjie looked funny. His black shoes shone, his socks were pulled up neatly and gartered below the knee with a flash of colour. He wore a tartan kilt and his sporran flopped as he moved, like a false beard. On top he wore the same khaki shirt he had been wearing all day, dusted with the same red dirt that was running through Alex's fingers into the sink.

'Did you ever wonder what's under a piper's kilt, Alex?'

'Undies, sir?'

'Are you sure? Look.'

The bagpipes carefully nestled under one arm, Benjamin moved closer by three shaking steps. Then he lifted the kilt and exposed his clean white Y-front underpants.

Alex looked at the man's bare white legs, which were covered with curly black hairs right up to where the underpants started. It was the first time he had noticed a man's hairs in that way. If Benjie counted as a man.

Benjamin stepped closer and took the boy's dripping hand away from the sink and traced it up his thighs against the prickly grain of all those tough hairs. 'Look, Alex.'

'Don't, sir,' pleaded Alex in a voice that was meant to sound polite but which came out husky and inaudible. He pulled his hand away and turned back to the water that was gushing into the sink as the man took a final step and pressed himself against Alex's pyjama bottoms. Then Alex farted in a loud bubbling trill. It was his only embarrassed defence against what might be happening to him. At that point Benjamin saw over the boy's shoulder what was in the sink. The dark hollow sockets of the skull fixed him with their gaze. It was washed almost clean, white save for some ingrained redness. The jawbone, held in place by Alex's hand, opened slightly. The mouth gaped up at him. 'He's Joe Skull,' Alex said. 'I've given him a name.'

Benjamin's stomach contracted. He laughed nervously and shrank back. His black shoes squeaked on the wet floor. 'They never lose the power to shock,' he grinned in imitation of the skull. 'Not a word of this to anyone, then, boy,' he went on, nodding at the thing in the sink. 'It's our secret.' He smoothed his kilt. 'Promise me, Alex, and I won't mention your mate here to anyone.'

Alex could not find the words of obscure gratitude to express the revelation of shared shame and blindness, both of theirs, in the ritual of initiation that Joe Skull had broken off.

'Thank you, Mr Benjamin,' was all he said, blushing awkwardly.

'Turn off the light when you're finished, won't you?'

A hissing sound came from the darkness as the piper came out of the washroom and down the dark corridor. All along the corridor were hissing voices mixed with stifled giggles. Disembodied voices, like snakes. Benjamin held his head proud and tall. The walls in the shearers' quarters were so thin that the voices seemed to come from everywhere and nowhere. He felt his way into the room where he would sleep. He climbed the ladder to his bunk. As he lay back in the darkness he heard what sounded like animals moving in the night, below him, as the boys crept back to their beds. In lisping imitation, Johnny Woodruff whispered: 'Did you ever wonder what's under a piper's kilt, Alex?'

Lying side by side on their backs on the deck of the dark tethered houseboat, the girls could sense the floating feeling of the boat as it rose and fell on the water. They floated themselves between sleep and dream, their imaginations as copious as the billowing Milky Way overhead. Stars, scattered like seed, sprouted into diamonds. The moon was like a brooch pinned to the bosom of the night. Wendy surfed the night on little surges of desire before an idealised image of Robbie Masterman that brought moisture between her thighs. Her hair sprayed out on the deck where she lay tight beside Jane, her most loyal friend, their raised knees touching, their thighs sliding, their backbones pressing against the boards in slow restlessness. Her fingers played with the dark bushy curls of Jane's head. Jane had one arm around Wendy's shoulders, and one arm reaching along Elspeth's slender arm on the other side. She was contemplating the constituents of the night: its blacks contained lights, its lights were a faded version of its black. As every other artist had done, Jane must become the night before she could enact it in ink and paint. She could do that while her friends were there to ground her. She did not know how to do it alone. Elspeth's flesh felt hot against the cool of Jane's arm. Elspeth's arms, running down the side of her body, her willowy legs, like paired oars, and her fine thick plait, leading from her head like a rope, all felt so long. She worshipped the pure void of the night, in which she longed to lose herself completely, leaving her body behind as if it were a mere plank as she crossed into a dimension of timelessness quite contrary to the patterns and constellations that Jane pieced together as she studied the sky. Orion, the Pointers, the Southern Cross and the Seven Sisters. The stars were the future patternings of their dreams and minds, the inky night their universe, the cool river breeze the breath of their bodies, in and out, long and shallow, as they lightened and floated off. In skin, teasing and prickling against skin, fingers tightening and toes interflexing, their spirit raft glided. Above the sluggish old river the bird soared, who became the morning-star, spirit of the people whose bones were unearthed that day.

5

ALEX was good at school work and happy to sit in his room with the hot desk lamp bending over him; or else he watched the black and white television obsessively. He argued with his father about the war in Vietnam using ideas he got from television and books. When his mother was in a talkative mood, after a few drinks, he argued with her too. Her arguments relied on free association to give rein to fantasy and rancour. His father felt uncomfortable listening. Then an argument would break out between Tim and Clarice Mack in a different register, and Alex would go back to his room or the television set. His sister Susan was spending her time with Robbie Masterman, who had become the captain of cricket at Alex's school. Alex went to dancing lessons with Elspeth, Wendy and Jane. He wished he could have invited Josie Ryan to dance with him, and go down behind the peppertrees at the back of the oval, where he would kiss her, but the Catholic schools had dancing classes of their own. Elspeth was competent and graceful in all things. Wendy made other people burn with desire and jealousy. Jane had the eyes, hands and ego of an artist. Alex was the top school debater.

The interschool debating tournament was held in the library at Alex's school, which had high mottled-glass windows like a chapel, an honour roll to those fallen in war where an altar would have been, and wooden pews for the audience of finalists, teachers and supporters, who were encouraged to mix over supper before the deciding debate.

Elspeth found herself sitting next to Cleve Gordon. Her team had been eliminated by Alex's in the last semi-final in a judgement that went against the grain for Joke, the girls' coach. Cleve's team was in the final.

'You remember Garry Adams?' Elspeth asked Cleve.

'Garry? Yeah?' Cleve replied.

'I thought it was you. You came to his birthday party one year, didn't you?'

Cleve laughed. 'You've got a good memory. Yeah, there was a girl there. Was that you? You've changed.'

Elspeth smiled. She barely considered that girl at the party to be herself. He looked at her admiringly. She had taken his side at the birthday party, but now she was beyond his reach. Cleve had changed too. He had life seriously in his hands.

'You still want to be an astronaut?' she laughed.

'You remember that too? Not now. I don't know what I want to be.'

'The first Aborigine in space!'

'Who said I was an Aborigine?'

'You are, aren't you?'

'You remember everything.'

'Space is reserved for the Russians and the Americans,' said Alex, butting in. 'They only put blacks in space like they put dogs in space.'

Cleve had learned it was better to grin than take on such goading humour.

But Elspeth was brazen with curiosity. 'Do you have Aboriginal religion?' she asked Cleve.

'What do you mean?'

'At Saint Joeys? Do they let you? Or do they train all that out of you to make you a good Catholic?'

'I'm just me.'

'What about *black* magic?' laughed Alex.

'Pointing the bone. That sort of thing?' continued Elspeth. Suddenly she remembered. 'Alex, you had some Aboriginal bones that you dug up from a place on the river. Didn't you? Whatever happened to them?'

Alex looked daggers at Elspeth. He had no idea she remembered. Back then was kids' stuff. But it was still his secret: the shoe-box in the bedroom wardrobe that contained Joe Skull.

'The school took us on an excursion to a property on the river where there was an ancient gravesite they attempted to excavate . . .'

Elspeth watched Cleve holding his face steady as Alex chattered to explain. Cleve's face revealed no response, except that behind the eyes, as blood drained a little from his face, a judgement was being made: of contempt, terror and shame.

'Weren't you scared of doing that?' asked Cleve.

Watching Cleve closely, Elspeth regretted exposing Alex in this way. But Alex sniffed in amusement. 'Not really. It was strange, though.'

'You didn't touch anything?'

'They dug them up!' blurted Elspeth. 'Whatever happened to those bones, Alex?'

'The school was going to take them to the Museum. They're lying around somewhere.'

'I heard you had a skull.'

'Who told you that?'

'Your Mum said so.'

'What use is something like that to you?' laughed Cleve eerily. 'You're crazy. It's not like the old days when the people used skulls as water carriers once there was no life left in them.'

'Is that true?' Alex was intrigued. 'Is that what they did with them?'

'In the old days they reckon that's how it was.'

Josie walked up with a plate of food. Elspeth looked at her vaguely and said nothing.

'Hi Josie,' said Alex. She had a cluster of freckles and some acne on her white cheeks. She wore glasses now.

'You swapping secrets with the enemy?' she said sparkily to Cleve, ignoring Alex. She and Cleve had not spoken since the night she surprised him ranting in the chapel. They saw each other from a distance at Mass. It was enough to be friends in silence.

'Sit down!' said Cleve.

'No thanks,' Josie said. She was far too tongue-tied to debate, but she could suddenly bite with a few saw-toothed words of criticism. She took her plate off somewhere else.

'What a freak!' said Elspeth. Then Ziggy appeared. He had turned up to watch Alex perform. He had left school when he turned sixteen and was flaunting his freedom from school uniform in a pink paisley shirt and purple velvet jeans. When he looked in their direction, Alex looked away. Elspeth was more unabashed. 'Ziggy!' she yelled. He pretended not to hear. 'Ziggy!' He turned stagily. 'It's Elspeth. Come over here and have something to eat.'

'The food's disgusting in this place,' he said as he came over, tossing his sun-bleached hair out of his eyes. 'Hi Elspeth.' He looked at Cleve. Alex giggled. 'How are you, Alex? Nervous? You'll be brilliant,' said Ziggy. 'I'll be back in two ticks. I'm going outside for a you-know-what.'

That was enough to make Alex go trailing after him.

There was a corner of the cloisters, dark and protected from the wind, where they could light cigarettes without being seen. They sat within the stone arch, backs against the wall, legs tucked up in front, facing each other.

'You should grow your hair,' advised Ziggy.

Alex's sandy hair was like a formless woolly wrapping around his head. 'We're not allowed to have it below the collar.'

'Pissweak,' snorted Ziggy. 'That's the trouble with school. There's plenty of stuff to learn. But I prefer to do it on my own terms.'

'You should go on television,' Alex said.

'It's only a matter of time.' Ziggy dropped his voice to a resonant bass. 'When I'm ready, man. I'm playing Hamlet. There's a director who wants me to do it. He's casting me in a professional production.'

'Really? Where? You're young, aren't you? Wasn't Hamlet supposed to be about thirty-five?'

'But young enough to have a father murdered and a mother posting to incestuous sheets.'

'When's it on?'

'I'll send you tickets for opening night. If you're still my friend.'

'Always, mate.'

Ziggy purred. 'Me too. Let's do something together. I want to. You're always so busy studying.'

Alex looked at Ziggy adoringly. Ziggy had style. 'You're going to be a star, Ziggy. I know that.'

'It's written in the stars. Look up there.' The cloisters disclosed a stretch of the evening sky. 'There it is. Z–I–G–G–Y. Can you see it? It's there for me. No matter what I have to do to get to it.'

Alex swung his legs down off the wall. 'Thanks, man. I better be getting back.'

'Break a leg or whatever you say. I don't mean it literally, stupid. It's a theatrical tradition.'

The library had a stuffy yellow glow and the air was stale. Drowsy after supper, people squeezed into the pews anticipating ingenious arguments for positions no one believed in. The motion for the final debate, between Alex's school and Saint Joeys, was that this house believes Beauty Lies in the Eye of the Beholder. Miss Jocelyn-Jones called on the first speaker and Alex walked calmly to the podium in his grey school suit.

'Ladies and gentlemen, when I grow up,' he began, lightly dabbing the smarting red pimple on his chin, 'one day soon –' there were titters already '– I will fall in love.' And the titters became splutters. 'Laugh if you like, because love *is* funny. It is desirable, so I am told, unpredictable, maybe inescapable. What makes it the great mystery is that there is no arguing with it. Only I can decide who I will love, and even I cannot decide, I can only experience it and proclaim it and when I do so you will probably think I am mad. What has this to do with Beauty, you may ask. I'll tell you. The object of my love is beautiful – to me, that is, but not necessarily to you. Otherwise there could be problems. More than that even, the object of my love is the most beautiful thing in the world, the benchmark, the epitome of Beauty – for *me*. I'm not talking about physical beauty or worth or suitability or any of the things that other people may comment on. I'm talking about an overall vision that is for me to say and me to know, for which all the other beautiful things, the moonlight and roses, the poems and pictures and songs, are only *metaphors*. Even God's love, I will shock you by saying, even our love for friends and family, becomes a pale imitation of this love of mine for the Entirely Beautiful.

'Love is blind, you will say. What if I change my mind? Does that mean my Beautiful was not really Beauty after all? Well, I am the judge of that too. If I see this as blue, ladies and gentlemen, you will never make me see it as red. You will not say I should love this one and not that one, or if you say so, you will have no power to enforce it. You might acknowledge that falling in love is the one exception, but let me in conclusion broaden the argument. Whatever we identify in our heart and soul as desirable, in nature or in art, or even a good idea, that is indeed Beauty. The capacity to find it lies entirely within our power. Beauty exists *nowhere* but in the eye of the beholder, and I challenge anyone –' Alex glowered at the opposing team, '– to tell me anything different. They will be wasting their time! Thank you!'

'I thought he had fallen in love a few times already,' whispered Elspeth as applause followed. Wendy pinched Jane's stockinged thigh under her skirt and made her giggle. Jane had her eye on Alex. Josie gave a demure smile and hung her head. Remembering how Alex used to dog her, when they were children, she accepted for herself the accolade of the Entirely Beautiful, for what it was worth from him.

The other speakers followed more conventional arguments, buttressed with quotations and facts, pro and con, relativism versus objectivity. One took a scientific line, one spoke of art and music, one talked about society, one about the manipulation of taste by consumerism.

Cleve was the last speaker for Saint Joeys. He stood robustly, gripping the podium in his light blue and dark blue blazer. He was his school's undisputed sports star, and had come good at English, whether handling words on paper or in public, as his debating showed. With a preacher's oratorical cadences, he began his slow delivery.

'It is the commonest thing in the world to hear people reckon that Beauty lies in the Eye of the Beholder. Even if they don't use those exact words, that's what people think. You can't argue with them. Even the fool has his reason. Maybe you think I look all right standing up in front of you. Do you look beyond that?' Cleve flashed his mocking eyes. 'When white men first came to this country there weren't enough white women to go around. The black women learned to run away pretty quick. Those blokes must have reckoned the black women were beautiful back then, before their white women came out and they came to see differently. The blacks could not even be beautiful like kangaroos and snakes are beautiful. So the ignorant whites destroyed the Beauty they could not see to create an ugliness that was Beauty to their eyes. "Beauty is Truth and Truth Beauty. That is all you know on earth and all you need to know", wrote a young Englishman called John Keats. He knew what he was saying. If you cannot behold the Truth that lies behind, what you think is Beauty is only a veil for your eyes.'

Cleve delivered these words with declamatory defiance. Looking across at Alex, he continued: 'I hear that one of our opponents has souvenired a black skull from one of the places along the river. I don't know whose skull it can be.' Alex blushed from white buttoned collar to the top of his scalp, his mat of sandy hair lifting from his skin. He was burning with embarrassment as the audience's eyes gradually turned, picking him as the one. 'I don't blame him. What I question is his attachment to this dead thing. I *do* question any Beauty he finds in it when he puts it up on the ornament shelf. It doesn't matter whose eyes you're looking through. That is Beauty of Wrongness and Foolishness, not the Beauty of Truth.'

They were clapping as Cleve went back to his seat. Josie patted her eyes with a screwed-up lace handkerchief. Elspeth applauded vigorously.

Then Joke, the adjudicator, allotted points to the speakers, giving Cleve a top score. Nevertheless she concluded that Alex's side had won the debate. Alex accepted the trophy for his team with a smug smile, commending the efforts of all the competitors.

Alex waited for Cleve on the library steps. He felt it was the right thing to be magnanimous in victory. But Cleve had slipped out through the cloisters. Alex went down to the bicycle shed to fetch his bike. He was longing to run into Josie. Then on the way he encountered Cleve walking slowly back with her. Cleve looked up, with a stern expression of solemn pride, knowing he had achieved something in exposing Alex.

'Do you want to see it?' Alex blurted.

'What's that?' responded Cleve.

'The skull you referred to.'

'We're on our way home,' Josie answered. 'Why would we want to hang around here anymore?'

'You can see it if you come to my place,' Alex said to Cleve.

'I'm walking Josie back,' he replied, as an excuse.

'It's only the other side of the park from her place. You can take her home first.'

'I'm okay,' said Josie. 'I'm okay to go home by myself, Cleve. You go.'

'I don't even believe the skull's real,' laughed Cleve.

'You spoke as if you knew,' Alex accused him.

'That girl said, that's all. Elspeth. I got the idea for a debating point. Fat lot of good. We deserved to win but that adjudicator bitch didn't want a riot on her hands.'

'Bullshit,' said Alex.

'You want to prove it?'

With that Alex lunged at Cleve, pushing Josie back in the process. Cleve was solid and well-positioned. With a light shove he sent Alex reeling backwards. But as he fell, Alex hooked his foot around Cleve's ankle and brought Cleve down on top of him. Alex was face down on the asphalt and his lip was smarting. Cleve struggled to pull himself away, righting himself in a rough exertion of strength. Alex, clutching his lip, rolled over in a ball.

'You'll be all right,' said Josie, kneeling down to see to Alex. 'No teeth missing. It was just an accident. Now get up.'

Then Elspeth came round the corner with her bike. Alex was dribbling bloody saliva onto the ground. He put out a trembling hand to Cleve.

'Sorry, man. I don't know what happened. I'd have a snowflake's chance in hell if I took you on.'

'You should stick to debating.' Cleve was grinning at him.

'Come and see the skull. I'll show it to you, honest,' Alex said.

'Can I see it?' asked Elspeth.

'I want *him* to see it,' said Alex.

They double-dinked as far as Josie's place. Cleve rode Elspeth's bike with Elspeth on the back and Alex took Josie. Then when Josie was safely through the gate, up the path and across the porch, where her blind grandmother was waiting with the light on, the others rode on up the hill through the dark park. Cleve got on the back of Alex's bike and weighed so much that Alex had to stand up to pedal. The bike swung wildly from side to side. Elspeth, alone on her own bike, got ahead in the dark and was waiting under a lamplight when they caught up.

'Fancy a bit, do you lassie?' sang out Cleve huskily as they veered at her.

Elspeth hooted with laughter. Then she rode swiftly ahead until she reached her front gate. The two boys followed.

'Better not come in,' she said as she looked from one boy to the other, the one familiar, belonging to her own people, the other a handsome stranger who came from a world completely outside. She felt a little dart run down her spine at the thought. 'Never know what Mum's up to. Sorry.'

Then Alex rode on with Cleve to his place. There was a light on in the front room and a muted raucous noise coming down the hall.

'Mum and Dad are watching television. Keep quiet and we'll go straight to my bedroom.'

'I shouldn't be here,' said Cleve, feeling the carpet underfoot, running his fingers over the flock wallpaper.

Alex switched on the desk lamp, shut the door of his room and told Cleve to sit down. But Cleve kept standing. Alex's swollen lip had started to throb. Cleve's eyes were so dark, thought Alex, like black oil, and his whites were bloodshot. His skin was a dull olive-brown. His hair, combed into place, was thick and wiry and he had a soft moustache on his upper lip.

'Do you want a Coke? I'll go and get one,' asked Alex in a gesture of hospitality, of acting the host.

Cleve was sitting at the desk when Alex came back with the drinks, looking at the geometry homework spread out there: compasses, a ruler, a set square, graph paper.

'What are you going to do when you finish?' asked Cleve.

'I'll probably do law,' said Alex.

'You already talk like a lawyer.'

'Me? You're the talker. How about you? They must have plans for you.'

'They want me to go into the seminary, once I'm certain of my vocation. Become one of them.'

'You won't do that, will you? That would be like becoming a witchdoctor.'

'What else am I supposed to do?'

'There's all sorts of things,' said Alex.

'Yeah? Name one.'

'You should do law. It would be useful.'

'Fat chance.'

'Go into politics.'

'Shuddup!' Cleve chuckled. 'Where's this famous skull?'

Alex brought down the green and white shoebox with split sides from the top shelf of the wardrobe. A bit of red dust trickled out. He put the box on the desk under the lamp and took off the lid. There was Joe Skull.

Cleve let out a hiss of breath. He did not move. Alex put his hands into the box and lifted out the skull. The dry white bone had a subtle graining of pink. The jaw was loosely in place, the teeth in their setting, the big flat molars and the smaller, sharper incisors. A couple of little teeth had come away and lay in the bottom of the box in a puddle of red dirt. Holding it carefully in his two hands, Alex offered the skull to Cleve, who still would not touch it.

'Jesus,' Cleve whispered.

'What do you think?' asked Alex. He wanted to ask whether the bone structure was familiar. It was an absurd question. He looked from the skull to Cleve's strongly moulded head. What did anyone's skull look like underneath their face and hair? It was something that you could never find out until they were dead.

'Is it old?' asked Alex.

'How would I know? It's not my Mum or Dad, if that's what you're asking. Well, I suppose it could be for all I know. It's probably not all that old. Some poor dead bugger.' There were suddenly tears in Cleve's eyes. He could not help himself. 'Put it away, please, mate.'

There was nothing Alex could say. He put the lid on as if the box were a little coffin and hid it away again at the top of the wardrobe.

'You're the only person I've ever shown it to.'

'Sorry, mate,' said Cleve, wiping his eyes. 'Don't know why I'm like this.'

'Sorry,' Alex said, putting his hand on Cleve's arm. 'Do you want a hankie? Here.' He pulled the grubby cloth from his trouser pocket and handed it to Cleve. 'What should I do about it?'

'How would I fucking know? Get rid of it. You shouldn't have it here.'

'Is it dangerous?'

'I'm warning you. If you sleep in here with it every night.'

'I gave it a name. I call it Joe Skull.'

Cleve shook his head and laughed. 'You're a sicko, mate. Get rid of it. Give it away. Before you get crook. I'm warning you.'

What Cleve said made Alex go cold. 'Do you have any brothers and sisters?' he asked Cleve.

'How would I know? I'm an orphan. Don't you know? My foster parents got me out of an orphanage. I've got no way of finding out who my real parents are. They could be like your skull by now. I might have heaps of brothers and sisters without even knowing. Anyone out there could be family to me for all I know. They're all family anyway, only not actual ones. You know what happens. People are just taken away.'

'Don't you remember?'

'I was a little kid.'

Alex jumped as the door handle turned. The door opened. It was his mother. The woman, swaying a little, put one hand against the doorframe to support herself. In a turquoise silk dress with her golden coiffure and her made-up face she seemed ready to fall into the room, into the circle of light shed by the desk lamp. Alex and Cleve looked up and said nothing, waiting for her to speak.

'Who's this, darling?' She focused on Cleve, who stood to attention. 'It's late, dear. You should have asked if you could bring someone home.'

'We just got back, Mum. We won the debating tournament. This is a friend of mine. I just wanted to show him something. Anyway,' said Alex, turning to Cleve. 'I suppose you better get back before they lock the gates. I'll take you.'

Clarice Mack wished there were words, bearable words, utterances, for what she wanted to share with her son – or with anyone. By the time she was ready to speak she was always floating too high or drowning too low to find the meanings she needed, and she was abandoned to her frustration. 'You're not going out again at this hour?'

'I'm dinking him home,' Alex insisted.

'Your father can drive him. Tim?' his mother hollered as she went off down the corridor to fetch her husband. 'Where is he?'

Alex raised his eyebrows helplessly. Cleve looked concerned. 'I can walk. I know the way. It's not too far.' He enjoyed walking by himself at night.

Then Mrs Mack returned with Alex's father.

'Where are you from?' Mr Mack asked.

'Saint Joeys.'

'Saint Joeys?' The man echoed Cleve's words. 'You're a boarder,' he said. 'No problem.'

Then Alex's mother shrieked, seeing the lip that Alex had been hiding in the shadow of his hand. 'What happened, darling?'

'Nothing, Mum.'

She ran her fingers over her son's split lip.

Mr Mack winked at Cleve. 'Got himself into a bit of a scrape, did he? You came out of it a bit better, I suppose. He'll learn. Well, come on now.'

'See you later, Alex,' said Cleve as he followed Mr Mack out of the house.

Back at school Brother Gavin was waiting for him once again with stern Christian counsel for breaking the curfew. He threatened Cleve with a belting. Cleve laughed. He could make mincemeat of Brother Gavin if he wanted, if his Christianity had not taught him to grin and bear what was served up to him.

6

A LEX'S mother cried and cried the winter's day her father died, while her own mother clung from her arm like a dog turning to a new owner. Her father had a heart attack at the races and was dead before reaching hospital, where he lay pale and surprised in his fine socks, slipped into a dead man's shoes, a memory of gentlemen's ankles on the Dublin docks. He had carried to Australia, as a twisting silk, the standards and values of Anglo-Irish custom that were as sacred as the Book of Common Prayer. An Irish seaman's son become eminent surgeon, he was a man within whose bounds life could be lived decently. Clarice Mack was devoted to her father, grateful to him for keeping the family's name good. In the grain town where he commenced his career, his wife had closed her door on the local community, keeping herself for a dancing teacher who came afternoons in a whirl of cologne, smoke and phonograph records. But by then there was money to send the child away to school. On the day Clarice was deposited at boarding school, aged nine, her father led her forward by the hand, while her pampered mother stayed in the car. It was her father's blessing that counted when she accepted Tim Mack as her husband. It was *his* pride that helped her cope when the children were born. Later, when she was depressed, her father gave her pills. Without him, her world made no sense, and she spun in her own space, incomplete within her completeness, a mystery she saw in Alex too. But because he was a boy he must learn how to act in the world at the same time.

Then, in the spring, Clarice decided to get rid of everything. It was not that the house was untidy. The hedge was clipped, the borders were neatly edged, the petunia seedlings sat in rich loam ready to bloom purple and pink for Christmas. The roof and trim were repainted in recent memory; the carpets, wallpapers and curtains inside were new enough. Everything was clean, even the guest bedroom and bathroom, ready for her mother, should she decide to move in. But the house was filled with things stored away and this suddenly struck Clarice as weighing her down. She went from room to room piling things up, feeling lighter and more enchanted the further she went. By midmorning, after she had downed a tumbler of vodka, sucking a peppermint to disguise the alcohol, she was doing nicely. Newly-wed crockery, Tim's school photos, furs, outmoded appliances, half-drunk liqueurs, picture books and children's toys, Barb Gillingham's gifts from all over the world, even her father's inkstained deskset: all must be shoved into limbo.

She took a load of treasures to the charity shop, and when she came back, she had another shot of drink to keep going. Her husband seemed pleased with himself these days, she thought, although he tried to hide it from her. She laughed at the idea that he was having an affair. She could not imagine how he would have time. Actually she was not so much jealous as disappointed. She shivered at how far she had come in twenty years.

Susan would kill her, she knew, if she touched any of the jumble of her daughter's sporting equipment, girl guide paraphernalia, dolls, science bits and pieces, shocking make-up, a Birthday Book, diaries left open to perusal, Robbie this Robbie that, all in use all the time, tribute to the girl's bounding energy. All Clarice could do was cull the wardrobe and, with a bundle in her arms, close the door on her daughter's life and leave.

Alex's room was different. It held smellier secrets, a consequence of the power a boy feels in touch with in adolescence, the pre-potency that Clarice sniffed as she began moving things around. Unwashed clothes, tennis shoes, the windowsill of stones, quotations from poets and philosophers neatly transcribed in notebooks, her son's odorous scrawled poetry. Her nose led her to the wardrobe, a moist dark trove in which anything might grow. She was wary of putting in her fingers in case they were bitten off. At the back of Alex's socks, she found the green and white shoebox. Digging her arms deep into the darkness, she pulled it forward. Cradling its split sides, she carried the box to the desk and cleared a space on the blotting paper where she could examine the contents. She lifted the torn lid. The skull, moon white with a fine veining of red, sat there like an extinct egg. She took only one look and looked no more. Unsteady from drink, telling herself to have another one, she put the lid back on and carried the box straight out the back door of the house. It leaked earth and bone dust all the way.

'Alas, poor Yorick!' she sighed, laying it on the back seat of the car.

She wove down the backstreets, hoping she was immune to other cars travelling at speed. It was not far to the tip. She cut through the park, down the hill, over the railway line to a road that sliced across the plain towards the port. She reached the tip without erring. It stank, not of adolescence but of fecund transforming matter, chemical and vegetable, leaves, rags and jagged glass, rusting metal and wood turning to rich humus in the afternoon sun. The mounds of rubbish were like a miniature range of mountains. At intervals a bulldozer took up its position and bore down on a rubbish mountain, flattening the garbage into a paste of soil that was studded with bright plastic and metal shards.

Clarice opened the car door and deposited her plastic bags and cartons on the side of the mound that she judged most likely to be the bulldozer's next victim. The old suitcase that she laid down her parents had taken to Europe on their first trip overseas together, while she stayed behind to complete her last year of boarding school. It had rusting metal fasteners, a stiffened leather strap and a collage of grand hotel labels: Montreux, Monte Carlo, Positano, Danieli, Eden, Ritz. Clarice didn't care either that she and Tim had taken the same clumsy suitcase on a family motoring holiday to visit the Snowy Mountains Hydroelectric Scheme. Time for it to go. She heaved it forward a little and it tumbled on its corner and slithered down the mountain of garbage to rest at her feet, where she gave it a last ineffectual kick.

Then she laid Alex's shoebox on the mound. She formed a pocket for it in a pile of vegetable parings and restaurant waste. No one would have guessed that the small insignificant box contained a skull and crossbones, or whatever it was, desiccating inexorably into pinkish salt-and-pepper dust.

She sat with the car windows closed as the bulldozer crept forward. It was best that she saw the bones buried. If they were found by accident, someone might get the wrong idea. Ask questions. It was best that she watched the remains return to earth. Part of the rubbish pile was smouldering. The bulldozer spread this slow-burning refuse into the next mountain that was its target as it crawled over the ground, mixing dirt and smoke with discarded matter, until at last the grader blade came to the slope where the old shoebox sat. Clarice imagined a pop as the steel teeth crushed it. Pop, like an eggshell cracking, or a grape in the mouth, or a butterfly's life. Burst, and then nothing left but a smeared, blackened mess, and the horrid roar of the machine. She had managed the clean-up without breaking any of her fingernails. But she could feel, as she nervously rubbed her hands together, fine dust from the skull box between the pads of her fingers, abrasive and dry. She could feel the fine grit from her fingers on the steering wheel. She tried not to grip the wheel too tightly. The car started to veer. Everything shuddered and swam. A car screamed to a halt almost in her path and honked her as she continued across the intersection.

She could not wait to get home, to wash the dust from her hands and steady herself with another drink.

Joe Skull was Alex's secret, something he protected in darkness at the back of his wardrobe. In the knowledge of what he possessed there was an untried, uncertain power. Now it was gone he felt alarmed that he had not carried out the responsibilities of possession. Temporary possession. Unconferred custodianship. He had always felt the time would come when those objects passed on into another's more rightful hands, but until that day they were his, provisionally, until he could identify the right person, and now that step had been taken out of his hands by another. He accused his sister of being in a conspiracy with those other people who knew about the skull.

'What would I want with your old bones?' Susan scoffed. She was a university student now and found Alex ridiculous.

'Give it back, you creep,' he shouted at her, red in the face.

She grabbed his wrist and twisted his skin in a Chinese burn as hard as she could. 'You're so immature. I didn't touch it. Do you believe me?'

'Let me go!' He yanked his hand away from her, realising how undignified he was being. 'All right, I believe you.' The last childish thing had been snatched out of his hands, and he was furious.

'Ask Mum,' Susan said. 'Maybe she knows something about it. She's been cleaning out the house all day.'

'Mum?' he scowled. To discover that Susan did in fact know something useful made Alex angrier than ever. His lower lip began to tremble.

'Where is she?'

'She's on the bed.'

Clarice Mack had taken one of her pills and lay on the bed with the curtains drawn and cold wet pads of cotton wool on her closed eyelids. She felt emptied after her cleaning mission, proud of how much she had got rid of, light and unballasted as she drifted like a cuttlefish on a drowsy tide.

'Mum?' ventured Alex, entering without bothering to knock. 'Have you been in my room?'

'What's that?' she murmured.

'Have you been in my room? Did you take anything?'

'It needed tidying. You shouldn't need me to do it for you, Alex. You're a big boy now.'

'Some things are missing. If you didn't move them, then some-one else did.'

'I took your dirty clothes away. You're reading some awful things, dear.'

'You shouldn't pry, Mum.'

'I found that box of bones at the back of the wardrobe. It's been there for years. It's disgusting.'

'You didn't touch it, did you, Mum? It's mine.'

Alex stood by the bed looking down on his mother's pale form as his eyes grew used to the dark. She tilted her face and the pads fell from her eyes. 'You can turn the light on if you like,' she said in slurred, weary words. The dim yellow bedside light gave her a romantic glow. 'It's gone to the tip.'

Alex went hot all over. His voice was raised, with a jagged edge. 'You're joking, aren't you, Mum? You wouldn't dare. Tell me where you've put it.'

Clarice frowned at the growling anger in her son's voice, the underlay to his coaxing bantering tone. She could not understand what concerned him so much. 'Don't get upset, darling,' she said. 'What did you want with it, anyway?'

'It's mine. I don't have to tell you my reasons.' Alex surprised himself with the strength of his feelings. His secret world – invaded, violated. The frustration he felt pushed up through him with the force of a piston. The sacred objects of that time of initiation between boyhood and manhood, between play and duty, stolen – and by his mother. 'Where's the box gone?' he demanded.

'Don't speak to me like that. I said it's gone to the tip.'

'Who took it there?'

'I was cleaning out.'

'Which tip?'

'The council tip.'

'The garbage tip?'

'That's right.'

'The dump?'

'The dump. What else were you going to do with that stuff?'

Alex was shaking. He could not believe he had not been consulted. It made a mockery of his incipient authority, his rationality, his maturity, when someone could just swoop in like that. His own mother. 'When did you do this?'

'I've got a headache, darling. Will you lower your voice, please?'

'You should have asked me, Mum.'

Her eyes crossed from side to side. Mother and son were as close as could be, like one person in shared understanding, which made her know what she had done to him. He was hostile. He would never forget this work of hers, this knifing of the dark threads that joined him to a world of imagination and power beyond her reach. 'I'm sorry,' she stammered at last, 'I didn't know it meant so much to you.'

Then Susan came in. 'It was Mum who did it, wasn't it? About time too. You've put a curse on all of us with that thing.'

Clarice got up heavily from the bed and went to her dressing table where she powdered her face and brushed her hair. They heard footsteps pacing up the hall. 'It's Dad home,' said Susan, while Alex stared in silence at the back of his mother's head and his mother stared into the mirror at her puffy face, puffy from drink and sleep and pills, and over her shoulder, in the reflection, at her son's dumb pain.

Tim Mack entered what was evidently a family hearing with awkward cheeriness. 'How is everyone?' he asked.

'I've spent the day slaving and get no thanks from these two,' replied his wife.

Tim looked around for an interpretation. 'She's been spring cleaning,' explained Susan.

'You didn't have to do that.' The man dropped his voice soothingly as he laid a hand on his wife's shoulder in something between a grip and a pat.

'She took my collection of Aboriginal bones from up the river and threw them out. She didn't appreciate their scientific value,' said Alex, mitigating the circumstances of his mother's crime.

'Of dubious value,' corrected his father. 'In the eye of the beholder purely.'

'You're fucked,' was all Alex had left to say as he turned around and pushed past his sister and father out into the hall. 'It's not fair!'

The gates of the garbage dump were closed and padlocked. Inside the high wire fence the manager's fibro hut sat like a palace in isolated pride in the flattened area of waste. Mounds of garbage smouldered in the dusk behind. Alex leaned on his bike against the fence, peering at the blurred and shadowy landscape for what he sought: a green shoebox or a stark white skull. Already he knew it was hopeless. What had been discarded in just a day was layers deep. The tip was like a hungry mouth that fed and fed on the remains of life, returning it to earth, rendering all the utensils, ornaments and sustenance that civilisation refined back into unformed clay; cast aside, sacrificed, laid to rest.

Simian fingers and toes pulled him up and over; he jumped to ground on the other side where the earth was damp and freshly pressed. He dug his toe against a chop bone. But that was not what he had come for. He ran across to the place where new rubbish was left and gazed at the slope of refuse rising before him. It was like a ramp to walk up which then loosened and fell away like scree; he stumbled and was up to his knees in it.

A rat on a neighbouring pile looked at him and turned on its elegant curled tail to disappear under the surface. In places smoke seeped from below and dispersed in the evening breeze like a kind of acrid incense, cleansed of the smell of decay. Turn back, Alex told himself; wade no further. To find Joe Skull was an impossibility like unto a rich man trying to enter the kingdom of heaven. He let out a howl of protest and hurt, and a histrionic tear dropped, like a pearl, from his cheek.

The grey netherworld of the low western suburbs sent up shafts of orange and gold as the golden jelly of the sun squished below the horizon line. The whole place was coloured with fire, turning refuse to apricot and salmon, mud to gilt. The drifting smoke, crawling over the rubbish tip, fingering its nooks and crannies, rose slowly into the flame until the sky was blood-red. He had looked everywhere, but the box was not to be found. He followed the track back to the gate. Joe Skull was sacrificed to the blood and mire and fire and gold of the council dump, broken back into the earth in a halo of redness; once a human, a powerful heroic figure, brought down by disease or defeat in the strength of prime, in another time, carried by Alex to one place, and carted off by his mother's outrageous and pitiful whim to this final inglorious annihilation. Rest in peace.

'Fight on,' Alex spoke aloud, as he strode towards the fence on two untiring legs, as Joe Skull had once done, over the earth of this place. 'Fight on and make your own victories.' A mongrel dog barked as he climbed over the fence to the outside and recoupled with his bicycle to pedal in sadness home.

~

Alex appreciated his mother's tribulations as a drama of the spirit, but could do little to alleviate the situation. Such were the fruits of the protected childhood Clarice Mack had given her children. But she was not going to alter to suit them. She would rather watch herself crumble in a hell of unwanted change. In her dreams, she embraced infinities of pain and desire, masks and monsters, Shakespearian savageries and ecstasies, a surging population filling the imaginative realm that her socialised mind suffocated. Tim Mack, promoted to corporate manager of the mining company, was in the business of entertaining clients and when it became too burdensome to bring them home, where his wife sailed between embarrassing charm and abuse, he took them out. It was to spare her or let her alone that he did it, perhaps to banish her as a naughty child or wicked witch. He scowled, and she was abased, until there was nothing else left between them except a grey and threadbare devotion.

On weeknights Alex sat at his textbooks under the hot yellow lamp. He expanded and contracted mathematical equations until his eyes would not stay open, then he cleaned his teeth and washed his face for bed. Susan had a car of her own, an unreliable orange Datsun, and was out. His father was out. His mother had left lights on as she lay sleepless in bed. When she heard Alex flush the lavatory she called out goodnight.

He came and stood in her doorway in his pyjamas.

'Don't strain your eyes,' she said.

He was a tall lean boy with a dreamy play of half-smiles and concealed sorrows across his face. He had a quality of hungry engagement too, that if he didn't lose too many battles would become a defiant charm. She was proud of him.

'Where's Dad?' he asked indifferently.

'I don't know. He won't be long. Susan's late. She's getting too big for her boots. Don't turn out the light too late, darling.'

His mother's head looked lovely against the skyblue satin pillow. Her obdurate and vulnerable expression, lips slightly tightened and an arching forehead, was comforting to him. He got into bed and read a few pages of the clay-coloured paperback he had bought himself after school, between buses, in the city, where he used to go for piano lessons. The shining, pebbly sentences soon weighed down his eyelids. *I see now that this has been a story of the West, after all – Tom and Gatsby, Daisy and Jordan and I were all Westerners, and perhaps we possessed some deficiency in common which made us subtly unadaptable to Eastern life.* He curled over and turned out the light. He kept his window six inches open to the night and a quiet corner of the back garden that, rustling and summery-fragrant, was 'sensual', he noted for his diary, as he flexed and curled, a coiled frond, in the warmth of the bed.

~

Clarice sat in the dappled shade of Barb Gillingham's garden. Barb's greying hair and her tough tennis player's body were products of experience, Clarice thought. Somehow Barb made all the parts of her life gel, from morning coffee to marriage, in ways Clarice could never manage. Perhaps appetite was the key, thought Clarice, as her friend passed the iced cupcakes.

A green cannonball from the sturdy walnut overhead thumped onto the white thigh of Barb's culottes and brought forth an oath. She pulled back the cloth to check her veiny skin. The varicose veins were like a root system breaking the surface. 'I'll have to get these done, I suppose,' said Barb, tracing the protruding ropes. 'How are yours?'

Clarice's thighs were still good. Only her distended tummy gave away the changes in her. She put on her sunglasses and looked across the lawn to the intense turquoise blue of the swimming pool. As her body grew heated from the coffee, she felt herself drawn with longing to soak in the pool's tingling cold.

'I did my laps first thing,' said Barb.

'I had to bundle Alex off to his last exam today,' said Clarice. 'Stop him getting flustered. But he's so organised really.'

'I ignore Elspeth. If she wants to study, she'll do it without me fussing. She's a stubborn cow.'

'Alex will go away to university next year if he gets the results he expects.'

'Is that his idea?'

Clarice took off her sunglasses and folded them up, showing her confused blue eyes. She gave no answer.

'Hard on you,' commented Barb. 'You'll miss him.'

'Tim says it's time for him to grow up.'

'I hear Tim's been doing a bit of growing up of his own lately.'

'What's that?'

Barb straightened her spine on the wrought-iron chair. 'He's moved up a few notches, hasn't he? He's a bit of a corporate figure, and all that.'

'What are you trying to say, Barb?'

'We're friends, Clarice – it's only what I pick up from Angus.'

Clarice decided to take the opportunity. 'Who is it? Come on, Barb.'

'If I knew, I'd tell you. Promise. You know me. Look, I shouldn't have told you this much. You won't do anything silly?'

'Like what?'

'Divorce.'

The word made Clarice cry because she knew she had no capacity to exist outside the arrangements in which she found herself. Yet in her whole inward being she was separate from everything. She started to sob like a sick animal in Barb's arms.

'You are a beautiful girl,' whispered Barb, encouraging Clarice's suffering to flow out. 'You're drinking a bit too much, you are, my girl,' said Barb. 'That's your trouble.'

'Tell me why I shouldn't,' Clarice bleated. 'No one helps me with anything.'

'Come on. Chin up. Straight back. Say again what you just said.'

'What did I say?'

'You said you need help.'

Clarice bit her lips. 'No one can help me,' she replied with a pained smile.

There was a point at which division occurred, at which the strong left the weak behind, at which life just moved on, leaving behind the remains of the world it had been feeding on till then. No matter how boundless your compassion, thought Barb, you could not help those who would not help themselves. 'Where's your grit, Clarice?' she asked harshly, unable to avoid showing her disapproval. 'Pick yourself up and get on with it. That's all you have to do.'

But the woman was like a netted stingray being dragged slowly up the beach into an element in which she could not breathe. Almost despite herself, she had decided to reject Barb's good sense. She looked again at the inviting blue light reflected from the swimming pool, then returned her dark glasses to her nose.

'I'm sorry about this, Barb dear. It's not your fault.' Clarice sniffed. 'Tell me who the woman is.'

'It's no one we know. She works in catering. In a pub, I suppose. The name I got was Audrey Ryan.' Barb hooted. 'A good Catholic name.'

'Not the ironing lady?'

'It would be, wouldn't it?'

'The slag!'

'That's right,' said Barb. 'You don't have to take her seriously. Now would you like a swim? It's a real scorcher of a day.'

'I'll sink after that cupcake. Oh well, why not?' Clarice never said a word more about it. She never inquired, nor accused. She took a sour pleasure in her secret knowledge and the illusion of power it gave her. That was enough. Only once, in a tender moment, she asked her husband if he loved her. Taken by surprise, he could only answer helplessly that he did, he loved her with all his heart.

7

NEAR the river mouth, running to the south-west tip of the peninsula, the Gillinghams had an acreage with a stone cottage that they planned to refurbish for their retirement one day. That westward-facing coastline of ancient hills and sandy beaches, beyond where the river emptied its sluggish currents into the ocean, was a reminder of other journeys, from other lands, to this place. For Clarice Mack, as she walked barefoot on the white sand, that shore took her across the water to the grain town where her beloved father had been the doctor, before she was sent away to school. The ocean spread its sparkling train towards where that town might have been, a small town just across the water, a sail ride away on a kindly day, and beyond it the islands that lay like stepping stones to the sky.

'Clarice!' called her husband. 'Are you going in?'

She shook her head. She was only wading in the shallows.

'The tents are up,' Tim announced as she turned back towards him. There was a separate tent for the parents, and a boys' tent that Alex would share with the older boys, Johnny Woodruff and

Robbie Masterman. Susan Mack was in the girls' tent with Elspeth, Jane, the Sunner girls and Sophie Masterman. The New Year camping holiday had become a ritual which the Woodruffs, the Sunners, the Gillinghams, the Mastermans and the Macks struggled to maintain. The men strode about like explorers, shifting the campsite from here to there and back again until at last someone hammered a spike into the ground to make a claim and from there it began. This time they had found an open patch of grass surrounded by she-oaks and nestled among sandhills on the other side of a sweeping surf beach. They carted fresh water across the paddocks from the tank at the Gillinghams' old cottage, identified a barbecue site, dug a dunny upwind and rigged up an army-disposal tarpaulin as a mess-tent. Friends, for ten or twenty years – schoolmates, colleagues, bridesmaids, best men – they all shared the sense that this life belonged to them. Unfolding canvas chairs and pulling drinks from the cooler, they were in business.

'Cheers,' they said, clinking their goodwill wishes round the circle.

The test match between England and Australia was playing on the car radio. The kids were on the beach. The women lay in their tents, brushing away the flies as they tried to read their holiday books. The men wandered off to poke about in the bush or go through to the beach, except Dr Woodruff, red-faced under a cloth cap, who was the one to stay put on his camp stool and keep the cricket score. 'Owzat!' he called, to proclaim that a Pommie wicket had been taken at last. After twenty years in Australia Don Woodruff, a Yorkshireman, barracked for the Australian side in the Ashes, never failing to feel wickedly rebellious towards Home. He considered himself to be as much an Aussie pioneer in his work at the Weapons Research Institute as any of the explorers or squatters before him.

Tim Mack had gone to the tent where his wife lay flat on her back with her eyes shut, feigning sleep. If he stepped inside, she would stir and complain about the other people there, and since he was in no mood for her negativity in the first flush of the camp's freedom, he moved on across the grass – pausing by the opening of the Woodruffs' tent to peer inside at Alison Woodruff, who had her knees up and a big fat novel propped against her thighs. Crop-haired Alison was the most athletic of the wives, the brainiest and the most vivacious. Clarice said she was like a blowfly.

'Cooling off in there?' Tim asked.

'Heating up,' she laughed. 'I suppose you don't read these steamy things?'

'I don't get much time to read.'

Alison grinned. 'Too busy with other things.' They had all heard the rumours about Tim Mack. 'You should learn to unwind, Tim. We're on holiday. It doesn't matter what we do with our time.'

'Once a year, eh?'

As they looked at each other, Alison's book slipped sideways. 'Where's Clarice?'

'Sleeping.'

'Good for her. It'll be a late night tonight.'

Tim looked over his shoulder at Alison's husband on the camp stool, ear bent to the cricket. 'You beauty!' yelled Don Woodruff.

Tim cocked his head cheerily. 'Another one out, Don?' He raised his eyebrows at Alison and turned away, tramping over the hills, unobserved except by his son, who recognised his father's determined gait on the sandy track to the beach.

Alex was sitting with Jane and Wendy in a shaded basin of sand below the crest of the biggest sandhill. It gave them a vantage-point.

'There goes Dad,' sighed Alex as his father's dark green T-shirt disappeared into the trees.

'Is your Mum okay?' asked Wendy.

Jane laughed. 'She's so gracious. So polite. Then she just fades out.'

'Her eyes tell you something completely different from what she says,' Wendy observed. 'It's frightening.'

'She knows what's going on,' contradicted Alex. 'You don't have to say everything you think.'

'You don't have to say anything,' declared Wendy, 'but if you don't . . .'

'Things aren't real until they're out in the open,' insisted Jane, 'until you can see them.'

'They're usually much more boring then,' said Wendy. 'If you don't say it, it's still a mystery, no matter how crass.'

'You can have a mystery between people even if you do speak about it,' argued Alex, 'as long as the perception is shared. It's when an outsider comes along who only sees the outside . . . then it's pretty embarrassing.'

'I need my dark glasses,' said Wendy. 'I'm going down to the tents. Will you two still be here when I get back?'

Jane stretched back on the sand to watch Wendy pick and swish her way down the sandhill, white sand tumbling in drifts where she ploughed her feet. With one hand Wendy caught up her honey-coloured hair, pulling it away from her neck to the top of her head.

'She's an exquisite nymph,' said Jane. Then she flashed her eyes at Alex, who was unappreciative where Wendy was concerned, and laughed sharply.

At the campsite Wendy encountered Dr Woodruff. He was like the camp guard, she thought, a kapo, his big hairy thighs planted wide apart on the ground and his fat bum stretching the camp stool to breaking point.

'Hot enough for you, Wendy?'

'I forgot my sunglasses, Dr Woodruff.'

'Would you like a cool drink? They're in the cooler here.'

Ignoring him, she went into the tent and rubbed some baby oil into her arms and smooth-shaven legs. She thought about lighting up a cigarette and relaxing on the stretcher-bed for a few moments, idly splaying her hibiscus-pink toenails and indulging a few sweet thoughts about Ivan her lover who was a fire-eater in a circus that toured the coast during summer. She would see him that night at the big New Year's Eve party in the nearby town. She heard the slapping of thongs. Then the scaly feet of Don Woodruff appeared under the flap, and his shadow slowly passed the tent. Gross old pervert. She put on her dark glasses and stuffed the cigarettes and lighter inside her bikini pants and stepped out to confront him. Dr Woodruff took one look at the girl and was slack-jawed. Her shocking pink bikini, the baby oil shiny on her skin and the thick spray of hair around the big glasses that hid her eyes made his blood race. He groaned a little as he found himself putting an arm round her shoulders. Love of my life, he thought.

'You found them then?'

The girl pouted, wriggling her body to dislodge his hand. The days when she found Jane's father funny were long gone. He made her want to throw up.

'You kids think you're immune to the sun,' he warned. 'You want to cover up.'

'I don't care how black I get, Dr Woodruff, as long as I don't peel. Peeling can be unpleasant,' she said as she flounced off.

'Little tart,' he stammered under his breath. Her bum wiggled its way through the empty camp chairs. He could eat her. She would like that. Only there would be hell if his wife found out.

Alex and Jane were lying side by side when Wendy got back, their fingers loosely entwined. They were brushing the sand off each other's feet with their toes.

'The darlings,' cooed Wendy.

Jane smirked at her best friend. 'We thought you weren't coming back.'

Dr Gillingham organised a party to gather driftwood and dry sticks for a bonfire on the beach. His wife was over at their derelict cottage with Elspeth and Susan. Barb Gillingham was quick to see how something could be remade as she led the girls through the house tapping, poking and prying. A Masterman-that-was, she had inherited from her illustrious forebears the conviction that anything could be made or unmade in this country. You earned the land by turning it into something. In her bones she had the memories of artisan and labourer, housekeeper and bookkeeper, as well as of squire and lady. The garden was overgrown with waist-high grass and a tidal surge of blackberry, roses as high as the house, tangled with boxthorn and wild olive, broken-boughed almonds, a grove of stunted orange-trees and one undulating fig.

'We'll get it back,' Mrs Gillingham swore, quite undaunted.

'Shame you can't just leave it,' said Elspeth. She never sympathised with her mother's determination to prove a point. 'Let it revert to nature completely and you could turn it into an Indian temple garden.'

'Start with spraying the blackberries,' ordered her mother, speaking to an imaginary groundsman, 'and burn the canes.'

Susan Mack nodded. 'You need some sort of plan.'

Then Mrs Gillingham looked Susan straight in the eye and said, 'I'm worried about your mother.'

Susan frowned. She wished her mother was more like Mrs Gillingham, sensible and down to earth. 'She won't help herself,' said Susan – responding in the manner demanded.

Elspeth, stepping away, found the paving slates of a path beneath the tangled growth and delicately followed it into the shady arms of the figtree as if she were already high priestess of her own sacred unkempt garden.

Clarice came out of her tent in her swimsuit and sun hat. The other women – Isabel Sunner, Alison Woodruff and Rosie Masterman – were at work preparing food for the evening. They let Clarice go, assuming she needed to clear her head. She had only to be a guest at their feast. Her bare feet seemed to touch the ground through a satiny membrane, not making contact, as if she were a curious organism all her own within the warm palpitating body of the world. Likewise her mind, under her widebrimmed straw hat, behind sunglasses and shining eyes, beneath her pancaked skin, was a world apart. She could not say where the emptiness was, inside or outside, as she walked in the baking light that throbbed with insects, dead leaves and grass crackling underfoot. Then a corner of her eye caught the snake lying like an unbarked stick across the path, a smooth, glossy king brown, the colour of wet yeasty dough, several feet long. Becoming aware of her, he quickly stopped his slow travel and turned in her direction, rearing his strong neck. Clarice froze, staring into the snake's eyes and open, fanged mouth, the snake frozen too. Ever so slowly she backed off three or four paces. At a certain point, aware of her movement, the snake lowered his head, lashed his tongue in and out for a few seconds, then raced up the sandhill through the pigface. She saw him go, his full glinting length flashing a trail over the ground. Then he was gone. Entranced by the apparition, she stood breathing and floating, her limbs shaking, and with regular shallow breaths she stepped forward across the snake's invisible track until she came with relief to the open beach and the dazzling, tumbling water.

Left and right up the beach she picked out people. Footprints radiated in complex patterns from the pile of wood for the bonfire that made an impressive cairn in the sun's acute angle. Each footprint was edged with shadow. The sea had its shadows too: a place for stepping off, she thought. Stepping into the shallows Clarice could feel the sea's undertow pulling at her ankles to topple her. She retreated from it, declining to swim, and walked up the beach a little way to sit on the sand, clasping her knees to her body, like a small black island under the brim of her hat. There was no end-point, only the silvery brightness washed down from the sky, no other land, no mirage of land, only immense shining emptiness.

Then she noticed two black marks transcribing a curve across the backdrop of light. A pair of pelicans came down over the waves on a huge span of wing, like two plump passenger planes. Then the foremost bird dipped into the water, upending, and got a fish. The bird, the female, surfed into shore, waddled up the sand and stood there gobbling, beak vertical in one axis with her long neck. The male followed suit, and the pair stood together feeding on the sand while a flock of lesser seabirds came circling in to feast off the shoal of fish herded shorewards by the threatening shadow of out-stretched wings. Kindly pilgrims, wondered Clarice, in search of a shriving? She remembered the myth of the pelican who gives her blood to feed her young. The fish in her shell-sharp beak was blood to be drained from her own side. Then the pelicans, having devoured the fish, took off up the beach, one behind the other, becoming two black marks again in the beginnings of sunset.

Peter Sunner and Angus Gillingham were coming along the beach, chatting earnestly about an investment partnership, when they recognised her.

'What are you doing, Clarice?' asked Angus.

'Did you see the pelicans?' Clarice replied.

'The place is rich with birdlife,' observed Peter.

'Right as usual, Peter,' she said. The pelicans in their getting and spending were probably better business managers than he was. 'I saw a snake too,' Clarice added, not expecting to be believed.

'A snake?' echoed Peter.

'Joe Blake,' rhymed Angus. 'Well, don't tell the others. It'll only scare them.'

Don Woodruff in an apron supervised the grilling of the meat. The table was covered with a blue and white check cloth for the occa-sion and spread with buttered rolls and salads. They drank fruity local claret from long-stemmed glasses. Peter Sunner liked to talk politics. He believed in government with a light touch by those who knew what was best for everyone. He wanted to move the chocolate factory to new premises and that could only happen if the state government provided a favourable loan. The chocolate, like the state's meat and wine, was the best in the world: he wanted to boost local exports. Standing with his old friends for their annual celebration, he was an innocent middle-aged man who did not understand how he could fail to get his loan and build the new plant. He was the first to propose a toast on that New Year's Eve, wishing for a change of state government in the elections the new year would bring. 'Time for a change,' he charged. 'Time for some politicians we can relate to.'

'Or preferably are related to,' quipped Angus Gillingham. Brice Masterman groaned.

'You're so hung up on material possessions,' said young Jane, who was hanging round for a glass of wine. The adults looked intensely at her in the long gypsy skirt she had put on for the evening, and thought back to a time when they had been as young, as unencumbered.

'As long as there's someone to pay the bills, young lady,' remarked Alison Woodruff.

The kids wandered over the sandy hills to the beach with news-papers and matches to light the bonfire. The matches blew out in the breeze, one after another, but little Sandy Sunner didn't give up until she had a spire of flame crackling and licking on the dark empty beach, driving away all demons, wishing boon for the coming time. The young people gathered in close, as if that pile of agitation and splendour was burning on the fuel of their youth. Alex brought his portable tape-recorder. Sophie did her imitation of Mick Jagger. Jane and Wendy began to move in long leaping steps, waving their arms like seabirds. Wendy needed neither fire nor music. She skipped along the moon-frilled edge of the sea in her own exultant dance.

Then Jane went with Alex into the sandhills. She walked ahead of him and stopped on a sandy slope that was the same pewter colour as the moon. She threw her head back to the sky and turned to face Alex, her teeth bared in a bright grin, as he stepped close to her. Their arms, swaying in the breeze, brushed with nervous energy and their hands awkwardly clasped. She pressed her mouth against his lips and teeth and put her tongue as far down his throat as it would go. Hugging each other in that rush of passion, they lost balance and toppled on to the sand. Jane put her hand down inside Alex's shorts while he grappled with her bikini top and moved impatiently to her knickers, yanking them from under her rucked-up skirt. There was sand on his finger as he rubbed her and she pushed him away. He had sand on his hot dick. She felt the grit on him as he pushed at her, rubbing backwards and forwards, chafing her skin with grit, chafing himself too, until it stung so much that he spat in his hand and rubbed spittle over himself. Then he was moaning and spurting all over her.

Jane laughed, low in the throat. She bit his lower lip and held onto it with her teeth. He lay on her as the stuff dried, sticking them together. Their breath was racing.

'You can smell it,' said Alex.

'You need to go for a swim,' ordered Jane. She stood up, walked to the top of the hill and looked down at the fire on the beach, burning in a small orange mound, and the black bodies moving mysteriously around it. 'What are we doing this for?' she asked, turning to look Alex in the eye. Her face was troubled. 'I feel like a smoke. I'm going to look for Wendy.'

With that she went ahead down the sandhill without once looking back at him, skiing her feet in the thick loose sand. She became a shadow on the beach as he watched her go down. He felt depressed, all of a sudden, and there was still a time to go before midnight.

Robbie Masterman had been lured by Wendy's solitary dance along the beach. Boring Susan was being a grown-up, sitting back at the camp, talking, and he wasn't interested in that. Wendy walked back with Robbie, daring him to drive down the coast to reach the surfing town where the big New Year's party was before the stroke of midnight. Taking him by the hand, she made him run.

Alex watched as the gaggle of adults came through the sandhills in a tipsy laughing procession with their champagne bottles and glasses, spilling out in a ring around the bonfire as they joined the children. He saw his father put an arm round Mrs Woodruff as he refilled their two glasses. His mother was not there. Dr Woodruff was responsible for the official countdown to twelve. Alex could hear him shouting above the roar of the waves as the tide turned noisily on cue. 10-9-8-7-6-5 . . . He wondered why Jane had not come back for him. One! Midnight! Happy New Year! Corks shot into the air. The shadows paired and kissed in a dance around the circle. People linked arms and their song drifted up on the breeze. *Lest auld acquaintance be forgot . . . for the sake of Auld Lang Syne.* He imagined the syllables of the old song of loyalty, transience and togetherness breaking up and blowing out to sea and falling in speckles of starlight on the broad pathway that led across to the west. He thought of his own absent friends, picturing them as if they were there: Ziggy tripping a festive dance across a ballroom floor that shone like the moon's reflection, the cynosure of all eyes; Cleve – friend or foe? – making his voyage forwards into a new sky; Josie, in hat and gloves, First Communion dress and veil, kneeling on the shore, the Blessed Immaculate; and Joe Skull out there somewhere too, mixing his molecules indiscriminately with whatever was. Then Alex brushed himself clean and went down into the campsite and helped himself to a beer. Robbie's car was gone. Jane and Wendy had driven off with Robbie, leaving him behind. Possessed suddenly by the conviction that he would be alone all his life, Alex skulked in anger through the circle of the camp, tripping and stumbling against ropes and tent-pegs, not caring if he pulled the whole lot down.

That was how he found his mother, slumped on the grass behind one of the tents, rocking and nodding to herself. The way she looked at him, he might have been no more than a blur in her delirium.

'Mum! What are you doing here?'

'Hallo Alex,' she said without a hint of surprise.

'Get up, Mum. The others are all down at the beach. That's where you should be.'

She looked at him in horror. Her son spoke in the hollow voice of the policeman, blocking all tenderness and compassion. A twisted smile crossed her lips, a bubbling laugh, her heart riven by his cold, rigid disapproval, which was like everyone else's. Her own son. If she crawled away to her tent, she would be regarded as having done herself a favour. Bloody Tim. Bloody leathery Barb with her talk of Audrey Ryan the barmaid. It was not her at all. Silly overexcited

Alison Woodruff was the one. Clarice had heard them go traipsing off together to welcome the New Year. Then, going in search of the dunny, she lost her way amidst all the knots and flaps. So she simply sank down on the grass where no one would find her. She had taken a couple of pills, on top of the drink, to turn herself into cotton-wool. She held out her hand to Alex and he tried to drag her upright, so roughly he might have dislocated her arm, but she fell backwards in a heap.

'Mum!' Alex shouted. 'Stand up, will you, please. Please, Mum.' He was begging like a kid for her to do what he wanted.

'Don't worry about me, Alex darling.' Her eyes, which matched the pearl earrings she always wore, glinted like her rings – the emerald engagement ring, the golden wedding ring, the diamond eternity ring, and the sapphire that her father had given her when she had her first child. 'I'll be fine,' she said. 'Go now. Leave me alone. You go and be with the others. Enjoy yourself.'

He was frightened by her. 'I'll get Dad to come . . .'

'I don't want your father.' She closed her eyes and smiled as he crept backwards over the crackling grass. 'Happy New Year, Alex darling.'

When Johnny Woodruff came into the boys' tent, Alex pretended to be asleep. Johnny peeled his clothes off and wriggled inside the sleeping bag. He had finished with Sandy Sunner for the night and was snoring within minutes. Brice Masterman popped his head inside the tent to check for his son's whereabouts. Don Woodruff was furious that his daughter Jane had gone off in drunken young Robbie Masterman's sports car without telling anybody and taken Wendy with her. Trotting back clumsily from the beach, Woodruff had imagined Wendy, alone in the girl's tent, unclasping her bikini top and preparing for bed.

'Don't ask me,' groaned Johnny. Alex lay there doggo. Johnny was sound asleep when his father came into the tent to find out where they had gone. Peter Sunner was concerned too – and Susan

Mack was in tears in the girls' tent, cursing Robbie for walking out on her. Woodruff was determined to fetch them back. Alex heard his father say that someone should go with Don to help him look.

But Dr Woodruff went off by himself, leaving his wife to settle beneath her queenly canopy of mosquito netting in her capacious tent and wait for her lover to take advantage of the opportunity that had arisen. Tim Mack checked his own tent, annoyed to find that Clarice was not there. Hot and horny, he could wait no longer. He put on his stripy pyjama shorts and rubbed his chest with citronella to keep the mosquitoes away. It was too hot to wear the top of his pyjamas.

'Alison?' he whispered, roaming over to the open flap of the Woodruffs' darkened tent.

'Tim? Is that you? Oh,' she murmured, as his weight hit the creaking stretcher.

Alex lay fully awake, listening above Johnny's piggy snoring to every noise of the night. He could not stop thinking about Jane. He was in love with her. It surprised him. He lay there wishing she would come back and be with him. A car sliced the tent sides with its violent headlights. There was the lone slam of a door as Dr Woodruff got out. He had returned empty-handed. Alex heard a rustle in the tents as Tim Mack hurried across to intercept him.

'They'll stay out all night,' growled Don Woodruff. 'The pests. I won't get any rest now.'

'It's a bloody shame,' Alex heard his father reply. Tim was hot in the face. 'Nor will any of us now, Don.'

Welcoming and steady in its rhythms as light came up, the beach was all Clarice's. Wide empty sand and ash-light sky. Between herself and the sea, between herself and her destination across that mighty covering of water, the other coast, the place in the west, the little town where she had lived before she was sent away, there was only ever the one relationship. The charred bits of wood from the bonfire were warm where she squatted to remove her jewellery. She did not want her rings getting lost at sea. She walked out without looking back over her shoulder to where her loved ones were, who would grimace and wail when they knew her journey. The foam tingled and tickled, like a chain around her ankles, her waist, her neck. Eye sockets and teeth of living bone stared calmly at her from the water. She would dive like a mermaid through fracturing green walls of water of a power so much greater than her own. She barely had control of her limbs as finally her body detached itself and she was tugged in a dream of return to join the other side, until the waves broke through her last drowsy resistance.

From a dream of the sea, rushing through his ears, Alex woke at first light, slithered from his sleeping bag and wandered down to the beach. The blackened ends of the bonfire lay scattered and forlorn in the dull light. He saw an upturned sunhat on the sand. A pair of sunglasses rested on the hat. In the upturned crown of the hat were rings – and the pair of pearl earrings. He looked to left and right along the empty beach. Where was his mother? The waves crashed high and superb over the thick blue heaving skin of the sea. He let out a yell. A confusion of footprints pocked the sand in concentric circles from the bonfire site but the tide had gone out since last night and there was a belt of sand with no marks save for one set of footprints that stopped at the low water mark. He walked out into the waves and yelled until his voice cracked. He was shivering, squinting to conjure into clarity the seaweed or driftwood or shadows or forms of any dark substantial thing. 'Mu-um!' Then he heard a gunshot from behind him in the hills, turned and ran up the sand for help, half-choking on the word that gripped his throat.

He was stopped in his tracks by Mrs Gillingham, pointing with her rifle at the limp dead snake at her feet. She had been up early, pottering about, when she came across the snake sunning itself in her path. She tiptoed back to her tent and got the rifle out from under the stretcher-bed. The snake was still basking there when she returned. Aware of her now, it reared its head. She bent her eye to the sights and squeezed the trigger. She was a good shot. She got it through the neck.

'Where's Mum?' shouted Alex in a voice of agony. 'I found her hat on the beach, and these –' he opened his palm and showed the jewellery. The others, disturbed by the shot, had come running to see what was happening. Alex screwed up his eyes to block the light and saw an image of the sun, crossed by a blackened moon from which a death's head looked out. 'No!' he shouted. No! No!

DANIEL

THERE was a break in the grape harvest when Joe, in his red beanie, took the kids back to town to see the family. Joe needed a bit of company. He liked to have a laugh at the stories the old people told. Rhonda, his eldest, was maturing so fast that he wondered whether it would be better if she stayed in town anyway. He wondered whether his two elder boys should not stay there too and go to school. There was only old Joe now to bring the boys to heel.

The aunties and uncles and cousins on the reserve had been willing to help when poor Mary passed away. It was Joe's decision to take the kids with him. The kids were all he had left. Bruno let his Aboriginal workers camp on the block. If they camped on the place, he could be pretty sure they would turn up in the morning. Bruno, who grew grapes for champagne, tried to keep on good terms with everyone. His wife cooked up pasta with tomato sauce for the pickers at the end of a day's work and she never objected if Joe took some extra tucker away to feed his five kids. They lived in a tent, sharing blankets, and Joe had no concern for how they filled their day as long as they stayed together.

Joe and Mary used to have a horse and wagon and camp along the river. They came from around that way, where the Darling joins the Murray and the waters snake south-west into South Australia. Mary lost her left arm as a girl when she fell out of a tree and gashed herself on the barbed wire fence below. They cut off the arm at the hospital, and she learned to cook and sew and do the ironing with only one arm, and nursed her children as well as anyone else.

Arthur and Danny were healthy, cheeky boys, with clean teeth and clear eyes, and someone usually managed to dress them in decent clothes. Their childhood along the river was free and open, and they were like that too. They played football, got into fights, chased other kids, went fishing in the river and cooked any fish they caught over a fire on the bank. It was their country, and there were things about it Joe had taught them. But they knew they were not supposed to go too far beyond, off into a world in which they had no place.

White kids from the surrounding fruit blocks rode into Wilga to catch the bus to school in the next town. They left their bicycles at the bus shelter all day, returning in the afternoon to ride back out to the fruit blocks and farms where they lived. Arthur and Danny would have gone to that same high school, only on the Vegemite bus, the bus that left from the reserve. The boys hated school, where they were made to sit at the back and use a separate blackboard from the other kids, but when they were in Wilga, Arthur and Danny would hang around the bus shelter during the day as if there was another journey of their own they should have been going on.

There were old bikes that could be identified with older kids. Then one day there were two new bikes that belonged to a brother and sister, Italian kids, who had been at the same primary school as Arthur and Danny and had just made the move to high school. The two brand-new bikes were left lying against the bus shelter, and Arthur and Danny knew the brother and sister wouldn't mind if they had a go. They hopped on the bikes and raced each other, like a crow chasing an eaglehawk, all around town, wheeling and skidding and having a great time. They took the bikes down by the river and threw them on the bank while they went diving for mussels. Then they just forgot about them. Finders keepers. When the school bus returned to Wilga in the afternoon and the brother and sister found their new bikes missing from the bus shelter, everyone with any claim to be concerned came out and tattled. The bikes were returned, but the parents of the kids who took that school bus could not stop talking about the state of those two eldest boys of Joe and one-armed Mary who had been allowed to run wild in the bush since their poor mother's death.

Joe took all his kids except Rhonda back with him to Bruno's block for the late picking. He did not want to lumber the folk in town with any more trouble. Then the Welfare came with papers. Any Australian in a suit and tie with documents was police as far as Bruno was concerned, and he led the man to the tent where Joe's lot lived. Bruno felt a bit uncomfortable snooping around Joe's tent while Joe was out in the vineyard bending over the vines with clippers and basket. He co-operated with the visitors so the matter would be handled quickly, without fuss, identifying the two eldest boys. The Welfare took Arthur and Danny away in the car to appear as delinquents before the court where they were classified as neglected children. Joe was brought before the court too. He was recorded as having nothing to say in his defence. What more could he do, if he had already done his best? When he returned to his work on the fruit block, Joe pulled such a long face that Bruno gave him a bottle of home-made plonk to cheer him up. At least his two boys would get an education this way, Bruno said to Joe, transported to a place hundreds of miles away on the coast.

~

They slept in a dormitory with eighty other boys. It was as if you were guilty just for being there. If you missed a meal, you starved. Outside in the grounds you could smell the sea. On the hottest days of summer, when the mercury passed the century mark, the staff of the Home took the boys down to the beach in squads of ten. That was the first time Danny swam in the surf. He struggled, in terms of right and wrong, to understand why he and his brother had been plunged into this place. He hoped he would prove strong enough to pass the test. He submitted numbly, trusting when the ordeal of confinement came to an end he would come through a new man surrounded again by his brothers and sisters and aunties and uncles and cousins, laughing with them, and his Dad, and his Mum. He drew his strength from thinking of them all. As long as he knew his family were there, in their country, far from this grey testing place, he could keep going. Arthur knew. Ahead of him up the line, or working at the vegetable garden, even when they couldn't speak, Arthur shared his world. But Danny never spoke much, even to Arthur. He bowed his head meekly when he stood beside his bed and they came to check that his things were folded properly, and Matron Campbell made him peel back his lips to show that his teeth were cleaned. You were not allowed to speak or sneeze or cough without permission. But he liked to draw. To doodle, to copy things. That could get you into trouble too, so he drew with his finger and left no trace, drawing and colouring in his mind's eye creations as big as the world.

He asked Arthur whether the others knew they were there. Arthur had no reply. They knew, Arthur said, but they probably did not have the right address. Never once was there word from the family. For the last six months in the home Arthur was taught how to lay bricks. When he turned fifteen, he left. He told Danny they had found a position for him as a brickie's apprentice. They had told him he would not be getting any money at first. Arthur said that for all he knew they might be sending him back out west, where the family was waiting for the boys to come home. He knew no more than that.

Then two pages of lined paper with writing every second line came from Arthur. Danny got one of the other boys to read it to him. All was well, it said. Everyone was good. They all asked after Danny. Rhonda had a baby now. She was living in Wentworth with her boyfriend. Lorna and Grace had grown up too. Dad was okay, Arthur wrote. He was not working any more. He had come back to live with the reserve mob. Lorna was mothering the whole lot. Lorna was twelve now. There was no work around, not for builder's labourers. No one in Wilga was building themselves bloody houses unless the government paid for them. No one wanted an Aborigine apprentice anyway. Everyone was good, but. They all sent their love to Danny. All was well. Everything was going to be fine, brother.

It was the last letter Danny got.

He learned not to speak at all in front of the staff unless spoken to, and then only a shy word with his head down. He made friends with the other boys in his electrical wiring class. They sat around with each other, or fooled about. But even in a crowd he could withdraw into a world of stubborn lonely dreaming as a way of killing time. Once he came to understand that there would be no second letter from Arthur, he decided that he would keep the stories of his family to himself. It was as if a tough skin had grown over that childhood life, and he began to think that perhaps the Home with its ways was all he could call his own.

Matron Campbell lived on the grounds of the Home with her husband, the roving Welfare psychiatrist. Dr Campbell was a thin man with an enormous nose, losing his hair. His wife was in her mid-thirties. She had a good head of hair that she waved herself with curlers. The boys called her by her first name – Judy – amongst themselves. She tended their routine ailments, giving them care they got from no one else. Her house had a fence around it and a well-loved garden where the boys sometimes saw her cutting a basket of flowers. On Sundays Dr Campbell mowed the lawn front and back with a hand-pushed mower. During the week the boys watched Dr Campbell come and go in his beige Holden sedan. On Mondays, weather permitting, Judy hung out the washing on the line. Observing the details of the Campbells' existence, the boys constructed a pattern of the life outside in society that would one day be given to them. In that way, Judy became theirs. Danny's. The boy was obsessed with her. In his fifteenth year, she was the only woman in his life. To be able to say 'Yes, Matron', 'No, Matron', 'Thank you, Matron' to her face even once a week with an adoring smile was how he survived. Not that she paid him any special attention. The boys talked crudely and ignorantly about sex. In the confines of the home it was a raw, painful business with no release or airing. Some of the boys formed pairs and protected each other when they were cornered by the men on the staff who took a special interest in them. Wanting to be clean, Danny turned inward on himself to find strength to endure the thrashings of desire that went through his body. But the well-upholstered figure of Judy would come into his mind. With open palms he would mould the air, imagining her solid curving form.

'Matron,' he said, calling at the infirmary one day, 'there's something in my eye.'

He had slipped and fallen during a hurdles heat and a burr had entered his eyeball.

'Let's have a look,' she smiled. She flooded the bloodshot eye with salt eyewash. When that failed to flush out the burr, she used tweezers. 'There, now.' She held up the tiny splinter for him to see. 'They feel huge, like you've got a plank stuck in your eye,' she laughed. 'Should be all right now.'

'Thank you, Matron.'

He was happy. His finger – the second finger of his right hand – started to move almost of its own accord. He was sketching her in the air. She looked at him, puzzled by what he was doing, and lightly touched his cheek.

'Go along now, Danny Boy.'

On the way back to the sports ground, he squatted down and drew Judy's curves in the dirt. It was a crude drawing and he brushed it away with his foot as soon as he finished. But that evening, as he hunched painfully over his homework, he began to draw her again, first doodling with his fingertip, then with a pencil in his science book. He did not draw her face. He could never draw that. Her curves were enough, two abstract lines that looked like a winding road running down the page, but not parallel, more like the twin banks of a river that swelled and narrowed. He found himself writing her name on the picture, Judy, only with the 'J' the wrong way round. He was so absorbed that he did not notice the supervising officer's approach until the cuffed hand came down on the notebook and snatched it up.

Next day the principal of the home gave Danny six cuts with the cane and called him a dirty little beggar who didn't know any better, a polluted savage with no respect. Danny was proud of the drawing and he worried that they might destroy it. They would show Dr Campbell, but he wanted Judy to see it for herself. How else would she know how he felt? It only took one rotten apple to give a place a bad name, said the principal. He had nothing against Danny, of course, he had barely noticed the lad, but since Danny would soon be leaving the home, Mr Price invited the psychiatrist to produce a report, based on the lewd sketch of his wife Judy, to confirm that the boy had perverted tendencies, was a bad influence on others and showed signs of being maladjusted to society. Mr Price attached the document to his own official report in which he wrote that although the boy was amenable, he was intellectually subnormal and had little aptitude for academic study. The reports went on Danny's file, which would go off with the boy.

Danny went to say goodbye to Matron Campbell, but was too shy to give her the drawing of her face he had done as a farewell present. It was not good enough for her. He would keep it himself to remember her by, the one he cared about most. On the day he left, he noticed her looking up from the clothesline in her yard, where she was taking in the washing, as the bus passed. Through the open bus window he could hear her singing. She waved, wishing them all good luck, all the boys who had turned fifteen. *Oh Danny Boy, the pipes, the pipes are callin'*. She was singing for him. He grinned, right into her eyes, and waved back wildly until the bus carried them on out the gate.

~

Mrs Fleyer's guesthouse had accommodation for eight boys in shared rooms. The Welfare, who paid the food and board, trusted her because she accounted honestly for her boys. She gave them breakfast, a packed lunch and a good tea, and she reported immediately to the probation officer if a boy failed to come back at night. Mrs Fleyer deducted the money for any extras – toothpaste, shoelaces, razorblades – from what the Welfare gave her. The late Mr Fleyer believed that if you gave people a basic sense of decency, it went a long way. His widow carried on this principle, but it was not always easy. She encouraged the boys to believe that her three-storey inner-city guesthouse was a place of opportunity. They must stand on their own two feet and look forwards. She did not want them going back where they came from. They must put all that behind them if they were ever to become good upstanding citizens of the country. She preferred young blacks as her lodgers to the white kids who were abandoned on life's wayside and could never throw off their miseries. She always gave Danny a cup of tea and a piece of cake when he came in after a day at work. He was a willing lad, which Olive Fleyer appreciated.

'He's got a splash,' the Welfare had said to her over the phone. 'But he's not as dark as some.'

Each morning Danny walked two miles to the trucking depot where he loaded and unloaded boxes for the store manager. He enjoyed seeing the men come and go, and hearing their talk, and it was not long before he was going out on local deliveries to help unload. Frankie, a Slovenian, would give him a smoke once they were out on the road. 'Life's a bitch,' said Frankie, who liked an audience for his opinions. 'And bitches are life!'

Frankie would curse Danny for being useless with the map, but when they reached a destination late, they would end up having a beer with the people at the other end. When the truck broke down, Danny could get it going again. He was almost sorry when the working day ended. He would talk to Mrs Fleyer about the store manager and Frankie and the parts of Sydney where they dropped and picked up.

'You've seen more than I have, young man,' said Olive Fleyer, nodding to show how impressed she was. 'Save your money and one day you'll have one of them homes of your own.'

'Nah, when I get money I'm going back home and see my sisters and brothers.'

'They'll lift all your money off you and you'll have to start all over again,' Mrs Fleyer laughed, shaking her head.

It was summer when Danny moved to Sydney and everyone complained about the heat. People flapped their clothes to cool their skin. Then the clouds would pile like icecream and the sky would slop down rain that made people streak down footpaths and run around in their cars with the wipers flapping like broken wings. Except for Frankie, who stood in the shelter of the truck depot smoking cigarette after cigarette until the rain passed. Frankie and Danny would talk about motorbikes and comment every time a decent motorbike passed. Admiration for a good motorbike was one thing Danny was not shy about. He wanted a motorbike he could ride all the way out west. He wanted a good pair of boots. Then he would hop out into the rain and not mind if he got wet through.

Danny liked Sydney. He liked the opinionated women, the old Greek men, the smart young girls in the tatty old terrace-houses who were not afraid to let their voices sing out over the streets, the rattle of after-hours sewing machines and the Chinese people behind grille doors where the click of mahjong tiles echoed. He liked the way people acknowledged him as having as much right to be there as they did – except when their blind eyes and cold gazes told him he was garbage. He rolled his eyes at those smart ones, got up in strange fashions like actors in a great big play.

But the girls up the Cross never bothered him. They knew who was for them and who wasn't. One Saturday night Matt, his mate, another of Mrs Fleyer's lodgers, went up to a black girl there and offered to buy her a drink when she finished work. He whispered to her that Danny was a first-timer.

'You can't fool me, a nice-looking fella like you,' the girl laughed. 'How old are you, anyway?' She was fourteen herself. Mary was her name. The same name as his mother, Danny told her. 'Cost you more than the price of a drink,' she winked. Then her Greek bloke came up and Matt emptied out his pockets. 'Mum's number one and Mary's number two,' the girl smiled at Danny. 'Remember that.'

Afterwards he sat on the edge of the mean bed with his shirt off and his pants on. Mary cheered him up by telling about the black American sailors who always asked for her. 'They call me their Little Black Sister. I'm the one they want. For real. They're our brothers, you know that.'

Matt and Danny were late getting back that night and Mrs Fleyer guessed they had been up to no good. She tried to separate them after that. That was when Matt told Danny he must learn to fight and run. If wrong was done to him, he must struggle, every inch of the way, to overturn the wrong and make it right.

It was Australia Day, January the twenty-sixth, the anniversary of the first governor's arrival with the English ships to occupy the land of smoke and no people for the King. No people were *his* people – but he didn't want to think about that. It was a holiday and he went out wandering as usual, down to the park and on through the deserted city centre, down canyons of buildings and shopfront awnings, on up the hill. A squad of Hells' Angels passed him on their way up the Cross, a dozen or more black riders with dead classy bikes that left him spellbound. As the black swarm of bikes climbed the hill and curved away over the rise, heading in the direction of the beach, he felt himself lift with them into a kind of ecstatic infinity, the shining blue sky echoing with the bikes' drone long after they had gone. He was transported. He was absent. Then he opened his eyes and he was there still, trudging up the hill with an empty gut. He wanted to find Mary and tell her all about the bikes that had flown past like a mob of black crows. But Mary had gone away, the girls told him. No one knew where. Little Black Sister had just gone and no one was asking where.

~

It was a sort of promotion, the store manager said. Paperwork. He wouldn't be going out on runs from now on. They had agreed to take a boy from the Welfare only to cover a vacancy over the Christmas period. The loading job had already been promised to Frankie's cousin. The cousin was lazy, just like Frankie. He did what suited him. He was not interested in starting until after the summer. Now summer was over and Frankie wanted his cousin to go out on the truck with him. Danny could stay in the office and learn the paperwork instead.

He sat at the table all of that day, letting the store manager's instructions fly over his head. He felt like he was in a cage. It reminded him of the Home. Only this time Danny recognised the anger he felt. Bloody Frankie. Typical whitefella.

When he told Mrs Fleyer what had happened, she said it was a worker's right to express an opinion, particularly if management had made a mistake. Danny asked if she would speak to the store manager on his behalf, but Olive Fleyer did not like to stick her nose in where she was not wanted. So he told Matt.

It was a hot night and Danny and Matt walked up and down under the rustling street trees cursing and swearing. It was the first time Danny had been like this. Matt led him off to the pub where they could get drunk with the old fellas. A man from La Perouse came in with a sack of oysters and his oyster knife and was sharing them round. But Danny stuck to his beer. He was on his third schooner.

'Scared of oysters?' The old man laughed at him as a wigetty-grubeater from out west. 'You know what you can do with a wigetty-grub.'

They reeled out of the pub. 'Fuck them,' said Matt. 'Smash them.'

Danny's head was spinning over the gutter as he emptied his guts. Matt held him upright.

'Is that you, Daniel?' called Mrs Fleyer through the glass panes of the door. She was in her dressing-gown. 'Where have you been? Come inside. You should be ashamed of yourself.'

Matt leered at Olive Fleyer. 'Dan's in a bad way.'

'Thanks to you,' she replied. Danny hung his head.

'No thanks to me, you old cow,' retorted Matt.

He took his packed lunch and left the house as usual at seven o'clock. It was not difficult to fill a day just walking the streets, sitting in parks, watching the people go by. He would not tell the store manager he could neither read nor write. The shame was too great. Church and tower, bridge and water, dockyard and schoolyard. He would stop one place and when he finished stopping there, he would up and move on, watching all the way. He hoped he would run into Matt, who had left Mrs Fleyer's after she reported him to the Welfare. At the back of the hospital, where he was walking, three nurses in stockings and caps were eating lamingtons from a bag. 'What are you looking at, darling?' they yelled out to him. 'You want a lamington, you come over here and get it.'

He counted the coins in his pocket as he went down into the long pedestrian tunnel to Central Station and came up in the station concourse where there were trains, all going off somewhere, and he couldn't tell which was which. Above the entrance was a huge information board with times, numbers and destinations: town after town. He peered for one he would recognise. Wagga Wagga. That would do. His father had worked at the army base there for a while during the war. Joe had talked about Wagga Wagga. Danny asked an old bloke in a railways uniform what the fare was to Wagga Wagga. 'Next train's in five minutes,' answered the guard, pointing to a line of people at the ticket window. 'You'll get your ticket over there, laddie, if you hurry.'

He went back down the stairs into the tunnel. He figured he could go out to the track while the train was still shunting and jump it that way. But when he came out of the tunnel, he was not sure where he was. He was running by the time he reached the park. He sprinted across to the far fence that backed the tennis courts; the tracks were on the other side. He clambered up the wire.

Then a white tennis ball sprang against the wire beside him and stuck there.

'Hey, mate!' called a Chinese boy from the court. 'Get the ball, will you?' Danny threw the ball down hard. 'Thanks, mate.'

Then he saw his train sliding from the platform. 'Shit!' he said. He was on the wrong side of the fence and the train went by.

The city streets cut like a gorge through the rock-face business buildings. At the bottom he found the army disposal store that had the best boots for motorbike riding. He checked the price. Four dollars short. He asked if he could try the boots on. The shop assistant asked to see his money first. Otherwise they did not want dirty socks in their good new boots.

That evening, over the washing up, Mrs Fleyer said that the trucking depot had telephoned to ask where he was. One false move, she warned Danny, and he would be in serious trouble. Then he began to ramble. Mrs Fleyer could not make sense of what he was saying. It was only words that he was mouthing, and words would get him nowhere. Every move he made was a wrong move, he told her. He only wanted to find out what he was supposed to do, and all they ever told him was that he done wrong.

Next day he kicked around the warehouses and yards until lunchtime when he knew that the trucking depot would be unattended. He checked with a whistle to make sure. The window of the toilet was open to the outside. He swung up onto the ledge and climbed in. He flushed the toilet, then he walked out the toilet door and came to the locked office door and pushed it open with a shove of his hips. The key was in the drawer where the store manager kept the petty cash. He opened it up and found the cashbox. He put it under his arm and took it out to the toolbench where he used the wirecutters to break it open. There was twelve dollars in the box. He slipped the money into his pocket, put the cashbox back in the drawer, locked it, locked the office door, pocketed the keys and climbed onto the toilet seat and out the window into the back lane.

In the afternoon he returned to the army disposal store and showed the shop assistant the money that allowed him to try on the best pair of bikie boots in the shop and walk out with them on his feet.

Things moved fast after that. Danny's probation officer cancelled the month's payment and advised the store manager to report the break-in to the police. Mrs Fleyer said that Danny had been upset by the way he was treated at the trucking depot but that his mood had passed since he got his new boots. He had been saving for them since he came to Sydney. A police car picked him up on the street. He told the court he came from Wilga and a request went out for information about the family. When no answer came back, the officer in charge recorded in his report that no family could be traced. 'You've got no family,' they told Danny, who was committed to Tamworth Boys' Home for two years.

He remembered what Matt had said about taking a wrong and putting it right, every inch of the way. They were lying about his family. They had only to go out there and ask anybody.

You were out of bed at six a.m., ten seconds after the wake-up alarm sounded, seven days a week. You stood by your bed while the morning officer came past with 'Good morning, Daniel.' On the order 'March' you went to your locker with your stuff, put your night things away and changed into your gym clothes. On the order 'March' you went outside and did your exercises. On the order 'March' you fetched your night can, emptied it, rinsed it and went for a shit. Breakfast followed, at seven a.m. And so by the clock and the rules, every day exactly the same. There was an understanding at the Home that you better clean yourself up by the time you turned seventeen, otherwise you went straight on to adult prison without ever having another chance to try your luck outside.

You stood at attention. You did not speak. You ran when ordered to do something. Nowhere and nothing was your own. You kept everything inside you and showed it to no one as if you were a soldier in a war against yourself. The top part might as well be dead. But the sap went down.

There was no trace of a tear or a smile or any other response. It was painful, growing inward when you should be growing outward. It was your only hope of survival.

When they interviewed Danny, he asked if they would contact his family. When they replied that he had no family, he asked them to seek again. When the answer came that in the history of his custodianship by the state there was no record of contact with any family, that was what it said in his file, he asked them to try again. Then at last an answer came in the affirmative. There was a family after all, as he always knew, and the Welfare would assess whether the family was fit to receive him back on his eventual release into society. But he could not wait that long. One day when he was with a squad weeding the sports ground one of the boys jumped the fence and ran away. The others stood by, watching him run. Then the head gardener shouted at the boys not to stand there but to run after the absconder and bring him back. Danny ran and ran. He was never going back. He ran until he came out to the main road and was seen by a passing farmer who gave him a wave. The farmer called the police and pretty soon they picked Danny up and took him back to the Home. For his trouble he was back to the full two years.

He was allowed to make pictures in the craft workshop, once he had sewn on his quota of buttons. As a way of relieving his own boredom, the teacher taught him how to paint with watercolours. They copied pictures from a book of Australian landscapes. To the teacher's amusement, Danny took Albert Namatjira as his model, Albert Namatjira, the only Aboriginal painter in the book, who died drunk and humiliated after all his fame. Soon Danny could produce a competent white gum tree in the foreground, purple mountains behind, and a space of flowers in between.

The Home was on a hill top. The road wound up from the roadside gate through paddocks where sheep grazed, through orchards and vegetable gardens, to a red brick archway with high gates of iron. Beyond that main entrance stood the historic main building, its brick glowing in the sunlight, as if it were the Kingdom of

Heaven. That was the last picture Danny painted there, the snaking black road, the arched gate, the red building, and the Cross of Jesus hanging from the sky above. He asked the teacher to write the name on the picture for him: The Prison on the Hill.

Danny walked out the gate early one February with a swag containing his few possessions and ten dollars in his pocket. It was 1969. That was the way it always happened. The boys were expected to walk into town and buy a train ticket to Sydney or wherever they were directed to go. Welfare's assessment of Danny's family was negative. He was advised not to return to that environment. The best avenue for him would be to go back to Mrs Fleyer's guesthouse for another stint, if she would have him, and find a job as an electrician's or a housepainter's mate. The idea made Danny laugh. He was free. He would do what he had to do, go home out west to Wilga at last. He would not throw his money away on a train ticket. The distance was five hundred miles. He would need every cent.

He walked through Tamworth to the other side and kept walking until he was far enough away from the Home to try for a lift. The locals would pick him by his clothes and his haircut and drive by. Someone from out of town on a long haul across the plains, en route out west to Adelaide or Perth perhaps, via Broken Hill or Mildura, was what he hoped for. He stuck out his thumb.

The first truck that stopped, Danny climbed inside and put out his hand.

'Beautiful manners,' the driver quipped, 'you just out of the Boys' Home, mate?'

They drove and drove. The bloke was called Moose and had a story. He had been a salvage diver in New Guinea and had made a packet. He was twenty-six and a bit of a dopehead. Then his mate had ridden his motorbike up a tree one night in Cairns, when they were back in North Queensland from Port Moresby for R & R. They were on the way home from the pub, off their heads, and the bike exploded, and Moose's mate was killed. 'That was it,' Moose said. 'He was only eighteen, but he was a really good bloke, so full of *life!*'

Danny listened as he looked at the road. The eagle's tattooed talons flexed on Moose's upper arm, where he had torn the sleeve off his shirt, as he held the wheel.

'You're a quiet sort of bugger, eh,' commented Moose. 'What are you seeing out there?'

Danny had his eyes full of the passing land.

'Sure is beautiful,' agreed Moose, carrying on his half of the conversation. 'Nothing like it. Wouldn't change it for anything in the world. There's a lot of it but, when you're trying to get from one side to the other.'

Moose dropped Danny at the service station where he filled up in the main street of Mildura. As Danny climbed down from the cab, Moose said, 'Give my regards to your folks when you get home!'

'Right,' replied Danny, nodding. 'You're a real gent.' That was all he could give by way of thanks.

Danny walked away from the rig to the roadside and looked right, then left, trying to decide which way he should go. Once he got back to the river he would know the way.

As the rig pulled slowly out of the service station, Moose gave a honk. Danny waved back. On his first day out he was lucky.

He stood at the junction. It was dry heat, over a century Fahrenheit. The flat land shimmered, the shiny tar melted and heaven was blue without blemish. He had no hat, only the grey cotton trousers and khaki shirt the Home had given him. As he waited, with one finger vaguely cocked against his leg, he thought of Moose's story. You had to feel compassion for that suntanned fella with shoulder-length hair that the sun had turned white. From a long way off he watched the beetling movement of a car as it grew towards him across the plain. It was a rounded old pale blue car, with South Australian number plates. The car slowed at the junction, as if the driver was not sure which road to take. He thought the car was going to pull over. A girl with honey-coloured hair put her head out the window and called to him with a smile. He could not hear what she said.

The car was full of kids – his own age. After slowing, it revved to accelerate again and his moment of hope for a lift was snatched away. The blue car melted out of sight into the mirror-bands of a mirage and was gone. It didn't matter. He didn't want to go with them anyway. They were going in different directions. Different roads. Danny turned his head back west towards the setting sun, where home lay.

· PART TWO ·

OUT ACROSS THE UNIVERSE

1

ENDY hung her head out the window, panting for cool air like a dog. On her skin she could feel the sun's fire fading from the burning air. The figure by the roadside cast a shadow in their direction, longer than a power pole, quite alone out there. As they approached, he put out his finger to hitch a ride. Wendy glanced across to see whether Jane would slow down. He was standing at an unmarked crossing, not wanting to take the main road, waiting for a lift back across country.

'Hey, slow down,' Wendy called to Jane. 'I want to get a look.'

He stood hatless, with a bag beside him – like a dark tree. His finger flicked up and he looked beseechingly towards the car.

'Wrong way, mate,' Wendy yelled. She had her head out the window. He would not have heard. He was darkish skinned and good-looking.

'He was going the other way,' said Jane. But his eyes followed them as they travelled away to the east, leaving him standing there in the dust.

'You never know,' retorted Wendy. 'He might have come with us anyway. Could have been interesting.'

'Only if he sat in the front with you,' protested Ziggy, who was being squashed by Alex's outstretched legs. 'There's no room here in the back. There's hardly room to breathe.' There was luggage round his feet, and all across the back. 'No room in the inn.'

Jane glanced in the rear-vision mirror. The image of the young man had started to quaver and break up in the fierce orange light of the sun that flowed down the road surface like molten fire. The huge circumference of sky became smoky and violet as Jane looked back. Then he was gone from sight.

An hour earlier, on a featureless part of the road, after they had left the river and the swamplands, in scant grazing country broken at intervals by tracks off to right and left, Wendy had noticed a temporary cardboard sign stuck on a post, pointing north at a right angle along a single sandy-pink track into the middle of nowhere. 'Turn off,' she had yelled. 'Stop. Turn off. I insist.' Jane was speeding by at a hundred miles an hour.

'It says The Walls of China.'

'The what?'

'The Walls of China! That's what the sign said. Chuck a U-ey. I want to go there.'

'There's a truck up my arse,' Jane screamed. A semi-trailer was looming from behind and she did not want to risk slowing or going off the shoulder of the road at speed. She had no choice but to keep on ahead.

'We're not going sightseeing in this heat,' Ziggy moaned from the back.

'It's not sightseeing. It's the Magical Mystery Tour,' Wendy protested.

'Well, you've missed it,' said Jane. 'Sorry.'

'Thank God.' Ziggy fanned himself. 'Straight on, driver.'

'What's happening?' murmured Alex.

The rig gave a sustained honk, looming to fill the rear-vision mirror. Ziggy swivelled his neck round to peer up at the driver. The great headlights blinked. Then the machine pulled out into the other half of the road, pounding them with a wave of air and noise, and groaned past.

'That fucking thing must be doing something like a hundred and eighty k's,' said Jane, gripping the wheel as the rig lumbered on ahead.

'They're all on speed,' commented Wendy. 'Go back, Jane. How about it? The Walls of China. It's an omen.'

'Not now, darling,' replied Jane definitively.

After ten hours on the road, all conversation had died. The ice bricks packed at the outset had long melted. The cool drinks were too hot to drink. Jane glanced at the temperature gauge of the old car as the dial edged towards boiling point. One hundred and ten miles per hour on the speedometer. The interior was like a furnace. Yet Alex was still trying to sleep in the back, breathing loudly, pushing Ziggy into the corner. Tim Mack had bought Alex the second-hand powder-blue Jag with worn leather upholstery and a blistered walnut dashboard as a reward for the university scholarship his son had won. He had decided it was best for Alex to leave home, to start his adult life in an environment without shadows – which Canberra seemed to promise.

Jane had been with Alex all summer. She was the one who looked after him. Her sobbing after the memorial service for his mother had allowed him to cry too, emitting terrible dry ejaculations of grief that Jane would never forget. She took him to parties, got him drunk and stoned, and danced with him wildly. Alex and his friends were bound together by what had happened to Clarice Mack as if it were their grief too. When it was definite that Alex was going away to university, the nature of the time became epochal.

Wendy had a boyfriend whom she had been cultivating in secret, in tandem with Ivan the circus performer, throughout the summer. His name was Alfonzo Vella. A few years older than her other friends, and more glamorous in her eyes, he had recently moved from Adelaide to Sydney for business and she had decided to pursue him. She did not feel entirely safe with him, which excited her, although she wondered whether in time she might not return to crazy, loving, fire-eating Ivan. She smiled at the choice. Jane, she assumed, would move on in time to more mature, more demanding relationships too. But for now it was all right that Jane should stay with Alex.

Alex could not imagine how he would survive in the new world to which he was travelling without the soul bonds of his old friends. He wished Jane would come with him to Canberra. She had applied to art schools in Adelaide and Sydney and, only a week before Alex was due to leave, a letter came informing her of a place at the school in Sydney that was her first preference. She made plans to leave at once, with Wendy, who was pleased at the prospect of Jane to keep her company in Alfonzo's Sydney flat to begin with.

Wendy had not even bothered to reply to the letter offering her a university place. Eventually someone would arrange a deferral for her. She would send her Mum and Dad a forwarding address. For now she didn't want to think about it. Everything in her upbringing was designed to springboard her into the world, but she rejected that. She wanted to do it all by herself, taking a shortcut with Alfonzo.

Then Ziggy made the decision to come too. He had auditioned successfully for a part in a play in Sydney. It was time he moved out of home, he realised, time he got out of Adelaide, and he was glad to make the crossing with Alex and Wendy and Jane. He was glad they were doing it together. And Elspeth, the remaining member of their childhood gang, had stood in the street outside her house that morning and waved them goodbye as they drove off.

Ziggy stared dreamily at the flat pale landscape they were passing through. Luxuriantly bored, he fanned himself with the *White Album* cover, slapping the stray bits of Wendy's hair that whipped him from the front. Jane was enjoying her turn at the wheel as the powerful engine opened up. The expanse of land excited her with its washes of lustrous colour, its rough markings of fences and occasional dwellings. The road was like a meridian line as indicated by a compass dial, and already in the rear-vision mirror she could see the sun setting on the places they were leaving behind, the midpoint of their journey passed.

'Can you see my sunglasses?' she asked, fumbling in her lap. The sun's rays needled her eyes.

'Hey, I want to drive,' said Wendy, lolling her head towards Jane.

'I need my sunglasses. Have a look in my bag, will you? If *you* were driving, we'd be in China by now.'

Wendy groped on the floor for the big woven bag. 'Wouldn't that be ecstasy!' she sighed. 'You're so bossy, Jane. Here are your shades.'

Wendy popped the dark glasses on her friend's nose and Jane clenched her teeth as she concentrated her gaze on the road ahead, adjusting her eyes to the green wrapping the lenses gave the world.

Ziggy opened his door, got out and stretched. He gave Alex's ankle a tug to wake him. Alex rubbed his face and looked around in confusion at this bright oasis in the night. Jane had the bonnet of the car up. 'It's overheating,' she explained as Alex crawled out.

'That's not surprising,' said Alex. 'So am I.'

'Careful, love, when you take the cap off,' said the mechanic. 'Better wait a minute for her to cool down. Those old radiators tend to boil over.' He fetched a dirty cloth and turned the radiator cap until there was a hiss of steam. The rusty water had not quite boiled dry. 'You'll need to keep an eye on the temperature. If she gets up towards boiling point, you'll have to stop and let her cool down. Make sure she's topped up with water all the time.'

'You hear that, Alex?' said Jane, vaguely irritated.

'Have you had this trouble before?' the mechanic asked Alex.

'Nope,' said Alex.

'Well, the outside temperature doesn't help. She's as hot as she gets.'

'Move the car out of the way,' Jane told Alex, giving him the keys. 'I'll see you inside.'

The truck-stop restaurant, cooled by a chugging airconditioner, was filled with men sitting at little tables eating good-sized meals. The mechanic's wife proudly displayed the huge oval-shaped plates with their serves of steak, bacon, eggs, tomatoes, lettuce and chips as she carried four at a time to a table. The men, whose routes crisscrossed the continent, were red-eyed, haggard and unshaven. On the noticeboard were messages, union instructions, prayers and photos from all over the country. The trucking and girlie magazines on sale, wish-you-were-here postcards, joke ashtrays, souvenir caps, toothpaste and painkillers made the life look seductive and freewheeling.

At the corner table Jane, Wendy, Ziggy and Alex were conscious of not belonging. The bright neon light exposed their faces. Flushed from the heat, Ziggy was acting out the role. That was the power Alex loved him for. It helped that Ziggy had long red hair and golden eyes and his mother's cheekbones. In his defiance of convention he set a high standard for Jane and Wendy to follow. Wendy went to the restroom to re-do her make-up while Jane was checking the car. The truckies took in their fill of her, talking among themselves about what they would do with her if they found her on the roadside asking for a lift.

'Give us a ciggy, Ziggy,' she said, returning to the table. She flashed the topaz ring Alfonzo had given her. She loved its changeable blue-green. 'I feel I'm out in eternity somewhere. You know? Miles and miles we've come already and still we're nowhere.'

'And *miles* to go before we sleep,' quoted Jane.

'Six hours to be precise,' added Alex. 'My stint at the wheel.'

'Pity you won't drive, Ziggy,' said Jane. '*I* won't sleep, because someone has to keep Alex awake at the wheel.'

Jane had simple, strong convictions, such as her commitment to Alex, her *choice* of him as someone for her. It gave her strength. She was at the mercy of a kind of ecstasy in her own ideas and perceptions, in the intensity and possibility of colours, in the magic act of putting on pigment or letting a line flow and engulf its object. Her friendship with Wendy grew in the ground of that ecstatic energy.

That was why she liked Ziggy too. That was why she was laughing when her hamburger with the lot arrived, with bleeding beetroot, grated carrot and fried onions. That was why she tossed her dark curls, chewed her thin dark lips, darted her blackbird's eyes and laughed.

Alex was different. He saw the grid laid over things. There were structures superimposed which were no doubt false but with which you must work, just as a driver must stick to the road system. He was interested in those grids and systems, and how reality itself might be changed by the structures of human perception and organisation. He saw the society they were heir to as guilty of suppressing too much of the unruly sea that Jane called ecstasy. He saw his own mother sacrificed to unreal social constructs. Yet in trying to harness unformed energies to improve the world, he was engaged by constructs himself. His long face, drooping nose and wavy sand-coloured hair gave him that melancholy, sardonic expression. He would grow argumentative with Jane's ecstasy, sometimes, needing it to serve a larger outcome. His ambition in going to Canberra, the national capital, was to change things, to expand the thin sanctions of Australian Society and let in the wide and the outlawed and the deep.

Wired after drinking the coffee into which the mechanic's wife had put two heaped spoons of International Roast, Alex drove for the next six hours. Ziggy and Wendy, crushed against each other, slept in the back. The radio played country-and-western and the temperature gauge flickered ominously towards boiling point without ever quite getting there. The sleeping towns they passed through had names formed from clumsy transcriptions of Aboriginal sounds: Wagga Wagga, Gundagai, Jugiong.

'Yes,' said Alex, as they took the last turn-off. It was as if they had crossed a border and escaped. They had driven more than a thousand kilometres from west to east. Seven hundred miles.

'Do you think you'll ever go back?' Jane asked him suddenly.

'No going back,' Alex declared, 'but we take it with us. The pressure of what we leave behind is always against us. That's what

the past is. It's the resistance. The friction. It's what is always pushing us backwards.'

'Ceaselessly,' Jane replied, going with the flow of his thought,
putting an end to it with that strange euphonious word.

The plantings were the first thing you noticed in Canberra – a carefully chosen mixture of native and exotic, deciduous and evergreen,
arranged conceptually in parks, around buildings and in public
places: new trees that so far gave slender promise of what was
intended. Plan and potentiality were everything. Manured and well-
watered with taxpayers' money and the energies of many, the city
was a precocious, anxious, shallow-rooted ideal. Like a spaceship
that had landed in a particular corner of earth and failed to lift off
again, it was making the first mutant utterances of a new language.
Its means were vernacular: three-bedroom brick house, clothesline
and barbecue in the backyard, ordinary shops, sprawling car-yards,
young families, transients. Blink and the national capital was any old
country town, except that no country town would have gone in for
such ordered frenzy of tree-planting.

It challenged Jane's anti-bourgeois aesthetic. She started drawing the faces of the desperate young mothers who stared from
living-room windows in outer suburban streets where there were
no buses, no shops, no people. She wondered what Alex would
make of it without her. For that first fortnight, she shared his bed in
the student residence, which was against the rules, but rules were
breaking up all over. Wendy shared a room with Ziggy. She got the
bed and he got a sleeping bag on the floor and never stopped complaining. The atmosphere was friendly, fast, tentative, and Jane
observed how the newly arriving students were like the forced trees
of the civic plantings too.

For Alex there was a dimensionless excitement to everything as
he flicked through the handbooks and guides, changing his course
enrolments over and over in contemplation of alternative life
scenarios. In the end he committed himself to economics and

Australian history, combined with law. That could take him any-where. To keep his soul alive he vowed to read poetry on the side: his favourites were Allen Ginsberg, Rainer Maria Rilke and Judith Wright. The thrill of the week was when he joined the co-op bookshop and bought his texts. Stacked on the desk in his poky room, his books formed twin portals to the assorted disciplines of knowledge. He gazed on them, when he was alone in the room, with deep satisfaction. When the fortnight was up and, as agreed at the outset, Alex set off to drive Jane, Wendy and Ziggy on their last stretch to Sydney, his books were the one thing he was sorry to leave behind. He imagined their ardour draining out of them in his absence.

Sydney was different. Stop-start, down clogged arteries, through unending suburbs, until, round a bend and over a rise, you glimpsed a shining segment of the bridge against the harbour's blue water. Driving on a rollercoaster until they reached the underground carpark at Rushcutters Bay and put the car in the space alongside Alfonzo's black Porsche, the powder-blue Jag still unwashed after the dusty plains. The view from the balcony of the apartment looked across the park to the forest of white masts in the marina, and beyond again was the dancing blue of the harbour and its hazy green islands and headlands in the distance. The pock of tennis balls, the creaking and knocking of yachts at their moorings, gulls crying and water lapping and a siren's shriek, and, from inside, the fluty whine of voice and acoustic guitar . . . *Round and round . . . round and round . . .*

'It's a real Sydney soundtrack,' said Ziggy. It was Saturday after-noon. Saturday night lay ahead and he wanted to have found him-self a bed by nightfall. 'Looks like it's so long,' he announced. He was going off in search of the address on a piece of paper in his pocket. Only Alex came down to the street to see him off. He put his hand on Ziggy's shoulder and Ziggy put his arm round Alex's waist.

'Go easy, man,' said Alex. 'Let me know where you are.'

Ziggy shrugged and grinned. 'Yeah. See you when I see you.'

Wendy yelled from the balcony. 'Bye-bye Ziggy!' She was dressed in a turquoise happy coat. Her boyfriend lay inside on the sofa watching her. Feeling his eyes, she turned back inside with a comic pirouette, winking at Jane who got the message.

Jane and Alex walked from the northern end to the southern end of Bondi Beach and around the rocks, pausing on the bluff to admire the vertical patchwork of pastel houses in the late afternoon sun. In the other direction the rockface was topped with green grass and the white tombstones of the old cliff-hugging cemetery. Out in front, the blue ocean that pulsed around the shore bore swimmers, bodysurfers and board surfers in towards the line of foam, bees to a hive, and the sand was flecked, like nougat, with coloured bits of towels.

They waded out together. Alex was scared for a moment, imagining his mother pulling him through a wall of water. As a wave reared towards them, they bowed their heads and dived into its body. They shook the water from their faces when they came up, conscious of marking their arrival at this furthest point east, the Pacific Ocean, after the crossing of the inland spaces. Salt water spiralled down into the passages of ears and nose, sluiced hair and groin, washed away the last arid outback dust. Alex thought of his mother, rolling with the tide, as he bobbed. Jane laughed at him, and made him laugh back until he swam over and grabbed her and she clung to him like a seahorse as they kissed in the swell. This was something she would cherish – an engulfing ecstasy she could paint.

They walked hand in hand along the line of shallows, dodging the leathery joggers who came panting like salmon fighting upstream to spawn. They were filled with pleasure in each other, and with being on the scene of this littoral where lives washed up, washed on, washed away. They came as if to offer themselves – flesh and blood for the messy theatre of life.

Then they drove back to the flat and crept into their room without disturbing Alfonzo and Wendy, and made love with the salt of Bondi charging their lovemaking. Alex held Jane's face in the night, drinking her in, and she pushed her mouth up at him, wanting him closer. The bed sheets were wound into ropes.

'I don't want to be tied down,' Alex said afterwards. He was setting off back to Canberra in the morning by himself. 'I love you. I am true to you in my innermost. But I want to be free too.'

And Jane agreed, surprising herself, without knowing exactly what was intended. It let her off the hook too. If they were true to each other, it felt real and convenient to say they were free.

~

'You would never get over something like that,' Elspeth said to her mother in a genuine state of wonderment, 'would you? It's such a dreadful thing.'

Barb Gillingham did not understand how anything in Clarice Mack's life could have been so bad as to warrant the taking of it, as people said. No matter how sure a swimmer you were, an accident could always happen. People simply disappeared in the ocean, like Harold Holt, the Prime Minister who was taken while surfing.

'Who are you blaming, Elspeth?' Barb replied. 'Don't blame Clarice.'

'I mean Alex.'

'He'll blame himself, poor boy.'

They were sitting in the kitchen of the semi-detached cottage in Adelaide that had been bought for Elspeth with money from the family trust.

'You must miss her, Mum, like I miss my friends.'

'We were friends always. From schooldays. An unlikely pair. But everyone's different.'

Barb would always miss Clarice, that was the truth of it. She coughed, frowning at her daughter's grubby cheesecloth dress. Elspeth had a style, not to say a will, of her own. She liked looking plain and refused to let her mother fix her hair or choose her clothes any more. Prudent in small things, Elspeth liked things done in the simplest possible way.

Barb quite failed to understand how even the Masterman wealth, that most fundamental of simplicities, could be regarded by Elspeth as a complexity so overwhelming that she might be prepared to reject it. She could not see that the inheritance she passed on to her daughter, along with the prospect of Masterman riches, included a determined yearning to have her own way, which was in combat with an equally ingrained dutifulness.

'The house needs a good airing,' Barb sniffed. 'It reeks of joss sticks, and that oil.'

'Patchouli oil,' revealed Elspeth, displaying outward calm.

'How can you wear that stuff on your skin, dear? No wonder you can't think straight, with that up your nostrils all the time. Anyway, it's your business, as long as you're not taking pot. You're not, are you, darling?'

'Stop worrying about me, Mum,' said Elspeth with her most radiant smile. But her eyes were empty, her mother noticed.

Elspeth had come to realise that what she was going to do was a problem for people. If she had not been continually asked, she would have forgotten that she was supposed to do anything. She was quite capable of filling each day and week. She could be engaged with books and things, and disengaged from other people and from herself. Life was surely only the surface of a stream. Reality was beyond. But there was also the question of what her parents would do with her. When she turned twenty-one Elspeth was due to become a director of the family company. Barb complained to her husband about Elspeth, but Angus was as silly and vague about their daughter as ever. It was his idea to buy her the charming little house in town to live in.

One day, while Elspeth was buying lilies in the street, a woman came up to her and handed her a leaflet. Elspeth found herself listening to the warm ripple of the woman's talk for half an hour without noticing the time, and she ended up promising to visit the meditation centre.

It turned out to be a cream-brick suburban house surrounded by miniature golden cypresses in an untended front garden, with Doric columns around the porch where temple bells chimed in the wind. The woman, whose name was Diane, introduced Elspeth to her friends. Their aim, she said, was to disperse negativity and fill their lives with light. Their hope was to become one hundred per cent perfect, as their Divine Leader, an Indian child, was one hundred per cent perfect. They asked nothing of Elspeth, or anyone else, except that they let their perfection shine through.

Elspeth kept her visits to the ashram a secret from her parents. When she cut her hair, she did not go so far as to shave her head, because that would proclaim what was not wilfulness but a private exploring. She did not wear orange, although her clothes had become more resolutely unfashionable than ever. All her closest friends had left Adelaide by now, and she stopped sending postcards to them wherever they were, although Mrs Woodruff gave her Jane's new address every time they ran into one another. It was too early to have to explain herself. And as the months passed, she submitted to the demands of the ashram community and its unstated power structures, opening her heart to light and her mind to universal oneness. She started planning her journey to India where she might be admitted into the presence of the Divine Leader. She prepared herself thoroughly, with Diane's help. Meat, sex, stimulants, novels, friends, society – let them go, lilted Diane, who was completely unencumbered. And property. Elspeth should have no further burdens to weigh down the person she really was.

'It's too crowded,' Elspeth said, explaining to Diane why she did not move into the ashram permanently.

'We need additional premises,' Diane agreed, 'but we also need to transcend our individual concerns. We all need to do that.' Elspeth looked placidly, with a faint frown, as Diane went on. 'It's possible to make a symbolic gesture of renouncing our own privileges for the benefit of everyone. If there's a true sense of community with the other devotees, if the longing to enter the presence of the Divine Leader is genuine. It would not seem a big thing, for example, to make your own house available. As an offering that you choose to make.'

Elspeth smiled broadly, amused, which was perhaps a way-station to spiritual lightness.

Diane burned incense the day they welcomed Shivakali, the name Elspeth was given, as a higher rank of devotee in their midst. Elspeth had the phone at her house cut off and filled in a form for the mail to be returned to sender by the post office. It created one less thing to worry about.

Then Alison Woodruff rang Barb Gillingham to warn her that Elspeth had gone orange. She had heard the news from Jane in Sydney, who liked to keep up with the Adelaide gossip. The melo-dramatic gloating in the woman's voice confirmed what Barb had always thought of Alison, but she appreciated having the alarm bell sounded. She rang her solicitor who said that whatever Elspeth might do would be legally invalid if a medical practitioner cast doubt on her sanity at the time. She rang Angus to prepare him.

'We don't want to restrict her,' Angus Gillingham said, 'we just don't want any funny business either.'

'You don't know where Elspeth's fantasies will end,' Barb replied. She had got the address of the ashram.

Angus bent to open the little wire gate for his wife, who charged up the concrete path through the unmown lawn to the front door and rang the bell. A girl with straggly, mousy hair opened up. She took one look at Dr and Mrs Gillingham and closed the door on them. Barb then knocked loudly, and two others, scalped and in orange robes, came to the door, opening it with vague half-smiles on their faces. It was dark inside and Angus picked up a sour smell of steam-ing vegetables. When he asked if Elspeth was there, the two devotees nodded in harmony, indicating that they knew what was meant. Without saying a word, they closed the door and disappeared. By this time Barb was furious. She rattled the door handle until someone else came padding down the hallway. The woman who opened the door had a red glass bead on her forehead. Her head was shaven, her expression was stern and distant, and the saffron robe of office was draped with some style over her bare shoulders.

'Elspeth?' Angus stabbed, not one hundred per cent certain that he saw through her disguise.

She stepped out on to the porch, pulling the door behind her, to shield those inside from the invasion. 'It's Shivakali now, Dad.'

'Are your things here?' asked Barb, as if the ashram were just another hotel room.

'What things?'

'You're living here, aren't you?' Barb insisted.

'But I have no things,' said Elspeth in a patient, clarifying tone.

'Good.'

'Why don't we go and sit in the car?' asked her father, leaning forward and lowering his voice so as not to be overheard. The wind chimes above his head gave a low tinkle.

'What are you here for?' asked Elspeth with an amused lilt at her parents' antics. She lifted her robe slightly as her sandalled feet tripped down the path and her sternness converted into a euphoric smile.

'We don't know what's going on,' said Barb, chasing behind. Angus unlocked the car and Barb sat with their daughter in the back. 'Your house is unattended. There's mail – you haven't given your house to those people?'

That was the moment in which Elspeth's eyes locked with her mother's in the old way. She smiled, not the empty smile of devotion, but a sharper smile of triumph. She had won this game. 'Not yet,' Elspeth said vaguely.

Barb gave a grin of relief. 'Then it's all right.'

'But the community does need an ashram in town. What do you think?'

The reality of property, a greater power than any other, remained part of the credo that mother had passed to daughter. So

Barb saw at once. Elspeth had evidently kept hold of that. She knew that the Divine Leader was prepared to sell her the promotion to a higher rank of transcendence. The same law applied everywhere. Yet with that knowledge she became interested in seeking transcendence on her own merits without paying any price. She wondered how her parents would move to stop that.

'Can't we go somewhere,' suggested Barb, 'instead of sitting here in the street?'

Her husband turned the key in the ignition.

'Are you kidnapping me?' the young woman asked.

'Come home for a while. Have a meal and a wash and sort yourself out,' intoned Angus with his doctor's cheer.

Barb reached across and fingered the third eye on her daughter's forehead.

'I always wondered how they get these things to stay on.' With her fingernail Barb dislodged the red glass bead. It fell down the back of the car seat. 'Whoops! Sorry, dear.'

'Don't worry about it, Mum. They sell them at K-Mart.'

So it was goodbye to Shivakali. She did not even put up a fight as her father drove off. That was something the Indian child had implanted. That was Elspeth. Not unless there was a point and you were certain of victory.

It was never clear when Elspeth looked back exactly why Shivakali with her third glass eye and her suburban divinity had come into her life and then vanished again as quickly, unless it was just as something she had found to *do* at the time – on her own.

Later that year, when she was on an even keel again, although reserving her capacity for one hundred per cent perfection, Elspeth went to Italy with her mother.

It turned out that Barb and her daughter travelled together well. In Tuscany mother and daughter hired a car, in gorgeous crisp weather, to tour vineyards and huddled hilltop villages. Sometimes Barb thought her daughter unresponsive, even shallow. Elspeth seemed to *need* none of it. Perhaps results could not be expected yet.

Their trip ended in Rome. Having done the Sistine Chapel with her daughter in the morning, Barb spent the afternoon at the hotel hairdresser. She could not but appreciate the man's flagrant flattery. Elspeth went out walking in her jeans and Italian shoes to the top of the Spanish Steps and on into the gardens where she bought herself a gelato and sat on a stone bench to eat it. It was too chilly to sit there and not look mad. From the belvedere the eternal city spread before her in silvery sunlight. Domes and towers shone like bubbles straining to break free of the foaming sea of history. She could imagine the whole thing going pop and an infinity of clean white light taking its place. It was pretty. But for what? It provided no question and answer – not for her, too airy and empty herself, too straightforward. Pop! She longed for something simpler.

The hairdresser had given her mother the glossy swept-back helmet hair-do of a Roman matron. It was something similarly uncompromising, but in a completely different form, as a mode of life, that Elspeth was seeking to suit herself.

'I can't wait to get on that plane,' said Barb with a happy sigh, as she stuffed her purchases into her bags.

'I wish I was going with you,' said Elspeth, sitting on her mother's monster suitcase to help it close. She had enrolled in a course in art conservation at a world-famous, underfunded Instituto in Urbino, home of the sweet spiritual painter Raphael. She was taking the bus there next day.

The twinkling eyes of mother and daughter met as the case snapped shut at last. Barb took life on her own terms. She hoped that inheritance would be passed on at least.

~

'Got any mint slices?' Alex asked, knocking on the door of René's college room and barging in. He was angry after trying to ring Jane in Sydney. It was after midnight and there was still no answer at

Alfonzo's flat. Alex knew that Jane had her own life in Sydney, but when she was not there to answer the phone he realised he had no idea, not where she was but *who* she was, no idea what substance the relationship between them had any more, and it made him cross.

René Baum, who lived down the corridor, had an endless supply of chocolate mint slices and cigarettes and was Alex's first port of call when he wanted a break from study. He had picked René from the beginning, by the voluminous brown wool dressing-gown he wore to the communal shower block. The other students in the block just slung a towel around their midriffs. René was majoring in Oriental Studies. His parents ran a cinema chain and lived in a house in Bellevue Hill with harbour views, and René had spent his childhood afternoons in dark picture theatres watching American movies. His parents had sent him away to university because they quarrelled all the time. They were getting divorced so Mr Baum could marry a younger woman, and René suspected the would-be stepmother of planning to diddle him out of his inheritance.

In their first major discussion René revealed to Alex that he had chosen his name on advice from a guru to ensure the best possible numerology.

'But what's your real name?' Alex insisted on knowing.

'I have no other name. I'm thinking of changing my surname too.'

'What else did the guru tell you?' Alex asked. Dawn was coming up.

'He said I should go East.'

'Then how come you're in Canberra?'

'It's the only place I could study Chinese and Sanskrit and Japanese.'

Language acquisition was René's way of growing a second skin. He looked forward to the day when he could lose himself so entirely in a foreign language that his native tongue disappeared. English, especially Australian English, was not his mother's or father's tongue anyway, which was German.

Alex had nominated himself as first-year representative on the Law Students' Society and joined Students for Direct Action. In jeans and duffle coat, with his hair a sandy afro, he spoke at lunchtime demanding Australia's pull-out from the imperialist war against the Vietnamese peasants. He called on all young men to refuse to register for conscription when they turned twenty. For him it was still a couple of years away. He was confident in his criticism of everything.

When René announced, in another of their talking sessions, that he had become a Maoist, Alex laughed him to scorn.

'You're just another middleclass wanker,' René said, interrogating Alex through his glinting granny glasses, 'getting up in front of those kids lounging on the lawns at lunchtime, sucking Coca-Cola through a straw. There's only one world revolution, mate, and, as the Chairman says, it's no tea-party.'

René dreamed of participating in the Great Proletarian Cultural Revolution. He had applied through the East Wind Bookstore, so far without response, to study in the People's Republic of China. It was his strategy to avoid being sent to Vietnam. He did not want the public spectacle of becoming a conscientious objector. In his tormented calligraphy he inscribed sayings from *The Little Red Book* on Chinese art paper and pinned them up around his room.

'You want to get down with the peasants, mate, and dig the good earth,' René chided Alex.

Alex was conscious of a degree of theatrical display in his behaviour when he addressed a rally, as he was conscious of the mental exhilaration in the evening meetings he attended, in the university bar, when radical ideas were pushed to their extreme, as if to conjure a total transformation of society. He was aware of the intoxicating power of camaraderie and solidarity in the activities in which he took part. In the bonds he formed with the other young men and women in SDA, he learned that it did not matter if no motivation was pure as long as the end was kept in sight. He was discovering himself as a politician. Then he would recoil as suddenly into the personal, curling up on the bed, talking with one of the women, hands warm around mugs of coffee, until he got all hot under the collar with desire and longing, but recoiled from personal emotion, condemning feelings as something too ephemeral to yield a satisfactory outcome.

Since becoming a Maoist, René rejected private life in total. He stayed chaste – cold and apart. Alex admired his awkward rigour, although he did not follow the example. It was as if René already lived according to the conditions of a life elsewhere.

On one of their all-night talks – the night when, instead of mint slices, they ate hash cookies and played *Stairway to Heaven* over and over on the turntable until at around three o'clock in the morning the Christian girl in the next door room exhausted her charity and started thumping on the wall – draped in blankets in the freezing small hours, René read the *I Ching* for Alex. His long dark hair hung down like a curtain in front of his long pale face in the shuddering light of a candle. Voicing the strange, percussive music of Mandarin names that corresponded with the trigrams Alex had thrown, René interpreted Alex's destiny.

Alex was a young fox moving out on thin ice. So said the *Book of Changes*. Alex recognised a reference to his political activism, his foxy feet pattering fast and light over ice that sheathed a dark and dangerous body of water. He did not raise the question of the problematic relationship between occult prophecy and dialectical materialism. It was René's oblique way of referring to his mother's drowning.

'At the back of our house in Bellevue Hill,' René said, 'when I was a kid, there was a kind of vacant lot that was once a market garden run by the Chinese.' He pushed his hair out of his eyes as his words ran swiftly on. 'It had gone to seed by the time I got there and was all overgrown. I used to escape out there because it was off the map as far as my parents were concerned and they would never find me. There was a trench filled with wild fennel where I used to hide and the remains of a bridge that the Chinese had built over the top, an amazing moon-shaped bridge made of rock and clay. I got high on the smell of the wild fennel. I just loved it. I used to roll up in a ball under the bridge and stay there for hours. It was bliss.'

'Back to the womb,' giggled Alex. 'That was before you ever heard of Chairman Mao.'

René leered at Alex. 'Right! You can't go back. The only way is forward, comrade.'

Alex lay back on the floor and stared at the metal rose on the ceiling. If activated by smoke in case of fire, he considered, it would burst into a shower and douse the room and the ink of René's revolutionary sayings would run down the wall, and the hanging calligraphy curl in the flames. Alex wished he had a whole other world he could content himself with, as René had found. His preoccupation was with the discontents of *this* world, which offered the only way he knew to take him away from himself. He needed the imperfect world around him, that he was rapidly learning how to manipulate, in order to blot out negativity.

With all his intelligence, Alex had not been able to see what was happening, or had seen and turned away because he had no faith in problem-solving. A mother's suicide, though no one ever called it that, was the absolute expression of the lovelessness of the universe. He had been the closest person to her when it happened, the one who might have saved her, and it had happened anyway, unstoppable, as if a curse were on him and her. Yet he knew he must not enter that black domain where everything seemed doomed and where the final outcomes were always the worst ones. He was not strong enough to survive there. He must stay away from that brink of despair, using active engagement to resist passivity.

After the night on which he told René Baum about his mother, Alex never mentioned what had happened to her to anyone else. As a student politician, he was becoming a tactician who enjoyed finding pathways to achieve outcomes. He was happiest working with the issues of here and now and the next day. Late at night at a gathering, back against the wall, beer glass and cigarette in hand, he would thrash out a question, pushing the boundaries back as if he were a commander on the way to victory. He attracted people that way, creating himself at the same time. If he kept doing it, always moving further from all those ties back to the world in which he had grown up, he might eventually put what had happened there apart from himself. He might eventually stop blaming himself. He might eventually burn away his anger and self-hatred. Then he would be able to accept coolly that every person was ultimately responsible for their own actions: even swimming out into the surf at dawn, leaving everyone else behind.

Alex had run into Josie Ryan in the street in Adelaide not long before he left for Canberra. He had been embarrassed by the encounter. She struck him as stand-offish and critical, as if she did not approve of his smooth appearance and disengaged manner. At this crossroads their ways were so divergent that it seemed like an end. For old time's sake, they duly wished each other well and passed on. Then out of the blue Josie's letter found him in Canberra.

I don't have your new address. That's why I wrote care of your old address at home. I hope it wasn't too much trouble to forward it. I passed the house and saw a For Sale sign on it and that made me hurry up and write before I lost track of you altogether. I apologise for being so tongue-tied when I saw you in the street that day. I'm not usually like that. I just didn't know how to say all the things that needed to be said. I didn't know what order to put them in. That was the problem. It's not easy for humanity to balance the good and bad of life, the worldly triumph and the woe, and know what is truly important in God's eyes.

I looked up your exam results in the paper. Then I read about your scholarship. You always were a clever bunny, Alex. You've been given great gifts and you must earn the opportunity to use them well. I pray that you'll find the strength and grace to use your abilities wisely. My results were good too. I give thanks for that. I'm satisfied. I'm not going on with any more study now. I don't see the point of it.

I heard about your mother, Alex, and that's what I really wanted to say that day we met, but how could I in the middle of the street, when you were composing yourself for your big journey? Mrs Vincaitis told me. I don't know how she knew. She never liked your mother, but what she told me was perhaps part of the truth. She said your mother was a troubled woman, a woman in pain, with no way out. I used to admire her from a distance and wish my mother could be more like her. Gracious, and a good mother to you, Alex. The loss must be hard to bear. I pray for your mother's spirit, and pray that God will succour you, Alex, in His mysterious way. I've got a job for the time being as a check-out chick! Isn't that wonderful? I'm under neon light all day. My grandmother passed away at the beginning of the year. She was seventy-seven. Do you remember Cleve Gordon, the dark boy from Joeys? He goes to the same Youth Fellowship group as me. He's studying Science at university. Not bad, eh? His foster parents didn't want him any more so he's staying with the Brothers. He still finds time for football. He remembers you. I hope you are settled in your new home by now. God bless and safeguard you, Alex.

    Love, Josie.

Alex didn't know what to do with the letter after he had read it twice. There was no place in his life for such a thing yet he was reluctant to throw it away. He folded it in four and slipped it inside his *Selected Poems* of Rilke, vowing to write a letter back. Which he never did. He told Jane, the next time he visited her in Sydney, when he had run out of things to say to her, 'Josie Ryan's got a job as a check-out girl. Can you believe it?' But Jane did not remember who Josie Ryan was. 'The girl I wanted to marry when I was twelve,' Alex said.

'She must have got sick of waiting then,' commented Jane sharply.

2

WENDY brushed her honey hair fast, teasing it out so it sprayed in an aura round her head. Eyes met smiling, knowing eyes in the mirror. She defied everything that Isabel and Peter Sunner had planned for her brains, health and beauty. Her imagination had carried her into a world of gold and silver, movement and light, fragrance and self-abandonment, that was in no way to her parents' taste. That was the condition she savoured as she swayed, lotus-position, on the thin cushion as the afternoon flowed on in mounting, breaking waves of time, and air wafted from the spicy beach, and she waited for Alfonzo to return to her, as return he must.

Alfonzo had glossy businessman's hair and a Zapata moustache that drooped round his large loose mouth. He had funny teeth, like a fish's, dark heavy-lidded eyes and a good tan. Lean and compact, he wore baggy white cotton trousers and a cream silk shirt that floated, unbuttoned, over his little pot belly. He paid for everything, for her duty-free perfume and cosmetics, the fresh food and drink she liked, for anything she wanted to buy. Clothes, sandals, hats, music, even the gifts she bought for him. Binoculars, roll-your-own tobacco, sunglasses. Whenever she wanted something, she asked for it and Alfonzo gave it to her, like the large emerald ring in a gold setting he had paid cash for at Changi Airport. Wendy thought that was funny. She remembered how she used to ask her father for money as a child, when her pocket money ran out, and Peter Sunner, citing Grandfather Wilbert's equation of labour and profit, would give her some on condition that she work it off. Alfonzo was never like that, he just gave it, with no strings attached, always cash, from a wad in his pocket.

Alfonzo's father still had the shoe repair shop in Adelaide and his mother cleaned city offices. They were hard-working people whose frame of reference was their own community. They did not much understand the values of wider society, except as refracted through the eyes of their fellow Maltese. But their son was an Australian like anyone else, a son of the new land who fed off the good times that bravado, racing hormones and his parents' hard-earned money procured for him. He and his mates all talked big, as businessmen, entrepreneurs, would-be tycoons. Appearances were kept up even when plans did not work out. With Wendy, the best-looking, sexiest, smartest, best-bred chick around, Alfonzo Vella became a Maltese prince. He even took her to meet his family once. This was a big mistake. His sister Leila jeered at Wendy and called her a moll through smiling gritted teeth.

Alfonzo took Wendy north from Sydney, first to North Queensland, then on to Bali and Chiang Mai, until they reached Goa and a community of hippies, healers and seekers who were intent on lifting physical pleasures into the spiritual. From their style of travel Wendy knew that Alfonzo's business was doing better and better. He did things in the neatest possible way, without confrontation, following the way of least resistance, channelling his cravings into the powerful current of a smooth-flowing canal.

Alfonzo had won Wendy with the value he placed on her, the esteem he let her feel. No other male in her experience courted her as he had done, with an intelligence that was sharp as peacock's claws, oblique and merciless. Her own intelligence was escapist, in rebellion against her Sunner upbringing which accepted only a narrow range of virtue and outlawed anything wild. In Alfonzo she had found the possibility to be different, in the face of her parents and society's scorn, and even the disapproval of her best friend Jane – living as his mistress, his woman, his all-quenching lover.

Alfonzo's syndicate brought in heroin from the Golden Triangle to Australia. It was a simple operation and the money was phenomenal. Alfonzo arranged for the Thai suppliers to have the drug supplied to the couriers in a ready-to-go form. At the other end he arranged for the stuff to reach a distribution point. He was still young enough to be a front man. With Wendy by his side he could travel around without arousing suspicion. He did not deal directly with the users and kept one step away from the naive young couriers, who could easily slip up. He never saw the stuff himself except for his own personal use – and Wendy's, after he started sharing it with her. He could control that, as he could control people.

Wendy grew adept at slipping through international airports and hotels, travelling light, packing a bag and leaving on a changed flight at short notice. Permanence and solidity were the only enemies. The imperative was to read the moment and respond.

~

Alex, growing restless at university, often went out walking on dark cold windswept nights, down avenues of leafless trees or through city colonnades where bureaucrats dined in crafty restaurants and lobbyists lingered in deafening bars. Impatient of other people, unable to bear his own company when he was alone, he walked like a madman, a solitary figure striding over hard ground. After a putsch he had dropped the ineffectual SDA, whom even René's Maoists denounced, and let himself be seduced into a wider New Left group. He itched, apprehensively, for a bigger arena, wanting the world to be different so he could show he was able to live in it as a mature and effective man.

He tried to push his facetious dialogue with René in the direction of something more personal, but René dismissed such matters as counter-revolutionary. René had been besotted with an American girl called Rebecca who was dumped by her diplomatic parents in his Sanskrit class for a semester. Sparks flew with caustic Rebecca – then she was gone before anything happened except an exchange of addresses. René remained a virgin for Mao.

Alex wanted to talk about Jane. Elspeth had sent a few postcards from Italy. His sister Susan had written only once to say she was over Robbie Masterman and was planning to marry a fellow pharmacy graduate. His father, Tim, had written too, to say that he was considering remarriage, once Alison Woodruff was free. The people in his life were moving away, he complained to René.

Perhaps Alex was moving beyond sight of the shore. He yearned for something more than this life of his. He didn't know what it was, he moaned, or where he might find it. There had been a zone of excitement, of emotional discovery, that Jane once gave him. It was withheld now. He twiddled his sandy mess of hair.

'You're turning decadent, comrade,' René said.

Ziggy sent down tickets to Alex for the opening night of a major production of *A Midsummer Night's Dream* in which he had been cast as Puck. He sent two to Jane as well, who was his only old friend in Sydney, now that Wendy was in Goa with Alfonzo.

Jane liked to draw on a portable sketchpad whenever the mood took her, painting whatever eccentric subjects she chose. At art school her work was framed by the demands of a course and the external judgements of a system that stood in for the world she would eventually have to negotiate. She must be herself: that was her strength; yet she must learn to be so in more complicated ways. That was the lesson explained to her by the Head of Painting, a painter called Michael Browne-Grey. Willing to learn that lesson, Jane spent more and more time with Michael, who abandoned his wife to spend more time with Jane in the Rushcutters Bay flat that she was minding for Wendy and Alfonzo. Jane told Alex all this only indirectly, in conversations about how her art was going, when he drove up from Canberra to see her. She was only trying something out. Why should she feel guilty? But it was noticeable that the time she spent together with Alex – on less frequent weekends and holidays – was working badly. Michael was hungry for his feminist goddess of youth, whereas Alex would have Jane only on their agreed, unclamorous, unpossessive basis. If that meant the relationship was dying, as Jane's feelings told her, so be it.

Jane invited Michael Browne-Grey to the *Dream*, so Alex decided to bring René as his guest. They stood about in the foyer chatting awkwardly and were glad when they could take their seats. Having heard so much about René, Jane shared Michael's reaction. They found him offensive. With his long greasy hair and smelly Mao jacket, he lacked all sense of style.

The production was a sustained hallucination in which fear, longing and dream folded into one another under the will of the Fairy King and by the agency of Puck. Flitting from scene to scene, Ziggy was superb. From re-echoing depths to shrill piping, he had music in his voice. His movement was lithe and metamorphic. The audience could not take its eyes from this dazzling embodiment of youth, this girl-boy, this fairy-mortal, this poised confusion of being.

Jane discussed the production in the foyer with Michael during the interval, amidst snippets of praise for Ziggy's performance from other people in the crowd. Michael got coffee for himself and Jane while Alex and René were smoking outside on the terrace. When they came in, they found the painter with his arm around Jane's waist. Alex wanted to say that paunchy Michael, his beard streaked with grey, could have been Jane's father. Dr Woodruff, Jane's real father, nuclear physicist and boy-man himself, was being divorced by his wife so she could be with Alex's father.

'*Lord what fools* these *mortals be!*' René whispered to Alex under his breath as they resumed their seats.

The performance culminated in a roar of applause when Puck

asked the members of the audience to give him their hands. The audience adored Ziggy. He was the discovery of the night. The star. When he came out to the bar afterwards, there was that special hush of salute. His friends took part of the elation as theirs. Ziggy hugged Jane and hugged Michael and hugged Alex and shook hands with René when Alex introduced him. Congratulations! Congratulations! People started shouting champagne. The director, Herbert Horsfall, a slender man with a crinkled face, who had, as he put it, rescued Ziggy from Adelaide, came over and gave them all wet kisses.

'Isn't he a wonder!' the director gushed, taking Ziggy's hand. 'Believe me. If he studies hard and works hard, this boy can do anything.' Then he floated off with Ziggy in tow.

René was spending the night in his old family home in Bellevue Hill, which was his mother's after the divorce. He asked if Alex needed a place to stay.

'A roll in the wild fennel in your backyard,' smiled Alex, making René scowl. 'Not tonight.'

'I want to talk to you,' Jane said to Alex. She had sent Michael home. 'When are we leaving?'

'We can't leave yet,' fretted Alex.

'Why not? What time is it?'

'What does that matter?'

'Don't leave,' Ziggy begged, throwing his arms round them. 'You mustn't leave!' He dragged the director back, who said he wanted to stay with them till dawn and watch the sun come up over Bondi Beach. Jane watched to see which way Alex would jump.

'Oh, I don't care,' said Ziggy, dropping his hands to his side. 'Why did Michael have to leave so early?' he suddenly asked Jane. 'I was so glad he came. He's such a good artist. Did he love the design?' Ziggy flashed his eyes at Alex. Neither Alex nor Jane spoke. 'Well, you two better be going if you're going. I really appreciate it that you were here.'

'You were amazing, Ziggy. Brilliant,' said Jane, hugging him goodnight.

Alex felt a pang at his friend's success. Ziggy reached out and kissed Alex on the cheek. It felt strange, and Alex slobbered a little, wanting to reciprocate.

'Go now,' grinned Ziggy, pushing Jane and Alex away.

'He's a very good actor,' Jane said when they were out in the street. 'The rest is trivial. He's a very powerful person too. Be careful of him, Alex.'

'And *I'm* not?' responded Alex, hurt, as they walked through the Cross. 'Is that it?'

'Don't be paranoid.' Jane took his arm. 'How would I know what you are? You no longer want me to know.'

'Only because you're no longer interested.'

Stung by what they had finally said to each other, they walked on in silence through the dark park to the water's edge.

'I won't fight for you,' said Alex. 'I can't.'

'I know you won't,' replied Jane disconsolately. 'I just want to know why it hasn't worked.'

'It is working. Part of that is that we have our own things to work out, which need their own spaces. The bond is still there. What about you and Michael, anyway?'

She snorted with laughter. 'You can't love. You don't know how.'

'I hate being like this,' he confessed. 'But you won't help me.'

She put her arms around him. He was a motherless child, after all, and for a moment he might have cried again, as he had sobbed in her arms before. She was looking over his shoulder at the confetti of light on the black harbour and knew that she needed none of this. She loved him. That would always continue. But Michael had stirred something deep and ambitious in her, which was more important now, if only by default.

'You were always the one who rode the carousel in the playground, giving the orders to whoever was doing the pushing,' he said. 'You remember that?' He laughed.

'Let's go to bed,' she replied. They made love, that time in Alfonzo's apartment, with a tenderness that came from having known each other almost all their lives. Then they turned away to the separate edges of the bed and slept.

'The purity of the revolution demands a thoroughgoing system that must pervade the meaning of every word and the intention of every action,' René argued the next night as he and Alex drove back to Canberra. They were discussing capitalist roaders and revisionary deviationism. 'Anything less is obstruction that preserves the old at the expense of the new.'

Alex could not imagine anything so radical, so totalising. Human will could only manipulate human nature so far. To achieve goals it was necessary to work pragmatically with what was at hand, making quantum leaps from time to time, as shock tactics, to break through into something new. That was his position now. 'If everyone believes in the same system, then no one believes it,' he said. 'That way lies falsity and mass delusion. Struggle is necessary, to move forward. I want something more dialectical, more changing.' He was talking about himself. What René wanted was something complete, like the system of Chinese language, a net to contain a comprehensive reality. For Alex it was the holes in the net that made movement possible.

Their heads were spinning by the time they stopped at the roadhouse in Goulburn for toasted sandwiches and coffee.

'The lovers are falsely manipulated by drugs and disguise,' René maintained, returning to their discussion of last night's play as he tore open a second sachet of sugar. 'That's where Shakespeare becomes a hegemonist – you know what I mean – a collaborator.'

'It's an incorrect analysis,' countered Alex, taking off his glasses and rubbing his eyes. 'For passages, moments, facets of their existence, the lovers are prepared to believe their dreams and that makes their dreams actually come true. It might feel like intervention from another order, the way it works in the play, but it has its roots in their hearts and minds. Nothing else is as real.'

As they left again on the road that night, buzzing with caffeine, the world and all its questions seemed something that their minds might just be big enough to encompass. Then after Goulburn, René suggested a short cut to bypass the slow, tortuous part of the journey along the shores of Lake George. He knew a back road that would bring them out on the other side.

'Even deviationism has its place,' René reassured him. Why not, thought Alex, willing to explore.

The road headed straight up into the hills and soon deteriorated into little more than a winding cutting through forest. But they pressed on, rather than turn back. The moon was high in the sky. It grew colder, and seemed lonelier, in the purring old Jaguar as they travelled further south and the altitude increased. René lapsed into silence. Reflecting on the relativity of reality that they had been discussing, Alex felt suddenly that every truth, every structure, *everything*, was contingent on a person's determination to believe in it. Suddenly his relationship with Jane seemed to depend entirely on how he and she believed. How they made it, so it would be; otherwise there was nothing – an abstract relationship, an eternal bond perhaps, but nothing real and there – nothing to rest on without the perpetual effort of making it there, and he did not think he had the desire, or the will, for that. He shivered. It made him sad to realise that this was probably a paradigm, *the* paradigm, that he would never love anyone in a way that did not depend on himself. Feeling it thus, and not being alone, he voiced it for René. 'Alone forever!'

'What was that, mate? Are we lost?' René muttered. He had fallen asleep. 'This road is taking far longer than it's supposed to.' The only light was the moon, and the crossing beams of the headlights.

'Alone forever! I said,' repeated Alex, and René yawned. 'I'm splitting up with Jane,' he explained. 'We can't make it work.'

'Because of that bastard?'

'Who?'

'Michael. The professor she's screwing.'

Alex was put out that René, who disclaimed any interest in affairs of the heart, who would never listen when he spoke about Jane, should have such a clear view. 'That's got nothing to do with it. It's me. I can't have a relationship with anyone. I can't share myself like that. If I can't love Jane, I can't love anyone and I know it's going to be this way forever. It's who I am.'

'Well done, buddy. Love the Revolution. That's far more important. You're lucky, in a way. Love the Great Helmsman.'

'Be serious, can't you?'

'I'm sorry. I don't see why you need to love anyone more than you say you do. Even if she's a fine woman like Jane.'

'I don't have your existential courage.'

René was quite unaffrighted by the immense spaces. 'You're bogged down in humanity. Look somewhere else. Be alone. Hey!'

The headlight beams had caught something white up the road ahead. Alex slammed on the brakes. The car slipped and halted in a cloud of dust. A white horse was staring into the headlights. Motes of fine dust swirled like smoke around the horse, a tall mare, silver-blue in the moonlight, a wild pony caught standing across the road in this narrow opening through the forest where no one would usually venture at night. She looked at the car, flaring her nostrils a little to conceal panic, steadily refusing to move, her dark eyes reflecting two bright points of light, as she flicked her tail.

Alex and René sat in the car wondering what to do.

'What a strange sight,' said Alex.

'Completely inexplicable,' said René. 'She's come to see you.'

'She's a brumby,' said Alex. 'Can horses see at night?'

He inched the car forward as slowly as he could, hoping the animal would step to one side. At the last moment she bolted, turned and climbed into the trees.

'Take it as a vision,' said René.

This strange and singular beauty was vouchsafed for them alone, a secret they shared, a wonder that would never be adequately conveyed when they told the story. The appearance of the white horse on the cold moonlit road was soothing to Alex's wound: the answering image of the single soul on its journey.

It made him suddenly think of pale Josie Ryan, all in white. She had written him another letter, this time to say she was becoming a nun.

'You brought this on yourself, friend,' concluded René as Alex drove on.

I did not write earlier because I have been in retreat. Now I am back in Adelaide. I have applied for a novitiate and been taken into our house here, the Order of the Sisters of Charity. I cannot explain my decision, if that's what you want to know, except to say I am confident that with God's grace it will turn out to be the right thing for me. It is a testing vocation. My calling is not yet fully tested. I wanted to let you know.

Alex looked again at the address and realised aghast that The Priory meant exactly what it said. He started to laugh. What an amazing and ridiculous piece of news! How could he be expected to take the decision seriously? Singular and anachronistic, yet so typical of Josie, sheltering under her floppy straw hat. The letter irritated him, as if he had been counting on her in some obscure way and now she put herself beyond reach for good. How could he respect her recidivist retreat into religion?

Later on I might have the chance to study at university, but not for now. At Youth Fellowship I listen to those university students discuss the things they care about. That's possible for me. Don't you dare think of me as being in a cloister!

He twisted his locks as he stared at what she said. A couple of strands of his hair fell on to the page. *Praise this world to the Angel, not the untellable: you can't impress him with the splendour you've felt . . .* He refolded the letter and slipped it inside his Rilke, together with her first letter, as a memento of the girl who could not go out in the sun.

~

Cleve spent summer with his foster parents, helping them out on the farm. It was a holiday, and they were kind to him, but the experience of his uneasy standing between guest and worker was enough to make it clear to him that his time with the Adamses was over for good. They were Christian people, but it was always only a provisional arrangement. He was glad to return to the Brothers, who were prepared to pay the costs of further study while he made up his mind where his future lay. He earned his keep by working as a groundsman at the seminary where he lived. It was a secure and content time for him. The place was familiar in its geography, its ritual and its cosy tone of rugged, eccentric monasticism. He might have found other subjects more stimulating, but since his bursary was to study science, he worked hard at Biology, Chemistry and Physics to achieve Pass results. In the back of his mind there was the possibility that he might move up to Medicine.

Study was made interesting by the mix of students. There were Colombo Plan exchange students who were darker than he was. There were women with whom he teamed up in the lab to carry out experiments. He joined the football team, the Christian fellowship and the History Club. He made up for not being able to study Australian History, his particular interest, by going to some of the special lectures.

Josie Ryan made him laugh when he saw her on campus. She had turned into a sharp-eyed young woman, on fire with idealism, who believed that the love of God could solve every problem.

'You must see me as a wavering soul,' he accused her, when she lingered after the fellowship meeting, as she always did, to talk to him.

'It's just that you're wasting your time here. You haven't found your true path.'

Cleve sneered. 'What's that then?'

Josie did not blink. The clear light shone steady from her eyes. She was right. If it had not been for the bursary, he would have thought about dropping out. The thing that changed him was a lecture given to the History Club one lunchtime by a wiry fellow from the Office of Aboriginal Affairs in Canberra, who talked about the Freedom Ride, when blacks forced their way into the public swimming pools of racist country towns, and about the referendum of 1967 when Aborigines were classed as citizens for the first time. It was the beginning not the end, the old man said, talking about survival and redress, about land and rights to land. But it was up to the people themselves.

Cleve went up afterwards and asked the beautiful old gubba, whose name was Nugget, what he could do to help. Nugget said that Cleve had the education and must make his choice. Once he finished his course, he would be one of a tiny number of Aborigines with university degrees. There would be a place for him. He would have a vital role to play. What else was he going to do anyway?

'It's the task of your generation to turn things round. It's going to be a bloody hard struggle,' Nugget said, shaking Cleve's hand in a promise. 'No point sitting around and fretting when there's something to be done.'

~

Hills of blown green glass, clouds like stairways to heaven, roads like tent ropes tying the landscape's contours to houses, villages, humanity: Elspeth looked out with a high sense of perspective from the window of the apartment she rented under the eaves of the Signora's palazzo, as if assaying the background of a painting with herself as the foreground. Her cheeks turned happily towards the warmth. Under the influence of Italy she was ordinarily fashionable once more. She had started sending postcards again, but she had not written a word to anyone about Giugi, the printmaker at the Instituto who had become her authority on the town. She always knew where to find Giugi when she had a query, or a story to unload, and he always let her perch on a stool at his workbench and obliged with a brusque response. Through Giugi she met an Australian family who lived in Urbino: Rod Dale, a Melbourne artist and his wife Margie and their two kids, who had been in Italian exile, as they put it, for three years now. Giugi made Rod's prints up for him. Under the influence of Italy, the artist had turned away from abstraction and back to figurative work, becoming interested in how the Italian masters could give both mass and divinity to the human form. He had painted his wife lying on their matrimonial bed. 'But Margie's too flat,' Rod said. He wanted to do Giugi's Umbrian body. 'Giugi's like a tree trunk rooted in the earth and holding up heaven.'

'Use only half that cheese,' Margie instructed as Elspeth grated parmesan for the pasta.

The men had gone to the studio. Margie could not help noticing those little signs of extravagance in Elspeth, when she used too much of the cheese, or ate more than her share of the olives that had been counted out. Margie was wife, mother and scrimping family manager. She had made a commitment to a husband and this was where it had taken her, when all she really wanted was for her own kids to grow up independent and unfussy. 'Five minutes till the pasta's ready,' said Margie. 'Better tell them, Elspeth. Do you mind?'

Elspeth was surprised when Giugi agreed to pose for Rod. But he had proved to be a fine and willing model, comfortably proud of his nakedness under the objective gaze of another man.

'Are you decent in there?' she called. She felt it only prudent to knock before walking in. The artist looked up, concerned that Giugi would be embarrassed by an intruder. The model was turned side on to the viewer in the bright light of the studio with his legs apart, as if pacing out a step, and his upper torso twisting forward away from the shadow, like a soldier caught by the eyes of someone in the crowd as he marches by, his body swivelling round ever so slightly. He was a stocky, muscular man with a goodly layer of fat. His rounded shoulders were twice the breadth of his waist and his legs were bowed like a weightlifter's in a travelling circus, thought Elspeth. His hairline bisected the crown of his head into light and dark hemispheres.

'Take a break, mate,' said the artist. 'Cover up.'

'Elspeth has no interest in a naked man,' declared Giugi. He pronounced the word as one syllable. Knacked.

'You would look better with a figleaf,' she said, looking him straight in the eye. Giugi had wonderful eyes. Canny eyes, she decided. 'Dinner's ready,' she said.

Standing before her, giving her a flicker of acknowledgement, Giugi pulled on his shirt and bent to pull on his jeans. He found Elspeth's puritanism powerful and provoking, when she had every opportunity to be otherwise.

At the end of the evening he walked her home. He wanted to take their relationship further. Was she willing at least to let that happen? Or was it her isolation, and a pressuring intensity that had grown between them during the meal, that brought her back to his studio with its white walls and grey floor? Elspeth wanted to explore the relationship with Giugi but did not want to sleep with him, preferring to stay choosy and aloof, yet worried that in refusing to recognise his desire she might put their friendship at risk, angry that she even had to take such considerations into account.

The light in the studio was harsh and white. The window was a dark hole. Everything was spare and strong and cerebral. She sat on the high stool at his workbench and he came and stood by her, stroking her hair. For a moment it was comforting, as if she were a child. Then she shied from his touch, like a pony, unable to allow him to continue.

'*Perché?*'

'You think I'm not interested in a man's body? You're right. I'm interested in your mind.' She stared at him with an ironical grin.

He smiled softly. 'You're interested in higher beauty.'

'Is that so strange?'

'I like that about you. You're no ordinary girl.'

'No, Giugi, I am.'

He came forward and kissed her lightly on the forehead. 'Is that okay?'

'No, Giugi.'

He took her hands.

'No. Please. It's late.'

'Okay,' he shrugged. 'You want to go home? I can wait too. I'm not going anywhere.'

The words echoed in Elspeth's head, like the sound of the footsteps on the cobblestones in the steep lane below the palazzo. That was what she found herself remembering about him. He was a patient craftsman, capable of using his intellect to move forward a position of balance. *I can wait too*. His words relieved the pressure. They were a gracious, open-handed invitation that disposed her to reply affirmatively. In three months' time they became lovers.

Her confidence in handling aged and damaged works of art gained too. It required a material understanding of how objects were made and of what happened to them then; it meant learning discretion not always to leave a piece alone, but sometimes to step towards it, using craft to achieve an unobtrusive renovation. Giugi helped, with his ingrained understanding that art was method as well as mind. Conserving things required subtle balances. It was a practice Elspeth quietly delighted in, once she got over her clumsiness, finding her own true form in the process.

On a spring Sunday the Dales suggested an outing. Margie took pleasure in preparing a proper picnic with sandwiches that would not fall apart, chicken legs, fruit salad in plastic containers, plates, paper towels, salt and pepper, chocolate cake, wine, wineglasses, and not forgetting a corkscrew to open the bottle. They took a bus to the nearby village that housed Piero della Francesca's *Madonna del Parto* and found the strange monumental painting on the wall of the little church next to the cemetery. The Virgin was standing in a tent with angels on either side of her holding open the flaps. She was looking down with concern, pointing to a slit in her gown through which her pregnancy swelled as the momentous parturition began. 'It's sliced open by Time,' said Rod admiringly.

They found a place to picnic, but it was cold in the weak sunlight and they ate quickly, then walked back into the village for coffee. The artist walked ahead with his wife – it was not the picnic Margie had hoped for – their arms round each other. Their kids played along the way, ducking into the roadside ditch, jumping out and hitting each other with sticks. Elspeth and Giugi lagged behind, walking separately from each other. They had been talking about the archaic ecstasy that seemed to erupt from Piero's painting.

Giugi stroked his chin. After a long pause, he said in his slow, clear English, 'If I asked if I could marry you, what would you say?'

Elspeth felt her body contract a little, as if from the cold. It was involuntary. They walked a few paces more. Then she made herself relax.

'I think,' she replied, reaching across the space for his big warm hand, feeling his tender skin against the snaky texture of her own, 'that I would say Yes.'

Elspeth did not immediately call her parents. It was Margie, feeling responsible for a relationship that she had encouraged, who wrote to friends back home. Margie could not be sure of the degree of innocence or calculation in Giugi's motivation. She did not think that Italians had all the answers anyway. She was concerned about Elspeth's privileged status in Giugi's world, when Giugi knew nothing of Elspeth's.

The news soon reached Barb Gillingham's ears that her daughter was having a fling with an Italian. It was the best way to educate yourself, after all, when travelling. But when Elspeth failed to respond to any of the hints in her mother's letters, Barb grew a little nervous.

Barb had her own way of doing things and expected others to fall in with her. So it continued through the meal to which Elspeth brought Giugi to meet her mother when Barb arrived in Italy. Barb conducted an animated conversation about art, Italy and the artist's life.

'But I'm only a printmaker, Signora Gillingham,' protested Giugi.

'And a paper conservator,' added Elspeth, happy for him to display his expertise.

'I've never understood from all El's letters what paper conservators actually do,' said Barb.

'Paper is a living thing, like skin. It grows old and tired,' Giugi said in a tone of compassion, 'but it can be cured.'

'Unlike skin,' cried Barb, knowing what a lifetime's tennis and swimming had done to hers.

Giugi held Elspeth's hand affectionately on the table.

'Elspeth has beautiful skin,' Giugi went on. 'Australia is a desert. I'll find out – when we go there – what the conditions are. Desiccation can break down the fibres of paper.'

'There's need for skilled conservators,' Elspeth threw in.

'Raphael always paints the skin so beautifully,' said Barb, blocking the drift of the conversation. 'Lucent and breathing.'

Elspeth laughed at her mother's language. Barb's strategy was to avoid all personal talk, covering all the other ground until there was no room left for Elspeth's fantasy of a relationship, of marriage. Giugi had not foreseen her patrician power. She was an experienced woman, full of character, fiercely protective of her daughter's welfare. For the first time, too, Giugi glimpsed how much money stood behind Elspeth. He had neither anticipated nor entirely welcomed this complication. He was an honest man after all.

Afterwards, in Rod Dale's studio, Barb exclaimed wistfully at the nude portrait of Giugi. 'Oh, he's an alluring fellow – just standing there!' She made Rod an offer for the painting – a gift for Elspeth later, for her birthday, when the whole thing had blown over.

On the eve of her departure for London, high in the apartment under the eaves, Barb turned and said calmly that her daughter would never marry the Italian man.

On being presented with her mother's flat-voiced certainty, Elspeth dug in. 'Why do you say that? When you know I will?'

'Not *marry*. He's a nice man. I adore him. But you'll change your mind, darling. You're portable. He's not. You are other things in other places that he knows nothing about.'

'We'll work all that out.'

'You like him because of his sense of balance. That means inflexibility in another context. I think you should realise that and decide to spare him the pain of not making the grade.'

Elspeth had been waiting for her mother's resistance. She found herself unprepared for its subtlety. 'What are you talking about, Mum?'

'I'm only guessing that you'll let him down lightly, once the course ends.'

'He wants to take me to Sicily in the summer.'

'Go then. Enjoy it. After that.'

'I can marry him without your consent. We only have to go up to the local church.'

'Of course you can. You're a grown woman.' Barb laughed nostalgically. 'You make your own decisions. Bring him back if you like. Unmarried. Your father and I will welcome him warmly. We'll see how he goes.'

'I'm quite happy to stay here.'

'You see. You don't really want to bring him back. He's a Catholic too. Not that it matters. That's only part of what I mean. But you need to go back, Elspeth.'

'Need?'

'To be who you are. Which is someone *even better* than the fabulous creature you are currently being here. You know that, darling. You'll go back. Australia's where we get everything from, Elspeth. We need to be there.'

'What will I do if I go back?' Elspeth asked in a sudden panic. She knew her mother's guesses and presumptions were prophecy.

She lay in Giugi's arms feeling completely happy and content. Their bodies were hot and brown after another day on the beach. Nearby were the temple ruins they had explored at dusk, roaming among the olive trees, pink oleander and wild thyme as the ancient stone darkened from honeycomb to bruised salmon-red. With him she was replete, she had no argument with anything. Nor did Giugi seem to need anything more. Yet in the darkness, in the hotel room, Elspeth was as full of afterimages as of the present moment that she proposed to give away. He knew so too. When the words were finally said, they would weep tears of grieving protest at the breaking of their bond and Giugi would warn her not to turn her back on the greatest happiness she might ever know. But he could not stop her. It was Elspeth's decision and it made her strong. She would remember it forever. Choice made her invincible.

~

Like birds of prey in their black and white uniforms, the police swooped under the fierce spotlights. The demonstrators cut the wire and ran on to the grass, yelling and throwing smoke bombs, fanning out from the opening in the security fence until they were overwhelmed by the black-and-white police diving in packs of four or five to run their victims to ground. Alex aimed his can of hairspray at the eyes of the pink-faced young copper who grabbed his hair, then the club thumped his neck and his wrist was wrenched, and the spray can rolled underfoot as he was dragged away. Valerie O'Rourke, one of the organisers, was screaming like a banshee, her red hair flying, as the police swung her through the air to the paddy wagon, their hands in her armpits and up around her thighs. She dug her teeth in and they were laughing, magpie beaks under the black-and-white caps of authority. The football crowd cheered and jeered as hundreds more demonstrators poured through the torn barrier, chanting in a frenzy, 'Stop the Tour!' But the massive, black-clad strength of the club-wielding police drove them back.

There were nearly a hundred demonstrators in custody at the police station that night. Hours after the match had been sullenly played out, the processing was still going on. Cold from shock, Alex peeled back his ripped shirt and fingered the spreading bruise on his shoulder. Beside him on the bench Valerie pulled up her skirt and showed the purple print of the hand that had squeezed her thigh. She had a graze on her face from a cop's metal badge. She was as white as a sheet and proudly tossed her tangled red hair.

The press were waiting outside to interview the ringleaders. The Union of Students, of which Alex Mack was president, had voted to disrupt the 1971 rugby tour by the South African Springboks. The government was determined that the match would go ahead at any cost. Force had won, yet the lack of restraint by the police, acting on politicians' orders, made martyrs and heroes of the demonstrators. For the benefit of the press outside Valerie began to sing a ballad of protest in her pure trained voice.

Alex rolled a cigarette, analysing the message their action would send out. The violent clash was headline news. The police taking down their details, now that the rush of blood had passed, and the thrill of proving a point through sheer numbers, already regretted making so much work for themselves. They could not even be bothered to confiscate the tobacco pouches from the pockets of these ratty, pampered middle-class types. Alex passed Valerie the neat cigarette. She was older than he was, and a little out of place with the students, for all that she exulted in being on the spot when the theory of direct action was put into practice. 'They won't lay any charges on us,' Alex said. 'They know the tour's a mistake.'

But his nerves were on edge from the sudden exposure to the fangs and teeth of Order, the other side of Law. Law became a kind of burlesque out in front of the structural oppression that existed in society when you experienced the means by which power was able to enforce its desires. What he saw in the violence that had broken out at the sports ground, what interested him as a political being, was that without those levers of brute power law itself was useless. Nothing could be achieved without also taking control of those levers, nothing of the pure justice beyond the law in which all those crammed under the bright lights in the police cells believed. As the crows and eagles had swooped for the kill, Alex saw the raw passion that politics could commandeer for its purposes, the hatred of a thing for its opposite, of black for white and white for black, the foul carrion on which all politics nourished itself.

Valerie stopped singing and smiled at him. She was also shaken. It brought out an unflinching spirit of opposition in her. She was doing research in the Economics Department of the university on unpaid female labour, having left her foreign-service husband after his first posting to a stodgy European city where being cast in the role of diplomatic spouse had thoroughly radicalised her. The nuns had taught her, even as they steeled her with the cut of their rulers and the barbs of their tongues, that women could do anything. Only knock away the barriers. Alex stared at the radical will that seemed to pulse just beneath the surface of the woman's skin as she waited defiantly for the constable in charge to call her name. He couldn't help thinking of Josie Ryan, in contrast, wondering what Josie could have done if she had not opted for the calling of retreat.

By dawn the protesters had all been sent home, their promising careers unblemished by even so honourable an item of criminal record. The police overreaction, in a society unused to such things, would only fuel the momentum for a change of government. 'There's only one way to go,' was how Alex pinned down his incendiary speech at the rally that followed. He was a lean, logical orator with a knack of belittling his opponents.

His profile rose after the Springboks demonstration. He was sought out by the group of academics, public servants and local politicians who were working for a Labor victory at the coming election. They envisaged a new style of administration, youthful, iconoclastic, vigorous in its social engineering, a watershed in the country's history. Debating beside Canberra's lake on long afternoons, downing flagons of wine with philosophers, policymakers and activists, he began to be intoxicated with the power that seemed ready to enter their embrace, at their disposal for just and noble ends. In those heady days, feeling themselves the true democrats of this new time and place as they tossed their ideas into the air – loud, drunk and unruly – they touched with their fingertips the platonic balance of theory and practice, of beautiful forms and the steps of betterment required to reach them. Values seemed to be theirs for the making.

As a party member of relatively long standing, Valerie O'Rourke won preselection for a Canberra seat that she was expected to win at the election. The whisper was she would be rewarded with a portfolio, to become the Minister of Social Change in the new cabinet. Alex talked to her about what she envisaged when they took government. It was now only a matter of months away. He found Valerie infinitely desirable and, brushing up against him in meetings and rallies and at drinking sessions by the lake, she responded to this energetic, intelligent young man. They danced together at a party one night, and as the dancing grew wilder and the lights went off, they were unable to keep their hands off each other. Her eyes blazed at his and they tongue-kissed on the dance floor while the others hooted them on. Then, too drunk to be embarrassed, they staggered out into the garden. They had been waiting for the moment when they would take this plunge and now it was as if they were falling into each other, falling through the darkness into something irresistible and unending, as they fucked on the grass, part of the new power that was coming their way. There was no commitment other than the pure excitement that kept bringing them back into each other's arms, until eventually Alex moved into Valerie's house.

The summer of the 1972 election victory was the first year he did not drive his old powder-blue Jag back across the hot dusty plains and through the riverland for Christmas with his family in Adelaide. Too many agendas were being drawn up in Canberra as the new government prepared to move. These were his people now, he belonged with them – and from Valerie he was learning more about determination as well as pleasure, more about hunger as well as ways to satisfy it.

Voted in by a landslide, Valerie O'Rourke was given the new portfolio of Social Change. She was the only woman minister, and she had to invent policy as she went along. Her time was fully taken up with travelling round the country to communicate the new vision. She needed other men, men who simply allowed her to switch off, relax and be someone else for a night. Alex stayed on in her house to water the garden and feed the fish. He was always there when she needed him, when she came back to the house wanting to swear and sing and gossip about it all in perfect confidence. Not a shoulder to cry on – during that transforming first year there was never occasion to cry.

Alex could stay on in her house rent-free as long as he paid his share of the housekeeping expenses. It suited him as long as he was committed to his study. When Valerie brought her colleagues to the house, Alex played the part of a housemate. He did not cook, but he was happy to go and get Chinese. He got to know all the senior people that way, as the bright young bloke who joined in their debates about tactics for evolving this or that reform. To help him out as he finished off his law degree that year, Valerie got him a part-time staffer's job in a politician's office. He completed his course with First Class Honours. Then the time had come, Alex and Valerie agreed, for him to find a place of his own. Time to start climbing the ladder.

~

'*We don't get huh-igh! We hold up the skuh-y!*' René wrote to Alex from People's China. He was studying in Changchun, former capital of Manchukuo, the Japanese puppet state ruled by the last emperor Pu Yi, a centre now of the People's heavy industry.

Beware Walt Disney. Beware Coca-Cola. Beware Led Zeppelin. Beware Stairway to Heaven. Beware Star Wars. Beware the things you know that the masses don't know. Beware the things you know that you do not know. Deviationists and capitalist roaders and other anti-party elements plot against our revolution ceaselessly. Soviet and American hegemonists and imperialists seek by every means to overthrow us. Only by submitting one hundred per cent to the teachings of the Great Helmsman can we embark on the first stage towards collective victory. I don't have to worry about food or clothing. A great-coat is all. I wrap up in woolly underwear and go out among the masses on my bike, trying to achieve anonymity. My Chinese name Bao means 'to wrap, bundle, or contain'. It's a pun on the word for 'embrace', China's embrace of me and everyone else within her mighty arms. If only Australia could discover her continental dimension, free from the old Brit insularity. In China everything comes from inside, everything from outside is quarantined. Scramble your texts. I am in love. One fennel dumpling was all it took. My roommate Xiao Pei shares everything with me. Everything that is mine is his, allowing for our different cultural backgrounds. I strive for the requisite disciplined and featureless purity of mind, modelling myself on him, my minder. Xiao Pei's proudest possession – apart from his peasant background – is a set of coloured pencils from Rumania. He sits on his bed in his spare time sketching scenes of the revolution in a state of blissed-out absorption. Propped on my bed, deciphering Water Margin, the bandit-hero classic, I love the oily smell of those coloured pencils too, the coal smoke and the cabbage and garlic smell of our mingled body odour in the fuggy room. At night we lie in darkness, wrapped in our quilts, expiring in a simultaneous exhalation of breath. A long way from our all-night raves of yore, comrade. Water Margin gives me the correct historical analogy for denouncing closet fascists. I study as this actual present projects into the future. I recall the empire with bitter tears. I investigate the complex meanings of Chinese ideograms. The future. Weilai. The come that has not yet come.

Yours in the eye of the Great Leader, training for life,
Student Bao
aka Comrade René Baum of the White Horse
Changchun Number One Languages Institute.

P.S. Changchun, by the way, amigo, can be translated as 'Sempiternal Springtime'. Fragrant armpit of the Middle Kingdom. In an historic nexus the design of the Japanese militarists' model city of Changchun was inspired by Marion and Walter Burley-Griffin's theosophical design for Australia's ideal city of Canberra. Did you know?

174 ~

P.P.S. The Party Secretary of Qiqiha'er, a hamlet up near the Siberian border, was devoured by a black bear last month it is rumoured. A group of counter-revolutionary intellectual youth from the south, condemned to labour reform in the great wastes up there, exposed the tasty official to the animal during an impromptu bear hunt that got out of control. You'll understand how precious such news is. Thought you should know, comrade.

By the way, if anyone asks, I plan to stay in this perfect continent apart forever. Miss ya, mate.

3

CLEVE Gordon opened the padlock on the gate in the high wire fence around the Portacabin that was provided for his office. He unlocked the screen door and went inside where he hung his jacket on the hook behind the door and put the electric kettle on. He opened up the back door to the flat empty yard, where the grass needed cutting and the garbage around the twin incinerator drums had still not been removed. That dry grass would be turned into lawn, Cleve vowed, as he walked out into the yard. Then he did a few push-ups in the early morning sunshine, before going back inside to button up his collar and put on his tie. The kettle was whistling by now. He poured hot water over the teabag in the mug, adding milk and two sugars, and sat down at his desk to look at the documents that had arrived in the latest great mustard-coloured envelope from the new Department of Aboriginal Affairs in far-off Canberra.

He left the gate wide open and at half past eight a woman and a girl came into the compound and stomped up the steps of the Portacabin.

'An early morning call, Doreen?' queried Cleve, sensing something was up. 'How're you doing, Narelle?'

'She's crook,' retorted Doreen. Doreen Tighe was one of the daughters of Auntie Betty Poole, the elder who had spoken out at the meeting Cleve called to introduce himself to the community. Her family was the biggest in town and she had relatives all over the district. Some of the people at the meeting had called Cleve a coconut, black on the outside and white on the inside. Auntie Betty just wanted to know where he had come from and why he had come. She said she was willing to be his ally, backing what he did with her age and authority if she thought it was right. She promised to sort Cleve Gordon out – which meant she would be watching him.

The previous evening, Doreen explained, Narelle had started wheezing and huffing as if she was going to suffocate. Doreen took her up to the hospital where the nurse on duty was too busy to contact the doctor. When the nurse finally phoned through to him, the doctor said asthma was not really an emergency at all and could wait until the junior doctor came on duty after midnight. But by that time another case had taken precedence: on a bend of unsealed road outside the town a drunken white kid on P-plates had rolled a car full of his mates. All Narelle needed was medication. The nurse could have given it to her herself if she had risked treading on the doctor's toes. But she made Narelle wait all night for the treatment, until she went purple in the struggle to breathe.

'The sun was up by the time that doctor got round to seeing the girl,' said Doreen, looking angrily at the lifeless bags that hung from her daughter's eyes. She was ropeable. She wanted the complaint written down properly, so Cleve recorded all the details. Then Ida Reardon, his secretary, arrived at work and made a big pot of tea to go round.

'That nurse,' Ida said, pouring out the tea, 'that two-faced white bitch, she better watch her snatch.'

Cleve crossed himself and laughed. No matter who said otherwise, Nulla was a town with lines drawn.

Old Nugget had not forgotten his pledge to Cleve. After the change of government, the offer of a job as liaison officer in Nulla had arrived for him on official letterhead from the new Department of Aboriginal Advancement. Cleve was needed. That was enough.

It was a flat riverside town with a population of about five thousand, an uptown end of solid stone and brick and a lower end of government housing, dribbling off into the old reserve area by the river.

When Cleve first arrived in the town, the Mayor poked his head into the Portacabin to pay his respects.

'How are you finding the new job then?' Wal Gorman asked Cleve jovially, rubbing his polished pate with his right hand. The Mayor wore a returned serviceman's pin on the pocket of his short-sleeved shirt for the occasion. 'If it's not broken, don't mend it. That would be my basic advice to a young fella like yourself.' He also ran the local meatworks and trucking business.

Cleve extended a hand, since the Mayor had not got around to doing so. 'I'm learning all the time, thanks – Mr Gorman. I'm discovering that the people can do with someone to look after their interests. There's quite a backlog to attend to.'

'Ah!' mouthed the Mayor, as if the idea had just dawned. In his opinion, Nulla was a tough but bounteous provider to the right people. The rest were parasites and losers. No matter that he gave employment to Aboriginals butchering horse flesh in his meat-works for lower wages than a white man would demand – Wal Gorman was not interested in whingers. 'The Lord helps those who help themselves,' he said, making his meaning clear for the new arrival, 'and so do I.'

'From the look of it, when they try to help themselves, they don't get very far,' retorted Cleve.

Mayor Gorman might have told the mixed-breed boy not to give cheek, but he would not get himself in a flap. 'We're all in this together,' he said with a steady grin. 'I don't believe in special treatment for anyone – black, white or brindle. It goes against a person's pride. There are enough hand-outs already.'

'Is that why you're so keen on a mixed community centre?' Cleve asked, directing the talk to the issue on his mind.

The Mayor's pink ears flapped on either side of his round head. 'It would be a bloody good thing for this town.'

'It's not what people wanted at the start, though,' Cleve went on, 'according to what I've been hearing.'

'Depends who you listen to.' Gorman's voluminous shorts, belted at the widest point of his belly, flapped around his knees as if to match his ears. 'It's an improvement on the original idea, you could say. Look, sonny, I don't care who you are or where you come from, you're a newcomer here. You're a blow-in. I've been working for this town all my life. I don't want any apartheid here, you know what I mean. As long as I'm the elected Mayor, my philosophy is that any money coming in is for the good of the whole town. The shire's priority has to be the basic improvements we need to keep the town alive. Upkeep of the roads first and foremost, before we drop off the trucking routes. That's our lifeblood. Upgrading the roads. Then there's civic amenities. You can't argue with that.'

In Gorman's view, the survival of the town depended on the likes of those who knew where to draw the line. That was how Nulla had survived to celebrate its one-hundred-and-fiftieth anniversary. He laughed. He would always blame the blacks if any do-gooder or busybody or government johnny asked about the divisions in the town. The blacks like to keep to themselves, he would say, as if that was their right. It was a free country.

Cleve gestured at the pile of paper overflowing the wire basket on his desk. He would have preferred to start with a clean slate, but there was too much unresolved correspondence, too many festering grievances, too much history. In sorting through the mess, he had come across letters about the Nulla Community Centre that Mayor Gorman proposed to build, diverting funds from an earlier proposal to build an Aboriginal hall. A cocky from the district who was running for parliament had promised the people money for a hall of their own. It was a vote-getter at election time. The hall was already under way when that funding dried up and the Mayor started talking about a community centre of his own at the other end of town. The politician, ensconced in Canberra by then, appreciated the efforts of his mate to keep Nulla sweet. But the change of government had since shifted the ground, as Gorman was given to understand when he lunched with his politician pal on a visit out East. The newfangled position of Aboriginal liaison officer was designed to monitor funding for towns like Nulla.

'There are better things to spend the money on,' said Cleve, taking up the Mayor's challenge. 'Like finishing off the black hall first.'

'Well, if everyone agrees,' observed Gorman, benign and unflappable. 'We don't want to import the bloody begging bowl mentality, that's all. It's my job as Mayor to bring all parties together.' It amused him to talk this way to the interloper. 'It's up to us, mate. You can't rely on the pen-pushers in Canberra. If you want my opinion, you'll let sleeping dogs lie. Take your time to get to know the place. Don't be a stirrer first up.' He cast his eyes at Cleve's pending tray. 'I'd be tempted to throw that lot in the incinerator.' He ran his hand over his smooth, shiny scalp. 'Come home to our place some time. The wife'd like to see you. Give you a meal.'

The steps creaked as he left.

Gorman's visit was enough to send Cleve delving back through the files again. Auntie Betty had said she would not be satisfied until the black community hall was complete, leaving Cleve honour-bound to salvage any government funding that was allocated for it. He wrote a letter off to Canberra and got back a non-committal reply. 'Thank you for your letter dated . . . The matter you raise has been noted and will be considered at the earliest opportunity . . .' That was the trouble with bureaucrats. They told you what was good for you and only gave you things you never asked for.

Cleve defined himself by a sense of mission and duty. His isolation at school and then at university had made him disciplined and formal in that way. He reacted sociably with the town, accepting invitations, attending meetings, joining in activities, yet without forming close relationships. He joined the football team with the idea of putting himself on friendly terms with the local boys, but his presence among them only complicated things, causing an element of jostling, when it should have been the local boys playing a leadership role and building their own confidence.

On Sundays he went to St Dymphna's, the red brick church built in opposition to the Church of England's classier stone edifice uptown. On Sunday mornings the women from the reserve down by the river would stroll through town with the kids, or drive their cars, for Mass at St Dymphna's taken by Father Frank, the priest who travelled the region in a Landrover. Cleve's regular place was down the back with the blacks, where he would stare at the shiny pate of the Mayor as he knelt at the altar rail. Mudguard Gorman, shiny on the outside, shit on the inside. Watching him take the wafer each week brought back Cleve's old sense of powerlessness. The way to fight it, he told himself, was not with momentary violence but through painful conviction and dogged campaigning. He vowed to continue writing letters to the bureaucrats in Canberra even if he got a reputation for being vexatious.

Then one winter morning at St Dymphna's, after he had been in the town about six months, Cleve noticed a young woman who was taking Mass very seriously indeed. She wore a white dress, a navy-blue knitted jumper, her dark hair was cut short, and her seriousness brought out a degree of theatrical conviction even in Father Frank. It was only afterwards, as the newcomer was walking out, that he got a proper look at her face. There was something familiar about her, but it was she who approached him first, before he recognised her completely, outside the glowing red church in the strong winter sunshine.

'I heard you were here,' she said. 'Have I changed that much?'

He gave her half a smile. 'Have you just blown in?' Cleve asked.

'A few days ago. One of our people got sick, so they decided to send me up early. At short notice.'

She looked across the wide street, empty but for the clumps and straggles of churchgoers on their way home. The clipped line of houses, their front fences all in a row, and the screen of high gums and pines behind, defined a kind of limit before the country and sky took over again. 'It's all pretty new,' she said. 'It's Josie Ryan, in case you've forgotten.'

'Yeah,' Cleve nodded eagerly. 'I know.'

She squinted. The sunlight was bright in her eyes, bright enough to burn, although it was still winter. Cleve noticed the gold cross that shone from her neck. Then she turned and grinned at a couple of the kids who were hanging round their aunties' skirts. The kids giggled back at her. 'Those kids are in my class. Gee, they're wild.'

'As long as they keep going,' Cleve said. 'Do you know anything about this?' He swung his arm round in a gesture that took in the town, the people, the place, all that history bequeathed and the work that needed to be done.

'Novice in name, novice in nature.' She looked candidly into Cleve's eyes. 'It looks like there's a lot the kids need out here.'

He looked back at her with surprise, then let his eyes slide nervously away. 'You better come over and have a talk. In a professional capacity.'

'I suppose I better. Anyway, it cheers me up to see a familiar face.'

Sister Mary Thomas was approaching to investigate. 'Keeping well, are you, son?' asked the old nun.

'Good thanks, sister!'

'That's grand.'

With that the old woman escorted Josie away. Cleve watched them go, shining white in the sun as they followed the worn grass verge of the road down to the convent school on the edge of town, with its carved stone cross above the doorway, its paved brick verandah on four sides, and the original rose-bushes. The Sisters of Charity had run the convent school in Nulla for a hundred years, welcoming the children of any parents. Cleve remembered how Josie had surprised him in the darkness outside the school chapel, her face so white then, her hair so dark, her eyes lit by a fierce glint. Now she was grown-up and serious, her short brown hair, freckled skin and rounded face like the markings of an animal that had moved into early maturity. A bush fowl of some kind, so Cleve reflected, amused, as he walked back to his bare house, carrying her image with him. She had surprised him again.

Auntie Betty was always pestering Cleve to find out where he came from, or, since he didn't know any answers, to help him find out. Auntie Betty was always finding family everywhere, chided Doreen with a laugh. The only thing Cleve could remember from the orphanage in the riverland was being hung in a sack from the clothesline when he was naughty. No one ever talked about the kids there having parents of their own. There were kids in that mixed-up place from everywhere, from Lake Cargellico in central New South Wales, the old Murrin Tank mission, to Pooncarie on the Darling River, and Wilga, and Wentworth at the Murray-Darling junction and Renmark on the Murray, all the way down to Point Macleay on the river's mouth in South Australia. A kid could come from anywhere and end up anywhere.

Auntie Betty's Uncle Davey, a man in his eighties, knew people in all those places, this mob and that mob, crisscrossing the back country like a river system. He had known people called Gordon back in the mission days. He wanted to know the name of Cleve's mother, and his father's mother's name. A kid often carried the mother's name if the father was an outsider. A whitefella. He could devise a history to satisfy his and Auntie Betty's craving for genealogy on the basis of people's migrations as they were made to follow one twist and turn of government policy after another. The story of one was the story of all. What counted was they were all in it together.

'You're one of us,' said old Davey, thumping his chest. 'No matter where you're from, you're one of us.'

Cleve laughed at the old man, whose face grinned through his flourishing white beard. 'That's for sure.'

The old man had a fat, scarred face and a big mouth that was missing its front teeth. A big roll-neck woollie stretched over his huge chest and belly. Sitting on the ground, he had pulled off his boots to be more comfortable. He wore red socks to match his jumper. With his grizzle of beard and hair, he might have been Father Christmas.

Cleve liked sitting on the riverbank drinking beers with the old boys in the crisp dry air of the bright winter afternoon. They watched the brown-green water flow under the low overhanging branches of the old gums. Leaves dragged in the water, touching blackened limbs that had already fallen, hands and fingers reaching up from beneath the water's surface. Uncle Davey and his sons and nephews, and the little grandchildren and grandnieces and grandnephews, and the other men and their families, had lines of memory and story that carried them all along that river, upstream, downstream, each line broken, frayed and mended many times.

The smell of grilling meat wafted over to the river. Lights came on, and hot showers steamed in the washing block. About five hundred people lived in the dwellings that made up the crowded settlement. There was a powerline in to the hot water tank, the outdoor lights around the barbecue area and some of the houses. When the bill wasn't paid, the Electricity would turn off the main powerline to the camp and there was no light, no hot water, no television. Then it became a problem for Cleve to fix.

Around the periphery of the camp, among the mallee trees, the vehicles were strewn: four-wheel drives, utes, sedans, old, worked over, stripped, abandoned, rusting in the grass where they had come to rest. Bursting carseats and armchairs in the thin scrub, forty-gallon drums and ploughshares. The shire council had instructed the garbage collectors to remove domestic rubbish only. Anything else had to be left there, so the circles of junk widened, fulfilling Mayor Gorman's vision of the place as a tip.

Among the scattered junk stood neat rows of white hives, busily humming by day with bees making good honey from the blossoms of winter-flowering wattles.

There was grilled mutton and rabbit to eat that night, and fresh Murray cod caught by the old women, with potatoes and spinach from the vegetable patch, and white bread and butter. One of the boys had brought in a couple of cases of oranges on the verge of going rotten, and folk ate them after the meal. Jason Tighe, Narelle's eighteen-year-old brother, had been in town to the pub for another slab of beer and a flagon of port for his mother Doreen to share with Auntie Betty. On a special occasion, on a Sunday evening, Betty was partial to a nice port. It was the church wine in the morning, she said, that always gave her the idea. She had learned how to drink as a young girl, when she worked as a maid in one of the homesteads. The old boss had given his blacks port at Christmas, Betty said. That was how she learned to drink and had never got drunk in her life. That was what she wanted to pass on to the younger women.

Narelle, dignified and silent, was hanging around Cleve. She wore plastic thongs with pink daisies on the toe, a blue-denim miniskirt and a loose pink pullover. Cleve asked how her asthma was. He couldn't help noticing her. She let her hair fall in front of her sunken eyes when he spoke to her.

'Eh?' he said. 'I missed your reply.'

'The cold air can bring it on,' she muttered.

'You better stick close to the fire then,' he said.

'The smoke can bring it on too.'

'Don't you give cheek now,' Jason told his sister.

Old Uncle Davey laughed. 'You're fair game, mate,' he warned Cleve.

'Do you know any language, Auntie?' asked Cleve, turning to Auntie Betty who gave a moan, rising in pitch, as if to say that it was her secret. She had known lots of things as a girl, from her mother and aunties and sisters. Then as she went through life, moving away from her family into service work, moving out again, to avoid the boss, finding a husband from a different mob, moving to his place and letting her life grow with her husband's people, that lingo had moved into the back of her mind. In dreams, or when she was alone, words might come out. It was only now she was old that language came back to her, not in single words, like a bit of gristle spat from the mouth, but in clumps, like a raft of leaves and twigs woven in the river's current. When she got with other old ones who still had their rags of language, they might be able to put something together.

She felt ashamed of forgetting what was surely her greatest trust, as she had once been ashamed that the lingo was ever hers. The church people had taught her never to speak it. You got in trouble if you did. She remembered scooping off into the bush with the other women when there were things they needed to talk about, secrets exchanged in a clicking, bubbling ripple of sound. When the lady from the university came with the tape-recorder, she hadn't wanted to tell her anything, until the younger women coaxed her. *The dagoes learn them kids their jabber, why do we feel shame?* Betty was embarrassed by her silly old woman's brain that could pass on too little, and still now she was scared to endanger what she knew by spreading it too freely.

'We might have been educated people,' Auntie Betty said, by way of answering Cleve, 'but we just battled on – battled through it all and come up out of the ashes.' She was proud. 'You hear that?' She cocked her bushy eyebrow at Cleve. He heard a high repeated cry. 'That fella's mupup. Owl. You hear? That's his call. Dear me, it's bad news.' Auntie Betty chuckled.

Cleve looked at her, puzzled, but she did not explain. Her eyes twinkled, as if it concerned him, and he looked away shyly. 'You can see the stars real clear out here, can't you, eh?'

Auntie Betty spat. She threw her head back to take in the whole realm of the sky above the trees. '*Kirralaa,*' she proclaimed.

'What's that?' Cleve asked.

'Stars in the sky,' she said.

'*Purli,*' croaked Uncle Davey, provocatively. 'That's what we say for stars.'

The language Betty spoke was a different one from old Davey's and they were always arguing about words.

The cry of the boobook owl came again, from further away.

'There's my sisters, see,' said Auntie Betty, pointing up. 'Two of them sisters was stolen away by a young fella, they were that worried about their other sisters, how they would worry when they found them missing. Then one day the young fella tells them two girls to go off and cut pine-bark, see. They say if they go and cut pine-bark he'll never see them again, and he says he needs pine-bark to make the fire burn faster. So them two girls go over to the pine tree and the pine tree grows and grows, with them sitting on the top branches, higher than all the other trees. Then they hear their other five sisters calling out. Yeah, they know them voices. All the other sisters gone up in the sky to look for them, and they reach down their hands and pull up them two missing ones.' Auntie Betty sighed with satisfaction. 'That makes all them sisters up in the sky. You see.'

Uncle Davey chuckled too. 'Crow's the clever one,' he said. 'Crow been fighting all this time with Eaglehawk. You know them two fellas never get on. Eaglehawk live all by himself up in a tree. He got two wives, Crow got no wife at all, and Crow's dead jealous. He asks Eaglehawk to go fishing with him in the river one day, there's this hollow log and Crow says to Eaglehawk, "You go in the log and chase out the big cod, and I'm catch him at the other end." But there never was no cod and Eaglehawk pops his head out the other end of the log, and Crow sticks his spear in and kill him. Then Crow go back and take Eaglehawk's camp for his own.'

Auntie Betty chimed in. 'Crow can be one real tricky fella. He kill Eaglehawk young nephew because the boy won't share a bit of kangaroo. When Eaglehawk brother find out, Crow say it's not him what done the killing. But Eaglehawk brother know Crow done the killing. Crow helps Eaglehawk brother dig the grave for the boy, to hide his guilt, and Eaglehawk brother ask Crow go down in the grave to dig it deeper. Then Eaglehawk brother put the coffin on top of Crow and bury him under the earth. The grave is all covered up and Eaglehawk brother know that Crow is under there but by the time Eaglehawk brother come back to find his two sisters-in-law, Crow surprise him by turning up. He got himself out from that grave by clever sorcery somehow and he come back to burn Eaglehawk's tree down. That Eaglehawk and them two women run for their life!'

'That's how Eaglehawk turned into the Morning-star,' Uncle

Davey added for Cleve's benefit. 'That's why you see him up there in the sky all by himself.'

'Eaglehawk is the Morning-star now,' repeated Auntie Betty. 'His big tree come crashing down and leave a big hole in the ground, where them bones of the big old animals from bygone times come up, the scraps of what Eaglehawk use to eat.'

Then Uncle Davey had a further detail to add. 'I reckon Eaglehawk got his arm burned off in that fire. Morning-star's all alone out there and he only got one arm.'

'The women stay by him,' insisted Auntie Betty. 'I can't see them with my old eyes no more, but they're still up there. His two possum women.'

'What's the word for eyes?' asked Cleve.

'*Mil*, we say,' said Betty. '*Mil*. It means seed.'

'You mean eye?' asked Davey. 'We say *miiki*.'

Narelle had gone to bed by now, and the other young ones had drifted away. The elders were nodding off to sleep in their chairs. The telling was over.

As he walked away from the lights and murmuring voices of the camp on the dark track back, in his black lace-up shoes, conscious that people would be watching him, Cleve wondered if that man Eaglehawk might be himself. He had always loved the morning-star, alone in the sky, bringing hope with each new day. He had greeted it like a brother, shining from the darkness on those lonely weekend mornings at St Joeys when he was the only boy left in the school. As he passed the closed house fronts of the dark town, dogs woke at hearing him and barked. He passed the convent school, still and silent in its shadowy moonlit grounds. Josie was asleep in there, in her star-bright candour. It warmed him to think of her, like a breath of air blown across coals. He wondered what she thought of him now. He wondered what sort of creature – bird, beast or human – would ever walk with him on his track through the world. What star-bride would he ever find?

He turned the key in his door, went inside his place and shut the door behind him. He went through to the bedroom where he groped for the bedside lamp in the darkness and turned it on. He washed his face, cleaned his teeth and took off his clothes, preparing for bed as he had done all the years of his life, climbed into the cold single bed, as he had always done, here alone in his own place, turning off the lamp at once so he would not have to face the cold bare room. It was an involuntary reflex to say a prayer, to ask the ungiving God for the heat he needed, begging for a fire to kindle and burn inside him.

Cleve laughed. 'This generation of kids is going to have everything that white kids have and still be black.' That was policy. He handed her the pile of the magazines and books at his disposal.

Josie was grateful for all the help Cleve gave her. St Francis Convent School ran on little more than determination and the minimum that the Catholic education system could push its way. 'Fancy you and I ending up in the same town,' she said. 'I still can't get over that.'

'I haven't ended up here, I hope.'

'Do you feel accepted now?'

Cleve shrugged. 'Course. They're my people.'

'You're saying so,' she answered. 'Do they agree?'

'I'm closer to them than you are,' he retorted, accusing.

'I know that,' was Josie's reply. 'I'm learning.'

She caught his tense frown. It had not been easy so far. The town might take her over in the end, but for now she regarded it as more of a stage on the way – the old, underprivileged school building and adjacent residence where she and Sister Mary Thomas were the only dwellers; the cypress, jacaranda and ancient white cedar; the bent peppertrees in the schoolyard that brushed the dusty ground; the crows that squawked overhead at midday, and the children of all shapes and sizes. There was a short-wave radio and a crackly colour television set in the lounge room. A library came round in a van once a week. From the beginning Josie had enrolled in a correspondence course. She would get her Diploma of Education by mail, with God to motivate her.

She sympathised with Cleve. He would be judged in the town not by his willingness and his faith, unlike her, but by concrete results and by the way he handled personal relations. On that would depend both what happened after him and also where he went next. That was the message she got as he stood on the steps of the Portacabin to see her on her way. And *he* looked at the piles of paper with more patient conviction after Josie's visit.

The matter of the unfinished black community hall had found its way to the member of parliament who made the false promise in the first place. He passed it back to Mayor Gorman for clarification. The Mayor had read Cleve Gordon as a lightweight opponent, but now there was a fight on. Over the phone to his pal in Canberra he painted the Aboriginal Advancement liaison officer as a troublemaker who was reopening old wounds in order to justify his existence at the taxpayer's expense.

New panes of glass were fitted in all the houses on the reserve where windows had long been broken. Auntie Betty could keep her place free of dust when the willy-willies whipped dust columns through the air. Once you stopped the grit blowing through a gaping window frame, the floor of compacted earth could be kept neat with a splash of water and a broom. By these results Cleve was encouraged to believe that someone out there in head office heeded him. He passed on a request from a girl who lived down by the river for Evonne Goolagong's autograph. The Department sent the girl a signed photograph of the Wimbledon Champion, care of Cleve. Yet the replies to his letters about the unfinished community hall remained as brief and uncommunicative as ever.

'The bastard swooped on our money,' Cleve groaned to Josie, unburdening himself when she came to collect another school parcel, 'to build his own bloody place. There's little enough funding to go round without that sort of behaviour.'

Josie grumbled too. She was disturbed to find her kids' dreams, black and white alike, ensnared by an almost total lack of expectation. She longed to build the kids' faith in themselves into a force of substance and power, and she felt frustrated by the church's niggardliness, and even sometimes by dear old Sister Mary Thomas.

Mary Thomas brought the soup, made with a pumpkin from her garden, in bowls to the table. The leg of lamb was resting in the oven. It reminded the old nun of grander days in Nulla, when the town had its own resident priest, a witty Irishman. She was in a mood to enjoy herself.

Father Frank uncorked the red wine and said grace. 'Some material comfort in return for the spiritual comfort we dispense,' he added mordantly. He was a soulful Pole who had never expected to be stuck in the backblocks when he graduated from the distinguished seminary in seaside Sydney. For this special occasion, on taking a break from his busy Sunday rounds, he was ready once again not to stint himself in partaking of the hospitality offered by the convent residence. Cleve, taking his cue from Josie, bristled at the priest's comfortable presence. Father Frank sensed this and offered Cleve no more than morose pleasantries. The priest was content to stay within the partial certainty that his religion and its adherents provided, neither converting others nor changing himself. Cleve, supposed Father Frank, burned like the novice with a commitment, that was also a need, to make the world whole.

Father Frank cut across the conversation to mention the hefty donation Mayor Gorman had stuffed into the collection box at church that day.

'Did he now?' said Mary Thomas, intrigued.

Cleve scowled. 'Maybe you can tell me why he's so keen on the community centre, Sister?'

'The council's already bought the land for it,' answered Mary Thomas. 'That's why. Wal Gorman sold it to council himself.'

'What do you mean?' Cleve asked.

'Belonged to his trucking business,' she went on. 'It's no secret. He bought it for a song off the old owners. Residential land it was then that they never got round to putting a house on.' She chuckled. 'Wal Gorman did them a favour and took it off their hands. Then it was the site chosen for the community centre and it was rezoned. No one was going to argue with that. The council bought the land off our Wal for a lot more than he paid for it in the first place. Bless him.'

'You never told me that,' said Josie, who, on Cleve's behalf, had quizzed the old nun about Mayor Gorman as they sat in front of the snowy television set one evening.

'There are some things that don't bear repeating,' Mary Thomas smiled. She had been saving it up.

Cleve was wide-eyed. 'He ought to be exposed.'

Father Frank poured himself another glass of wine. The vice of idealism was to find pleasure in others' iniquity. 'Only God can make the world whole again,' he intoned in his peculiar accent. 'It's too much for us.'

'But it's our job,' insisted Josie angrily. 'It's given to us.'

After the meal Sister Mary Thomas sent Josie and Cleve to sit outside under the peppercorns while she cleared the table. The priest went to lie down.

'It's a joke,' snorted Cleve.

'The first stage is to understand. That's what you're going through now. You're only beginning, mate. Then you have to get tough,' Josie counselled.

'That's fine talk for a nun.'

'I'm facing the same problems.'

'Sometimes I feel so powerless I wonder what I'm doing here,' Cleve confessed. It was strange how he could show Josie his weakness in this way. Perhaps, he thought, it went back to the time she had witnessed him bawling at Christ on the Cross that night and had not blamed him. 'I don't even know who my people are,' he went on. 'They ask me and I don't know. Where do you come from?

Who are your relatives? They should be my people if I'm going to work for them, but there's a barrier. I love them and that, but sometimes I feel I'm just another blow-in like Gorman says. But there's nowhere else. I refuse to pass myself off for a whitey or some wog with a mystery background.'

The more pain Cleve let show, the more Josie's compassion flowed to him. From the restless way his expression danced across his face, over his brown skin and his deep brown eyes, she felt she could read his soul. Yet she could not define him or say who he was. 'As you serve people, you become one of them. As you walk with them, you share their spirit. They share the spirit with you,' she said. 'You cross over boundaries that way.'

He hung his head, shaking it from side to side in protest. 'It's not that easy.'

Then he put his hand on hers. He needed to touch her – or someone – and she let his hand rest on hers on the warm wooden bench where they sat for a moment. Then she clasped his hand, shook it in a handshake of support, and nervously withdrew.

On Monday morning Cleve found Wal Gorman parked behind the desk in his office with a broad, shriven smile on his face.

'G'day, son. I expect you've come to explain what you're playing at writing letters off behind me back?'

'Credit where credit's due,' responded Cleve with dead calm. 'I was just curious to know how the council decided on the site for your new community centre.'

'*Our* new community centre. Well, you won't find it on any back file.'

'It's common knowledge, anyway. It was your land and *you* chose the site.'

'You better watch what you're saying if you don't want to end up in court, Mister.'

Cleve was losing his temper. 'It doesn't look too good in anyone's book,' he said, his voice rising.

Gorman only laughed. 'If that's the tone you're going to take, there's no point talking about it. Just forget it, son. The land belongs to the shire council now. It's all been sorted out and it's not going to change whatever your mates in Canberra say. It's history. You're new to Nulla, like I said to you before, and you're blundering round when we ought to be working together.'

Cleve felt himself burning up as he listened to the Mayor's complacent words. Then his rage overtook him. 'You're a fork-tongued devil,' he snapped.

'First time I've been called that,' Gorman clucked.

Cleve was on the verge of grabbing the man, but he held back. 'You're a lying racist bastard,' he said.

'Whoah! Steady, now. We don't need none of that. Okay? Got the message,' the Mayor said, lumbering to his feet to open the door and dismiss Cleve. 'Just remember one thing. It's not your town. You're an employee here. It's *our* town. I trust you'll learn. You're pretty smart for a boong.'

~

The art works were hung on the rough unclad walls of the unfinished black hall and a lighting system was rigged up. Since it was a mild day, it did not really matter that the roof had not been made ready and the windows and door frames were missing. Cleve gave a little speech to congratulate the exhibitors, who were nervous and excited and proud when it came to the business of being photographed with their art works, not just for the town paper but for the big regional paper in Wagga Wagga. It was the first event of its kind in Nulla. All the high school staff came and many of the students. Friends and relatives of the artists were there in force, stickybeaks, activists, supporters and doubters. Josie and Sister Mary Thomas were there to applaud Cleve's speech. The visiting officials from Wagga Wagga and Broken Hill shook their heads in disappointed concern at the state of the building. It was the first time they had looked inside the black hall. *Still unfinished?* That was when Elspeth walked in.

The works of art were on sale to raise funds for the hall. A notice in the district newspaper had caught Elspeth's attention. She was living, now, on a property not far away – a grazier's wife. She seldom had occasion to visit Nulla. Its mean, raw, running-down quality put her off. But this time she had made the effort to get there for the opening of the art exhibition and quickly selected two watercolours she wanted to buy. One was a dream landscape of unearthly colours in which a river ribboned through a desert scene, not stopping at the horizon but spiralling up into an indigo heaven that was abundant with golden sun and silver moon and stars. The other was a black and white print of a woman with a blank white face nursing in her lap a girl with a blank black face who was nursing in her lap a little white doll.

Both pictures were by the same artist, a young woman who had studied art at high school, otherwise a bad student who talked all the time in class and could never be bothered with reading or writing, whose only talent was for making pictures. It was a relief when she turned fourteen and was not made to go to school anymore. As the camera flashed, the shy young artist stood with a blank face beside the tall smiling woman who wanted to buy her pictures. The pictures would stay on the wall until the show ended, with red stickers beside them for all to see, prize exhibits that someone had paid money for.

After posing for the photograph Elspeth went over to Cleve.

'Good speech. I didn't know you were here. I suppose you don't recognise me, do you, Cleve?' But he did, of course. 'It doesn't matter,' she said. 'I wouldn't expect you to, without some sort of hint.' She smiled faintly, embarrassed, and out of courtesy, to relieve him of his embarrassment. 'We've all changed. I'm Elspeth. Elspeth Gillingham. Do you remember – from Adelaide?'

Cleve stared hard at the woman's beautiful face. Her eyes were like green stones, he thought. Then all at once the twist of her long neck made the connection. He could see her as she had been, and remember her exactly.

'You were only a school kid then,' he said, to excuse himself.

'Congratulations on the show,' she replied. 'You're obviously doing good work here. It can make all the difference. There are *lovely* things. I *love* the two pictures that are coming to me.'

'Thanks for your support. Elspeth. It's great. It will mean a lot to Kerry. The artist. But — where have you come from?'

'I live here. Not *here* — but not far away. That's my car outside.' The eyes of the town had already taken note of the new Volvo station wagon she had driven up in. 'Yes, all that,' she added knowingly. 'Our place is two hours' drive back west. I don't usually come in this direction. Is this where you — come from?' she went on brightly.

Cleve stammered that he had been sent out to the town only a year ago, by the Department of Aboriginal Affairs.

'My family has had land out here for generations,' Elspeth explained in conclusion. Cleve was aware of other people wanting his attention and he could not think quickly enough what he should say in reply. She put out her hand to shake his. 'Come and see us when you've got time. Findlay is my married name. I've got a husband now. But I still go by Gillingham.' She smirked and bowed her head to him before she ducked through the crowd and made her exit.

From across the room Josie Ryan watched the startled, intense conversation between Cleve and the woman, whose hair was cut in a neat line across the bottom where it used to be long and straggly, who was heavier, and whose face had changed. Elspeth had gone from being a schoolgirl to something else — a stylish, guarded young matron, Josie noticed. Elspeth didn't see Josie. But Josie — from the corner of her eye as Elspeth passed — stripped away those layers in a glance.

It had been easy for Elspeth Gillingham, after returning to Adelaide from Italy, to find herself married to Andrew Findlay, one of the boys she had grown up with. Andrew had turned out to be mild-natured, kind, reliable and the right age. For scions of similar stock to entwine affirmed the core of clan and caste. Elspeth was regarded as having made a wise and pleasing move after some earlier foolishness. Andrew, of course, knew what she was worth. Andrew was considered to have done very well indeed. At the wedding Barb and Angus Gillingham struck about the right balance, Barb dabbing tears and Angus grinning. Jane Woodruff came from Sydney to be principal bridesmaid. Elspeth's second cousin Sophie Masterman was the other bridesmaid. Robbie Masterman was the best man.

The newlyweds took themselves off bush to a place beyond the riverland called Whitepeeper to set up house together, in the same homestead, as it happened, where Elspeth's mother had been born. It was grand, remote country. Elspeth could be alone with herself and Andrew could grace her new role. Some of the wedding guests wondered how the skills young Elspeth had gained in Italy would translate in the Australian outback, where there was little need for art conservation. Her mother came to stay at regular intervals, hoping for the baby that must be part of the arrangement if it was to work. Andrew, Barb knew, was only one of the verandah supports. As brick-faced Robbie had said in his best man's speech, Andrew was a good recruit. But even shrewd Barb, coughing on her cigarette, could not tell whether her daughter had ever really come back from wherever she had been on her inner and outer journeys – or whether she was lost from the world for good.

For Elspeth there was no contradiction or loss, however, when at night she could stand alone on the old verandah at Whitepeeper and look up at the thick sowing of stars in the still clear sky, and feel nothing intervene between her and the full extent of the cosmos. She had wanted such emptiness all along. She could hear it groaning. She could feel its dust in the worn timbers under her bare feet. In that position, chastened and diminished by a confrontation with the void, Elspeth felt strangely and strongly that she achieved a certain ordinariness at last.

4

WENDY rocked in the cane chair on the wooden deck of the house on stilts that creaked and sighed among the trees like a ship. Sequins of water glinted through the palm tops and flower-dropping figtrees and the vines that grew from bough to bough, like the webbing between her splayed fingers as she peeked at the green dazzle. The humid heat of North Queensland made her drowsier than ever. Taking her hands from her face, she pulled her feet up into her lap and buffed her frosted toenails. Then she tucked her feet under her thighs and, curled into the chair, continued rocking. She was sleepy after staying up all night and her thoughts floated, among the treetops. She and Alfonzo had gone down to the beach for the dawn enchantment of colours and coolness, then they ate mangoes and oranges on the deck, drank bitter coffee sweetened with honey and went down to the beach again, swimming in the morning heat to rinse the stickiness. Then Alfonzo had showered and dressed, combed his hair, and driven to the Cairns airport.

The wooden floors were covered with bamboo mats and cushions, strewn with towels and lengths of cloth that Wendy did not bother to pick up. There were out-of-date newspapers and magazines floating about, and a small pile of paperbacks. No need to unpack properly when at a few days' notice they might be moving again. Their clothes hung from a pole in the room with the spare mattress. They slept in the big bedroom, with the windows open all the time. The empty house was like the dry carapace of a sea creature. Through the cracks, from its skin, came the smell of wood and bamboo and rotting vegetation, salt and sea and Chanel No.5, and their bodies.

Huge red mangoes, streaked with green and orange, hung from the trees, filled the palm of the hand, sat in wooden platters through the house, the first of the season, with avocadoes, bananas and crimson tomatoes. As the mangoes ripened, she would eat them, a whole one at a time, peeling back the skin to reveal the potassium flesh into which she sank her lips. She never lost the thrill of fat, ripe availability – in Adelaide mangoes were a tropical rarity – laughed, in the mirror, to see the orange fur sticking to her lips and chin after she had eaten one while naked on the deck in the morning warmth, her legs apart, careless of the juice. Then she would shower in chilling, tingling rainwater. Mango princess. Mango life that would go on forever. The union of mind and body in a blissful dance, unrelated to the harnessing of body to mind in order to labour and produce. No aim outside the moment. Her father and mother had worked hard all their lives. Wendy laughed to think it was for this.

For it was not her parents who had given her this ecstatic freedom. It was Alfonzo whose glossy hair waved down his neck, whose torso was moulded by a herring-bone of fine dark hair, whose skin was warm walnut against which gold shone, against which teeth and eyes were bits of shell. When he came back from the airport, he hung up his white linen suit and wrapped a sarong round his waist and padded across the deck with a tequila sunrise and a joint, and in a sitting position they made love until her helpless giggling turned to nasal growls of ecstasy. How he loved to see her eyes close, breath charging and her hair a flicker of fire, her breasts in his hands, her body engulfing him. His special prize, nestled in his groin, the mascot that brought him luck in all his dealings. All he needed was his bejewelled, braceleted consort to be waiting for him.

So they pushed each other further, each day, each time, with Wendy demanding that Alfonzo let her repeat the best thing of all, whenever she wanted. If he would do it for her. She never liked to see the needle herself. To Jane it seemed that Wendy was wasting her life, but she tried not to be judgemental when they spoke on the phone. She might admire it as a grand joke, if she did not think that Wendy would be better off going back to Ivan the fire-eater, who was always waiting for her. If Wendy really wanted to make one long joke out of her life, Jane thought Ivan was a safer way to do it. He was a circus performer. He would catch her when she fell. Ivan was funny and Wendy had conquered him forever on the New Year's Eve of the year they finished school, in that surfing town on the peninsula the night Clarice Mack drowned. Jane always made a point of letting Ivan know where Wendy was. She encouraged him to maintain contact for the day when Wendy would escape Alfonzo's clutches.

~

Dusty and pitted, the long road out to Whitepeeper would have been impassable in Cleve's car in wet weather. But today it was fine. Cleve nestled Elspeth's pictures on the back seat and drove with a sense of freedom, out on his own, through the low bluebush flats and scrubby mallee country, and the sandy undulations where wattle and belah grew, watching only to avoid the stumpy-tail lizards that paused in the middle of the road. Elspeth's husband, who was coming in for lunch, greeted him as he drove through the gate and up the long avenue of misshapen old Monterey pines. Andrew Findlay had a nice welcoming smile. His face was a ruddy peach colour. They shook hands and he helped Cleve in with the pictures. Elspeth intercepted them on the steps and gave Cleve a kiss. She took the two watercolours into her hands, checking them one after the other, and led the way inside. It was her place, and her husband followed her cheerfully in his grubby moleskins, blue cotton shirt and bandless bush hat.

Cleve waited for a dog or a cat, or a child, to come exploring round his feet in curiosity, but none came. The grand old homestead was of primrose weatherboard with a green corrugated-iron roof, a wide verandah and neat white trim. Out of sight, behind a line of gums, was a shack where the manager lived with his family; and beyond, in the dry grass of the home paddock, lay the rough-hewn slab shearing shed where armies of sheep had yielded their golden fleece to the early pastoralists.

'There goes my Raphael,' laughed Elspeth, taking down an oil painting of a bow-legged nude man from the dining room wall without further explanation and trying Kerry's watercolour of the blank-faced nursing mother in its place.

They ate at a polished cedar table set with silver cutlery and big china bowls – pasta with Elspeth's bolognaise sauce.

Andrew proved to be a talker, naively interested in Cleve's work. 'What I don't understand,' he said, 'is how come there's this chronic unemployment among the Aborigines when there's always a short-age of casual labour round the district when you need someone. It doesn't compute.'

'People won't hire a black when they can hire a white,' replied Cleve.

'People can't afford to pay the wages,' Andrew went on. 'In the old days the blacks camped on the property under the cocky's protection. That was your great-grandfather's approach, wasn't it, El? They were always around.'

'The missions changed all that,' said Cleve.

'That's when the rot set in,' agreed Andrew.

'It doesn't help anyone to work for less wages, though,' Cleve argued. 'Unless we get the same pay and conditions as everyone else, we'll always be behind.'

'It's all very well in theory,' said Andrew. He considered himself benevolent, but didn't like the blacks asking for too much.

'We got union battles to fight as well,' added Cleve. 'It's true, that's hard.'

'Nulla must be pretty racist,' said Elspeth. She wanted Cleve's opinion. Without really thinking about it, she saw herself with Cleve, outsiders, and was uneasy with the line being drawn in Andrew's conversation.

'The bloody Mayor of Nulla has been siphoning off Aboriginal benefits into his own pocket,' Cleve began, by way of example, as Elspeth served the coffee and banana cake, 'with the say-so of council. That's why the hall where we had the art show has barely got to lock-up stage.'

'Mudguard Gorman,' said Andrew, confirmed in his belief that all government was corrupt. 'Sleazy bastard.'

'He's voted in every time,' protested Cleve. 'That's what makes you sick.'

'No one can be bothered to stand against him. He's frightened them all off,' declared Andrew. 'Who'd want to do a job like that? Not me. Mudguard can have it. Anyway, mate, I better get on with it.'

After Andrew went back to work, Elspeth brewed a second pot of the strong espresso stuff that made Cleve's heartbeat race. They moved outside to the deep wicker chairs on the verandah that surveyed the garden's straggling array of flowers and scents. On all sides stretched the thousands of acres that made up Whitepeeper. The Emperor of the Bush had leased the land from the Crown nearly a century ago, forging his chain of pastoral possessions. The grazing country was to north and east, across the great sunken plains. At its southern extremity the property ran through to a sluggish tributary of the river that had been dammed to form a lake. Westward it disappeared into uncleared bush.

'It's splendid isolation,' Elspeth explained. 'I love it. No one to tell you what to do. At night the place is alive with sounds. Do *you* feel close to the land?' Elspeth asked him. 'How old were you, Cleve, when you first went to live with the Adamses?'

He closed his eyes as if removing himself from the place for a moment. She looked at him curiously, straining to guess what he might be thinking. 'I didn't know you knew about all that,' he said at last.

'My mother told me. She knew from Mrs Adams.'

'The Adamses dropped me like a hot potato. It was all because of their little girl, who got leukemia. I was just part of the bargain with God, but she died anyway. No, they're good people. I owe them something. They took me from the Home when I was a kid. Three or four, I suppose.'

'You must remember something.'

'Nuh. Nothing.'

'It just seems strange that you came back to this part of the world. Those Adamses used to have a place down the river from here, according to my mother, near our Masterman cousins.'

Shaking his head, as if to throw off a demon, Cleve turned to her with a forced smile. 'I'm not being rude or anything. It's just that I don't know anything about it so there's nothing much to talk about. Imagine that, can you, when you know all about your great-grandfather and your cousins and all them. *This* place could be *my* place for all I know.'

Elspeth stood up. 'Come on, get in the car and I'll take you on a tour.'

'No, I should be heading back.'

But she insisted. 'I'll grab the keys. We won't take long. I want to show you something.'

They bumped as Elspeth drove the Volvo wagon fast over the tracks of the property, stopping only for Cleve to open the gates. In the corner of each paddock was a tank and trough fed with water pumped by windmill from an underground bore. Hoof tracks scored the earth around the troughs like spokes, where prickly pear and boxthorn, scraggy wild geranium, fig and bamboo thrived on the moisture and stock droppings. The paddocks were defined by dead-straight lines of barbed wire that crossed the rise and fall of the country with no regard for natural contour. The track wavered, through three huge fenced paddocks, until they reached the crest of a low hill where Elspeth stopped her wild driving and offered Cleve the view to behold.

On the far side was a shallow basin, a saucer, a great flat dish of caked pink mud dotted with bluebush and saltbush that stretched for miles into the distance. It was bounded by a shimmer of white, broken into bands, like a mirage.

Elspeth pointed. 'See those hills in the distance,' she said. 'We call them the Walls of China. They are the finest sand.'

'What about in front?' asked Cleve.

'No one knows for sure. It's called Lake Moorna.' There was no water in sight, only the dry glitter of the sunken plain.

'Does it ever fill with water?'

'It's below sea level. Water sometimes lies on the surface after heavy rain. They say it's been dry since the last Ice Age, 15,000 years ago. We can drive across it if you like. It's not salt.'

A track cut across the middle of the depressed plain to reach the wall of sandhills on the far side. As they drove, a pair of emus came striding into sight, disturbed by the car's noise, making their escape in huge strides through the low growth of the plain, pointing their beaks ahead as if for take-off, the bustles of their tail-feathers bouncing behind. Elspeth stopped the car while the emus ran out of sight, funny and vulnerable for all their speed. Then, reaching the base of the sandhills, she and Cleve got out and walked.

The white surface had been eroded where the wind sliced the hills open into gullies. Within the gullies were further, deeper gullies and crags. Beneath the surface the sand shaded in layers from pale buttery cream to darkening orange and red. A few bushes grew in the mounds of loose sand. Mostly the surface was hard crust. If they had ever been greater, the hills, reduced by time, were now neither high nor steep. On each side they extended for miles in an eroded body and where the erosion had formed small cliffs, the strata of past terrains became visible in rifts of white clay and red ochre that cast up fragments of bone and shell.

Cleve stubbed his foot against a knob of white bone that the wind had exposed. He bent down and tugged at it. It was embedded in the crust. Cautiously, he dislodged it. It came out clogged with damp soil and fine roots. To consider its shape, he stood up tall, looking around, conscious on every side of the extraordinary formation of the place, the only elevation in an ocean of dry plain. Then he laid the bone back on the ground.

Elspeth came over to find out what he thought of the place she had brought him to. 'Why is it called the Walls of China?' Cleve asked her.

'That's what it looks like from a distance. It's a bit of a local tourist attraction if you know how to find it – miles off the beaten track.'

'Private property?' he replied.

'They just come barging in,' she laughed. 'Once in a blue moon.'

As she faced him, her green eyes hidden in a quizzical furrow, her attention was caught by a faint buzzing sound in the clear sky. She looked up and saw a small plane passing overhead. It circled and came over them again, lower. They had been spotted. Cleve looked up at the plane as it dipped.

'Wouldn't you love to fly one of those things!' he blurted.

Elspeth waved. The intent drumming of the engine seemed to fall on them from the still, silent space above. For a third time the dark sliver of the plane crossed the sky. Then, evidently satisfied with what had been seen, the plane flew on.

'What was all that about?' asked Cleve.

'Planes come over prospecting for minerals. Looking for certain distinctive formations,' was Elspeth's explanation. 'It must look wonderful from the air.'

'They're not going to dig it up,' said Cleve. 'This place is special.'

'They can't go digging it up without my permission first,' Elspeth said.

On the drive back to the homestead Cleve mentioned that Josie Ryan had turned up in Nulla as a trainee nun at the convent school. Elspeth had not been aware of her at the art opening. She had never been a friend of Josie's. Her gang had always joked about the pale girl under a hat who had to take her blind grandmother for a walk. Elspeth told Cleve that Jane Woodruff was teaching at art school in Sydney, and painting; Wendy Sunner was in North Queensland; and Alex Mack was working in the Department of the Prime Minister in Canberra.

'The Prime Minister?' repeated Cleve. 'There'd be some fun and games there.'

'Yes,' sighed Elspeth. 'It's getting rockier, isn't it? Where's all the money going to come from?'

She was happy that Cleve had come, she realised, as she stood on the tufty lawn at Whitepeeper and his car disappeared in the dust of the road. He was a man from whom she could learn something, a man she actually *liked*. Not that she didn't like her husband Andrew, who was a good companion to her. But Cleve was a man with a cause and she liked that.

Cleve liked Elspeth too. She would prove a useful ally. She was an attractive, elegant woman, even if ultimately she lacked courage, he suspected, like all the rest of them. But he had always admired her, and he found that being with her made him feel pleased with himself and grand somehow.

The day was dark by half past five when Cleve got back to town. Doreen Tighe was waiting outside his office and dragged him over to the police station at once. It was Cleve's job to stand up for them.

A truckload of men had come over from Wentworth to make trouble. Nulla had beaten them at football the previous Saturday and in the celebrations after the match one of the Wentworth women had gone with the rival captain. The woman's brothers didn't like that much. There was another reason too. The horsemeat trade was in decline and the meatworks in Nulla were threatened with closure. Some of the blokes who went over to Wentworth for the football match had made enquiries about work at the abattoir there. That meant taking jobs away from Wentworth men, if the

Nulla men were willing to work for less. The Wentworth mob felt it was not up to outsiders to go behind their backs to the abattoir bosses. They decided to drive over to Nulla midweek to sort things out.

After a rowdy barbecue down at the reserve, they headed into town for a drink, starting with the black pub, then the mixed pub, until at last they decided to pay a call on the white pub uptown, the so-called Members Only club. When they were refused admittance, they kicked up a fuss. The elder of the group, an old-timer called Joe who had been roaming the district all his life, was happy as Larry after being on the grog all day and told the manager that he could stuff the club rules up his arse. He was the one the club manager chose to swing his fist at. Poor old Joe, the oldest and most helpless, was quick to punch back and it was on. The club bouncer joined in, the Wentworth footballers sprang to old Joe's defence, and that was enough to bring the police, who lost no opportunity to elbow and kick a few blacks as they pulled the brawling parties apart. Apprentice police sent out from the city, keen to leave their mark, they managed to haul old Joe and a few others into the paddywagon and drove off in triumph with them. Which brought more men up from the reserve to head for the police station and demand their brothers' release. By nightfall the whole town was in an uproar and everyone was looking for Cleve Gordon.

The police locked up the younger men, who were the most dangerous. Some of the others were let go because there was nowhere to hold them. Old Joe, who was accused of starting the whole affair, was drunk as a skunk, incoherent and barely able to stand. The police sergeant, who had been in the town longer than anyone, said the best thing to do with the poor old bugger was tie him up to the post outside the police station until he sobered up. It was the post in the yard where horses had been tethered in the old days. They tied him up there like a dog and he soon started howling to prove it.

Uncle Davey was already giving the sergeant an earful when Cleve came bowling in. The police station, lock-up and courthouse, the oldest and grandest structure in Nulla, was run-down on the inside. Cleve slammed the door behind him and it fell on its hinges. Shelves bulged with unattended paperwork, equipment was antiquated and grubby. The sergeant's girlfriend swore, bashing the wrong keys against the faded ribbon on the manual typewriter, as she took down the statements of those charged. The grey fluoros highlighted the stained, flaking walls and the dirty dank corners.

'A bit of a brawl outside a pub! Happens every Saturday night all over the country. Is it worth all this trouble?' asked Cleve, interspersing himself between Uncle Davey and the sergeant.

'They come over here to make trouble,' insisted the sergeant. 'We were responding to a call, mate. The stoush was on.'

'You've only got Aborigines in here.'

'They're in here for their own good.'

'Stirrers. We don't want 'em here,' said the voice of Wal Gorman over Cleve's shoulder. The Mayor had come through from the cells having made his own assessment of the situation. 'They've got till morning to sleep it off, then they can get in their truck and piss off back to where they come from.'

'You'll drop the charges?' asked Cleve. 'They're visitors from out of town. They don't know the rules here.'

'That's for later,' said the Mayor. 'That's the sergeant's decision.'

'Why not let them go and sleep it off down by the river?' argued Cleve. 'Do you need all this?' He gestured at the sergeant's girlfriend struggling with the typewriter.

'It's statistics,' said the sergeant laconically.

'Fucking statistics,' yelled Cleve, blowing a fuse and turning for the door. 'Come on, Davey.'

But Uncle Davey still had words for the sergeant. Cleve headed out the door by himself. Outside on the scrap of lawn that led to the roadside he saw old Joe tied up to the horse-post. The rope went tightly round his ankles and his wrists, skilfully tied, not to be undone no matter how hard the old man kicked and prised and yanked. In the end Joe had given up standing on his roped legs and sank down the pole into a heap on the ground. He was wearing his team's loose green football jumper over his fat chest, the red beanie on his head, khaki work trousers and his worn old leather boots. He wet himself, lying there, nodding off, his beanie at a rakish angle, the smile on his half-open mouth gaping wide.

Cleve stopped, his anger turning to pain. There was no point going back inside the police station for another altercation. He took out his penknife and hacked at the rope. Joe's bloodshot eyes stared out at him from their bags of flesh. Their eyes met in that flash of communication, Joe's gaze claiming Cleve with something stronger and more intimate than the imperative of compassion. Then the rope was carved through and Cleve pulled Joe to his feet and dragged him as best he could across the lawn to his car.

'Hey, what do you think you're doing?' bellowed the sergeant, coming outside to investigate.

Cleve ignored the policeman's yell as he bundled old Joe into his dust-caked official car and drove off to the Portacabin, a safe haven, where things could be sorted out. Cleve fixed up a comfy chair for the old man and made him a cup of tea. Auntie Betty arrived around midnight, concerned at what was up. She took one look and told Cleve to go home and sleep. She would sit with Uncle Joe and see that he was all right, poor old bugger.

Cleve was distressed. Trust his luck, to be absent from his office when it all blew up.

'As if you could have stopped it, son,' said Auntie Betty. She peered at the bleary-eyed old man nodding over his cuppa. Then she gave Cleve a beady, searching eye. 'If Auntie Betty says you going home to sleep, that's where you going.' He had no choice but to obey.

He checked at the police station on his way. Now that Gorman was gone, the sergeant was willing to let Cleve into the cells to talk to the other men in the lock-up, on condition that there was no more trouble. The men were pretty unhappy. Cleve hoped they would not do anything desperate. They would be free in the morning and would hear no more of the charges if he had his way. The men said the prison stew was dogshit. They requested hamburgers.

The sergeant said that the stew made by his girlfriend was decent tucker. It was getting on for two o'clock in the morning. Hamburgers could wait.

'You brothers get some sleep if you can. Like I'm going to do,' said Cleve. 'We'll have you out of here and back home tomorrow if I have anything to do with it.'

Cleve took himself home at last where he crashed on the bed, tugging his shoes off, scarcely bothering with his clothes. He was dead tired. As he sank into sleep, he saw the two faces, Elspeth's and old Joe's, tossing him and turning him from one side to the other, and then at the end of hours of semi-wakefulness Josie stepped into his dream to put out her hand and lead him away.

When Cleve arrived at the office in the morning, Auntie Betty was bright and chirpy as a parrot. The old man was up and about too, feeling good. He was smoking his first cigarette for the day and drinking a cup of tea strong enough to stand a spoon up in.

'We been talking all night,' laughed Auntie Betty.

'Yeah, we been talking all night all right,' chimed in old Joe with a chuckle.

Joseph Jones was the man's name, Auntie Betty told Cleve. From Wilga to be precise. He used to roam all along the river, picking on the fruit blocks and vineyards from season to season. His people always prided themselves on being dependent on nobody, and Joe had got his mission exemption, his dog tag, and gone out on his own. Joe's wife, Mary, died young, of heartbreak, after she lost her kids. The lighter-coloured one of a pair of twins was taken as an infant and the girl was stolen when she was just a baby. Mary never got over it, but she did her best to rear the others, all five of them, keeping them clean and healthy, the kids Joe was left with when Mary died, the kids he took with him out to Bruno's block the time he got work picking grapes for champagne. That was where the Welfare chased him up and took two more. Auntie Betty told all this sad story with old Joe putting in bits along the way, correcting her and changing parts, all with a big grin, as if his whole life were the grimmest comedy.

'There was Rhonda and Arthur and Daniel and Lorna and Grace,' Joe repeated their names.

'The kids took their mother's name,' Auntie Betty had found out. 'They took Mary's name for their family name. Mary Gordon. You say your people most likely come from round the riverland, Cleve. That's Wilga. Wilga's where the riverland blacks ended up.'

Cleve's mind was rushing to follow what Auntie Betty was saying, rushing in the face of the resistance his mind was putting up at the same time.

'Cleve,' croaked Joe, 'that was his name. The little fella who was taken away.'

'Cleve Gordon,' Auntie Betty chimed in. 'You're looking at him.'

'Bullshit!' swore Joe.

'You're a bit slow off the mark, Cleve boy,' said Auntie Betty. 'Don't you remember anything? Do you remember your mother?'

Cleve was breathing fast. He had his hand against his chest. 'Nup. Nothing.'

'What do you mean?' scowled Auntie Betty.

'Only when I think of what she looks like,' stammered Cleve, 'it's really strange, I can't see her face but I know it's her. I don't need to see her face. I can feel her body. I can feel her arm round me. Like she's only got one arm.'

'That's Mary,' whispered old Joe. He was scared now, as if the information had been drawn out by some sorcery. 'She lost her arm when she was a girl. She only had one arm and she reared all them kids.'

Cleve stared at his dad, but Joe was too ashamed to meet Cleve's eyes.

'I knew it the second I saw the two of youse together,' said Auntie Betty. 'Look at each other, youse two. I just *knew* you was family.'

Cleve felt winded. Denial would have been easier. He felt his legs give way. He was on the floor, on his knees, his arms reaching out, grasping the old man's ankles, pulling himself up to lay his head in his father's lap.

'There there, sonny,' said old Joe, patting Cleve's head to comfort him, welcoming this discovery as another thing in his unruly life that he could do nothing but accept. Auntie Betty had known all right. She was beaming over them, basking in the thanks due a workaday angel who has done her job. She had known from first sight.

Cleve wanted it to be true too much. He was like a child again, ready to take on faith whatever he was told. The men from Wentworth were released from the lock-up that morning and got their truck back, and Cleve drove with them in convoy, with old Joe up beside him in the passenger seat of his dusty white commonwealth car. His dad. Joe talked all the way about his wandering life, his people, his family. Cleve listened without asking questions. He just wanted to hear, latching on to any bits that might connect with him or identify him. He listened as a child listens to stories, taking the whole thing on trust yet, within that belief, finding practical difficulties and things to worry about. The old man rambled, avoiding areas that gave him pain or embarrassment, evading the moments of reckoning, and Cleve's curiosity overwhelmed him with questions to be asked later.

As they approached Wilga, after leaving the others and the truck behind at Wentworth, Joe said casually that this was the last place they had seen Cleve as a little boy. Cleve felt himself shiver. Joe said he was out picking grapes down the road at the time. Mary was at home with the kids. Joe told the story as he had heard it so many times from his wife. Cleve's story.

When the Welfare swooped all you could do was hide the kids or grab them and run, Joe said. The Welfare had the power to steal kids and make them fit into white society. The policy was to take them as young as possible before their own people could influence them.

For each of her births Mary Gordon had gone out into the bush with other women in order to avoid the hospital. She was so proud when the twins were born, Cleve and Daniel, both boys fairer than their older brother Arthur, even if other people said twins were bad luck. It was the same with her daughters. Rhonda, the first girl, was dark. Pauline, the girl who came after the twins, was the fairest of all the children. When word came that the Welfare was snooping round, it was always Pauline they worried about. Girls were the breeders. But girls could be trained into domestic servants who need never be mothers themselves.

When they saw the Welfare car coming in the dust along the road, word spread like wildfire through the settlement. 'Run, you kids, run!' Mary yelled, scooping up baby Pauline under her arm. Even the darkest child, Arthur, could not risk staying at home. The Welfare never left empty-handed.

Cleve was a smart little three-year-old. He knew where to run. He had his hiding place in the chook shed. Little Daniel was more confused. He wanted to follow Cleve, his older twin, as he did in everything else, but their mother told them always to separate if the Welfare came. Daniel ran down towards the river to the logs of fallen trees where he hid when they played hide-and-seek. Rhonda and Arthur ran ahead towards the river. Mary and the baby followed in the same direction, but at a slower pace.

The Welfare car stopped and a man in a navy suit, a lady in a nurse's uniform and the driver in creased khaki shorts and long white socks stepped out. They were striding round the yard. Mary ducked behind the broad trunk of a tree and pressed against its bark. Then the baby, squeezed against its mother's heaving bosom, began to cry. The Welfare man was marching towards the river, his feet crunching the bark and leaves. Before Mary could gag the baby's mouth, the man had made a beeline for the tree. Mary was too frightened to run. The man came round behind the tree and gave a smile to discover mother and child at their game.

'Is it a boy or a girl?' he asked as he reached out calmly for the infant.

With her one strong arm, Mary held tight as the Welfare man's hands pulled the baby away. Pauline was crying her lungs out. At last, fearing the baby would be hurt, Mary let go.

~ *213*

'I appreciate how difficult this is for you. You're doing the best you can, but they'll have a better life with us,' the man said. 'A better chance. You must try to be a good Christian woman and understand.'

He crossed to the car with the baby and passed it over to the Welfare woman who settled in the backseat with the crying bundle in her lap. The engine was running. Cleve heard his mother's cries and was terrified. The worst had happened. All that mattered was to get Pauline back. He dashed out of the chook shed and saw the black Welfare car sputtering down the track in a cloud of dust and his mother standing in its wake, covering her face with her arm, wailing. The settlement was deserted otherwise. The little boy raced with all his might after the moving car. He drew near the car. The car was slowing. The car stopped. The car was reversing towards him.

'Cleve! Come back!' his mother shrieked from far away behind. 'Cleve! Get out of the way!'

The car door opened. Cleve thought he could dive in the open door and grab Pauline. But the man in the navy suit stepped quickly out and opened his arms wide. He seized the child. The door slammed. Cleve was kicking and squirming and punching and biting in vain. The car moved off.

He was breathing the dust of the road. He heard his mother's screams. He saw his mother fall on her knees on the track, her face covered with an arm glimpsed through the window as a car pulled away. Cleve writhed, the air filled with howling – the image locked in the back of his mind until now.

He drank with old Joe that night, sitting with him on broken chairs in the cold hut. He laughed with the stream of people who came to have a look at him. Raw, edged laughter interspersed with head-shaking and strange silence, all on an empty stomach as they drank. His sister Rhonda introduced him to her two kids as Uncle and found a family resemblance. But Cleve didn't look like Danny, she said, Danny was better looking. Old Joe rambled and Cleve kept on thanking him for going out into the darkness and bringing him back before it was too late. For that was how Cleve saw it, the drunker he got, and he kept shaking the old man's hand, not letting go, in thanks. He was going to be together with the old man for the rest of his life, he swore; they would do everything together to make up for all the past; they would be best mates.

They refilled each other's glasses. For a while Joe let Cleve hold him. Then the old man got cranky and said he had other kids and grandkids to worry about too. He was not Cleve's twin brother. And in that moment the gap opened again for Cleve, who gave his edgy laugh and gulped his wine. Then the old man was gone and Cleve found himself sitting among the others, his head spinning. He stood up, knocking over the chair in a fury, and stumbled outside. Was the old man gone again? No! He could not let that happen. Old Joe was wandering among the trees and the dead car bodies with the flagon of wine. Cleve staggered after him and caught him by the shoulders and held him tightly. He put his arm round his father like a drunken mate, took the flagon from Joe's hand and drank from it, wine running down his neck.

'Get out of it,' growled Joe, grabbing the flagon back. 'I got to learn you, boy. I got to learn you everything where you come from. I got to learn you everything that I know.'

Cleve put his arm round the old man's neck and gave his grizzled cheek a long slobbering kiss. He held the man exultantly, hanging off him like an infant, nuzzling at him until they toppled over on the grass with a thud. He was never going to let the old man go again, father and inseparable son.

'If Mary was still alive to see this,' groaned Joe, winded from the fall, 'and we were all back in our old place.'

'We can get it back, Dad,' whined Cleve in a high-pitched voice. 'I'm telling you, old man. We can get it all back.'

Old Joe's arms were flailing about as he struggled to free himself from Cleve's grip. He got up out of the grass, staggering as he found his balance. A couple of dogs came running, barking at the disturbance.

'Shuddup!' yelled the old man, chasing them back into the settlement with their tails between their legs. 'Get!'

Cleve lay on the grass. The mallee trees were circling, their silver feathers brushing the sky. The sky was turning. The ground beneath him would not stop falling away. He had never been like this before, plunging like an eaglehawk through the darkness without end.

'Learn me,' he called after old Joe in a soft plaint. But it was too late. 'Learn me, man.'

Cleve shouted at the top of his voice as the old man made his way back into the settlement. There was a tinkle of women's and children's laughter from the nearest hut. When no answer came, he sank back into the silence and closed his eyes. He woke in the morning when the sun coming through the trees touched the back of his neck. His body had turned during the night. He woke on the hard earth, face down in the grass.

By the time he got home to Nulla next night, Cleve had met so many people and heard so many stories that his head was reeling. The Wilga mob had been waiting all this time for the missing ones to come home from their long journeys. For Cleve it had the force of a miracle.

He was sitting by himself at the kitchen table, letting the reunion sink in, when there was a knock at the door. As he went to answer the door he wondered what else could be in store for him. He opened up to find Josie standing there with a container of soup that she had brought for him.

'The light was on,' she said. She felt awkward about disturbing him at home. Over her uniform she was wearing a pink angora jumper. 'I heard from Ida Reardon. I thought you might want to talk. Tell me to go away if you want to be alone. I'll just leave the soup.'

'No, come in, Josie.' He greeted her warmly. The soup was welcome in his bare kitchen, and she was right, he needed to talk.

Before she sat down, she gave her verdict. 'It's the work of God.'

'It could be that,' he responded with a smile. 'If I deserved it.'

'You do deserve it, Cleve, and more.'

'I can't hold it all in. It's overflowing. I haven't only found my old man, I've found a whole family. A past. A history. I've met some-one else in myself who was a stranger to me before this. Can you understand, Josie? Am I talking sense?'

'I never knew my father either,' she said, unforgiving of what had been done with her best interests at heart. 'My mother kept him away. Then he was gone.'

'You grew up with your own people, though.'

'Yes, I did that.'

She sat with him at the table as he ate the soup. She was eager to share the surge of his feelings, to celebrate the occasion's joy, to help him unburden doubts and renewed longings.

'My Mum's dead,' he said, 'long dead, and there's still a brother and a sister missing. There's grief in it as well – as well as the sense of relief.'

'It means you belong, Cleve. You belong here with the work you're doing.'

'I've still got so much to learn. I went out to Elspeth Gillingham's place only yesterday and she showed me round her property out there. There's all that to learn about too.'

'What do you mean? You don't need to get mixed up with her,' said Josie, almost with a sneer. '*She's* not your people.'

'We're all in it together,' replied Cleve, trying to explain. 'That's the reality. That's what we have to tell ourselves.' He was already feeling his power. 'You come from one place. That's your starting point. Knowing your starting place means you can make the jour-ney to somewhere else, to a better place.'

Josie's eyes glittered brightly. 'It's your journey, Cleve. It's not other people's. I only hope I can walk with you as you go. That you and I will be permanent friends.'

'My journey's for everyone, Josie. *Specially* you.'

He no longer knew the meaning of the words he was saying. He felt at that moment as though he had the universe and all the ages whirling inside his head.

'God has blessed you, Cleve Gordon,' Josie stated with total conviction. 'I love you for it.' Speaking so, in his presence, it was as if she were lifted off the ground.

~

That winter Cleve received a letter from Canberra. One of the letters he had written to the Department of Aboriginal Advancement concerning the unfinished black community hall in Nulla had been intercepted by an officer in the Department of the Prime Minister responsible for monitoring Aboriginal issues. Goaded behind the scenes by old Nugget, his key adviser, the Prime Minister took a keen interest in Aboriginal affairs. Kangaroo and emu – the federal coat of arms appeared at the top of the letter. The contents of the letter were as short and unequivocal as Cleve had learned to expect of bureaucrats.

The government is distressed to hear of a delay in the completion of the Aboriginal community hall in Nulla as originally envisaged by virtue of a proposal to redirect funding to an alternative project without appropriate consultation with the initiating funding bodies. The government trusts that every effort will be made to remedy the departure from the agreed schedule caused by postponement of the work. The expenditure of any funds transferred to the Nulla Shire Council for this purpose is to be acquitted forthwith and unexpended funding made available to continue the work as soon as possible. The government looks forward to the completion of the project and acquittal of funds at the earliest opportunity.

Cleve let out a whoop of joy. It was victory. He marched straight round to the Mayor's office and waved the letter in Wal Gorman's face. Gorman had received his own version of the letter in the same mail. It was inadvisable to defy the Department of the Prime Minister – not yet, at any rate. He rubbed his polished pate in his usual way and said to Cleve, 'Well, it looks like it's time we got a move on with that hall for the reserve people.' It need be of no particular concern to Wal Gorman, who consoled himself that he was not out of pocket personally.

Cleve showed the letter round town, making sure everyone knew. He was puzzled by only one thing. The letter was signed Alex Mack, Executive Officer, Department of the Prime Minister, Canberra. He had no complaints about the outcome, but he wanted to know whether this Alex Mack was the same Alex Mack from Adelaide, as he assumed it was. Elspeth had said he was in Canberra. Cleve wanted to know whether Alex Mack had been aware to whom he was writing.

'Well, I'll be blowed. Alex! Fancy that,' said Josie when he showed her the letter. 'Course it's the same one. Friends in high places, eh?'

Cleve sent a note of thanks to Alex, care of the Department of the Prime Minister in Canberra. He never got a reply. He might as well go down on his knees at church on Sunday.

Spring in Nulla was heralded by outbreaks of wildflowers – flannel flowers and daisies and orchids with pinching fragrances rising from the damp pink earth. People woke to sunshine and pottered in their gardens before breakfast, picking snails from the dewy vegetables, and ate their tea in twilight at the end of lengthening days. After taking Joe home the first time, Cleve had been back to see the people at Wilga only twice. That was enough for the time being. While he was impatient to know more, he did not want to ask what they were unready to give. They laughed at his bender that first visit. He took his cues from Rhonda, his older sister, who was the talker, the carer, the family authority and chronicler. Joe was too old to care any more, after a life which had overloaded him with things to care about. He was unable to take any more responsibility. He felt too much shame.

Rhonda hugged her long-lost little brother warmly and laughed with him and made him feel welcome. She had moved back to the

Wilga settlement when the father of her children walked out on her. But she did not plan to stay on forever looking after her old father. She wanted a house of her own. Rhonda's laughter as she talked of things in the past created more holes than she filled in the jigsaw that formed in Cleve's mind. For the time being he was content to absorb the implications of the new person he was discovering in himself. But he felt what he had missed out on: a family's togetherness, struggle, suffering and love; the experience of his people, over decades. He had lived differently, and felt sorely deprived.

Strangely, the discovery of his family took the edge off his commitment to his work in Nulla. Now he wanted to curl up inside his identity and just be himself, rather than serve as a representative. That was where Josie's intensity sometimes irked him, as if he were not enough just as he was.

'You must be proud,' she declared. 'You're finding your path.' She was always pushing him towards his mission. She considered her relationship with Cleve, and her support for his work, part of her vocation. There was no room for personal passion. But she was infatuated with him.

He found it easier to be with Elspeth, who talked about things like the joy of mark-making, about art and preservation, on the occasions he visited Whitepeeper. One day they drove a hundred and fifty kilometres to see the rock art on the sides of a gorge he had never even heard of. Hands outlined on the rock wall. Ringed eyes staring from another dimension, spirits' eyes, like the gaping holes of a blind man. She was concerned that the images would deteriorate unless they were properly protected and cared for. Traces of kangaroo, fish and birds, in ochre and charcoal cross-hatched with white pigment. Broken human beings filled in with red.

'We probably shouldn't be here at all even gazing on them,' said Cleve.

In his own good time, helped by knowledge of his family, he was learning to bear the burden of his job. Still the best time was to sit with the people down by the river, eating and drinking under the trees, kicking the football with the boys, playing cards, singing and telling stories, getting stoned. He loved to swim in the river on hot days, to swing out on a rope and drop into the water with the kids, to swim upstream and dive back into the current from a high fallen log, to race from one bank to the other. Under Auntie Betty's guidance the people down there made him feel he was at home in their place. He was no stranger anymore. As she had promised when he first came to the town, Auntie Betty had sorted him out.

5

ALEX deciphered the careful script of René's letter. It was postmarked Hong Kong and had been sent by sea through a third party. It had taken eight weeks to reach him.

I hope this finds you, comrade. Maybe you could send me a smoke signal to let me know. Well, the revolution continues. Without any warning we find ourselves in the countryside in an apple-picking brigade — all the foreign students and our Chinese classmates and teachers. I don't know if it's to reform our thoughts or put us out of harm's way or improve the productivity statistics. The French and Italian anarchists went on strike at the compulsory physical labour and, as class monitor, I had to lecture them until they came round. Student Bao to the rescue! Every morning we walk out to the orchards where our ladders from the day before are still leaning against the trees and go on with the harvest. The apples are such pulpy little things that they're bruised all over by the time they make it onto the back of the six horse-power commune tractor and are carted away. What state can they be in when they reach the Soviet Union? The Chinese students laugh to think that their fickle

Big Brother in revolution would even accept them. It's a great source of pride.

But the atmosphere has got so strange after the death of Mao that in a way it's a relief to subjugate oneself to timeless toil. The mornings are primitive, especially with chapped hands. No toast and Vegemite. The smell of manure increases as the day warms up. Luckily the farm work in this muddy muted landscape helps detach the mind. We have an hour's rest at lunchtime when the canteen workers trot out into the orchards with pannikins of steamed dumplings. But I can never just switch off and snooze, even though I'm up all night listening to the shortwave radio I keep hidden in my bag. It's not illegal. I just like to keep it private.

That's how I heard the news of Chairman Mao's wife and her closest allies being arrested as the Gang of Four. It came through on Radio Australia. So I guess you already know all about it. Considering my duty as class monitor, I passed the news on to Xiao Pei, my little mate. The bastard denounced me in front of everyone for listening to counter-revolutionary propaganda. Maybe it was his way of passing on the news. There'd been nothing in the official media at that stage, and this place is so remote that there's no way of picking up any whispers or back lane gossip. Our poor brigade leader was left without any correct version of events to refer to either. Everyone denounced the radio news as a vicious rumour put about by Aussie running dogs. I felt sorry for them. I know the capitalist media lies, but not like that. It must have been truly disturbing for the Chinese to hear the news that the world had collapsed – that's what it means to them – courtesy of a foreign shortwave radio broadcast.

We've been having meetings ever since. That's why I'm not out picking apples today. Most of the teachers are continuing to speak with loyalty and praise of the members of the Gang of Four. They want to wait and see what happens. But a few of them are starting to reveal a little bit of a different picture, what they really thought, or so they say, as a prelude to changing their stance. Within a fortnight, I predict, the very people who were most active in screaming anti-Deng Xiaoping slo-gans will start vehemently denouncing the Gang of Four and praising

Deng Xiaoping. I have come to understand the mentality only too well and I consider it outrageous and sickening. The ideological struggle is exposed as charade and farce. Even the hardline cadre responsible for our political instruction has made the change overnight. I told her to her face that I find it difficult to accept this one-hundred-and-eighty-degree turn-around. She just laughed. I told her she was making all values meaningless if she could just change them like a suit of clothes. She laughed at me as if I was a complete dumbo and had proved beyond question the idiocy of even the cleverest outsider. So much for all those years of language study.

I had to write to someone, old buddy, even if you never get it. I'm betrayed, but I can't leave the place alone. I can't go back so I'm staying on. When the apple harvest is finished, we move on to grape-picking. When our university sorts itself out, we return to class and something new starts.

~

Wendy rocked in the cane chair, drowsier than ever. Alfonzo had touched her to the quick, like a hot wave breaking, as she crossed her legs around him. Again it was the creation of mind from matter. She would have his child, in keeping with their push forward into experience. She told Jane when she phoned her in Sydney with the news that she could feel the seed starting its journey of growth inside her. The two women could not stop giggling. Would it ruin Wendy's life? Did that matter? It was decided in the manic defensiveness of their giggling. Alfonzo howled with joy and pride when she told him, stomping out a circle on the deck, flinging his arms in the air.

'I hope I stay attractive,' Wendy frowned.

'You will always be beautiful,' he laughed, looking beyond her to his child.

Wendy enjoyed going into town in her loose thigh-length shirt, picking up her needs from the little shops. She ate huge amounts, disinclined to stint herself. It was harder to abstain from the drugs that might damage her baby. Alfonzo's pride in what she had become made him pamper her more than ever. She would spend hours sitting on the sand with her legs apart, watching the offshore currents and the crossbreezes hold the water in contrary directions at once. She loved watching this phenomenon of the sea, its complex patterns of motion as within her the baby grew and moved.

~

The visit to North Queensland was time out that Jane would normally have resisted. As a promising young artist with a career, she rejected motherhood for herself as the worst possible handicap to a woman's achievement. She was ferocious about the obstacles she faced as a woman artist in Australia, where big fish fed off emerging talent in the small fashionable pond.

Her career was boosted by her relationship with Michael Browne-Grey, an ageing pioneer, but she had moved away from him now to a younger, more radical group of women artists and curators for support. Her work challenged the masculinist traditions of Australian oil painting and she was starting to be recognised.

Alfonzo, guessing that Jane disapproved of the baby as she disapproved of Wendy's involvement with him, did not welcome her visit nor trust her. But it was too late for Jane to have any influence over Wendy, and fundamental to their friendship that she should not try. Wendy demanded her presence and Jane would be attentive and helpful only as required. She wanted to know that the hospital was booked, that Wendy was seeing the doctor regularly, that there were no anticipated difficulties.

'Mum and Dad don't know yet,' Wendy threw in, as an aside.

'They don't know!' Jane shook her dark curls and peered at Wendy with magpie eyes.

'We decided it was easier not to tell them. They'll only want to make us get married.'

'What if something happens?'

'Nothing's going to happen, is it, darling?'

'What's Alfonzo frightened of?' asked Jane, jumping to the real reason Wendy's parents had not been told. She would have preferred Wendy as a single mother. There was at least honour in that. 'Do *his* parents know?'

'They will know after the birth.'

'Then you're taking a lot on yourself. Are you sure Alfonzo's going to stick around?'

'Why wouldn't he? He's paying for everything.'

'What if he *can't* stick around for some reason?'

'How do you mean?'

'You know where his money comes from.' Wendy wished Jane would mind her own business. A consort did not delve into such things. But Jane would not be fobbed off. 'It's dangerous for you and the child. You need a contingency plan.'

'You mean I should run away?' giggled Wendy.

They were sitting on the deck drinking jasmine tea. The wind stirred the timbers of the house and Alfonzo appeared in worn jeans, barefoot as usual, his cerise shirt open and flapping. Jane looked awkward, as if she had been overheard. Alfonzo, dark and smiling in a sinister way, appeared to her as a magician who could read people's thoughts and saw women in half.

'How's our kid been today?' he asked, putting his arms round Wendy's neck and laying his hands on her belly.

Jane looked out to sea.

'You're not going to leave me?' Wendy asked, clasping Alfonzo's hand.

'Is that what she thinks?' he replied, casting his eyes at Jane. He laughed. 'My own flesh and blood – how could I leave you?'

Jane turned round to face him. 'I was only asking in case anything happened.'

He glowered at her for an instant. 'You're behaving like a mother-in-law. We don't want a mother-in-law, do we? There's going to be a spectacular sunset tonight. It's the eve of a storm. We should prepare ourselves and go out and watch it. The colours of minerals on fire. Jane, you could paint it.'

Wendy thought it bourgeois of Jane to be offended by Alfonzo. Morality, she thought, was itself immoral. In all his years Alfonzo had not tripped up. If people were vulnerable to exploitation, that was their decision, their choice, their risk-taking, their death-wish. There was big money to be made, and what big money was ever made out of tender regard for other people's susceptibility? You could not protect people from themselves. Wendy's only problem was with the risk. She did not want her parents involved. She delighted in Alfonzo's cleverness at being able to live with enviable ease. Alfonzo's parents had always told him that princes and lords and the pale-eyed upper class of this new-old society, with their smooth hands, ungiving talk and dull taste, had a right to live free from the system's yoke. Alfonzo had managed the ascent to that aristocracy in a single leap, rapier whistling, cape flying, a swashbuckling pirate-prince reclaiming his true inheritance. The aspersions Jane cast were galling. He would give her some stuff, free of charge, if she wanted it, as he did for Wendy's other friends. He was nothing if not magnanimous, and he expected other people to be grateful, including Ivan the fire-eater, his defeated rival in Melbourne, to whom he regularly sent angel's dust.

Jane walked through the grove of trees carrying her pad, pens, pencil and charcoal. Mangoes were rotting all over the ground. She had been producing huge oil paintings depicting domestic landscapes – suburban houses, backyards, back fences, back roads leading to school gates, factory doors, church porches – but all rendered on an heroic scale, as contemporary history paintings that depicted the lives of working women. She exulted in her skill with paint, thick, roughly plastered on, with knife as much as brush. Dawn and dusk, noonday, the light before an electrical storm, extremes that hinted at imminent apocalypse, expressed in colours that she borrowed from the great post-impressionists: Cezanne for the brown of roadside mud, the green of winter hills behind a housing development, factory brick red; Bonnard for the pink of a corrugated iron fence, the yellow of a schoolhouse, the blue of kids' pyjamas on a clothes line; Van Gogh for the purple of a church spire, the orange wheel of the sun. But the point of view in her paintings drove her crazy. She was looking from outside, when she wanted to be inside the things she painted. Her training had stressed view, composition, placement, when she was groping for a kind of displacement, leaving no one position from which to see and compose – the vision of the eye of a fly. And she wanted those dimensions to include history, so that the scar tissue of the past would tilt up against the present, as if the earth were ripped open and its secrets thrown to light.

She stomped through the mango bower squelching the yellow-orange flesh underfoot, dodging the wasps that were drunk on the juice. She had eaten mangoes since she arrived, keeping Wendy company, who loved them and craved them. The lemon-coloured mangoes were sharper than the massive plum ones. The sinuous arms of the trees reached up and out like the Indian gods who peo-pled Wendy's world. Green mangoes hung from them like so many globes of Venetian glass. How could Jane depict it? The slithering, glowing abundance, the warm shadowy caves that formed and unformed as light moved and hid.

Pushing out from caves of green to white blinding sand, Jane peered through sunglasses to the far end of the beach. Graders were clearing seagrass and coastal mangroves. In a cleared patch, a scoop was dumping sand in the back of a truck. When its load was full, the truck churned along the beach. Men at work. A construction company quarrying the sand. The noise buzzed in her ears. Here was the wound she was looking for, the delving of mighty blades into virgin sand, the slicing in and carving out of a landscape, and back from the beach the profuse rotting presence of the abandoned mango orchard.

In the middle, as Jane imagined her painting, rendered with shining light brushwork and hard white knifework, stood the figure of Wendy: fire-red spirit suspended in mango-flesh. Rapidly she sketched with the charcoal, not removing her sunglasses since the true light was too bright. It was a portrait of a woman she was reaching for through the ripening mango and its hard seed.

She conceived a whole series, portraits that incorporated landscape into the work with integrity and critical edge: a new kind of environmental allegory.

Michael, when Jane showed him her ideas, correctly read the determination in her excitement. Stroking his trimmed beard with one hand as he gently felt the skin round her navel with the other, and she tightened her muscles, he accepted that he had only one final purpose to serve. He was on the committee to recommend a prestigious commission for a new insurance tower in Sydney. That was what Jane wanted. The commission would signal an artist whose work had demonstrable monetary value in this newly pricey Australia. It would bring Jane to international attention.

'Would an insurance company go for this sort of work?' Jane asked.

'That's the whole point,' laughed Michael. 'They'll love it.'

In advising Jane to put in for it with a work from her new series, Michael was promising her; he was also, he accepted, ruling off the page on their commitment to each other.

~

High above the city that was ablaze at sunset, people drank champagne and ate hors d'oeuvres to celebrate the unveiling of Jane Woodruff's *Mango Dreaming*. The painting filled a wall of the boardroom like a gorgeous, painful daydream. The artist looked brilliant in a scarlet crêpe gypsy skirt and a tight black top, big gold moons dangling from her ears.

'That's Ziggy Whatsisname, you know, the star of *Iceberg*.' People pointed with their champagne flutes. 'He's even better looking in real life, don't you think?' Ziggy's first feature film had been acclaimed as the best Australian production since *Picnic at Hanging Rock* and had won a prize at Cannes. He had a deep clear tan and his sunblonded red hair, cut in a long straight fringe, shone like fire.

He wore a beige linen shirt with a Mao collar that sat nicely on him. He swam every day. He must have kissed or shaken hands with everyone in the glassed-in skyscraper rooftop before he got a proper look at Jane's painting, in which the mango glowed and the goddess form in the middle of the orange shape had the quality of burning oil. Jane came over and took his arm. 'You know who it is. It's Wendy,' she said. 'Did you hear, Ziggy? She's had a girl. I'm flying up in the morning.'

Ziggy's cool cheekbones counteracted his almost pouting mouth. 'No,' he gasped, creasing his face. 'Already? That's wonderful. Give her my love.'

It was an easy birth, as it had been an easy pregnancy. Wendy spoke to Jane on the phone, rejoicing at the little girl she had produced – a gift, like her fortune and her happiness. Alfonzo was flushed and proud, with champagne and cigars, unable to wipe the grin off his face. He had called his parents who sent a huge arrangement of orange roses. Jane felt it was the right time for Wendy's parents to know too. But Wendy warned Jane not to tell them. She was completely happy with things as they were, not ready for anything more, as she struggled to learn how to suckle little Cassie.

'I hope she'll be all right. Poor darling,' said Jane, squeezing Ziggy's arm.

Then Alex walked into the room. He was wearing a public servant's dark suit and had just stepped off the plane from Canberra. Jane shrieked with delight. She gave him a big friendly hug. 'You got here! That's great.'

'Hi Ziggy,' Alex grinned warmly, putting his arm on Ziggy's shoulder. 'I didn't know if you'd make it. It's like a reunion.'

'Wendy's dropped the baby,' said Ziggy. 'Did you hear?'

'Wow!' said Alex.

'I'm flying up tomorrow!' Jane could not stop laughing. 'We should all go!' She could have taken off from the roof of the building, like a helicopter, with her old friends.

'We should send her something,' said Alex. 'What an extraordinary thing. One of us is a mother!'

'I certainly won't be doing it for a while,' said Jane, with another burst of laughter. 'Anyway, *Mango Dreaming* is still Wendy's painting, despite all the money the corporates have paid for it.'

'Congratulations, Jane,' said Alex. He glanced at the painting. 'It's stunning.'

'Before I fly out in the morning Cynthia's bringing an American collector to have a look at it.'

'Cynthia?'

'Cynthia Temple. The owner of the gallery. My dealer.'

'Cheers.'

They clinked glasses.

'Come and see the view,' said Jane, linking arms with Ziggy and Alex, dragging them over close to the glass wall of the building that dropped sheer to the street thirty storeys below. People were flowing towards the Quay on their way home, to the buses and trains and the ferries that headed out across the burnished water of the harbour. The stepped-up buildings on the opposite shore reflected light back in a mirror mosaic, mobile, insubstantial, a ziggurat of shine and glamour.

'It's like having wings!' said Ziggy.

'Where are you staying, Alex?' Jane asked. 'You could have stayed with me.'

'They put me up at the hotel. I've got a meeting in the morning. You're too busy.'

Between Alex and Jane there was still the vestige of awkward intimacy, although it was six years now since they had been together. Alex looked much older, his hair waved, his eyes flicking humorously about, his remarks ironically considered. After Labor was thrown out in 1975, he had weathered the change of government, staying on to become the boy wonder of the Department of the Prime Minister. The experience had fixed his confidence in his capacity to make things happen.

'Well, I hope you're coming on to dinner. The least you can do, Alex,' Jane countered. 'There's just a few of us – Cynthia, Michael – lovely man, he was on the committee for this, Stephen Fazzoletto –

the *Herald* critic – and some arts people. They've booked a restaurant in the Cross. Why don't you come along? Ziggy, you have to come. Otherwise when will we see you again?'

Ziggy was leaving for London to make his stage debut in a West End production of *The Wild Duck* – a part he got on the strength of his soulful Scandinavian quality. He would rather have been in a musical. Yet coming in the wake of the brilliant reception for *Iceberg* in London, it was a break he could not afford to pass up. He tossed his hair at Jane and Alex. 'I've got a call for a shoot at five o'clock in the morning. If you can guarantee I'll make it in presentable shape, I'm on.'

'Looks like there's no choice,' smirked Alex.

They found themselves crowded into a noisy, fashionable restaurant, where the wisecracking young staff in their bleach-fresh white aprons, exclaiming in delight over every selection from the menu, were eager to bring them anything they wanted. Wine was poured and another bottle ordered as soon as a bottle appeared on the table. Crusty bread, olives, prawns, rock oysters, mudcrab, grilled fish, fillet steak, chips, greens of every kind, served in piled bowls and on huge plates, stories shouted down the table as it all went on and everyone became drunker and wilder and artfully disarrayed. It was typical Sydney. Cynthia made a speech to her client's good fortune. She said you must always throw yourself at life because life would always catch you in its open arms. Then came the desserts, all mango and chocolate, and the shower of credit cards to divide up the outrageous bill.

Alex stood up and, scattering the other credit cards, placed his own on top of the bill.

'Allow me,' he said, smiling at Jane. 'I'm up from Canberra for an important meeting. Government business.'

The others laughed. There was applause all round.

The sacking of the Whitlam government and the return to power, by election, of the Liberal party, had produced a rougher, less scrupulous society. The eye was always on the main chance. At every opportunity people were asserting their right to take the next step up the ladder, with an uncaring energy that affected culture and personal relationships as well as politics. Alex had done well, in Canberra, to make the transition. He had bought a flat of his own. He wondered, getting drunk at dinner and joking loudly with Jane to remind everyone that they were old friends, first lovers, whether he was not still hankering after her. Despite interludes with a few Canberra women, apart from Valerie O'Rourke, he had tied himself to no one. Having kept her seat, Valerie had gone to the Opposition benches and stayed in the shadow cabinet after the election. Alex pondered. Jane was on a different trajectory now too. Was it too long ago for the flame to be rekindled, he wondered. Would it suit her? And if it didn't happen tonight, would the moment come round again on fortune's wheel? He felt good being in Sydney. He felt good, sitting in his dark suit beside Ziggy, his other old friend, who was soaking up the eyes of the besotted restaurant.

Life in the capital had taught Alex how political power worked in its several phases: the power of senior politicians channelled through the projects they personally wanted to see realised, or through the people they were loyal to, or who were loyal to them; the power of the bureaucracy, greater than the power of politicians when it came to where the money went and what actually happened, but hedged around by process, complexity, inertia, rivalry, accountability; the sway of public opinion, through media, lobby groups and the unpredictable shifts of community attitudes; all these Alex could manipulate and ride now, to serve his masters one way, the party another, and himself yet another. He had seen many of his contemporaries bail out because Canberra was not about money or hedonism or the adventure of your own creativity, except in coded ways, but he did not really expect anyone to care that his own faceless successes were, in their own way, as great as Jane's and Ziggy's public, self-achieved triumphs. It was enough that there should be a moment of awed silence when people heard he worked in the Department of the Prime Minister. Politics depended on the fearful attraction of those close to power.

In the morning, he would meet his future backers, those who would owe him and those he would owe, after the next turn of the wheel. It was slippery, thrilling stuff and the stakes were high.

'I'm glad I came along,' he said to Jane as he bumped up against her in the scramble to leave the restaurant, once he got his receipt for the bill. He put his arm around her and she leaned into him. But he felt her pull back. 'I love you,' he said, leering at her.

She looked round for the others. 'What now?' she asked.

They were out in the street where it was raining and people were grabbing taxis. Two taxis took them on to the nightclub – Jane, Michael, Stephen the newspaper critic, Ziggy, Alex and a couple of people who had been picked up from one of the other tables.

Lights spun in the blackness. The music was loud, the place half-empty. The art critic, who was a regular, found them a table. The others hit the dance floor. At last they could reveal a skin beneath the manic masks of the evening. Jane was off-duty, dancing with Ziggy. Round each other they circled, gazes dramatically glued, pumping their limbs. When they finished, they laughed all the way back to the table. Then they danced again, Jane with Alex this time, Ziggy alone.

Alex tried to talk to Jane as they danced, jumping up close to shout words in her ear or standing in front of her, mouthing words that she might understand above the noise. Being drunk, he took the opportunity to say some of the things about her that ran on in his head. Their relationship had dwindled away in indifference, as each pursued other paths and tried themselves out with other peo-ple. It had never formally ended. They had each been hurt, and the hurt was something they pushed aside as they moved on, before admitting that they might have discarded something valuable with-out considering the consequences. Jane was not really in the mood to indulge Alex's shouted analysis, but she let him go on. They behaved as if they were different people from the kids who had grown up together; new people encountering each other in the eager, uncommitted way that happens. Yet there was also the submerged stratum of history, of what they had been through together, shared almost by accident. They knew so much about each other from the past, yet what they knew were things that had been put aside in maturity, rejected or transformed. It was not the substance of their adult selves but a residue of the experiences that had got them where they were. Alex's mother's death, when Jane became his lover, was a part of himself that he had buried. Their parents too, Tim and Alison, had ended their affair and Alex and Jane had jettisoned the accommodation they made in case they turned out to be stepbrother and -sister. They were both in a world of their own determination and choice now, without a need to return to what had made them – except in dreams, or dotage.

'I want to thank you!' Alex was shouting at her. 'Thank you for everything.'

Laughing, she pulled him close to kiss him. 'Who would have thought?' she whispered. 'Here we are.'

'Will I come back to your place tonight?' he asked.

'Will you?' She paused. 'To try again?' she giggled. The choice was to leap up, wings outstretched, into those unknown arms of life, or to look back over her shoulder – and what would she turn into then? No, she kept her focus. 'Stephen's got some other plans, I think.'

'Stephen?' Alex blurted. 'What about Michael?'

'That's all over. No, I need some comfort. That's what I get from someone new. People you know too well don't give you that. Anyway, Cynthia said I should look after Stephen.'

Alex understood that Jane, shouting over the music, was denying him the luxury of a retrial. Her artist's gaze never turned a blind eye to lapse or weakness. That was the crime of which she had mentally convicted Alex when – on her own instructions – he had failed to fight for her.

'You're flying up to see Wendy?' he asked. The old subject was over. Jane nodded. 'Give her a big hug for me. What a crazy thing to do. A baby with Alfonzo!'

'Right,' said Jane. 'Didn't you say you've got a meeting in the morning?'

'Don't worry, Jane. It's my night out. I'm okay.'

It was three in the morning when Jane left with Stephen. Ziggy was chatting at the bar. Alex sat alone at their littered table waiting for him to come back.

'All alone, mate?' commented Ziggy when he came over. He ran his hand over Alex's head to rouse him.

Alex's head was spinning. He looked up at Ziggy with his old rakish grin. '*You're* still here.'

'Always,' Ziggy laughed, and tugged at Alex's arm to haul him to his feet. 'Let's get out of here.'

The rain had stopped, leaving the air fresh and nipping. The regular slicing of car lights and tyres in the wet empty streets gave a pulse to the night as groups of people stumbled across the road in front of the cars, holding hands in a chain, and solitary people swayed along the footpaths.

'Jane's gone off with that art critic,' growled Alex.

'Does that worry you?'

'There's no accounting for taste, is there?'

'You seem pretty out of it, anyway.'

'No, that's no excuse. That's never been a problem.'

'Really?' Ziggy exclaimed. 'I mean you must have had enough. Do you want to go home? Or go somewhere else?'

'You didn't tell me you were going to London, Ziggy.'

'You never asked. Yes. Next month.'

'For how long?'

'Quite a while.'

'You mean you're not coming back?'

'Not unless I have to. I have to keep learning. I have to push myself.'

Alex shook his head, as if shaking this news down inside him. 'Can't you do that here?'

'The challenge here is to keep on top of things. That's different. Success here is treacherous. That's what Herbert Horsfall says. Theatre here is a clique. Film and television the same. They suck you in so they can spit you out later. They're interested in talent only if they can control it for their own ends. There's nothing to pit yourself against.'

'You're cynical already.'

'I see it for what it is.'

'What about Herbert?'

'Oh, he's different. That's why he's telling me to get out.'

'The creative contribution you could make here is so much bigger, surely? *Here* and *now*. You're needed. You could do such things . . .'

'Later, man.'

'Why don't you do something for Australia?'

'You've become such a patriot down there in Canberra, Alex. The reality's international. You know that. Mama and Papa are very pleased that I'm going back to Europe. They were threatening to move from Adelaide to Sydney to look after me.'

'They must be so proud of you.'

Through his drunken vision Alex stared at his beautiful old friend. He saw Ziggy as a trapeze artist swinging through the air. He didn't want to lose him, yet he could not but salute him as he soared away out of reach. It had always been Ziggy's imperative.

Alex stumbled forward and gave Ziggy a tight long bearhug. He loved what Ziggy had given his life, ever since they were kids at school. So much of Alex's showing off, like when he had eaten dirt during the eclipse of the sun in an attempt to show that you could stop things from harming you, so much of his performance, had been for Ziggy, the scathing, doubting, imperious judge.

Alex hugged Ziggy so tight, as if squeezing their shared childhood to hold it from changing, that he lost his balance. It was Ziggy, lightly disentangling himself from Alex's grip, who saved them both from toppling to the ground.

'Come on,' said Ziggy. 'I know where we can go.'

They were inspected by the bouncer, who flickered his eyebrows in recognition of Ziggy Vincaitis and opened the red door. Downstairs a cavernous space was filled with the dancing bodies of men. Lights roved the crowd, picking out a face or a head or a flying hand, a tilting shoulder. There seemed to be no walls or end. That first instant Alex found it funny and Ziggy squeezed his arm to reassure him. This was a fervent rite, not a comedy show, the brassy music so loud that they were dancing even before they had pushed through to the crowded dance floor.

'Wait,' ordered Ziggy. 'Don't go away.'

Left by himself, Alex continued to dance. It was a way of keeping from looking like a fish out of water. He had been to bars before, but never anywhere as unabashed as this. In the Department of the Prime Minister, and at key positions throughout the government, were razor-sharp, fancy-free men like these, nodes on a network, and Alex was never averse to going for a drink with them, hoping he was the sort of person for whom they would go the extra distance. Dancing alone, he attracted a few glances, when the cruising light picked out the faces or the eyes that were on him. The smell of desire was strong: shampoo and aftershave, smoke and dope, sweat and hormones. Then Ziggy grabbed his hand and led him into the darkness of a second space, lit only with pins of light, like stars, where men danced in each other's arms to slower music, groping, before sinking to the sides, into couches and up against walls.

Down a corridor to the toilets out the back, they passed a further space, the pitch-dark back room, from which moans and gasps emerged, and a cocktail of odours including what for a second smelled like hot dark chocolate. 'That's where they do it,' explained Ziggy.

He bundled Alex into the empty ladies' cubicle and locked the door. He prepared the line of cocaine he had scored from his friend and showed Alex how to snort it through a rolled-up twenty dollar note. The powder produced a cold sensation on the inside of his nostrils.

'Half the people here seem to recognise you. Doesn't that worry you?' Alex asked. 'What if it gets into the press? What about your reputation?'

'Everyone is here. Judges, television personalities, members of parliament. It's a small town.' He was moving the crumbs of cocaine into a neat pile with the money straw. 'That's one reason I'm looking forward to London. The anonymity.'

Alex grinned, feeling a wave of well-being break over him. 'Sure, Ziggy. Relative anonymity.'

'You have to start somewhere.' Ziggy arched his brows in an expression of delicious cynical innocence. He could do nothing about how the world was, except know it exactly. 'If you're cute, this is the place.'

Then a fist started pounding on the cubicle door and a falsetto voice begged, 'Git out of there, you two. I've got my period!'

Ziggy's departure for London was a juncture. He had absorbed his friends' hopes into himself and was going off alone now. That Alex and Ziggy were together, for one night, seemed to signpost the crossroads which they had reached.

Alex was dishevelled, his sandy hair standing up in sweaty tufts as he danced, his business shirt unbuttoned to the ribcage, his tie trailing out of his suit jacket's pocket, his eyes staring and bloodshot. Ziggy was in better shape. He knew how to maintain appearances, a little louche but still elegant in his beige linen shirt. It would go for drycleaning in the morning. You only ever wore a fresh garment once.

Herbert Horsfall had cast Ziggy in *Iceberg* for his red hair and high cheekbones and golden eyes; and because he was sexy, had good technique and the charm to touch and work an audience; and because he was ambitious to claim a more rightful inheritance for himself than his immediate environment provided. Herbert had ticked off these requisites for success one by one when Ziggy first performed in the *Dream*. But even that combination of attributes was not so rare. It was the extra thing Herbert saw that ensured his commitment to the boy. Ziggy was a perfectionist. He had the capacity to strive for every detail to be right. Whether in performance, daily life or in his relations with the world, he paid extraordinary attention to detail. When he was a kid, this might have seemed like precocity or affectation, but he was laying the groundwork. He was learning. The fanaticism of his preoccupation with getting even the shadings right was not simply aesthetic. It was a concern with the rightness of things. By achieving a rightful order in things, Ziggy felt he was on the path of righteousness. Truth and clarity were the pillars he would one day walk through – so Herbert Horsfall understood. That gift underlay Ziggy's vocation and would make him great. It was a priestly function, the director saw as clear as day, which would make Ziggy Vincaitis a star.

Ziggy's golden eyes sparkled at Alex through the murky smoke. Alex reached out and held Ziggy loosely. It felt, for him, like a moment of enchanted trust. They shuffled, wrapped in each other's arms, propping each other up, exhausted. They were cheek to cheek, then mouth to mouth in one long unbroken kiss.

Alex blinked as he finally pulled away, shaking his head.

'Let the bird of freedom fly, brother,' quipped Ziggy with a deprecating snigger. 'Let's go.'

The taxi took them to the little terrace house in a lane in Surry Hills where Ziggy lived. His housemate was asleep. As quietly as they could, without turning on the lights, they crept past the closed door into the bare room where Ziggy slept on a mattress on the floor. Ziggy opened the window to let the cool air in. Already an iridescent hint of the new day was feeling its way across the sky. He lit a candle which, agitated in the draft, summoned up phantom shadows from the room's corners. At low volume he put on his favourite tape of the moment, Ravel's *Pavane pour une infante défunte*. They pulled off their smoky, sweat-drenched clothes and lay down on the mattress. Ziggy held Alex, whose heart was pounding and whose head burrowed into Ziggy's neck. His bristly stubble scraped Ziggy's skin. Then Ziggy sat on top of Alex and closed his eyes.

Alex moaned with the sensation. 'Ziggy! Do you want that? Is it all right?'

'Not too hard!' Ziggy winced. 'Try this.' He reached for a phial of amyl, unscrewed the top and held it to Alex's nose.

Alex sniffed. Then Ziggy took two sniffs himself. The pain turned to mounting, cresting waves of pleasure. 'That's it,' Ziggy gasped. 'Oh, Alex, kiss me.'

Alex was conscious of being drawn into darkness and heat, of being held there. His hands clawed and teeth bit to keep himself from sinking deeper into a dark warm burrow that seemed to have no end. Chocolate waves were engulfing him. Waves of desire, waves of release. He screwed up his eyes. When he opened them, he found Ziggy's face running with tears. He licked his friend's tears, and when he closed his eyes again, sheets of lightning flashed across his inner vision. Then he saw the burning rim of the sun eclipsed by the black disk of moon. Luminous within the sphere of the moon was a shining skull. Joe Skull. Yes, oh yes, oh yes, Alex. Ziggy. Baby. Coddling Alex in his arms, Ziggy rocked their two bodies, and it felt right. 'It feels so good,' said Alex, groaning.

'You're an old pro,' snickered Ziggy, rolling cigarettes for them both.

'I've never done it before,' protested Alex.

'I've wanted to do that with you for a long time. Will you love me forever, mate?'

'It felt as though I left my body. I saw a skull against the moon. Blocking the sun. Does that mean guilt and shame? When I was a kid, I kept that Aboriginal skull that I dug up. I kept it in my room. He was my mate, only I never realised it at the time.'

'I was supposed to be your mate back then.'

'My secret imaginary mate. He went to the tip in the end.'

'No!' exclaimed Ziggy in camp horror.

'You remember. It was my Mum who took the skull to the tip. I sometimes wonder if that was the curse. Why she died. I hated her for that.'

'You don't believe that.'

'I feel such guilt, Ziggy. I don't know why.'

Ziggy put an arm round Alex's shoulders as they lay together on the soiled mattress smoking their tight rollies. Ziggy seemed to have tied a string to Alex's innards and to be drawing out things he had never said before. 'What are you, Alex?' he asked.

Alex gave a muted raucous laugh. 'What sort of question's that at a time like this?' He looked down at his navel, crusted with Ziggy's drying cum. 'I don't know. I could be anything or nothing. I don't know what my identity is.'

'Then you're dangerous.' Ziggy's tone turned serious. 'I love you, Alex, and maybe you love me too. Don't forget me, will you?'

'How could I? You took advantage of me, didn't you. You bastard, Ziggy. Of course I love you. I wouldn't be here otherwise.'

'You wanted it too,' said Ziggy, giving Alex a slap. 'Are you feeling okay?'

'Yeah, I wanted it,' Alex went on. 'It was strange. I had a feeling of total abandonment and at the same time I'm wanting to fight you, to master you and absorb you into myself.'

'That's what I get off on. When you want to possess me, then I've got you. We're joined forever. Now what time is it?' Ziggy asked. 'They want my face at sunrise to promote anti-acne lotion.'

'Shit, it's after five already and I can't even talk straight. I've got a breakfast meeting. Can I borrow one of your shirts?'

'Summon the energy, Alex. Ride the energy. You'll be fine.'

'Two aspirins, black coffee, Vitamin B and Vitamin C,' Alex recited.

Alex revived with a hot soaping shower and a clean shirt. His eyes were a bit pink. He barely had time to fetch his briefcase from the hotel room where he was supposed to have slept the night. There were messages – from Valerie, from Collison, from Reg Rufus, from Senator Lewin himself, each wanting to go over things with him in private before the meeting. In an accidental piece of good judgement he had not given them the chance.

At one end of the goldfish bowl mezzanine a Hong Kong tour group was eating its breakfast. At the other end two men and a woman were waiting at a window table that looked over old Woolloomooloo to the shining harbour, through lush greenery and massive Port Jackson figs that gave the impression of predating all this white man's hugger mugger. Alex went straight to Valerie O'Rourke and bent over her from behind to give her a kiss. She brushed back against him kittenishly, reaching a hand up under his chin. 'Late night?' she purred.

Valerie always looked good, professional, interested in everything that was going on. There was his boss, Simon Collison, his mentor in the Department, a fifty-year-old Canberra *éminence gris* of cautious behaviour and shrewd instincts. Collison had steered his Department's accommodation to the Liberal government when Labor lost power, and now he was being courted by Labor again, where his first loyalties discreetly lay. Without a greeting, he nodded at Alex to sit down.

The other man, whose round, jowly face beamed as faces do when used to being beamed at by other faces, was Senator John Lewin. The remains of his sleek dark hair were plastered round the sides and back of his head. He was the Shadow Minister for Resources and Environment and courteously stood to shake the young man's hand. Behind his jovial expression was a more penetrating gaze, quick to make assessments. Senator Lewin and Alex had talked on occasion in Canberra. This was the first time they had met to do business.

'Order something for yourself, Alex,' suggested Simon Collison. 'We're waiting on Rufus.'

The men had ordered large cooked breakfasts of eggs, bacon, tomatoes, hash browns and toast from the à la carte menu. Valerie had a croissant and orange juice in front of her.

Reg Rufus came in waving the morning paper in front of him and swearing. He was the organiser, the indispensable and feared numbers man. As a backbencher in Opposition, he was one of the party's powerbrokers – a big fat man whose life was devoted to securing power for his mates. His family lived in Sydney, so he had gone home to the wife and kids overnight. He was squeezing in a working breakfast on his way to the airport to fly back to Canberra. Mates were, in his belief, the best cause in the world. If your mates didn't have power, it would fall into the hands of enemies, as was the case now in Canberra.

'He's just not up to it,' groaned Rufus, not waiting to acknowledge any of the people present. Once again the leader of the party had failed to make political mileage out of the soaring unemployment figures. Rufus slumped down gloomily in the chair, which barely held his bulk. They were all loyal cronies.

After being thrown peremptorily into the wilderness at the last election, the party was desperate to win government back. Their analysts told them they could do so if they had a new leader and made a new appeal to the people in the middle, to mothers of young families, to youth, to middle-class idealists, in selected urban seats. That appeal, looking ahead to the 1980s, was the Environment, a new concern which their opponents, bound by support from the rural sector in the coalition of government, could not afford to take seriously. Labor's policy on the Environment was Senator Lewin's responsibility. In the Department of the Prime Minister, Alex handled Environment, Heritage and Aboriginal issues under Simon Collison's direction, proving his loyalty to the party by white-anting the present Prime Minister from within. Taking the advice of his bureaucrats, the PM was more and more out of step with majority community opinion on such issues. He kept getting it so wrong that it was enough to lose him the next election, if only the Opposition had a credible leader to put up against him.

Reg Rufus had a plan. 'If the Environment policy's right, John will be sitting pretty. He'll go into the next election untarnished by unemployment and the other intractable things and he can snatch fucking victory from the jaws of defeat.'

Rufus had arranged for a vacancy to come up in a safe seat in the lower house about six weeks before the most likely date for the next election. When that happened, Lewin would resign from the

Senate, contest and win the seat in the House of Representatives at a by-election and be in position to challenge the incumbent leader. Rufus had the numbers worked out. From there he would sweep the party into office. In other words, Alex was looking at the next Prime Minister of Australia across the breakfast table, who gave a gracious nod, faintly curling his lips, as the strategy was revealed.

'There's no one else,' smiled O'Rourke.

'The essential part is getting the Environment right,' Rufus went on. 'It's the only baggage John's carrying. That's where you come in, mate.' Rufus looked Alex up and down. 'Simon reckons you're the best person around for that. You know the sensitivities seat by fucking seat. John reckons he can work with you.'

Alex saw at once the position he was being put in.

'You'd take leave from PM's and go on to John's personal staff. Sorry about the drop in pay. You can see how important this is. You're not going to breathe a word of this to anyone, comrade?'

Valerie, who was sitting beside Alex as they had sat so often on the sofa in front of the television in her Canberra house, adjusted her seat. She bumped Alex as a reminder that he must never do anything to cross Reg Rufus.

'We know how much you owe to Val here –' Rufus was unstoppable, '– so she came along this morning too.'

Alex had always wondered when Valerie would call in the debt. He figured that it depended on the nature of her feeling for him. If she was actually in love with him, she would want her pound of flesh. If she was a mate, she would let it go, until she needed something that only he could give. The longer she waited, the more likely he would have the capacity to deliver with interest.

Rufus was speaking again. 'You might have hoped to work in Val's office for the election run-up. Most probably Val will stay with the Social Justice portfolio. That's an important area too. I'm not denying that. Probably more to your taste than Environment and all that basket-weaving stuff. Still and all. I wanted you and Val to have an opportunity to discuss it so we can all feel good about it. We've all got open minds, son.'

Valerie put down her coffee and moistened her lips before speaking, with the privilege of past intimacy, directly to Alex. 'I'm happy either way. I'd love to have you in my office, but what Reg is outlining I find really exciting. For you as well. I'd like you on my team, but the party's interests come first. It's your choice, mate.'

Handing Alex across to Senator Lewin, moving her protégé closer to the heart of power, Valerie showed herself as a good judge of talent.

Before Alex could respond, John Lewin weighed in. 'You see how much faith we – I'm acting on Simon's advice, I share his assessment from what I've seen of you in our casual chats around the traps, Alex, so I say we – you see how much faith we're putting in you. I'm quite confident you can deliver, if that is what you want to do for us. I'll appreciate it personally, of course, and consider it quite within your rights to ask what we are going to do for you in return.'

Then Reg Rufus cut straight across the man's smarminess. 'What John's saying is that we'd want you to be cut in.'

'The division of the spoils in the event of victory,' Valerie interpreted with a smile. But Alex had no need of her conspirator's intervention.

Senator Lewin was leaning forward. 'Which way do you plan to go, Alex?'

'Preselection next time round,' suggested Rufus, yawning at the technicalities, 'if you want politics. Or you could head up a bloody government department, as appropriate.'

'We'll need top-level administrators in those areas,' explained Simon Collison, with the bureaucrat's regard for the appearances of propriety. Young Alex Mack would have to be seen to deserve his rise. 'Things went wrong last time through lack of expertise. In Environment, Heritage and the rest –' Collison's voice trailed off in ultimate disdain for such Micky Mouse areas, leaving John Lewin, moving further forward, to repeat the question. Under the table Alex felt the prickle of a grey worsted knee rubbing against his thigh. Just a feeler. The future Prime Minister. Alex blushed at the honour. Or was it to test, to find out what he was made of?

Reg Rufus chuckled. 'If you're worried that Val will think you're a bit of a tart to go rushing into the arms of the Environment, well, all that's understood between friends.'

'I'm not a politician,' Alex said. It was one of the few things he said at the meeting.

'Too early to tell,' quipped Val.

'He's a firstclass policymaker,' observed Collison.

'So that's it,' declared Rufus, and the deal was done. If and when Lewin won the election, Alex would have his pick of government jobs. Rufus was already on the way to catch his plane. He shook hands all round to seal the deal. Although he had not warmed to Alex, he was confident about what he was doing.

Collison had a nine-thirty meeting with the state government. Someone was needed to escort the would-be Prime Minister to his next commitment. Alex did not want it to be him. He needed to crash. Valerie would not have minded a chance to talk over what had happened with Alex either, but she had appointments too. Which way are you going, they were all asking each other. Alex succeeded in sending Simon Collison and Valerie off in a taxi together, which left him standing outside the building with Senator Lewin for a confirming moment.

'I feel comfortable with you on board,' was the Senator's way of putting it. His hand was cold and soft, squeezing Alex's.

'It's a privilege, John,' said Alex, speaking straight to the heart of his benefactor's ego.

'We'll get there, eh! Together!'

The Senator looked around for any possible audience, observers or spies, as he stepped with all his emanation of public dignity, which would soon be power, into the idling taxi. Alex listened for Lewin's cheery instruction to the driver. 'Broadway. News Inc. Thanks, cobber.'

As he walked through the revolving door into the hotel lobby, permitting himself a wide and refreshing yawn, Alex wondered whether these powerbrokers would have made the same proposition to him had they known how he spent the night. Power did not stop its roll for such things. If there was a mess later on, power merely rolled over the squashed bodies of those in the way. But he might have been more tempted by preselection for a safe seat in parliament had he not come from fucking with Ziggy Vincaitis, who had consummated their relationship at last. Or violated it. Some things were best kept out of the way. Which way did he want to go in anything? Up, was the lift button he pressed, feeling like a helium balloon, inflated with promises and hot air.

~

Alfonzo was good with the baby. He pressed her against his heartbeat as if she were part of him. He turned out to be better fitted to the domestic routine than Wendy, who made an uneasy and restless mother. He kept Wendy company while she fed Cassie, or got up in the night, sometimes letting Wendy sleep on, wrapped the baby in a blanket and took her out on the deck where he would pace up and down with her in the warm night breezes, in the clatter of the leaves, or take her down to the beach in the hope that the waves would stop her crying. But if she was hungry or had wind, the waves made no difference.

Once Wendy woke in the night and found Alfonzo and the baby gone. She called out blindly and, grabbing a flimsy robe, ran outside, ran down to the beach where she could hear the baby crying. Alfonzo was walking about, holding Cassie tightly in his arms, as if deafened to her cries by the roar of the sea and the magnitude of the night. Wendy seized the baby from his arms in a tender scoop and rocked her on her breast, cooing, 'It's all right, it's all right.'

'I couldn't sleep,' he said. 'She was calling.'

'It's too cold for her out here.'

'She's wrapped up,' he replied angrily, putting a hand to Wendy's neck.

'What the hell are you doing?' she asked him, unsettling his arm.

But he put his arm round her shoulders and they walked

together back to the house, the breeze wafting Wendy's hair and picking at her robe as she held the baby. Wendy felt Alfonzo's possessiveness in the pressure of his hand on her shoulder. He would never let them go. And the baby was more important to him than she was. The baby was the one good thing in his life, a pure and innocent thing that held the hope of putting a new, decent appearance on his existence. But Wendy knew Alfonzo was jealous of the distance that had opened between them since Cassie arrived. She could not do anything about that. There was not enough of her to share.

Kicking the sand with her feet as they crossed the beach under a sky of stars swept free of cloud, with the weight of Alfonzo's arm heavy on her shoulder, Wendy looked at the crescent moon. It was like a high-prowed canoe. She gave the laugh of a child, bewildered by her incapacity to resolve her thoughts. Alfonzo's arm did not move.

6

ONE day, when she was by herself in the homestead at Whitepeeper, Elspeth came to the door and found two men who asked whether she would mind if they camped out at the Walls of China and did some exploring. They would not disturb anything, they promised. From the small plane he had flown over the property, Fritz Vogel had seen through the surface of the land with his X-ray eyes to pictures of time beneath. Now the geomorphologist wanted to get closer. He laughed with his eyes in gruff, ironic modesty, rubbing his grizzled beard and staring at Elspeth as she made up her mind.

Nicknamed Fritz in childhood for the local Barossa sausage, Vogel had spent his life in the bush, continuing the tradition of his missionary-scientist ancestors in his own way, as a true Australian old-timer who was interested in everything and believed in nothing. He did not believe in civilisation. His geomorphology was a means of exposing human vanity to the cheerful indifference of physics and chemistry and the epochal range of creation. He merely nodded when Elspeth agreed.

His companion, Ralph Kincaid, was different. Humble rather than modest, careful and organised in all he did, the anthropologist had come from an exhausted Welsh coalmining village via Cambridge University to a lectureship in Australia, where he found himself digging again, as his fathers had done, only this time through millennial layers for the fragile leavings of an indigenous culture that was not his own. He measured what he did from a distance, with the greatest respect for the smallest thing that might provide a clue. Now Senior Curator at the Museum of Australia, Kincaid was the foremost scholar of what he affectionately called Australia's Prehistory. Was there any time *before* history? Kincaid scrupulously referred to the period before writing, for which there were no written records. But it was his professional mystery to know that all was writing – stone-tools and flints, rock carvings and fossils, lines painted on bodies that mimicked lines found drawn across the earth – to be deciphered vertically as a site was dug.

The hints at Lake Moorna were littered over the surface too. Middens of shells, one hundred miles from the nearest river, five hundred miles from the sea, petrified firewood, teeth and vertebrae of extinct megafaunal wombat and emu and kangaroo.

With Elspeth's permission, Kincaid and Vogel made tests and took samples, preparing to corroborate a theory back in the lab. Before the last Ice Age that great prehistoric lake had contained fresh water for possibly ten, twenty or thirty thousand years. Its shores, fringed with reeds, had been rich in mussels and shellfish, its surrounds lushly pastured and forested; its hills may even at times have been capped with snow. Here, in what was now a flat, parched, barren landscape, people could have lived a pleasant lakeside existence abundant in fish, flesh and fowl.

Then, towards the end of their dig, the discovery was made that Kincaid and Vogel scarcely dared hope for. They did not attempt to remove anything at first. Kincaid insisted that they should record as many details as possible while leaving excavation for a later, better prepared expedition. They were curious and impatient, however, and eventually conceded, each weighing the question with the other, that some small samples could be removed temporarily for laboratory examination. It was thus from one or two carefully isolated bones of a skeletal body left in the sand that she was found. A young woman, cremated, her burnt bones marked with red ochre for subsequent burial. And if there were rites of burial, there was the evidence of human consciousness creating meaning beyond itself: a story of dying as the completion of a process that began with birth and continued in an afterlife for the dead or the bereaved, in this world or some other. That was the message of the creature they named Moorna Woman after the lake where she had lain for thousands of years.

Fritz Vogel and Ralph Kincaid could not contain their excitement when they drove over to the homestead to pass on the news and take a hot bath. When she heard the details over dinner, Elspeth realised that what was there was beyond possession by anyone. She was justified after all, she said to Andrew, with whom she had argued about it, in giving them permission to carry out fieldwork at the Walls of China. She was now the custodian of Moorna Woman's shrine.

When his own personal file arrived from the archives of the Department of Aboriginal Advancement, *Cleve Gordon, date of birth recorded as 10th of March 1952*, he could not bring himself to open it straight away. He took the file home and spent the evening going through it, trying to connect himself with the papers that bore his name. He read in one document that his parents, being unable to support their children, had requested the authorities to find another home for their little 'yella fella', to give him the chance of a better life. The report confirmed that the children were in a state of neglect and that alternative homes would be required for the other children too. The Welfare's elaborate kindliness was justification for breeding people out. It was recorded that the child had specifically asked to be transferred to the Catholic orphanage where he could be like all the other little children. Cleve did not recall that. Nor had any reference to his Aboriginal descent been made at the orphanage. The Adamses never pretended he was their own, but only slowly, secretly, at first, had he begun to think of himself as black. That was when he started seeking out the people in the city park after school.

His file recorded his progress until he reached the minimum school leaving age of fifteen. After that it was silent, the Welfare having done its duty by Cleve Gordon. There were no records of other family members. And asking old Joe about his twin brother and missing younger sister was like interrogating a wombat. He could not even say whether they were dead or alive. Rhonda told Cleve that their eldest brother Arthur had died in hospital of hepatitis B. She told him about Danny too, about the time Danny came back to them, a few years ago, and was picked up by the cops for stealing a car, and resisting arrest, and was taken away again.

Rhonda moved into Wentworth with a white bloke called Lance Strickland who gave her a roof over her head. Old Joe, who had been counting on Rhonda for his old age, stayed out of the way at Wilga. When he drove over for the housewarming, Cleve could see that Rhonda had it rough with Lance. Her face was puffy and she had dark rings around her eyes. But Rhonda wanted no pity.

'Anything I can do?' Cleve asked the woman he called sister.

'Just because they reckon you're family now doesn't give you the right to interfere,' Rhonda replied with a laugh.

The file on Daniel Gordon took a long time coming and was far thicker than Cleve's own. It recorded every stage of Danny's institutionalised life, and the inability of anyone who wrote the successive reports to see hope for this young man. Cleve was repelled and angered by everything he read in his twin brother's file. It was too bald, too grim, to make any sense by itself. And the file did not include Daniel Gordon's present whereabouts, which unsettled Cleve.

Of Pauline Gordon, the missing younger sister, there was no trace, no file on anyone of that name.

~

Josie pushed through the crowd of people at the celebration to offer her laughing congratulations to Cleve. The community hall was completed at last.

'You're a hero,' she said as she raised her beer can.

Sister Mary Thomas watched the two of them together. She wondered if Josie's devotion was a sin, or whether it was less Cleve himself than the cause of Cleve that engaged the young woman's spirit. Mary Thomas did not oppose the association as long as there was no gossip. For the young women who came to the school, the town was a testing place, as she remembered from her own time. Isolated and exposed, you came to know your maturing needs and reactions in every fibre of your body, which was a good thing too if you were to make your vows. Then the town became your family and you did not expect to part from it until you went to the Sisters of Charity retirement home in the Blue Mountains. The struggle was to keep the school going, and for that Josie had to stay.

But Josie could no longer take faith on trust, unaskingly, as Mary Thomas did. There had been a change, by virtue of her association with Cleve. *He* was her commitment, not the world. She asked herself difficult questions and demanded rigour in the answers the church gave. In this regard she was influenced by Cleve. She was ready to look again at what she had set aside to enter the novitiate. That was her act of choice – then. Now she fancied herself as a soul blazing in the flames of intellectual debate and wondered how she could live that fantasy and still stay on the path she had chosen – a dilemma, she admitted to herself, that meant movement.

Josie did not discuss her faith with Cleve in so many words but as his politics became more radical she bore witness to his hardening realisation that God was only grace for the human struggle here and now. That was what she saw in the pools of Cleve's eyes, the set of his jaw, the spring in his short wiry hair and the tension of his mouth.

~

The satisfying immensity of God, the beauty of Christ, the real presence of Cleve, the fertility of the earth she worked with her hands, her own multiple selves as a woman, each one capable of achieving its fulfilment: these were the things that floated in Josie's mind as she knelt alongside Mary Thomas, weeding in silence in the vegetable garden behind the schoolhouse. It was November when the old nun tripped on the hose. Over the pile of weeds in her arms, Mary Thomas failed to see it lying in ambush, like a snake, on the brick path to the garden. She fell and broke her hip. As soon as she reached the hospital, carried there on a stretcher in an ambulance, the doctor gave her a painkilling injection for the agony, but Sister Mary Thomas was immobilised. The next day the ambulance drove her to Mildura from where she was flown to Adelaide for a hip replacement in Calvary Hospital.

Like most of the rest of Nulla, Cleve came out into the street when he heard the ambulance siren. It was seven in the evening, a lovely warm violet twilight with the smell of newly mown lawns sweet in the air. Cleve had mowed the lawn around his office during the afternoon. Grass grew fast at this time of the year. When he found out who was in the ambulance, he walked over to the convent school to see what he could do to help the situation. Josie was surprised to find him waiting for her when eventually she got back. She had waited with Mary Thomas at the hospital until the old woman fell asleep. She was still in shock from the spectacle of the poor old nun moaning helplessly, before the painkiller took effect.

She poured out a glass of sherry for herself and one for Cleve. There was nothing else in the place. She found some cold chicken in the fridge and prepared a salad, snapping off and washing leaves from one of Mary Thomas's lettuces. Josie wanted to talk.

'I could end up staying here,' she said as she raised her glass to Cleve, acknowledging in her tone that it was her dread, yet a fate that beckoned if Sister Mary Thomas did not convalesce properly.

Cleve smiled at her agitation. 'Were you planning on going?' he asked back.

'I'll be needed to run the school. Single-handed. I know I sound selfish, worrying about myself like this, it's only that I always thought it would be my free choice, to stay or go.'

'You're good here. You could do a lot more with the school. Anyway, you don't have to do whatever they tell you.'

'Yes, but I never thought that job would come to me.' She put the plates on the table. 'Sit down. Eat something. It's late. Are *you* staying, Cleve? We'll all move out some time.'

'Why do we need to?'

'Because there's work to be done!' she almost shouted.

'There's important work here too,' he replied gently.

Josie finished her glass of sherry and poured them both another.

'I'll stay if you stay,' she proposed. 'I don't know that I'm ready to do it on my own.'

'Being a nun must be lonely,' he responded. 'It's a lonely vocation.'

'Are you turning me down?' she laughed.

'I only meant that you don't leave yourself much room,' he explained.

'What about you? It's not easy for you either, is it? All eyes are on you in this place, in your role, first DAA liaison officer. They're all waiting for you to slide.'

She tidied the meal things away, clumsily made a pot of tea, and turned off the bright kitchen light to stop the moths and insects batting against the wire screens. They sat in darkness and Josie continued to speak fast and strangely to Cleve about what they could do in the town, what they could do in the world, what they could make of themselves and their visions and beliefs through their powers of acting and doing. She poured out her wrangling religious doubts, not about her vocation, but about the form of things, the strait-jacketing of a system that provided all the answers, and her conviction that even the orders of theology must be changed. She and Cleve were suddenly free, and power-ful, together, as if in their talk this night they could create a new earth and new heaven.

At about eleven o'clock Cleve got up to go home. Josie was exhausted from the emotion of Sister Mary Thomas's accident. She was overstimulated too, yawning uncontrollably then giggling at herself. She did not want Cleve to go, and he was as reluctant to leave. Nervously she stayed sitting when he got up and, reaching for his hand to hold him from going, bowed her head, turning her face away, to prevent their eyes from meeting.

'Josie,' Cleve said, firmly squeezing her hand.

'Don't go,' she whispered. Then she bounced up, standing squarely in front of him, and looked him in the eyes, her short wispy hair tangled round her face. She took his other hand and they stood together for a time, their clasped hands swinging, before he brought her two hands together in a double clasp that became a troth.

'Too much has happened,' he prevaricated. 'You need some sleep.'

'I'm tired,' she shrugged. 'No, I'm happy.' Then she could stop herself no longer. 'Stay a bit.' She kissed him on the lips. A little peck. A trial. Once. Twice. He put his arms tightly round her and when their bodies touched, with the soft flesh and hard bone pressed together, their mouths meeting in a kiss, it was impossible any more to heed the barriers they had set up.

'No,' he moaned. 'Not you. Not this, Josie?'

'I want you to stay,' she said.

'Is it all right?' he asked. His hands were running all over her. 'We shouldn't,' he said, burying his face in her shoulder.

'My darling, my darling,' she murmured in his ear. 'There's nothing wrong. There's no sin.'

He left in the dark, praying that no one would see him. A dog barked, then gave up as he passed quietly through the sleeping streets. Lying in her bed, Josie gave an impatient, blissful sigh as she bade her farewell to the Immaculate, the Virgin Mother.

With Sister Mary Thomas away, Josie took over the workload at school but every waking moment her mind was pulled in to contemplation and anticipation of Cleve. He was the same. In those days and nights they recklessly pursued an uncertain passion, unable to control the delights and compulsions they opened up in each other as they pushed what they had started towards conclusion, testing not only each other but also the decisions they had made about vocation, faith, work and partnership. To be with each other on those mild nights of early summer in the old school buildings only accentuated the loneliness and repression of their lives in the town, which meant recognising that neither of them thereafter could go on in the way they had done.

After ten days in hospital, Mary Thomas returned to Nulla and started to walk again with the help of two sticks. Josie ministered to her. Cleve might come to the convent for an evening meal, linger and then leave. Sometimes, going down the brick path behind the schoolhouse to the vegetable garden, he and Josie might tear at a bit of their passion in a hurried kiss and Mary Thomas, sensing the changed current of feeling between them, might have guessed what was going on.

One evening, on the pretext of collecting DAA materials for school, Josie called at Cleve's house, after Mary Thomas had settled for the night. With the blinds down, the curtains closed and the lights on in the front room, they had the opportunity to lie in each other's arms on the thin mattress of Cleve's iron-frame bed at the back of the house. The encounter was fleeting, furtive. Only within the close sphere of their togetherness were they unashamed, or unperturbed by what they were doing. When she got back from Cleve's house that night, Josie went to her convent bed in a troubled, irritable mood. Sister Mary Thomas was calling for her, calling out her name in a dream.

When the team of geomorphologists, archaeologists and anthropologists from the Museum of Australia came on their expedition to Whitepeeper to excavate Moorna Woman, Elspeth alerted Cleve. She thought, as Aboriginal liaison officer, he ought to know what they were finding there.

Later Cleve told Josie what Elspeth had told him about the discoveries at Lake Moorna. Prehistory was outside his range; what could be made to happen in the immediate future was his concern. But Josie was curious and asked if she could go with him to the dig. She had retained her cold, intrigued hostility towards Elspeth.

The track was a long scar across the dry bed of Lake Moorna, pointing like an arrow towards the curving lunette of the Walls of China. A settlement had grown at the base of the sandhills: tents, cars, trucks, people, and ropes and orange plastic flags to mark off the excavation of soft sand, where mounds of darker earth were thrown from under the pink surface.

Elspeth had claimed for herself the role of documenting the occasion and went about taking photographs. Ralph Kincaid, who hoped to keep a tight rein on any information about the site, could hardly refuse her that desire. Nor, despite his concern that some important and fragile object might be crushed, was he able to deny her equestrianship either. Elspeth rode her pony around the site. She bent from the saddle and shook Cleve's hand before he had time to introduce Josie. Then the two women shook hands, Elspeth reaching her tanned arm down.

'Haven't we met before?' Elspeth asked. She was fair-haired and stylish where Josie was dark-featured and brusque. Elspeth seemed bred in her jodhpurs, where Josie by contrast was strangely natural, like running water. The novice made Elspeth feel there was a pulse missing in herself. Josie's skin was so white. Elspeth had too many powdered-over lines and shadows.

Ralph Kincaid reacted warily to Cleve Gordon, who was introduced to the excavation team as the local Aboriginal official. Fritz Vogel slapped him on the back.

'Do our people know what you're doing here?' Cleve inquired uncomfortably, as was expected of him.

'Back in Melbourne they know,' replied Kincaid. 'We haven't been able to find the right people to ask out here. Maybe you can help us with that, Mr Gordon. Mrs Findlay says there's no one around who knows anything about this place. As far as her knowledge goes. It's a long time ago we're dealing with. It would be a pretty remote connection to anyone alive today.'

It was Ralph Kincaid's supercilious joke.

Over at the main digging place people were bent over a trench or standing in a pit, prising things loose, bringing them to the surface, placing them immediately in special containers and labelling them. There was a hubbub of excitement, and faces wore worshipful expressions. Bone by bone, section by section, Moorna Woman was raised. Cleve looked at the bright bones, perfectly preserved and recognisable through the pink earth. He brought his face up close to smell what was deposited there. Sand trickled back into the hole as people moved about. In the layer where the bones had been lying nothing had moved since the grave was made. That particular composition of soil and conditions, dryness and heat, had protected the skeleton from time immemorial until now.

'Makes Jesus Christ look like yesterday,' Josie said, giving voice to her awkward wonder. Cleve reached back to touch her, to steady himself, as he bent over the pit.

Josie was amused to see the party of men paying such homage to a woman. They reverenced her body, then dismantled it and removed it piece by piece into their containers for transport to their faraway laboratory where they would examine her for the power they could derive from her secrets. These scientists were her suitors and wooers. How could they ever know what she was: virgin, priestess, mother, whore, queen or goddess?

During the elaborate dig another figure had been found nearby, a younger partner named Moorna Man. His body had been coated in red ochre before he was laid in the ground, uncremated, a stretched-out corpse. It was another ritualised burial.

At lunchtime Andrew Findlay drove up with hampers and Elspeth poured out red wine for all those who would drink. Water would have been better, thought Josie, who was needing her hat. It was too hot for wine, the sky cloudless and the air still, the land disappearing to vanishing point in shades of cockle-shell pink, pumpkin and terracotta across the sunken expanse. The only sound, apart from the shouting and chattering of the intrusive humans and the yapping of their dogs, was the long repeated cry overhead of a solitary crow. Josie picked at her food and listened as Fritz Vogel told Elspeth what he knew of the local history.

According to Vogel the last Aborigines had left the area in the 1920s. The overlanders had dispersed the blacks who put up the resistance. Then sheep and the rabbit plague had destroyed their traditional lands, and disease and white people did the rest. The last people had worked for Elspeth's greatgrandfather, living half their lives in a bush camp on the property. After that some others came back, wanderers, itinerant workers. People moved on from place to place until the time came when no one could say the whereabouts of the last people who belonged to this particular place, or the last who spoke its language, if there were any speakers left. Whitepeeper, Vogel added, got its name from the green-grizzle-haired old guide who led the early explorers through the land with yamstick and firestick, the elder who was captured by Vogel's compatriot Ludwig Becker in luminous watercolour before the artist succumbed to dysentery and death in the bush. Fritz Vogel had a prospector's mentality. He asked no one's permission to make his discoveries. But by way of self-justification he lamented the lost old people whose permission he would have sought if they had still been around.

'Time immemorial we were all brothers and sisters, anyroad,' he concluded. 'One big family.'

'But not today,' Elspeth sardonically reminded him, as if she were speaking on Cleve's behalf. 'Who do *you* think owns the site, Cleve?'

'You own it, don't you?' Cleve tossed back.

'We're the leaseholders,' she said carefully, 'but what do we own? We can't own thousands of years.'

'That's one for the lawyers,' groaned Andrew. 'They'll probably take another thousand years to figure it out.'

'It's the secret that's valuable,' whispered Josie. 'That's what we're really seeking.'

'What secret?' asked Elspeth.

'The knowledge,' Josie said.

'She's right,' Kincaid pondered aloud. 'It's the knowledge we're after and whoever is in a position to make that knowledge available to the public has a moral claim to the material.'

'I don't know about that,' said Cleve. 'I don't know who can say.'

'Anyway, we mustn't waste the daylight.' Kincaid directed his remarks at Cleve. 'This is a most important day. I'm glad you could come along.'

In the glaring afternoon heat the visitors continued their work. Andrew lost interest and drove off to check the water for the stock. Elspeth took Cleve aside and asked him to come back another day when the scientific party had gone. She wanted to talk the meaning of the site over with him. From the stilted reactions of the professionals to Cleve's presence, Elspeth saw that the immense resonances of Lake Moorna were more complicated than she had realised. She wanted the advice of this capable, courtly man.

Josie ran her eyes around the great shining saucer of land and sky, alone at the foot of the dunes, while Cleve heeded Elspeth. Moorna Woman's bones were inseparable from the place itself, she reasoned, inseparable from this concavity, this once-upon-a-time lake of plenty, this low vessel that bore her, this almighty pockmark on the earth's surface. This – all that she saw, high up into the sky – this site, this formation of God's earth, gave Moorna Woman to them not as a prize, but as a trial – ambivalent and testing, Josie felt, as if it were the stirring in her own body.

'What did she want?' Josie asked, when Cleve came back to her.

'She wants a different perspective on what she's dealing with. I'll have to seek counsel.'

'It is a test,' Josie said. 'She has been revealed from out of the earth in order to test us.'

Somewhere along the road back, where a grown-over track led off between two fences and the slightly rising ground was wooded with low sparse belah and rosewood, Cleve turned and found a place where they could be out of sight. They climbed through the fence and walked into the bush through the thin crackling grass until they found an open place to spread the rug, where there were no ants. The light was dappled through the shading trees and the ground was scattered with soft, curled grey leaves that were like ash. They passed the softdrink bottle and ate slices of the cake in Josie's bag, sitting side by side, touching each other, leaning against each other, feeling no apprehension here in the bush away from town as they undressed and lay naked on the rug, holding each other, feeling their intimacy expand to fill the sky.

For all the fearful stories that were told around her as a girl, Josie never thought it would happen to her in these unorthodox circumstances. She had imagined herself immune, she supposed. Others in this predicament lived far away in place and time – like medieval Eloise and Abelard. She thought of her mother, Audrey unmarried Ryan, whom she had always judged so harshly. She cried over it in bed at night. To have a child would change her life and not to have the child, she admitted, would change her calling. What sort of example would she be setting to the weak flesh of others if she had an abortion against God's will? The very word itself was sin.

'You!' Cleve spluttered when she finally told him. Then he saw how upset she was and he brushed her arm. 'But you can't have a baby –'

'Not now,' she said, 'not like this. But I'm going to, unless I do something about it.'

'It's no Immaculate Conception then?' Cleve rejoiced.

'It's my problem,' she stated firmly.

'It's *our* problem. We've been bloody irresponsible. We could get married. If you want to go through with it. If you want to have it. Damned if you do and damned if you don't, eh?'

'You're not suggesting I don't,' she said flatly. 'Do you think it's a joke?'

'You ought to know what you want,' he said, starting to get cranky.

'I want you to pretend none of this ever happened.'

Cleve shook his head. They were in it together. Yet Josie saw that it was not something he would ever have chosen – not her, not her child – when he was uncertain enough about his own life. She had faith that she could help him, but it must be something he chose. His commitment to work for those he acknowledged as his people was a fragile vow that could shatter easily and leave him sinking into powerlessness, uselessness and self-destruction.

She developed a cold logic about it. 'If I wish to continue my work, my vocation in holy orders, then I cannot have this child. Which is more important?'

'You'll get rid of it? It's against everything the church teaches. I'll marry you, Josie,' Cleve said.

'That's not necessary.'

Josie cried again that night. Cleve was willing to marry her out of gallantry but it was not what he wanted. He did not love her, although she had tried to make him and had only caught herself in the process.

After two days of thinking he said to her solemnly that if she wanted to leave the order, he would marry her. They would have the baby together. They were on the grass outside his office by the Portacabin steps. If they spoke too loud, Ida Reardon would hear what they were saying. The child would be Aboriginal. Was Josie prepared for that? There was modesty in the way he asked her and she might have blessed him for it.

'I can give you a home of sorts,' he promised, 'once I'm promoted to Wagga Wagga. You'll have to tell Sister Mary Thomas It's better to bring it out into the open.'

'She won't be too surprised.'

'Others won't like it.'

Josie saw how people would use it against Cleve, to damage his reputation. She left it at that, asking for time to think. And time was pressing. She saw that Cleve was opening a way for both of them but she wanted Cleve to soar higher, to be what he was capable of being. It was too early for him to stop finding out who he was. She knew he was kind and decent. She worshipped him. But she did not know if worship was love.

She told Cleve he must not try to stop her, nor ask any questions, nor discuss what had happened with a living soul. She was going interstate for an abortion. She had no grievance with him. She cherished him in her heart. It was her decision and she took full responsibility.

'You'll need money?' he asked.

'You can give me some if you like. But listen to me, Cleve. I might repent but I don't regret anything.'

'How could I regret either?' he answered her. He had tears in his eyes. 'I hate to think of what will happen to you.'

'Don't think about it. There are more important things. No one need ever know. Ever.'

The event was given to her, in solitude and mystery. She would not take it to Father Frank for confession.

When Christmas came and the school was silent for eight weeks, it was perfectly natural for Josie Ryan to pack her suitcase, put away her personal things and take the bus out of Nulla, changing buses at the next town, all the way to Adelaide. She need not have said anything to Mary Thomas. But on the evening prior to her departure, sitting together at the table for the last time, Josie told her what she would not even tell Cleve. She would have Cleve Gordon's child. He had offered to marry her out of duty, but she would not accept his offer and stand in the way of his prospects. She did not tell Mary Thomas that Cleve did not love her. She said that as far as Cleve was concerned she would terminate the pregnancy during the summer holidays and would continue her novitiate and her work in this school and this town or in another.

Sister Mary Thomas drew breath. What was done to flesh was never undone.

But what she actually proposed to do, Josie went on to explain, was far different. She had discovered that her vows were impossible for her. The right thing was to back away. She was going back to her mother in Adelaide to have the child which would grow in the love of its heavenly father without it mattering that the earthly father was absent. She would continue to study and to teach when the child was born. She would not abandon her work for the world. But she could not deny the child that life she and Cleve had given it, even if Cleve were left free and would never know.

'The child will be part-Aboriginal,' said the nun.

'Yes,' replied the young woman.

'You must let it have that. You must not deny it that.'

'It must have everything,' said Josie, shaking.

'Can't you be honest with Cleve?' begged Sister Mary Thomas.

'He doesn't want it,' insisted Josie. 'Not now. Not yet. There's too much else he has to do. It mightn't seem fair, but it's for the best. For now, anyway.'

Sister Mary Thomas looked with sharp understanding at the young woman. 'Bless you, girl,' she said.

Hearing those words, Josie took the old woman's hand in hers and fell to her knees, laying her head in Mary Thomas's lap where she could smell the plain washed uniform that she would never wear herself. 'Thank you, dear one,' Josie murmured from her heart.

'Will you see him before you go?'

'In the morning.' Josie bit her lip. 'I can't see him now. Not and still go through with it.'

Cleve came early and offered to drive Josie as far as Mildura. He said he had some business to do there. He did not care what comments people might pass, seeing them drive off together.

'Thanks, I've already booked my ticket,' said Josie.

'You should have thought of that earlier,' added Sister Mary Thomas. She made a pot of tea and was rather cold with Cleve.

'The order has paid for my travel all the way back to Adelaide. Thanks, Cleve, but it would not be right.'

Cleve snorted. Going off to have an abortion, Josie had a funny sense of right and wrong.

Sister Mary Thomas saw that Cleve had something on his mind and shuffled out to her vegetable garden on two sticks, leaving the two of them alone.

'I reckon you shouldn't be doing this,' he said, grabbing Josie. 'You haven't even seen the doctor yet.'

'Don't be rough,' she replied, shaking off his grip. 'I don't have much choice.'

Cleve scratched his head, then opened his hands before her in a gesture of helplessness. 'Why won't you marry me? It's my colour. Is that it? Did you just want to try me out?'

He was angry, and Josie's blood rose in response.

'Saints preserve us. How can you be so dumb? Do you think this is what I wanted? This is an ordeal I must go through. At least I have the will to make the decision and live with it.'

'You're only on about proving something to yourself, Josie Ryan. Why won't you stay with us, until your time comes. It doesn't matter what anyone says. We'll look after you.'

'Down by the river?' she asked forlornly. 'What good would that do any of us, or God's work, if I went and lived down by the river with your people?'

'You don't know God's work,' he said. 'You just think you know best.'

'Don't make it any harder, Cleve.'

Tomatoes hung among the sticky leaves like orange lights, glistening with the silver trails of slugs. Mary Thomas stopped herself hurrying back inside, hearing voices raised. She hoped Cleve would prevail, would prove himself, but she knew Josie was obdurate. He was acting out of chivalry, nothing else, and the young woman could never accept him on those terms. She was too proud for that. Josie Ryan had her own free will still.

A departure from Nulla of any duration was marked by minor formalities. It was a town in which arrivals and farewells notched an endless line for those others who simply stayed. The people from the reserve by the river, aunties and uncles and kids, and some of the struggling white mums and their little ones, formed an escort to the bus. Cleve carried Josie's single suitcase, and Sister Mary Thomas followed at a snail's pace on her sticks. Josie was the only passenger to be picked up in the town and she barely had time to kiss all the kids goodbye before the bus engine began to shudder. She shook hands with Cleve. Then he bent forward and kissed her on the cheek, clutching her. He was trying not to cry. Last of all she bundled her arms around Mary Thomas, pressing her cheek against the cheek of the old woman, who whispered: 'Bless you, dear!'

As the bus rumbled away, Cleve felt the swish of Sister Mary Thomas's habit by his side. His heart was wrung. Sister Mary Thomas looked him in the face and spoke fiercely to him. 'Shame on you, Cleve Gordon! Shame on you for what you done to that sweet girl!'

He hung his head, letting her blows of denunciation fall on him.

'It didn't ought to be like this,' he blurted when he lifted his head. Division, only division, ruled his world.

She changed her tone. 'Come and have a cuppa with me.' The old woman's mouth was twisted in an eerie grin. She was satisfied that he was capable of being contrite. But he was not ready for Sister Mary Thomas's comfort. What he wanted to do was go to the black pub at the other end of town and get plastered. Because as far as he was concerned, Josie was doing the right thing.

Cleve drove in the dust of the bus that took Josie Ryan back where she had come from. After a few drinks he had decided to go looking for old Joe.

He stopped by Rhonda's place first. Lance Strickland answered the door, looking dead evil with crusty eyes and five days' ginger growth on his wedge-shaped face. He told Cleve that Rhonda was asleep in bed feeling crook. Lance didn't let Cleve get a foot in the door. He told Cleve to look for Joe round the shantytown at Wilga, down on the dump where he belonged.

When Cleve found him, old Joe was sitting in the collapsed chair on a patch of dirt in the sun, napping. He had been having a blue with Rhonda about a benefit cheque of his that she had taken, giving him nothing in return, not even a square meal, just a white-sliced peanut butter sandwich, as if he were a lousy kid and not her old father. So he had walked off from Rhonda and Lance's place and found his mates down by the river with some beer, and when that was gone and there was no more, he had no choice but to stumble back home where he still had his own lumpy bed. He was pleased to see Cleve, this son of his, this stranger who drove up in a big white car. Old Joe put an arm round Cleve and said he was just in time to take him off to the pub. Cleve was in just the mood.

The fantastical, confused memory went back before the settlers arrived, the squatters, the overlanders and the explorers, back to the beginning. Old Joe knew the old people who fought in the area, their chiefs, warriors and women, their languages, their totems, their good tucker. He knew all that lore, not in any clear or organised way, but as a jumbled dream in his head. He knew, as he knew rock and sky, the shape of the law that underlay the stuff that swirled in his brain. That was what Cleve wanted to ask. As the whispering about Lake Moorna grew louder and more public, Cleve was disturbed that no one knew what the site meant, no one who really belonged to it.

After his visit to the dig, when Moorna Woman and Moorna Man were exhumed, he had tried to talk to Auntie Betty about it. She wailed when she heard of the bones being dug up. No matter how old they said the skeleton was or how carefully they handled the bones, she could not understand why anyone would want to do such a thing except sorcerers bent on bringing evil. There was a place out there where the old people would take the young to instruct them in sacred things in the old days, where she had been taken as a protesting girl once, in the same vicinity, not a place of sand, a place of water rather, in a gorge where trees swayed above a pool like dancing bodies and the walls were carved and painted. That, Cleve guessed, might have been the rock-art gallery Elspeth had driven him to see. Auntie Betty told the story of the giant red kangaroo who was chased by spirits across the land in the direction the waters ran when the rivers were in flood. The kangaroo left his footprints in the string of lakes that dotted the land, said Auntie Betty, dried lakes now that only filled with water when it rained in bucketloads and the land was flooded. Then people could see the route the red kangaroo had taken on his flight into the westering sun. Cleve nodded slowly, astonished to find lakes that had vanished in the last Ice Age figuring again in the old woman's yarn, her story mapping the land from time immemorial. When he asked her which people belonged out there, Auntie Betty said nothing. In her imagining it was a place of sand where the ghosts had been disturbed. Only an evil man would belong out there. *Her* people belonged with the river, as Cleve's father did. Her husband's people had belonged on the grassy plains to the north-east, like Cleve's mother's people. No one belonged out there in the middle anymore.

But Cleve only half-believed Auntie Betty. That's why he sought out old Joe. On his second glass of cold beer in the gloomy pub, Joe leaned forward like a conspirator to Cleve and said: 'That land belongs to us.'

Cleve's eyes shone in response to the dark brilliance at the heart of Joe's cloudy bloodshot eyes.

'Which land?' Cleve asked.

'All of it. From the Murray to the Darling and all its streams. All that bloody country. They came here. They never even asked us. They say they *took* it from us is a lie too. It still *is* ours. Always was, always will be. Trouble is, nothing we can do about it.'

Old Joe smacked his lips.

'Maybe you're right, old man,' said Cleve, returning from the counter with two more cold glasses, 'but it's too abstract. Can't you be more specific? You been telling me about the different mobs – the Pakaantji, the Marawara, the Ngyaampa – all the different mobs mixed round here. If there was a map, whose land would Lake Moorna be in?'

'There's no map, son. It's because we're all mixed up in it that it belongs to all of us.' Joe grinned. 'I know. If it belongs to anyone, it belongs to old Joey here. Prove that it doesn't.'

'Can you prove that it does?'

'It's my say-so, boy.'

'You need more than that, mate.'

'That's your job,' concluded Joe. 'You're the clever bugger. You know how the gubbas think. It's your job to go get it back.'

'You mean Lake Moorna?'

'Nah, all of it. Another dead one,' sighed Joe, clicking his tongue over the empty glass.

'If it's yours, it's mine,' said Cleve.

'Right you are,' quipped Joe with a wink. 'We're all family.'

Cleve changed the subject then. 'Why don't we go and find Danny? If I can find out which jail he's in, we can go and visit him.'

Joe's face became expressionless. 'Don't know where he is.'

'We can find him,' insisted Cleve. 'You can't just forget about him.'

The brash cheeky charm Joe was displaying a moment before passed as suddenly as if it were no more than a bit of fine weather, gone never to return, the misery setting in again, loss heaped on loss that Joe had suffered in his life, since the taking of those first kids broke his dear wife Mary's spirit and nothing Joe could do to change things. A shadow of misery spread purple over poor Joe's old skin. He feared what Cleve was saying. He could not face the blame that Cleve, the son he never had, might heap on him.

'And Pauline's gone too,' he muttered almost inaudibly, whining a little. Even when one loss was put right – Cleve, the family's stolen son returned, still not quite believed in by the befuddled old man – there remained countless other losses, uncompensated, inconsolable.

Elspeth could not help thinking of Whitepeeper as inalienable Masterman land. The Emperor of the Bush had been a tough trading rogue, yet a monumental figure too, as far as his great-granddaughter was concerned, whose claims were indisputable compared with any of those that came after.

She wanted to consider how the terrain might have evolved over the millennia, declaring natural boundaries of its own. She wanted to draw the moral contours, and formulate an understanding of the situation. Standing on the verandah of the homestead, she could not hear the messages of the mute land. Encouraged by Brice Masterman, the chairman of directors in Adelaide, Andrew Findlay had sold off stock when rain did not come and the country could not cope. It meant sending mediocre beasts to bad markets. Andrew was not by nature a battler. He was happy to live from day to day on a certain amount of fat. The day would probably come when he would give up struggling altogether. Then they would have to move back to the city, leaving the manager to do the work. After a while Whitepeeper would be incorporated with other Masterman Holdings properties. Or they might sell. What could not be seen from year to year was the inexorable decline of the family's Bush Empire, not through the fault of Brice Masterman as third generation scion, but by laws of change and attrition over which there was no control. The effort to preserve and value what had been inherited merely served its slow and steady disintegration.

Ralph Kincaid's correspondence from the Museum of Australia indicated no end of interest in Lake Moorna. It was the earliest recorded site of ritual burial practice anywhere and he was being pestered by requests from people all over the world who wanted to visit it. Writing to Mrs Findlay in cool confidence, Kincaid was unaware that his letters afflicted her with greater doubt than ever about what she should do.

Elspeth spread her map out in front of Cleve Gordon in his office in Nulla. For him her action was a line of smoke signalling that the land was up for grabs once again as it had been back in the pioneering days. That, indirectly, was why she was coming to him, yet without saying so. Cleve saw that it was up to him to get that land for the right people. The simplicity of Elspeth's logic, seasoned like the best timer, was a quality that held him in her thrall, giving him faith in her impulses and motives. He told her that the local people were not clear about the meaning of the site and had warned him that it was a thing of power and danger.

'It will take some research,' Elspeth said. She wanted him to be more definite than that. 'A different kind of research from Ralph Kincaid's. Research among living people. The answers may not be readily apparent.'

'There *are* answers,' Cleve responded, as if to honour Elspeth with a promise.

'Yes, but what are they?'

~

When the new school year started, Josie Ryan did not come back. Sister Mary Thomas told Cleve that a new teacher was promised to take Josie's place after Easter. He had been offered a promotion to the regional office of the Aboriginal Lands Council in Wagga Wagga. When Josie did not come back, he wrote to her mother's address in Adelaide, but there was no reply. He asked for her address and telephone number from Sister Mary Thomas who fudged. It was as if Josie Ryan had disappeared into thin air. He worried about her, missing her company. On hot nights he found himself lying in bed imagining being with her. But when he decided to leave Nulla too, it was as if he were deciding to leave the memory of her behind.

They gave him a wild and raucous send-off in their hall – the Cleve Gordon Memorial Hall, they ribbed him – Auntie Betty and Uncle Davey, Doreen Tighe, Narelle, Jason, Kerry, the football boys and all the kids who were like family to him.

After he left Nulla, he found that Josie did go out of his mind.

He stood with Elspeth on the edge of the lake. The dig site was like a graveyard where the gravediggers had been interrupted in the midst of their work. The expected funerals were yet to come in this ancient wind-swept expanse.

'Where do you come from?' Elspeth asked Cleve. 'Have I asked you before?'

That's the billion-dollar question,' he joked in reply.

'Do you know?'

'Everyone comes from somewhere,' he said. 'I could come from somewhere out here, I reckon.'

'*Here*?' she repeated, her body stiffening as her feet pressed the earth, so that *here* meant not what was in her gaze but the very spot from which they seemed to grow.

'Maybe round here,' said Cleve, not wanting to force a precise claim.

Elspeth stepped several paces away from him onto the lunette. Where did people come from? She and Andrew had been trying to have a family for all the years of their marriage. That was its purpose. She had assumed a baby would happen with the same kind of productive efficiency that her family reared stock. On days like this when her black and grieving mood told her that once again she had failed, the world seemed to deride her and she felt such rage at the invisible forces that made things. She found it hard to accept that it was unlikely to happen, that she might as well have been a barren case of skin and bones, despite the flux, an empty ghostly presence that crossed the land leaving no trace.

She wished it was not on one of these days that Cleve had come to say goodbye. Without knowing, he was sensitive to her mood. He came up slowly behind her as she stood there, like a slender stake in the silvery land. He could not help stalking her and, when she turned to look at him, putting a hand out to touch her.

Startled, she said recklessly, 'I'm from round here too. My grand-parents had their kids here. My mother was born in that house.'

His hand was resting against the small of her back. In her present state she could have thrown herself into his arms and wept. She could have thrown herself at him. The failing was hers. Andrew was not to blame. She believed that Cleve could change her, that he could give her what she wanted, make her into what she craved to be. He was like a water-diviner who could find the fertility in this dry salty country.

But she held herself back. She would do none of that. With her iron will she hooped herself in. It was too late. None of that could happen. It was an impossible, disturbed dream. Elspeth stepped away from Cleve's touch with force and his hand fell to his side. She walked briskly up the sandy pink slopes of the Walls of China to where she could look back at him from a higher vantage point. He had not moved from the spot. He stood waiting, a straight dark figure in the low light. He desired her, but he did not know whether she was friend or enemy. The sun was setting over the sunken plain. It blinded her to see his black silhouette outlined against the burning gold. They stared at each other, alone out there, feeling a force of recognition pass between them.

DANIEL II

DANNY Gordon had a Koori mate called Oscar who could read and write. They never worked out exactly what their relationship was. They were mates, anyway, and since Oscar was due for release he asked Danny if he could do anything for him. Danny's answer was go and see his sister Rhonda. Send her his love. Tell her he was fine. Tell her he would be home soon and would come and find her straightaway. Danny made Oscar promise and Oscar's promise was a serious thing. He tracked Rhonda Gordon down out west in Wentworth where she was living with Lance Strickland. Rhonda was none too pleased to see Oscar, but the least she could do was invite him in for a few drinks, since he brought greetings from her little brother. When Lance was out of the way, Rhonda told Oscar that the man was bashing her all the time and would not leave her alone. She had tried to get away back to the old place, with her father at Wilga, but Lance came after her and beat her up. He had a real violent temper on him, Rhonda said, he was real jealous, he treated her like his bloody dog and she was miserable.

Oscar asked round a few other people and they all had the same story. He went out to Wilga and they all said the same. 'Rhonda thought she was moving up town and now look what she's got herself into.'

In the pub Oscar met one of Lance Strickland's mates who said that Rhonda Gordon was a lazy fat slut. Hearing that talk made Oscar feel crook for Danny's sake. He didn't know what to do. He felt he owed it to Danny to do something. He didn't know if it was the right thing to tell his mate. Better to leave him in ignorance. Danny couldn't be much help from where he was. On the other hand, Oscar figured, Danny would be out soon and if he went blundering after Rhonda without knowing the situation, it could only make matters worse. Besides, Oscar was the only one who could tell Danny the truth.

Danny waited until his art session to ask the therapist to read the three pages of Oscar's letter. He could not read it for himself. The therapist was alarmed by Danny's reaction. She had never seen him other than calm, passive and fairly cheerful. If anything, she noticed, he didn't react to things. In one of her reports she had described him as emotionally deficient and deprived. She was surprised to see the spasm that came over him as she read out the big careful cursive script of Oscar's blunt letter. Danny shuddered in front of her. His jaws ground. His eyes rolled back until only the whites showed. There was no doctor on duty. One of the warders, authorised to act as a nurse, had a look at him. 'Bad news from home,' was the explanation. No one but the therapist read the details of the letter and no one remembered to record the incident in the daily log. It was nothing out of the ordinary.

When Danny woke from a long sleep, his cellmate asked what he was going to do.

'I'm going to sort that white bastard out,' Danny vowed.

From that day on a change came over him. He became brooding and tense. His cellmate asked to be transferred. Danny Gordon's childhood world was filled with people who were familiar and loved him, an easy world that was changing to make it harder for his people to live their lives and survive, a big, open, real world, filled with customs, stories and relationships, a world that could feed a growing child. Then that world was taken away and replaced by a different world in which he was the least wanted part. They would rather he did not exist. Yet the system existed for his sake. The warders and administrators, officials and teachers, social workers, trusted landladies and employers, all had their place in preventing his life out there in the world that surrounded his world of confinement, and since they would not set him free, he became the more determined to live by his own rules, the rules from his own world, which were the only rules he knew.

What they treated him as was a slave, despite all they said. They were his masters – all of them. What they hoped for him was that in exchange for bread and water he would be able to function as a second-class labourer, a beast of burden, forgetting who he was. That was already inside his head. He knew he could not read nor write. He knew he could not hold down a job. He knew he had no money and no chance of getting any. He knew his family were spread all over the place and did not want to know about him. Except for Rhonda. He knew, if he went out on his own, that he would always come back asking for a meal and a bed and a roof over his head. He knew he had bad thoughts. He saw bad things. He must suffer always. Yet he knew he played good guitar. He painted a good picture. He played good football. Men trusted him and came to him in need to talk about the hard way through the dark world. He knew that people respected him as a human being, even when everything said he was worth less than almost any other human being on God's earth. So a light seemed to glow within him that the confining world could never see. *They* said he should slowly die. He said, before he died, he would make *them* invisible.

Danny sat on the bunk-edge, hunched over himself, hugging his knees, rocking. He was counting the days till he got out, when he would go and save Rhonda, who merged with indistinct memories of his mother to stand for unconditional love and loving kindness such as he had known nowhere else in his life. Rhonda, his big sister, who rescued him from the Welfare when he was a kid. Rhonda, free as a bird, who somehow made sense of his useless, worthless, locked-away life.

He was let out of jail with his few belongings and his unlovely prison clothes. An unemployment benefit was supposed to come through but had not done so and no one had been notified of his release. There was no one to notify. He headed for the river. He liked to be travelling west. The east had not been kind to him. He hated the city and the sea frightened him.

The truckies who gave him lifts bought him meals or gave him smokes or small change when they heard he had nothing. The country he knew, at least, from the two or three times he had traversed it in his life, drawn in his flesh like a pattern of scars: good places and bad places, black, white, his people, other people, mates and cunts, right and wrong. His resistance endured deeper than any rock while his charm played like sunlight over a hillside and his imagination, like the sky on a bright night, created piercing patterns against an endless dark. His capacity for action was like a stone thrown through the air with perfect aim to knock out an enemy's eye. Like a seed shooting.

He slept rough for two nights on the road and had little to eat. He quenched his thirst from the taps in public toilets. He was tired and hungry when he reached Wilga. Old Joe Jones hugged his son in a hero's welcome and invited him down to the pub. But Danny only wanted to know about Rhonda.

'That's her business,' Joe said about what was happening. 'That's only a bit of nothing. Don't you go butting in.' Rhonda was in a shocking way. Strickland was a devil. But no one wanted any more trouble than they already had: battles with the government, battles with the townsfolk, sorrows with their parents and kids and brothers and sisters. It was enough to get through a day with a bit of money in your pocket. Old Joe gave Danny his canny grin. He knew how to shut up this loony jailbird prodigal son of his. 'There's someone looking for you – looking hard. One of the family come back to the roost. Your twin brother that was taken away when you were too young to remember.' What Joe said stopped Danny in his tracks. 'I never talked much about him,' Joe went on. 'You didn't need to know about him. You didn't need that worry. Not when there was so much else after your poor mother died.'

'Where is he?' Danny stammered. His face had reverted to the expression he used in prison when he was being accused of a new misdemeanour. He never knew he had a twin brother. But the world was full of things he never knew, facts and stories, and he did not doubt his old man.

'He's around. He's the Aboriginal officer over the way,' said Joe with mocking pride. 'Cleve's his name. Cleve Gordon.'

'We've got the same name?'

'Course you got the same name,' Joe laughed. 'We better give him a call. He'll be tickled pink to hear you come back.'

They telephoned Cleve's office in Nulla. Ida Reardon said he had already moved out. They called the office in Wagga Wagga. Somebody there said Cleve was away at a meeting in Sydney. Joe left a message. 'Tell him his old man rang . . .'

Danny lay awake that night wondering about this brother, out in the world all the time, while he was locked away in a world within, this version of himself to whom he was a phantom. He had not expected anything like this. Joe said they were not identical, they did not look the same at all, even though they were born the same day by the same mother, first Cleve, then Daniel. It troubled Danny mightily to consider whether this brother had been entering his mind and directing his thoughts, whether all these years his brother had been taking his thoughts and sucking his energy out of him even though he never knew. He wondered if his brother had been a comfort to him, or a curse and the cause of the loss he always felt.

In the morning, after thinking all night about these things, Danny woke and walked out into the day feeling confused and incomplete, as if he had been mugged. He reacted by focussing his thoughts. He must not waver from his path. He must not lose his way in this immense and complex world when it was *his* role to save Rhonda. Not his brother's role.

The square of thick buffalo grass was bright green outside the house in Wentworth where Rhonda and her kids lived with Lance Strickland. Geraniums ranged along the front porch, scarlet, orange and purple against the darker green concrete. Through the fly-wire of the open front door Danny could see down the dark corridor to the back door, open to light. Lance came out of the bedroom into the corridor. Hearing the latch on the front gate go clunk, he headed for the front door to investigate the intrusion. His large shadow loomed as Danny approached the front step.

'Who is it?'

The man stood behind the screen door. He had seen Rhonda's little brother Danny years ago, but did not remember him. The dark man who stood on the other side of the wire mesh looked like just another one of Rhonda's mob come to bludge.

'G'day, mate. Is Rhonda home? It's Danny.'

Lance opened the door and the two men sized each other up. Without being invited in, Danny stepped over the threshold into the house. Lance would have blocked the man's entry, but he moved sideways cautiously in the corridor to let the man pass, sensing a blind element in him. Rhonda came out from the bedroom. 'Bugger me,' she said. 'Daniel! Your mate Oscar said you was coming back.'

Rhonda wore tight jeans and sandshoes and a flamingo-pink T-shirt with a golden bird printed on it. Her eyes glittered at Danny's. Her belly bulged like a football in the tight studded jeans. The T-shirt stretched with her breasts. Her hair was thick and alive from the brushing she had given it. But it was her face that was dif-ferent – fatter, rounder, yet shrunken and aged at the same time. She put her arms round him and gave him a long tight hug, losing her-self in him. He did not know how to respond. He had been away since he was eleven, except for once.

'Oh I been missing my little brother,' Rhonda moaned.

As she released him, he examined her lined, puffy, pickled face. She could read in his eyes the distress at how he found her. She knew he had been hearing stories about her.

'You know Lance? My husband,' she asked uncomfortably.

Lance was a lanky bloodnut, with red freckles on his milky skin and a watery look in his grey eyes. He had a long scoop of a face, and a simple empty expression fed on frustration. 'I think we met,' he said.

Danny made no reply. He would not shake hands with this white bastard who was treating his sister bad.

Rhonda brought a bottle of beer from the fridge and three glasses. Lance sat on the green moquette couch in the living room and sulkily lit a cigarette. Dust rose from the seat when he thumped it, wanting Rhonda to sit beside him. Danny sat opposite on a canvas chair that pinched his back. Lance offered him a cigarette after he had lit his own – a formality merely – but although he was craving a smoke now, Danny said no thanks. Then when Lance put the packet down, he reached over and took one for himself.

'When you got out, Danny Boy?' Rhonda asked.

'I come straight here,' replied Danny, his mouth tight.

'We lost track of you all this time,' nodded Rhonda cheerfully.

Lance raised his glass of beer, which had quite a head on it. 'Cheers,' he said. Rhonda sat down beside Lance and his hand gripped her thigh.

'Yeah, Oscar said he saw you,' continued Danny intently.

'That bloke,' snorted Lance. 'He saw us and we told him where to get off.'

'It got me pretty worried,' said Danny. 'What he wrote.'

There was the sound of kids squealing as the backdoor slammed and Rhonda's two children came running in from their game. Rhonda made them stop and say hallo to Uncle Danny. The boy and girl stood side by side grinning shyly and Danny smiled back in excitement.

'What have you got for us?' asked the girl, the older of the two.

Danny winked. 'I dunno about that.'

'You kids go and play. You're always wanting something,' said Rhonda. 'Get out, you hear!'

The girl twisted on the spot, making a face, then grabbed her brother's hand and ran outside.

'You don't want to believe every story that's flying around,' said Lance in a testy, bitter tone. 'Some people just can't accept things the way they are.'

'I don't want to hear bad things happening to my family,' said Danny. 'Makes me feel real bad. I come here to check for myself that things are all right.'

'Things are all right, brother,' Rhonda replied with the force in her voice that she used to disguise what different words in other tones might have revealed. 'Don't you worry.'

Danny took a sip from his glass of beer. He was not used to alcohol. 'If he ever lays a finger on you –' he began.

But he stopped when Rhonda started to laugh. It was a harsh, full-bodied laugh. She was shaking so much that Lance joined her in a low hissing chuckle as the ripples from her body worked up his arm. 'Oh dear,' said Rhonda, wiping tears from her eyes.

'Yeah, what?' asked Lance, challenging Danny's threat.

'We don't want you putting your nose in here where it's not wanted,' said Rhonda again with that shrill force in her voice. 'We can sort out our own problems, brother. No one asked you to come round here meddling, did they, eh?'

Danny put the beer glass down hard on the table. He could not look his sister in the eye. He stood up and looked at Lance, pointing a finger at him. 'If you so much as touch her –' His voice was cold.

Lance lashed out in reply. 'I touch her all the time, mate. That's how she likes it.' He gave a jeering laugh. Danny was about to lunge at him when Rhonda jumped up and placed herself between the two men.

'You piss off now, Dan,' she whispered, in a different, low voice. 'Please.'

The quaver of her panic seemed to snake down into his throat.

Her eyes blazed into his, his sister's plea grabbing at his heart. Without saying a word, without looking back at either of them, Danny stamped out of the house into the fierce daylight, screwing up his eyes as a shield from the furnace of heat and brightness.

There were parts of the straggling, divided town where he could walk without anyone worrying and parts where he was not welcome. He knew the minute he set foot over the line. Yet he could see through all those things. It was only the address of the house where Rhonda lived that had given him a destination. Outside of it the town with its strange, pompous grandeur was a meaningless place for him. He walked past the jail with its crenellated turret, and the honey-gold church with a clover-leaf cross perched on top. He remembered that squat church from childhood, the stained-glass lights moving over the white walls and shiny floor and over the heads of the people, magic coloured spangles, making you feel safe under the protection of the holy shepherd. He remembered the feeling of that world. It was a reminder of the cup he must drink as he stood on the dry verge outside the church.

He headed back along the river with a deep tow of concentration. He found his father asleep on a blanket down by the river and sat down beside him, then after resting his legs for a while, he turned right round and walked back to Wentworth again. There was only one action he could take.

Dark fell suddenly as he came through the trees. The town lights were on across the river. Gamblers were making their way to the casino for Saturday night and the pubs were busy. The noise and smell of cooking came from the caravan park, the houseboats, the kitchens behind the pubs and behind the houses that fronted the street with doors and windows open to yards and low fences. Everywhere people were pursuing their purposes, purposes barely definable to Danny who walked like the shadow of a reed down the wide strips of grass that divided those streets. He knew he would find Strickland. The man had no excuse. Danny had warned him.

He knew that Danny would not let him go until he faced the evil he was doing to Rhonda.

Danny slipped into the noisy pub through the door that led from the men's dunny and the back lane. That way no one saw him enter. Lance Strickland stood with his legs apart in a corner of the bar drinking and laughing with his red-faced mates. He held his long pointy head high, his lank fringe tossed back. The mean grin was a slash across his face as he told stories at the expense of Rhonda and her folk. He did not see Danny Gordon come in at first, nor acknowledge him when Danny nodded along the bar. Then, with a finger in the air, Lance beckoned him over. The bloke was there with malicious intent, Lance knew, but he was confident of himself anyway and not a man to walk away.

'You looking for me, are you?' asked Lance brazenly, having no doubt of Danny's purpose.

'I want a word with you,' Danny replied. 'That's all.'

'Here's as good as any place,' the man said. 'What are you drinking, mate?' Danny was silent. He did not move. Lance went on. 'Look, you and I have got more in common than perhaps you realise. We both care about your sister, don't we? You're wanting to give Rhonda a helping hand. She appreciates that. But we don't like you listening to stories when you don't know anything about what's going on. Take the time to find out what's going on first. She means it when she's says it's none of your business.'

The more the man spoke, the less Danny was listening. He could not believe any of these words that were the devil's complications and justifications. He nodded to the exit. 'We'll talk about it outside.'

Danny felt the eavesdroppers in the pub pressing in on him as he turned and went out into the lane. He wondered if Lance would follow him.

'You're not going to bother with a cranky Abo, are you?' said one of Lance's mates. 'We're coming with you if you do.'

But at last Lance went out into the lane by himself, where Danny was leaning against the brick wall in wait.

'Look, I don't know what's eating you, mate?' Lance's mouth crinkled.

Danny moved forward, away from the wall, to face his enemy down the laneway.

'You don't know the damage you done,' Danny said. 'You think you can get off that easy.'

Lance was rubbing his left hand over the closed fist of his right. 'Me? Is that so?'

Fit and strong after his prison years, Danny sprang forward in a violent flash, pushing Lance off-balance. In the same movement he aimed a punch at Lance's head, concentrating the blow. The man fell back, his feet pulled from under him, and hit the concrete edge of the guttering in the lane with a thump, head first. He was knocked out just like that. Danny stood over him, the power to destroy pounding in his body. But he didn't kick him or hit him again. He grabbed Lance's two feet and dragged him to the end of the lane and round the corner where the garbage tins were. Then he ran.

The ambulance was never prompt on a Saturday night. By the time they found Lance and got him to hospital, the head injuries had killed him.

Rhonda cursed her brother Daniel as she wailed over Lance's body. He was no brother of hers. She had told him to keep out of it. He was crazy. He was a bloody lunatic. He should have stayed in the lock-up where he belonged. He had no idea of the price of life.

Danny picked up a car and drove across the border into South Australia. The police caught him three days later and threw him in another of the grand old river town jails, not far from the place where his father used to pick the grapes for champagne.

He lay curled on the bed in the bare cell, rocking himself. The concrete was pitted and stained. He fingered the carved graffiti on the walls, scratched out and painted over. Grey river dust caked the frosted glass of the barred window and cobwebs were slung across the corners. He was back in the lock-up again. It smelled of piss, and he was triumphant. He had released Rhonda from bondage to that devil and she and her kids were free to go back to their family where they belonged.

He heard the big feet of the constable approaching his cell, and the jangle of keys.

'You've got a visitor,' roared the voice outside as the cell door was unlocked. 'He comes with the authority of the Aboriginal Legal Service,' he announced sarcastically. Allowances had been made. 'You're right, mate,' said the constable, locking the visitor inside.

Danny looked at the man, his own age, lighter-skinned and stockier, with a plump face and deep-feeling eyes. He looked solid and proper in a jacket and tie, clothes that Danny had never worn. His hair was parted to one side and slicked back. Danny stood proudly to meet him.

'Daniel,' said Cleve. 'Do you know who I am?'

'Are you my brother?'

They looked down at their outstretched hands, big and brown. Then Cleve gave a disparaging laugh and threw his arms around Danny. Unused to physical contact, Danny merely stood and let his brother hold him.

'Don't you believe me?' sighed Cleve, shaking his head and laughing all the time. 'What's wrong? I can see myself in you. I can see Joe.'

Danny had never had much time for looking at himself in the mirror. That didn't matter, though, because he could *feel* the likeness in Cleve, the identity, the presence in this other man of a part of himself. So he let this Cleve fella hold him, rested his chin on Cleve's shoulder, let his cheek scrape against Cleve's rough cheek.

Cleve had turned round and walked straight out of the office to his car when he got old Joe's message, reaching Wilga late that night. The family was in an uproar. Rhonda was wild with rage and despair, howling at Joe and blubbering over the kids. She had lost her love. She had lost her man. She had lost the home for her kids. She had lost the only second chance in life she was ever likely to have. She blasted her idiot brother for coming barging in where he was never wanted. Why could he not have left them alone? They never wanted him back. He ought never to have come. He had been in for too many years and they should have kept him there.

The family rallied round Rhonda in support, echoing her terrible words. She swore she would testify against Danny until he came to trial for Lance Strickland's murder. She vowed to repudiate her brother's action with a vengeful ferocity and make all the family take her side. There was no good in it otherwise. Danny was no kin of theirs. He was scum. He was not fit to live.

Danny talked about how he had been prevented from contact with his family or with people from his old world and how his faith was never shaken that they were always there waiting for him to be part of them again. He talked about the person the institutions wanted to make him, an anonymous individual, with nothing, who was shoved out into the vast cold sea of society and left to find his bearings, forming whatever connections were possible, expected to be alone in the end, someone who lived, worked and died and left no trace behind. They would have cut his balls off if they could find the excuse, or burn out his brains. If they could they would have kept chains on his feet and hands.

'You survived all that,' said Cleve, absorbing Danny's distress. They had been born on the same day, in the same place, to the same mother and father.

Cleve remembered a little boy by his side. He had never known whether it was in the orphanage or in the foster family's home or later or earlier. All his life there had been an absence or a presence running beside him like a shadow that he could never grab and see but which he could never dispel. It was only in reaching a slow familiarity with this other shadowy being through adolescence and young manhood that he had come to himself. Danny had never been taken from himself in that way. He had grown up roaming across his country with his father and brothers and sisters. He knew the world that fed him before it was taken away and he was forced to carry in himself everything that remained, deep down, as society tried to annihilate it. That was the way Danny remembered Cleve, curled round him and nudging him from inside himself. After joy came sadness, sharpened by the knowledge that they were two and their union came too late.

Danny boasted about Lance Strickland. Cleve did not want to hear. For Danny his action was not born of passion or violence but coolly premeditated within his own righteous private clarity. It was the sweet and lucid action of a hero. Cleve could not bring himself to tell Danny the family's reaction. He only said that Rhonda was back in Wilga with the family, which was what Danny wanted to hear.

If only he had sought harder and found Danny earlier, Cleve raged. He could still have intervened. What was the use of his position otherwise? After a lifetime of separation he found his brother in this corner of utmost powerlessness in a wretched country jail cell. Suddenly – again – the options diminished to nothing. What could he do for Danny now? He sat on the bed clutching and stroking his brother until the constable came jangling his keys to let them know that time was up.

I could have saved you, Cleve told himself over and over again, if only we had found each other earlier.

Danny stared hollowly into space. He was reassured to have the arm of the family around him. He accepted what was happening to him – emptied of action. He knew there was nowhere else for him to go and nothing else for him to do.

From what *he* saw with *his* eyes, he was saved already.

· PART THREE ·

· THE WALLS OF CHINA ·

1

LUCKY ones had their drivers drop them right in under the awning by the front door to avoid getting wet. Almost everyone else, no matter how well equipped with umbrellas, buttoned-up raincoats and waterproof boots, was a little damp from the sudden downpour. Manhattan was after all an island breakwater to the almighty storms that late winter brought squalling in from the great ocean. The Atlantic rain paid no heed to the fact that a city stood in its path with towers of glass and spires of steel as high as the stormy clouds. Nor did the dumping rain make allowance for the density of human life, the difference of high and low, native and foreigner, rich and poor. For Jane Woodruff, rushing down the slippery sidewalk to make an appointment, the rain made no difference anyway. Hatless, coatless, without umbrella, she got her hair spattered, her calves soaked; and water creeping under her collar, she felt as high as if she had ridden the crest of a huge ocean wave from Australia to New York in a single roll. The gusts of spray and spume about her face, the wet buffeting of the crowd and the rain spitting off the road and bouncing from the fire escapes were like a continuation of her voyage. Carried along by the rain's pelting force, she walked with her head back, exalted by the soaring height of buildings that rolled upwards, like carpets, to a sky that might open up like a clear and shining deity, or was sometimes veiled and ungiving, or at other times, as on this evening, roiled in unappeasable power. The rain fell in shining silver wires from the building tops – flailing streamers tossed from a dark churning source. Lifting up her gaze, she giddily felt herself driving back down with them, plummeting vertiginously to the miry street. She had never had such a sense of the vertical as in New York.

The doorman was amused by her as he ushered her inside. Her curly dark hair flounced as she shook off the raindrops on her way through the revolving door. 'Dripping and all!' he said. Her outlandish expensive dress was darkened with damp. But it would not be too much to say, on this gloomy evening, that she glowed. She was pleased to find a padded chair waiting for her by the fire in the bar, and Cynthia Temple, laughing at Jane's incompetence, already settled with a drink.

'No umbrella? You're joking!'

'Where are they when you need them?'

'You can always buy one!'

'The prices double when it rains,' complained Jane. 'I refuse to buy an umbrella when it's raining.'

'That's exactly when you need one.'

'You see my problem.'

Cynthia lit a cigarette as she pulled the page from the *New York Times* out of her bag. She was as excited as Jane by the review for the SoHo opening and had already called Sydney, waking her assistant in the middle of the night, to read out the good bits that would be fed to Stephen Fazzoletto for the local press.

At a time when American painting, not so long ago the most potent creative force in the contemporary art world, has lost its way, comes an artist from the bottom end of the globe to show us the essentials of the art in all its majesty: color on a flat surface celebrating the visual experience of the world. Exhibiting for the first time in New York, Australian artist Jane Woodruff shows up conceptualism, arte povera, neo-Dada *and all the rest that passes for art here today as so many emperors without clothes. Perhaps it is the isolation Down Under that gives such exceptional boldness and passion to the artist's paint. Woodruff has said in an interview that, even as she welcomes a presence for her work in New York, she does not feel compelled by the maneuvers of a contemporary art practice derived from dialectics within European and American history. She defines her subject as freedom from history. Hence her loving elaboration of huge fruit, flower and marine forms as allegories of newness, mandalas of birth, growth and elemental creativity, in severely knifed paint to produce sumptuous brocades of clashing and, at last, harmonizing color. Pierre Bonnard meets Georgia O'Keefe. In the most striking work of the show,* Mango Dreaming II, *the sheer activity within the rendering gifts the viewer with the paradoxical serenity of meditative absorption. Coming from a land that still needs the archaic power of paint to turn natural force into images for humanity to value, Woodruff offers a way forward to us all.*

'Value to the tune of twenty-thousand US dollars, I hope,' commented Cynthia with a grin, 'if those museum people acquire *Mango Dreaming II.* You've come along at the right time, my darling.'

'He sounds like such an arch-conservative,' said Jane.

'Horses for courses,' replied Cynthia. 'Let them find in you what they like. The paintings are bloody good and this will certainly make the people back home sit up and take notice.'

'They have to make us into primitives, don't they?'

'We're the innocence they have lost. Historyless is how they imagine us and happy for being that way. If only they knew. The only reason we exist is because of fucking history!'

Jane drained the martini Cynthia had ordered for her, ate the olive and ordered another drink. 'I herald a new age,' she said. 'Well, I hope so.' The crude, colourful dissections of Jane's paintings showed her sharp, exuberant curiosity about life, shaped by grow-ing and saturated with meaning, like the mango seed that she knew would sprout and grow when it was chewed and suspended in water. Perhaps never again would she express herself so completely in painting, or express so attractive a self as she rose like Venus from the sea. She must relish the moment for all it was worth and understand how far she had come up the steep steps of art's pyra-mid. 'Cheers,' she grinned, dry and warm now, ready after the sec-ond martini to meet the collector who was preparing to acquire *Mango Dreaming II*.

Peter Mustafed was taken with the stories told by Jane's work.

'Australia was first depicted by men,' she said, 'nineteenth-century European explorers who took possession of the land with a panoramic gaze, placing each specimen and category within a universal hierarchy, as if they were acquiring the whole environ-ment for a natural history museum from the first day. I want to undo all of that. Painting as a woman I can't be part of that cold, abstracted, conceptual kind of exploration. I don't see myself as any sort of pioneer in that sense, a point of origin along a line of process and perspective. I refuse to be interventionist in that way. My energy comes from the continuum, the cycle of life, seeds nurtured, harvested, made into food –'

'So that's the mango?' asked Peter Mustafed. 'The food and the seed.'

'That's right,' smiled Jane. 'It's a kind of feminist version of Piero della Francesca's *Resurrection*, if you want to get art-historical.'

'I see,' he nodded. 'So you feel free to do that?'

'The mango flesh is the aura.'

'Well, that's very primitive,' the collector went on. 'You could call it anthropological.'

'But Jane's technique belongs to action painting. That's what's so wonderful.' It was Cynthia's turn to talk. 'Because that seed is an act. Is in a state of activity. It has no other condition.'

The two women were excited after their martinis and the violence of the rain outside the restaurant and Peter Mustafed, the collector who was preparing to donate Jane's work to a private museum of contemporary world art, was thrilled to be the discoverer of a new artistic front.

'Piero della Francesca, you say? I thought you dismissed the Western high art narrative as irrelevant to your concerns. Isn't that your position?'

'The *narrative* is irrelevant,' declare Jane brashly. 'Where there is a natural affinity, a crossing of energy, that can be incredibly powerful. Of course. Artist to artist direct. Piero means a lot to me. But I would never claim a line of descent or even a mediated relationship. It's just a grab.'

The gentleman laughed, then his features settled back to their usual look of boyish concern. 'I like the way you say that. What about your tribal art in Australia? How does that inform your work?'

'Aboriginal art?'

'Yes, Aboriginal art, that fascinates me. I saw a couple of extraordinary objects.'

'Objects is what they are,' said Jane confidently. 'Sacred objects. They are not art in the sense of self-expression or commodity.'

'That is what makes it work,' replied Peter Mustafed, clear and sure in his connoisseurship.

'Recently,' added Cynthia, 'some Aboriginal groups have started to adapt their traditional image-making to modern media. Acrylic on canvas, screenprinting et cetera. It's a weird and wonderful hybrid.'

'Sounds intriguing.' The collector's brow furrowed and a faraway look came into his eyes, as if all his involvement with art were but an act of compliance with his stringent personal creed. 'I'm truly grateful to make the acquaintance of you two ladies. I congratulate you on *Mango Dreaming II*. It is an important work and it will take the museum's collection into the new world where it needs to go. This is the start of something enduring, I am sure.'

Cynthia solemnly acknowledged the man's tribute. Like the New York rain, fortune came in a downpour and could last for days. Then it would stop just as suddenly, the sun would come out, the rain would have left no trace, and if you were lucky there would be a tinge of green. But for now there was only rain.

Jane could not help giggling. She and Cynthia were going back to their hotel twenty thousand dollars richer, on a sixty-forty split with half Cynthia's forty per cent to be split further with the SoHo gallery owner. The rest of the stay in New York was theirs to enjoy. Jane gave Cynthia a kiss goodnight and Cynthia gave Jane a big hug, refusing to let go. Jane was grateful. She was reassured by Cynthia's big reliable arms around her, always.

From her hotel room high above the city, Jane looked down through a gap in the towering buildings opposite at the iron roofs behind the theatre facades, plastered with garbage, and was where she wanted to be, high up and above it all. She felt easy and graceful on the pinnacle where she had alighted, although the distance travelled was remarkable. Other women, other Australian artists, drowned themselves on the way, or bashed themselves semiconscious against a brick wall, or renounced themselves and their people in order to become something else for others. Jane would never have to do that. She was living proof that things were different for the first time in history.

To push and pull her raw talent into powerful shape had taken singlemindedness and singleness. It was the measure of her talent and ten years of solid work. But her personal relationships had been unable to accommodate the force of her ambition. Alex Mack, experimental companion of her youth and the first indication of what men would fail to give her. Michael Browne-Grey, teacher, mentor and ex-grown-up-lover. Others too, when it suited. The more important alliances were with the few unenvious curators and critics – and Cynthia. A top dealer and a tough operator, Cynthia saw Jane as the high priestess of a new age who was giving sensual soul to Australian women's power for the first time. Women had been visible hitherto in Olympic swimming, champion tennis, the feminist struggle and bel canto singing, but not in art until now. Cynthia worked tirelessly, with a conviction about the artist's achievement that answered Jane's own faith in herself, and Jane channelled her energies – even if it meant falling into a cold empty bed on this night of triumph in New York.

The telephone rang at four in the morning. Wide awake, she listened to the prickly void of the international line waiting to connect.

'Hallo my darling.' The voice was husky and strange. She knew at once from that familiar greeting who it was. 'You're in New York.'

It was darling Wendy calling from Cairns.

'I'm in New York and it's great.'

Wendy knew how significant the show was to Jane. To call at almost the right time and connect was Wendy's way of sharing and affirming Jane's triumph. 'So far away,' she said then, more plaintively, and her voice switched. 'When are you coming back, darling? I need you here.'

'Is something the matter? Is it Cassie?' Jane had a sudden flash of the baby, whom Wendy had made her godchild.

'I want to take her away from Alfonzo.'

'Shit. What about you?'

'If I can. Look I don't want to talk. He'll kill me when he finds out I've even rung you.'

'I'll come as soon as I can.'

'Tomorrow?'

'Oh darling, is it that bad?'

'It's for real. I need you now. Has it been great for you in New York? I bet you're a big hit.'

'I'm a hit, darling. Don't worry. It's wonderful.'

'You'll come, won't you?'

'Make me cut my holiday short, you bitch. Don't worry. I'm on my way. Why do you have to do this to me?'

'Don't say anything when you get here. Okay? Cassie and I are leaving him. You're coming to take us away. That's final. Oh-oh! Gotta go. Bye now.'

'Bye!' Jane breathed. Click. Then there was only the prickly crackle across the void again.

For a moment she lay in the silence. She felt as if she were levitating. Then she turned on the radio and let New York babble away. At five o'clock she turned on the light and started to pack. By six o'clock in the morning, when the newspaper was pushed under her door, she was ready to sit cross-legged on the bed and skim the news while she gave Cynthia another half-hour.

At six-thirty she knocked on Cynthia's door and broke the news that she had changed her flight and was returning to Australia that same evening. The important work in New York was done. Cynthia could mop up. *Mango Dreaming II* would hang on a vast white elegant wall somewhere in the city while Jane was called back to its source.

Cynthia swore and yawned. She felt lousy after the previous night and could barely see. She hated imperatives. Flexibility and negotiation were her way. If Jane could hang on for a couple of days, she would move her appointments forward and they could travel back together, making the epic flight less stressful. Cynthia's wisdom was that a crisis usually passed into anti-climax.

'Not this time,' said Jane. 'I promised her. She's got no one she can trust. It's one of those things I have to do. Sorry to mess you around.'

'It's okay,' grinned Cynthia. 'Now can we meet in a few hours, when I've got myself together?'

Jane spent the day doing the Guggenheim and the Museum of Modern Art. The best way to prepare for the flight was to make meaning of the time. Something seriously dangerous was going on. Jane had recognised the note of unequivocal extremity, the mother's plea, in Wendy's voice, but for all their powerful intuitive communication she could not visualise the specifics of the scenario and the fastest journey would not get her to Cairns for another forty-eight hours. She feared that Wendy was using heroin again. It was more than eighteen months since she had fallen pregnant and given the stuff up. Jane cast around in desperation for someone else she could call, just to get some more information. She thought of Wendy's family in Adelaide. She could not ring Peter and Isabel Sunner, whom their daughter had disowned when they found out about Cassie and tried to interfere. She thought of Ivan the fire-eater and called his place in Melbourne but he was not there. He could be anywhere. She thought of the old gang . . . Alex . . . Ziggy was in London . . . Then she remembered Elspeth, who still always sent postcards. She assumed that Elspeth was in touch with Wendy by postcard too. She found a phone number for Elspeth Gillingham in her old address book, at Whitepeeper in western outback New South Wales.

The reports of Jane's successful New York exhibition had already appeared in the Australian papers. Elspeth had the newspaper open in front of her on the kitchen table as she picked up the phone.

'Jane! How amazing! I was just thinking about you,' said Elspeth with surprise. 'Congratulations.'

Wendy had thought she could control the situation, but she knew now that it controlled her. She could not resist Alfonzo physically or emotionally. She had nowhere without him – no house, no money, nothing. Cassie, she knew, he regarded as his own achievement and possession, quite separate from her. But the greatest happiness was still to be with him, with their little girl nearby, and to make him as happy as he made her. He would give her the stuff when she was too agitated to do it herself, returning her to the river of ecstasy that ran through the heart of their relationship.

Alfonzo often talked about how good his own mother was with babies, talking sentimentally of all the things his mother and father had done for him and his sister Leila when they were children. He talked of the Maltese way in which kids were brought up by their grandparents. Wendy knew it was his plan to take Cassie away and have her brought up by his parents in Adelaide.

She was in no position to fight this. As long as she was with him in this condition, in the cage he kept her in, Alfonzo would consider her an unfit mother. If she stayed with him, it meant the child must go. The only way was to leave with Cassie herself before it got to that. She had imagined that move, every step of the way, convinced it was the right thing, but she would never actually do it. She even tried to talk to Alfonzo about it in a roundabout way. She asked if they would ever move away from their tropical paradise back to one of the cities down south where they came from. She asked if they would perhaps be forced to settle overseas one day. She knew the day would come when Alfonzo would have to run and hide, taking her with him and sending Cassie to his parents for minding.

He scowled at her. 'Don't worry,' he said. 'You're getting so paranoid these days. Don't worry about *anything*.'

Knowing by his hollow evasion that she was deeper and deeper in, she mockingly acted her part. 'Okay, honey. I'll check Cassie.'

Then one of Alfonzo's couriers was arrested at the airport. The police were on to him. He was smart enough to have covered his tracks, but he started to panic. He only told Wendy that he had invited his father and mother to come and stay with them, without telling her what was wrong.

'Your parents hate me,' said Wendy.

'My parents love you. It's my sister who hates you.'

'Why do they have to come now? They've never been here before.'

'They've never seen North Queensland. Listen, they can help you out with Cassie. You and I need to take a little holiday somewhere. Where would you like to go?'

The time had come. Wendy needed to be told no more. They were coming to take Cassie away. It would happen while she and Alfonzo were on holiday. She must escape before it was too late. Yet she did not have the strength to carry out that move by herself. If he knew that she was planning to leave him, Alfonzo would do everything in his power to stop her going. He would punish her, bash her, bash the baby. He would refuse her the hit she needed until she was incapable of anything. She rang Jane in New York, and a few hours later she got that phone call from Elspeth. Elspeth was dying to see Wendy's baby. She was on her way. She had only been waiting for an invitation, she said.

'That's great,' squealed Wendy. After she hung up, she told Alfonzo that Elspeth Gillingham was coming to visit.

'Elspeth who?'

'You know. My old schoolfriend. Elspeth something else now. She changed her name. I can't remember what she is. Elspeth Gillingham.'

'Does she know how to get here?'

'I gave her the instructions.'

Alfonzo groaned. 'When is this? This is not the best time. Why now? Where's she coming from?'

'She lives on a farm somewhere in New South Wales.'

'Jesus. So she's driving here?'

'I don't know! She's on her way.'

Alfonzo was furious. 'I don't want this woman coming here, Wendy.'

Wendy giggled. 'You'll like her. Her family used to own half of Australia. She's cool. She used to be an orange person. Her parents dragged her off to Italy to get her away from it. Or was it the other way round? She found religion when her parents dragged her away from her Italian lover. I can't honestly remember any more.'

Elspeth drove from Whitepeeper to Cairns in twenty hours. She was a good driver but she nearly crashed the Volvo wagon a couple of times from fatigue in the later stretches of the trip, in the small hours of morning, playing one tape after another, stopping only to refuel, eat something, drink coffee. Unconditional loyalty impelled her, personal links expressed in tacit schoolgirl vows that defined who she was. Jane would not have called Elspeth out of the blue unless Wendy was in genuine crisis, so Elspeth hurried to answer the call. Wendy had told Alfonzo that Elspeth was leaving her husband. That was a lie. But as always Wendy came close to the bone. In simply getting up, going out to the car and driving off, with a note left for Andrew, Elspeth realised that there was nothing keeping her to him.

Alfonzo found Elspeth less weird than Wendy had made out. His show of hospitality disguised the violence of emotion the unexpected visitor brought. For lunch they ate Thai-style parrot fish with rice and wine, and mangoes on the deck afterwards. Through the rubbery clatter of tropical foliage was the sparkling ocean which charmed Elspeth. Alfonzo was being a charmer too – but Elspeth had taken an instant dislike to him that amounted to loathing.

'You're here by yourself,' he asked. 'Where's your husband gone?'

'He's fine,' she replied, insouciant. 'He's looking after the sheep.'

The baby charmed her most of all. Even Alfonzo's features found favour as refracted in the infant's dark eyes and golden olive skin. But thank goodness Cassie had Wendy's sharp amused expression and, presumably, her mind. Sitting by the cot in the afternoon, Elspeth admired Cassie dreamily, and when Wendy came to check her there was a chance for the women to talk. Fourteen-month-old Cassie could be trusted not to pass on what she heard.

'I'm *not* paranoid,' said Wendy. 'He's planning to separate me and the baby. He's got his parents coming to take the baby away. I don't know what he's expecting to do with me. Dump me in an ashram in Goa or set me up for a drug bust. Declare me unfit to raise my own child.'

'Can you and Cassie leave with me?'

'He'd kill me.'

'Not while *I'm* here.'

'We won't tell him. We'll go whenever you're ready.'

'When? He won't leave us alone,' whined Wendy.

'You're not his prisoner, are you?' Elspeth asked.

'I can't live without him. You don't know how it is.'

'There are ways to deal with that. You've got to think of your baby.'

'You don't understand, Elspeth.'

'You've got to decide what you want.'

Elspeth glowered at Wendy with the same imperious no-nonsense demand that Barb Gillingham would have made. Wendy must choose what was sensible.

'Okay. We'll do it tomorrow.'

'Jane's on her way. She'll be here tomorrow. Don't you want to wait for her?'

'He thinks *Jane's* coming to take us away. He's afraid of Jane. If we are going to do anything, we have to do it before Jane gets here.'

Cassie, in her disposable nappy, lay on her back in the cot, uncovered in the warm, mild night. She was quiet. Her little hands and feet struck Elspeth as perfect strange creations, as if they were fruit or some other entity in their own right, complete and miraculous.

'She's an adorable little thing. So peaceful and innocent.'

'Look after her, whatever happens,' begged Wendy in a whisper.

Without a word, Elspeth squeezed Wendy's hand. Wendy was crying. Silent tears pouring down.

'Fuck,' she sniggered, 'my mascara. He'll know I've been crying.'

It was as if they were schoolgirls again. Wendy had always hated being caught. She hated the idea of evidence. She never wanted to leave traces.

Alfonzo came in and put his arms around the two women beside the cot. For a long time he said nothing, sensing what they were planning. He sighed over the baby. At last he spoke, 'She's irresistible already, isn't she?'

In the afternoon they went down to the beach, Cassie in a papoose tied to Alfonzo's chest. They walked barefoot along the soft white sand. The breezes off the sea played with their hair and flapped their skimpy clothing. At the far end of the beach they sat on the sand and let Cassie crawl about naked. Wendy lay flat on her back and squinted at the shining sky. Alfonzo sat hunched, shirtless, letting his tanned skin bake. Elspeth, behind dark glasses, took Cassie to the shallows and, holding her up by the arms, walked her through the tingling bubbles of foam, laughing in elation.

In the direction they had come from, the curving bank of shimmering coastal forest revealed a broken view of their house, its windows mirroring the sunlight. A flock of ibis lifted from that same green bank, squawking as they descended to the beach for a strutting, scavenging promenade. As they walked back Wendy said to Alfonzo that Elspeth wanted her and the baby to go south for a break. Elspeth was willing to help with Cassie while Wendy got some much-needed rest.

'Sounds good,' smiled Alfonzo. 'But I don't know when you're going to get time for that. We've got so many people coming up to see us. How long is Elspeth planning to stay?'

'As long as I'm not in the way,' Elspeth said, 'I love it here. I'm in no hurry to leave.'

Alfonzo wondered how long it would take him to win Elspeth over.

Elspeth saw from the way the secret plan had been carefully, casually revealed that Wendy was incapable of disobeying Alfonzo. She saw the way Wendy artfully distorted the proposal to put the blame on her friend. Wendy was a chronic liar with no grip on the truth. She lived like that, surviving by altering things in her mind all the time. It was, Elspeth understood, her last remaining wile. The baby papoose was strapped to Wendy now, but it was Elspeth's turn with Cassie. She carried her in her arms, walking ahead of the others back to the house. The child might have been her own.

At last, from sheer exhaustion, Elspeth lay down on the mattress in the soothing currents of air in the spare room and fell asleep. Dusk was just passing and the light was purple. She had vowed to stay awake and keep watch, staying straight for that reason. She saw herself as the baby's guardian, but she had not slept for two days and could not help herself drifting irresponsibly away.

~

Wendy was sorting through her racks and boxes of exotic clothes and jewellery, vain and childlike enough to be unable to contemplate a move, or even a decision, without considering the personal effects essential to it. Alfonzo came in from smoking a joint on the deck and told her to relax. Why would she not come and sit with him? The baby was asleep. There was no hurry. They could enjoy themselves. Alfonzo ran his hand over Wendy's honey hair, stroked her cheek with two fingers and ran a firmer hand down to her waist.

'Hey beautiful, you're not really thinking of leaving me? You'll never get it as good again.'

'You talk as if I'm finished.'

'As long as you stay with me you'll have a man who worships you. Everything I do is for you.'

'Don't, Alfonzo.'

'You're not going to run away?' He held her and kissed her. 'You can't live without me either. It's like the fairytale. We're the three little bears. Papa Bear and Mama Bear and Baby Bear. I've got some really good stuff for you.'

Wendy sighed, resisting him. 'That would be so lovely. But not while Elspeth's here. I don't want her to know about that. Please.'

'Elspeth's crashed out. It's night-time, baby. There's a whole beautiful night ahead. Listen to the music.'

Wendy felt the craving within, the desire for release, the need to feel good. There would never be a time when she would not long to repeat it, for as long as she lived. She wanted to glide down that river of plenitude where she could untether herself from the enslaving complexities of existence and float, trailing golden limbs and hair, like a princess, in the adoration of Alfonzo, where all her tears would dry, her fears be lifted, and she would be brave and powerful again.

'I wish you hadn't mentioned it,' she said to him. 'It would be so-oo lovely.'

Alfonzo lit the candles in the dark. He lit the sandalwood incense. He closed the door to Elspeth's room and to the place where Cassie slept in her cot. He closed the double slatted doors to their bedroom. He prepared the needle.

It was top, top stuff, he told Wendy, who sat in a ball on the bed, bouncing like a monkey in anticipation. Her teeth were chattering.

He smiled and kissed her. She was away. He was not really sure of the quality of the stuff. Not a hundred per cent. It was double the amount she was used to. They made love, then he left the room. Later, when he checked her, she was in a deep sleep and he could not rouse her. Better not to try. The fat candles burned creamily on either side of her bed. The air was thick with fragrant smoke. She was lying, face up, head on the satin pillow.

Elspeth looked through the window and saw the morning-star wink at her from the violet sky. The house was quiet. She got up, stretched, orientated herself, and walked to the open window where she breathed the fresh dawn sea air. Pricking her ears then, she listened more carefully for the hidden sounds of the house. She longed just to hear the baby's muffled breathing, but she could hear nothing. She crept out of her room and went looking for Cassie. Her head was thick from sleeping so deeply and she felt confused. By mistake she opened the door to Wendy's bedroom. It smelled fetid, the scent of wax and something else. Elspeth saw Wendy's hair, like a mop, on the pillow. There was only one person on the bed. She whispered Wendy's name. There was no response. 'Wendy?' she whispered louder, going inside. But there was nothing. She came closer, listening for breath. Still nothing. She reached forward in the terrible stillness and touched Wendy's dry hair and forehead. She tugged at Wendy's shoulder. She sniffed in alarm. There was vomit all over the pillow. Wendy was cold and immobile. There was no sound of breath – no response. In a savage heave Elspeth pulled Wendy up by the shoulders and flung her back. Then she backed out of the room and blundered next door to where Cassie lay sleeping, tucked under her cover, undisturbed.

'Alfonzo!' screamed Elspeth. She stumbled out on to the deck where she found him curled up asleep in his hammock. 'Call an ambulance. Wendy's dead.'

In an instant Alfonzo was wide awake and on his feet. He ran to the bedroom and took one look at Wendy, then returned to the deck. 'Jesus!'

The sun was popping over the eastern horizon. Pausing for a moment, he pressed his hand over his face.

'Call the ambulance,' shouted the woman. 'Or do you want me to do it?'

Elspeth dialled the emergency number and handed the phone to Alfonzo. There was an argument over the telephone about whether it would be better if he brought the victim in to the hospital or whether the ambulance should come. No, it was better to try first aid straight away while they waited for the ambulance. If she had vomited, clear her passages and attempt mouth to mouth.

This Alfonzo did lovingly, as Elspeth witnessed, putting his mouth to Wendy's fouled mouth with a lover's passionate kiss and massaging her heart and chest like a lover. But it was all a useless show. The ambulance arrived in a matter of minutes. The paramedics put her on a stretcher and transferred her to the back of the ambulance van, where she was hooked up to their equipment. There was little hope. It was a sham. The man was a known drug dealer. It was a straightforward case of drug overdose.

When they were ready to leave, the ambulance men told Alfonzo to hop in the back too. They assumed he would want to be with the woman, his de facto, the mother of his kid. But Alfonzo hesitated.

'What about Cassie?' He was worried all of a sudden.

'I'll keep an eye on her,' replied Elspeth flatly.

Alfonzo was unnerved.

'Something wrong, mate?' snapped the ambulance man, impatient to be off.

'You go,' said Elspeth. 'I'll stay with the baby. People will think it strange otherwise. If you don't go with Wendy.'

Alfonzo's eyes slotted back and forth. She was right. He did not trust Elspeth an inch but was quick to follow her calculation. If he wanted to keep the police away from him, he must show the right sort of feeling. So Alfonzo burst into tears and allowed himself to be bundled into the back of the ambulance beside his princess.

'She's a doll,' said the paramedic in the back, nodding at Wendy's serene face. It was his way of offering condolences. She had been snatched away. When it was a young woman like this you always thought they might just wake up again. 'Poor kid.'

By the time Alfonzo got back from the hospital, Elspeth had cleared out and taken Cassie with her. She had gone in to sit by the baby, where shock and grief and fear came gradually to the surface. She picked up the baby and pressed her close to her heart, consoling herself as much as the infant, who started to cry. In a panic, to comfort Cassie's starving cry, Elspeth found the milk that Wendy had expressed into a bottle the day before and warmed it on the stove. As Cassie hungrily took the milk, Elspeth felt her bond with the baby grow. She remembered Wendy's plea to Elspeth to look after Cassie if anything happened. She remembered her promise. Wendy had known. She had been entrusting her child to Elspeth.

It was not entirely a thought-out action on Elspeth's part, but not entirely an irrational compulsion either. It was simply that once she had taken the baby up in her arms she could not bring herself to put her down again. There was no time to lose if they were to get away before Alfonzo returned. Callous as she felt at abandoning the dead mother, her dead friend, Elspeth knew it was time to be tough and practical. There was too much at stake. And Jane was coming. Jane would sort everything else out.

Cassie was asleep again as soon as she finished the milk. Elspeth laid her in the bassinet. There would be no more milk where that came from. She grabbed a big bag which she stuffed with everything the child might need, including a random snatch of Wendy's possessions as keepsakes. The blue-green topaz ring was by the bedside table and Elspeth put it on. She didn't take the emerald one. The house was wide open, filled with air and light, looking as if it had been ransacked when she finished. The telephone was ringing.

It rang and rang. Urgently. Elspeth ignored it as she carried the sleeping child with tender care to the car. What a weight! She settled the bassinet on the backseat, threw her own bag on the floor and without wasting time to go back and close the doors of the house, she climbed into the driver's seat and drove off.

Having re-routed her journey from New York, Jane reached Cairns late in the afternoon. She had changed into a white T-shirt and a full long black skirt at one of the transit lounges along the way.

Alfonzo was in the house in the white linen suit he had put on for entertaining the police.

'You,' he said to Jane by way of greeting. That was all.

'Where is she?' Jane asked.

'She's dead,' he told her, and started sobbing again.

'You killed her,' said Jane.

'Piss off,' said Alfonzo, wiping his eyes. 'Get out of my sight.'

'Not until you tell me what happened.'

She could barely comprehend what he told her. She did not believe him, yet she knew it must be true. All she could think was that she had come too late. She came rushing all this anxious impatient way and she was too late. Disaster had driven its hideous course through the house. The causes of Wendy Sunner's death were recorded as accidental choking following an overdose of heroin combined with alcohol and medication, self-administered. The body was lying at the morgue after the autopsy. Alfonzo was arranging a funeral and cremation at the earliest opportunity. Next of kin had been notified.

Suddenly Jane felt a wave of pity for Isabel and Peter Sunner. Although it was years since she had seen them, she could picture the policeman knocking at their door in suburban Adelaide and their flustered reaction, more embarrassed in front of the fretting cop than anything else, and Mr Sunner reaching for one of his bon mots. *Those whom the gods love die young.* Jane pitied the Sunners almost as much as she pitied herself.

'That crazy woman's stolen the baby,' Alfonzo blurted. 'What the hell was she doing here? Did you put her up to it? Don't you know that kidnapping's a crime? Does the bitch think she can get away with this? I've got the fuzz coming round any minute.'

Alfonzo wanted his child back at any cost. He had called his mother and father and told them to get onto it. He had ordered his contacts to get working on it straight away. His network of friends and relatives would sort out Elspeth Whateverhernamewas. For himself, he could not afford to stick around. The evening after the funeral he had a flight booked out of the country, using one of his other passports. The time had come to return and purify himself in the temple at Goa where he and Wendy had spent their most ecstatic times, where together they had become the twin-bodied Godhead of the thousand arms.

Jane and Alfonzo looked at each other, their gazes filled with hatred and blame. Jane saw the man's bruised, haunted eyes and the lines that scored his skin, sallow beneath the tan. His face had caved in. Now he was an exile from the world he had sought to enter and make. He was a ruin.

'You bastard,' was all Jane could say. 'You bastard. You fucking bastard.'

'You shut your face before I smash you,' Alfonzo snarled back at her in agony. 'I'll smash you before this thing's over. I promise. What have I got to lose? I hold you personally responsible. Dyke bitch.'

Jane taunted Alfonzo with her smug, tight smile. The retribution was already happening, as Elspeth's car sped along the back-country roads with the baby in the back and great plumes of dust rose in its wake like smoke from a sacrificial pyre.

2

Z IGGY was intrigued to see Alex's familiar scrawl appear under the Australian coat-of-arms on thick white Parliament House letterhead.

She was so young and beautiful and full of life and promise. Somehow she got on this highway and couldn't get off. It should have been just a roadstop for her. She would have moved on given time. It's just such a waste. Jane is completely traumatised. She knew what was happening with Alfonzo and wanted to get her out but Wendy wouldn't let her. She was so happy with the baby. We have to respect Wendy's decisions. We have to value her life as it was. She burns like a flame forevermore. She always loved you, Ziggy, right from the first day you walked into the schoolyard. You gave her joy. You know that. I miss you, mate.

Love, Alex.

The sheet of paper, black on white, had been folded in four and Ziggy smoothed it out in front of him. He blessed the frayed meanings it feebly conveyed. So far away, Ziggy felt able to experience a purer grief. Having embarked on a different life and career across the sea, he might never have seen Wendy again anyway. If she had been taken from the world, she had not gone from this other world of his, a plane of re-imagined reality where she would always exist and he would always adore her, golden and young.

The high window let a square of pale cold light fall from the white sky onto the worn green carpet of the flat Ziggy rented. He waited for the sun to warm his bones as the shadow of the building opposite slowly receded across the floor. The second-floor flat in a severe West End street showed its faded opulence in the carpets and matching green curtains. It was bare in the absence of furniture that Ziggy could not afford to buy. He had cadged a few good pieces for his basic needs, including the oak table on which Alex's letter sat like a speckled bird in the sun. Ziggy liked the space of the flat, as he was vaguely proud of the excessive rent.

Jane had already telephoned, when she got back to Sydney after the funeral, in the middle of her night and Ziggy's afternoon. The old black phone that sat on the floor on the green carpet had rung and Ziggy, happening to be at home, picked it up to hear Jane's solemn, stately voice. Something to tell you, Ziggy. Some difficult news. I'm afraid. Wendy's dead.

'The ceremony was this afternoon. We're all completely shattered.' She waited for his reaction down the silent phone.

'I don't believe it,' he managed. 'I'm not going to believe it. No! What happened?'

'That's the trouble. We don't know exactly.' Jane grew more excited. 'I was in New York and she called me from Cairns. You know, where she was living up there with Alfonzo and Cassie, her baby. She begged me to come as soon as I could. Straight away. From New York! I guess she wanted me to help her leave him and I got there too late. She OD'd. Alfonzo's a monster. He told the police she did it herself. But he must have given her the stuff. The needle was the part she always hated doing for herself. Ziggy, you know how she liked other people to do things for her.'

'What are you saying, Jane?'

'Elspeth had gone before I got there.'

'Elspeth? Was she there?'

'I rang her from New York. It was going to take me two days to get there. Elspeth had already been and gone and taken the kid.'

'She what?'

'She took Cassie away to Wendy's parents in Adelaide. She says it's what Wendy wanted her to do. It was the only way to stop Alfonzo. He had the police at Elspeth's place in the country within hours, looking for her. But of course Elspeth wasn't there and her husband Andrew had no idea what was going on. Clever Elspeth was already in Adelaide at the Sunners' place with the kid. Wendy and Alfonzo were never married, you see, so Isabel and Peter are the next of kin.' Jane laughed. 'I wish you could be here, Ziggy. Why aren't you here?'

'I don't believe what you're saying. It's horrible. It's not your fault, though, Jane.'

'I was too late by a day because of bloody New York.'

'How was New York?'

'A triumph. Funny, isn't it?'

'You can't blame yourself. Is there anything I can do – for Wendy?'

'There's nothing you can do, darling.'

'Will it go to court? Is that what you're implying?'

'I don't know if it should. We've got to think about what's best for Cassie. Alfonzo doesn't matter any more. The bastard. How's London, anyway?'

'I wouldn't be anywhere else.'

That evening Ziggy privately dedicated his performance in *Richard II* to Wendy. He carried the pain in his own body, as if she were with him, and kept bursting into tears. The character of the suffering king was one of Ziggy's parallel existences, rescued from the childhood world that had been destroyed over and over in his parents' flight from their ancestral lands to the no-place of Australia. From there Ziggy had made his own way back – abandoning school, escaping his parents' dominion, out into the streets and across the deserts and seas and on to the boards in order to reach a new world where he could transform this cruel, always repeated process into a glittering enactment that released him each time –

> *. . . sometimes am I king;*
> *Then treason makes me wish myself a beggar,*
> *And so I am: then crushing penury*
> *Persuades me I was better when a king;*
> *Then am I king'd again; and by and by*
> *Think that I am unking'd by Bolingbroke,*
> *And straight am nothing . . .*

He bowed for the cheery applause, head down humbly, up smiling, blood draining from his face. He tossed back his titian hair and turned his reddened eyes to the circle. Again he bowed abjectly and came up with a fresh warm smile but his skin was as pale as a ghost's.

On stage Ziggy Vincaitis combined hypersensitivity with the fearlessness of the outsider. He was in exile twice-over, from Lithuania and Australia, not to mention from the pure fantasy world that he considered his rightful inheritance. But he was never out of work. Born by chance in the operatic city of Salzburg, he had now captured the London stage with a nameless quality that enabled him to carry for an evening not only the audience's dreams and desires, but also its pain.

Oliver Blow, the composer-librettist, had grown accustomed to coming backstage, impressed and charmed, after Ziggy's performances. He had started sending flowers for opening nights, maintaining a formal relationship with the young actor. He didn't push too far. For all his politeness and wit, Oliver Blow was a formidable figure in the theatre world. He made his own rules, bringing not only a new seriousness to musical theatre in his crossover from classical composition, but also new popularity and profit. So much money had he made in fact that, however eccentric, his judgement went unquestioned. Blow's spectacular version of the Grail myth in contemporary idiom was to be his most ambitious production yet. 'Wagner with Tunes' the industry christened Sir Perceval. Everyone wanted to be in it. That was when he found Ziggy. A portly, middle-aged Yorkshireman, with an oily mane, massive shoulders and the sable beard of a Holbein courtier, Oliver Blow filled the dressing room in his black leather coat and trousers, pinching Ziggy with his huge onyx ring each time he extended his hand in whispered congratulations.

Ziggy was already good at guessing the content of what Oliver said. There was a sympathy between them. Hammering out a relationship, they sat round in cafes and bars gossiping intently about the state of the stage as if it were the only thing that mattered, until one day Oliver said to him, 'You are my Sir Perceval, Ziggy, but I don't precisely know who my Perceval is yet. That's the thing I want you to show me. When will you be free to come with me to a special place where we can discover who *he* is?'

'What do you mean, Oliver?'

'There is an island I want us to visit together. A place where I'd like us to spend some time.'

Ziggy smiled at the man's riddling way. 'An island? Is it far?'

'It's about as far as you can go. He who is tired of London,' nodded Oliver sagely. 'But there are other things you need to understand, dear boy. More things in heaven and earth and all that. Shall we do it?'

'Is the island yours?'

Oliver smiled.

The ferry sailed from the docks of a granite city where a solitary boy with a lamp was fishing from the end of the long pier in the fog. He seemed to wave. The ferry crossing was made once a day to service the community of that extreme place – little more than a cold, low, windswept scattering of rocks that jutted from northernmost water. It was a land of emerald rock and russet heath, crumbling off the edge of earth into sage-green sea, where the whiteness of a screeching sea-bird, the silver flash of fish or the blaze of orange lichen were notes of colour like music wrested from silence. That was why Oliver Blow loved this place, which he considered his own. The huge bearded man with his black leather coat and green tweed cap was like a seafarer, returning with a red-haired young stranger in a padded blue-plastic down jacket and a crimson beanie, as they walked up the flagstones from the ferry's docking place. Oliver unlatched the stiff wooden gate in the mossy wall and turned the key in the door of the cottage. In the dark interior he tore open the faded curtains on windows set deep in the stone to seaward. The whitewashed walls were darkened with smoke. Ashes were dead in the grate.

The slate floor rang as Oliver fetched wood. The inside surfaces were no different from the world outside. Then once the fire was drawing in gulps and crackles, he unlocked the door that led to the piano room. He pulled open the thick curtains and in the pale white light the sombre black instrument lay like a lustrous barge. Oliver opened the lid and sat to play the first prelude of *The Well-Tempered Klavier*, notes stabbing and ringing as he played the piece through until, as he lifted his hands in pious conclusion, only the pedal kept the last chord faintly alive.

'Welcome to my island.'

Ziggy simpered nervously. There would be no leaving this domain, no escaping Oliver's island, until the two of them departed together in five days' time.

That night over dinner, by flickering paraffin lamplight, Oliver talked about his life. His father was the parish priest in a seaside retirement town and Oliver an only child – 'like you, Ziggy' – born to parents who were already old. As soon as his legs were long enough to work the pedals, he played the church organ and then attended choir school, progressing from treble to alto to tenor, in a singing education that immersed him in the traditions of English holy music, which became his natural style. But at the Guildhall, where harshness and surface prevailed, no weight was given to the traditional mastery. So Oliver ran away, across Europe to the asylum of Vienna, and was accepted by a teacher who had studied with Schoenberg. Madame Roth was a Jungian, rumoured to have been the lover of Anton Webern before the Americans shot him by mistake at the end of the war. She showed Oliver music as the severest master. In Effie Roth's oft-repeated phrase, music must combine the mastery of the mystery and the mystery of the mastery. The truth of the saying was guaranteed by its pedigree. Madame Roth got it from Webern, who heard it from Schoenberg, who learned it with Mahler, who knew it from Wagner and Liszt and Schumann, who took it from Bach, who got it from God. But not the Christian God, Oliver belly-laughed. The God of the old religion.

'The old religion?' asked Ziggy.

'You know what that is,' answered Oliver, his eyes ablaze. 'You know it in your bones, Ziggy.'

Ziggy laughed out loud. Oliver had him entranced.

During the short space of amber light that was granted in winter Oliver took his visitor on a tour of the island, anti-clockwise, on a path that led from the settlement between tumbled walls of stone and returned by way of a last rugged stretch of misty coastline. As they walked, Oliver explained that the island had been the feared haunt of the old religion before the fanatic Christians, quite late in the day, almost succeeded in driving it out. 'There were bears here too,' continued Oliver, 'great black bears stranded by the last Ice Age, after they had moved across from the northern wastes of Asia. Wherever that bear appears in female form, she is worshipped. The mother bear who licks her cub into being from a lump of clay. One of her claws can disembowel a man. A German boat came on shore here during the war and only the men's bones were ever found, stripped of flesh. It was a victory for which the local people dare not claim credit to this day. The bear did it, they say.'

'Imagine bears on a small island like this,' said Ziggy. 'You couldn't hide them.'

'Centuries before Christ, all across the north, the she-bear was protected and worshipped,' intoned Oliver, ' – the Guardian, the Great Mother. You red-haired Vikings are not unrelated to all this either.'

Ziggy giggled awkwardly. He had never thought of himself as a Viking.

'You're not saying there are bears still around?'

'Not as such. But their spirit is here, I believe.'

'Is that why you brought me here, Oliver?'

'Is that why you came?' Oliver pointed at a rocky outcrop near the highest point of the island. 'The ruin of the church the Christians built on the site where the last of the bears were slaughtered is up there.'

'Ooh, are there bears' bones?' Ziggy asked in a show of excitement.

'We shall see the place, but not today. The fishermen will tell you the story of the iron swords that slew the last she-bear of breeding age, there on the mound, when the Christians came bearing their message of light and the dark old forces were driven beyond the edge of land.'

'The fishermen? They'd say anything.'

'Are you scared, Ziggy? Do you sense something?'

'I had a bear once,' said Ziggy. 'A black wooden bear that came in a Red Cross parcel when I was in Salzburg. A hard, pricking toy bear that sat up almost as big as me.'

'As a Lithuanian you are close to the old religion,' proclaimed Oliver. 'What is also called the Gothic. Lithuania is one of the last places in Europe where paganism thrived. The church was never more than a veneer there.'

'You're right. Papa used to talk about that,' Ziggy recalled. 'Mama knew all those old secrets.'

'That is what you must acknowledge, Ziggy. That is what Effie Roth taught me in Vienna. There is a stern and secret order behind things. Stigmatised, travestied, repressed. You are brave enough for it, Ziggy. I know you are.' Oliver was singing a line of atonal melody as he danced a shuffling step forwards. He swayed near to Ziggy, opened his arms and, with a smile, hooped him in an iron-tight hug. 'You're not sorry you came, are you?' he asked. 'Sir Perceval. It's grand to have you here.'

'Careful,' said Ziggy, pushing Oliver away. 'You'll crack my ribs. What's that thing you're singing?'

'It's a Chinese song setting by Webern. Can't get it out of my head.'

'Such a strange sound.' Then Ziggy put his hands on Oliver's shoulders and ran his fingers lightly down Oliver's expanded chest. 'I'm drawn to you. You know that, don't you?'

'You recognise the fact that you can go no further by yourself,' replied Oliver. 'You need a discipline from outside. A master who is bigger than you are.'

'But not a bear,' yelped Ziggy, turning away from the path and feeling light. 'That's ridiculous.'

'Absolutely a bear, my dear,' boomed Oliver from behind, his words the links of a chain that made Ziggy turn again and walk back, as if that were the movement he must make.

Next morning Ziggy lay in bed until the insistent repetitions from the piano, never quite resolving into music, drove him to get up. Oliver had been at the piano since before first light. Ziggy splashed his face in ice-cold water, cleaned his teeth, brushed his stiff hair and went out. He sniffed himself. He was starting to smell like a fisherman.

The overcast sky was fleecy-white, the pewter sea quiet and dull. His fingers were blue and unresponsive in the sluggish air as he perched like a cormorant on the pier and wrote *Dear Alex* in small writing. He had bought a faded postcard of a green and blue summer scene at the island store. He only wanted to record a tourist snapshot of himself, all rugged up, on the icy shore of a far-flung island where a rich and famous composer was leading him up the garden path of occult mysteries. *Merlin in black leather*, Ziggy wrote. That would tantalise. He would write Alex a long letter after the adventure was played out. And himself? *The chaste knight undergoing trial*. He laughed. Was he intimidated? He was in awe of Oliver's manifold talents, his prowess. Composer-librettist, Oliver was also producer, director and entrepreneur and would no doubt be dictatorial about the scenario he wished to act out with Ziggy. But there was something else about the man and his will, his absurd heroic ego that took a world to satisfy, something unloved and silly that Ziggy knew he could touch. Oliver was right. Applauded every night on the London stage, Ziggy craved a more secret, more lasting transfiguration, that came from beyond him, of a self the audience never knew.

The snowy seagulls dipped fearlessly for fish, mewing as they curved against the breeze. He wrote a jolly card to Jane, and a rapturous one to Herbert Horsfall about the sheer extremity of the place. He wrote a card to his mother and father in Lithuanian about the fish he and Oliver had eaten for supper the previous evening, before Oliver retired to the piano room. His mother used to sing about a golden ring inside a fish's belly. *I keep waiting for that golden ring to appear on my plate,* Ziggy wrote.

He could not go back to the house while Oliver was composing, so he set off to explore the island, but even as he walked he imagined he was hearing those same strange tones in the sounds of the outside world – an iron rod blown against a wall, a banging door, bootnails on cobblestones, a chimney that howled like an organ pipe, wind rushing through the plaited hedge, the whipping of a tether-rope, a boat's sides knocking at the wharf. Gull cry, pigeon rubato, ewe bleat and the eerie overhang of silence as the cold came down. He thought, in contrast, of the place where he had grown up. Adelaide, South Australia. He never thought of it as his place. It was as inimical to the Gothic as any place could be. Was that why he had always dreamed of escaping? The classical city of a society conceived on an enlightenment model. Grid of reason laid down according to logic and geometry. Site where the people's democracy could prosper through the promotion of civic ideals. He had been flattened by the weight of those regular golden blocks. Not just Adelaide, but Australia, conceived as a place where society could rid itself of its flawed elements, creating the circumstances for transformation, not to gold as the alchemists had dreamed, but to a more serviceable metal of good citizenry. Turning its back on the diabolical and the demonic, shearing light from dark, severing the tree of life at the roots. Denying the deeper flow of sap down and back. Australia worshipped budding flowers and new leaves that would wither as soon as they were picked. No wonder he was a stranger there.

He put out his hand to catch some of the single flakes of snow that drifted down. White clouds descended like a downy bedcover. The snow settled in white specks on black stone, black earth and green heath. He was approaching the mound at the centre of the island and recognised the rocky outcrop that Oliver had pointed out. Through the snow he could see two ruined stone walls, parallel, roofless, with Gothic windows and a broken span between them. He stepped inside that space and looked at his feet, planted in the snow, then he threw his head back and stared into the sky. It was as if there were an entity apart from himself, out there, into whose presence he was being brought. He shouted suddenly the lines from *Richard II*.

> . . . *Whate'er I be,*
> *Nor I nor any man that but man is*
> *With nothing shall be pleas'd, till he be eas'd*
> *With being nothing* . . .

His voice, so strong on stage, was small in the gathering dark, each warm vibrating word muffled by snow and swallowed by cold as soon as it left his lips. The snow was falling in a strange thick mist now. He had, he realised, no idea how to get back. It was very cold, but a certain euphoria at the thought that he might be lost made him feel warmer. He walked back to where the path had been and, pulling his jacket closer round him, headed downwards more briskly. Soon it was dark. He bent forward into the softly falling snow, his face stinging with cold and snow covering his hair. There were fuzzy yellow balls of light up ahead. They were dancing at about waist-height. He called out. Then he was frightened. He imagined bears, freed from their chains, dancing to get him. He could hear sounds now. He called again, louder, and there came an answer. He recognised the full-chested tenor. With two companions, swinging their torches in shafts of light that crisscrossed the dark, Oliver was approaching through the snow.

'I had to get the boys out,' he said like a prim schoolteacher, grabbing Ziggy by the collar and shaking him. His black leather coat was buttoned to the neck.

Ziggy grinned like an idiot as a way of greeting the two ruddy-faced men who made up the search party with Oliver. 'The snow came and it got dark,' he blurted, then slowed himself down. 'I would have found my way back. I'm sorry you had to come out.'

'You'd have been lost in the snow, dead of hypothermia and rigor mortis would be setting in,' pronounced Oliver, 'if you'd been out much longer.'

'It's a small island,' said one of the torchbearers.

'It can surprise you on a night like this,' said the other.

Oliver gripped Ziggy's arm and escorted him home to the cottage where one lamp glowed and the fire was down to its embers. Ziggy sank down on the hearth rug.

'It's not a bearskin, is it?' Ziggy groaned.

Oliver nodded. He had bought it in Vienna. It was supposed to come from Siberia. 'I've got a paw too,' he said, hovering before Ziggy. 'Beautiful old thing, mounted on oak. Claws razor-sharp as the day she was hunted down.'

'When was that?'

'A hundred and fifty years ago. More – she predated Wagner.'

'That's disgusting. Unhygienic. You're crazy, Oliver.'

Oliver beamed as he handed Ziggy a whisky. 'You shouldn't just go wandering off, you know. You don't know what's out there.'

'I've got a good sense of direction, usually. I love this place.'

'You're responding to something different here. Cheers. You're a smart boy. You think you know things. But you have the capacity for an even greater understanding. You are only now pushing through to the other side, to that special knowledge of how things are. Perhaps you are not ready yet.'

'That's where you come in, isn't it?' Ziggy said as Oliver took a seat by the fire, his leather-clad legs staked apart on the floor. A tender transparency seemed to come over him, for all his riddling talk.

But Ziggy was still perplexed by Oliver's calm, elliptical words. He was willing to go where Oliver led, to experience what offered. More than that. He craved, as Oliver had correctly guessed, a higher discipline that would perfect and empower him, making his gifts hard and permanent. Oliver's magnificent, obdurate success attracted him. It made him want what Oliver could give, with a compulsion that he was willing to let materialise, for this stretch of time at least, on this island, in this laughable holy setting. But he was uncertain and embarrassed about exactly what Oliver might come up with.

'You'll have to try and explain, Oliver. I don't really know what you mean,' Ziggy prompted.

'You need to understand the bonds that link us and the obligations we are bound by to the powers we worship. Not just you and I, but our whole invisible brotherhood. There is a chain of service that binds us one to another down the ages, a secret order of bondage, akin to the discipline of music itself, passed down from master to student until the student becomes the master in turn. Do you know what I'm talking about, Ziggy? Whatever the sources of my music, there is a lineage back to dark original times.'

'Did you bring me here to tell me that? I thought you only wanted to see if I was good enough for the part. For Perceval. I can do it, Oliver.'

'Of course you can. It's so much more than that. I wanted to see if you could *be* Perceval. Which means enter that realm of purification through abasement.'

'You've lost me again.' Ziggy gave a faint smile. 'Why don't you just come out with it?' Did Oliver merely want to seduce him? If so, Ziggy was impressed by the grandiloquence of Oliver's line. He was excited by Oliver, flattered, amused, enthralled, and wanted to do him honour in return.

Oliver gazed at Ziggy beside the fire. With his mat of red-golden hair, his high cheekbones and his clear golden eyes, there could be no doubt that he was the knight. Ziggy had the composure and nobility of a serious explorer that you scarcely hoped to find in an actor.

'Out there. In the snow,' Ziggy went on, aware of taking a deeper step. 'I felt uplifted.'

'You should not have gone wandering without me. The local people don't approve. There have been casualties.' Then Oliver got up and crossed in front of the fire to stand by Ziggy. 'I am speaking of a special relationship between us. I want to show you everything and give you everything. Don't be alarmed. You will be my Perceval. If you are willing.' The timbre of his voice had changed completely.

Ziggy raised his eyebrows. Oliver's obsessive solemnity made him want to laugh. He cast his eyes sideways as Oliver moved a few inches closer. 'Why don't you play me the music you've been working on, Oliver. Is it fit to hear?'

'It's the Perceval music. The ascent of the mountain in the second half. The knight is trying to purify himself of the violations of the world when he meets a grizzly bear on the mountainside. She enchants him and he dances with her.'

'You're not serious? It's our story exactly,' quipped Ziggy.

'Do you want to hear? Bring the lamp.' Oliver led the way into the cold wooden piano room and sat at the keyboard. Ziggy held the lamp behind him. Light rippled over the black and white keys where Oliver's hands were already running. He hummed and rocked as he thumped the big chromatic chords. Wagner, Ravel, Prokofiev and the Webern intervals. Ziggy could hear all the sources as Oliver hunched over the instrument, loving it. 'It will work,' he moaned as he came to a break. 'Won't it? What do you think?'

Then before Ziggy could reply Oliver had started to play again, and would not stop.

In that dim cone of light Ziggy was transported back to his music lessons with Solomon T. Cross in the upstairs room behind the church in Adelaide. The child stood in a happy dream at Mr

Cross's shoulder while the teacher pounded the chords of his great unknown masterwork of virtuosic pianism, the *Ode to Albert Namatjira* that had won the Broken Hill Eisteddfod of 1946. The teacher was singing, ash falling to the keys from the cigarette in his mouth, dandruff to the dark shoulderpads of his jacket, as the snowflakes had fallen on Oliver's grizzly bulk as he came out into the night with his torchbearers to find Ziggy. The round pink spot on Mr Cross's head was bobbing in a space outside time that the clownish fantastical man had shown Ziggy all those years ago, a man whose music no one had heard, unlike Oliver Blow's, whose determined, demonic creativity went out into the world to work on hundreds of thousands of souls, earning fame and fortune beyond Solomon T. Cross's wildest imaginings.

'I'm exhausted,' said Ziggy at last. But Oliver did not tire. It was nearing dawn and the paraffin lamp had burned out. The whole of *Sir Perceval* had been presented in outline. 'Let me sleep with those sounds ringing in my ears.'

'Sleep then,' ordered Oliver. He closed the piano and ushered Ziggy back through the door of the draughty room to the dead fire. He pulled back the eiderdown and Ziggy fell into bed. Oliver covered him, tucking in the quilt around him, and hugged himself to keep warm as he watched Ziggy sink into sleep.

The house shone with white light in the morning.

'Put this on,' said Oliver when Ziggy opened the door and went to go outside, 'or you'll catch your death.' He handed Ziggy his long black coat.

Ziggy put the coat on obediently and stepped out onto the snow-covered stones. He had no shoes on and his bare feet left a clear print in the crisp virgin snow. He wanted to feel the cold, but with a yelp he hopped back inside.

'It's so beautiful,' exclaimed Ziggy. 'Virgin snow.' He clasped his hands as if in thanks. 'A complete transformation overnight. Did you know it would be like this?'

Oliver was bathed in the steam from a cauldron of water that he was boiling on the stove.

'Close the door and keep warm. I'm heating some water for you. You may wash at your leisure in the tub in front of the fire. There you go. In you get, my lamb.'

Ziggy's toes tingled as he tried the hot water after the snow. He balanced on one foot and rubbed the other to warm it. Then he took off Oliver's leather coat, pulled off his nightshirt and lowered himself into the steaming water, bending his legs and curling his arms round his knees, his groin prickling at the heat. The light from the blazing fire burnished his taut skin as he soaked in the blissful bath until he was flushed and drowsy. Then Oliver poured a second cauldron of water into the tub. His skin scalded. 'Ouch!' squawked Ziggy.

'Don't splash now,' said Oliver, steadily filling the tub to the brim, 'and you'll be all right. Don't forget to clean behind the ears and in all those other crevices,' nagged Oliver, immensely pleased. 'Who's a pretty boy then?'

'All right, Mother. Now where's the towel?'

Oliver caught Ziggy's dripping body in a big outstretched bath towel. 'Dry yourself with this. Then put the coat back on or you'll catch a chill. I want you to come with me.'

The piano shone like a slab of black ice in the light reflected from the snow outside. Oliver pulled up a high-backed oak chair that scraped the floor and set it hard against the curve of the piano's body. 'I want you to sit here,' he ordered. Manhandled by Oliver, Ziggy fell on to the chair. Then Oliver was on his knees beside the chair, rattling something metal. Ziggy felt a cold steely bite around his leg.

'What's this?'

'New day, new game, my son.'

Before Ziggy could kick it away, the lock was fastened. There was one ring closed around his ankle and the other around the piano leg.

'What on earth are you doing?' Ziggy yelped.

330 ~

'Just relax. Don't panic. See how you like it.'

'This is absurd, Oliver. It's freezing in here. I've just come out of the bath! So this is how you get people to listen to your music?'

Oliver grinned. 'You're my prisoner, Ziggy. I want you to stay here and see what it feels like. Just a few moments. Don't go away now.'

Ziggy bared his teeth and chuckled. 'Well, I'm hardly in a position to run away, am I?'

The metal ring was tight around his ankle. It was impossible to wriggle his foot free. If he pulled the chain taut against the piano leg, the circlet around his ankle cut into his flesh and the beast of a piano groaned a little on its castors. He shivered as Oliver adjusted the black coat snugly around Ziggy's neck and over his bare chest.

'May I enquire what the rules are of this little game?'

'I shall leave you here to savour the sensation of being a prisoner. Imagine you're in a dungeon. In the Colosseum, if you like. About to be eaten. And your remains flushed into the sewers as you deserve. You are tired after your impromptu excursion yesterday. You are relaxed after your bath. The conditions are perfect.'

'This is ludicrous, Oliver. I'll die of cold.'

'You have my coat. A little discomfort never hurt. Would you like me to fetch the bearskin for your legs?'

'That stinking thing!'

'Do I have your consent? That's the first and only rule.'

'Well, if you insist.' Ziggy giggled in a slight panic.

'Too tame for you? I'll only stop when you give the signal.'

'Oh no, I didn't mean that. No, no.' Ziggy laughed nervously. 'What's the signal then?'

'Don't you know?' Oliver cackled, baring his teeth. 'You worthless scum.'

It sounded funny in Oliver's Yorkshire accent. 'Now that's not very nice,' whined Ziggy in insolent reply.

Oliver left the room and closed the door behind him. Ziggy could hear him moving about on the other side of the room. Then there was silence. 'I'm cold,' Ziggy shouted. 'Fuck you, Oliver. Poor

Tom's a-cold.' He rattled his chain but there was no response. If Oliver never returned, he would perish of cold and starvation. His teeth were chattering like an old sewing machine. It was a farce. He would piss on the ancient floorboards if Oliver did not come back soon.

Eventually Oliver came back. 'It's quite warm in here actually,' he said, taking off his jacket and tossing it across the piano. 'You shouldn't complain.' He pulled off his fisherman's jumper, then his long-sleeved vest, and bared his torso. Then he moved towards Ziggy, who twisted on the chair away from him, shivering more violently than ever. The chain around his ankle was biting into him. Then Oliver took Ziggy's nipples between thumb and forefinger and squeezed. He twisted the nipples, both at once, until his nails began to cut flesh. Ziggy squirmed and clenched his teeth. The waves of sensation reached every part of his body. Then he burst into tears. 'I'll do anything you want, Oliver.'

'How's that?' asked Oliver with a contented smile. 'You don't mean that, you piece of shit. So you like it, do you? I want to see you beg for this honour.' Oliver tipped Ziggy to the floor. The ankle chain was stretched to its full extent. 'On your knees.'

It was the posture Ziggy adopted to enact King Richard's humiliation at the hands of his tormentors, before he smashes the face-glass to smithereens. He felt the familiar control and transport of performance invest his grovelling. 'Easy does it,' whimpered Ziggy, his eyes streaming. 'Good God, what's that?'

It was a spiked wooden club.

'Look, scumbag,' instructed Oliver. 'It's the morning-star. An old name for this particular instrument of torture. These things were always done at first light, as the morning-star rose in the sky.'

Ziggy was shuddering.

'Trust me,' said Oliver. 'Don't move.' Oliver dragged the morning-star back and forth across Ziggy's hairless chest, lightly, scratching and tickling.

'Don't,' squealed Ziggy. 'No, Oliver.'

'Do you accept?'

'I accept,' said Ziggy, back in the part.

'That's better.' Then Oliver took the key from around his neck and unlocked the hobble from Ziggy's ankle. Ziggy hunched over to rub his ankle where the skin was raw. Oliver took his tousled hair and pulled his head up so his eyes were looking forward.

'What do you see?' Oliver asked. He was standing in front of Ziggy's bent body, bare-chested. With his finger he traced a line through the mat of hair over his torso, down the centre of his ribcage, parting the hairs precisely to reveal a raised scar several inches long.

'A scar,' said Ziggy. 'Was it open heart surgery?' he added, unable to keep the mockery from his voice.

'Scarification,' explained Oliver, 'done with the claw of the bear. My proudest possession.'

'It must have hurt? You didn't do it yourself, Oliver? That's going too far. No, I think this is where I get off.'

'Are you interested?'

'No, Oliver. I've got my career to think of. The movie cameras. There's no hair on my chest for me to hide behind.'

Oliver chuckled. 'It would be a hairline of blood, nothing more. How do you feel?'

'Empty. Is it over now, Oliver? Will you tell me the bloody signal, please?'

'No, it's not over. It never can be. That's the other rule.' Oliver's breath was heaving.

Ziggy replied with a tender smile. 'It's over for now, Oliver. Please.'

'There's one last ritual to which you must submit,' Oliver said, 'if you are to offer yourself. I must cut you.'

They crunched the hard snow underfoot. The night was still, as if holding its breath. They passed beneath a broken arch to enter the space between the ruined walls, atop the mound at the centre of the island.

'Look up,' said Oliver, taking Ziggy's hand.

Through the open dark space they saw the half-moon gleaming brightly in the clear sky. They stood together in silence, staring upwards, heat passing between the palms of their bare clasped hands, master and disciple, parent and child.

'What do you hear?' Oliver asked, as if putting a catechism.

'What is it? A kind of rumbling. Is it the sea?' Ziggy wondered. But it was something else – an inexplicable sound from the earth itself.

'Now bare your chest.'

'It's freezing.'

'It only needs a moment. Do it.'

Oliver unzipped Ziggy's down jacket and unbuttoned his shirt to reveal hot skin which he splashed with whisky from a hip flask. Then, trembling, he took the bear's claw, which was as sharp as a razorblade, and cut Ziggy's skin in the centre of his chest. Ziggy held still and made no sound. He felt no pain. But Oliver's stomach was churning. When it was done, Oliver bent down and took a handful of snow that he clamped against Ziggy's heart. It burned along the dark line of the wound, and Ziggy emitted a guttural laugh. His body and Oliver's beside him were like fires flickering within that coldness, flames dancing within that darkness. Then the cold hit and he felt stunned, but overcoming his faintness, he stood up straight as a sword. He understood that the bond Oliver was forging with him would carry him beyond to impersonal powers. To music and art, to discipline, to the old religion, to mysterious truths – a bondage that would stay with him until his dying day. He felt as if the world of illusion, in which he had always lived apart from the everyday world, had been revealed in strength and clarity and high order. It had been given substance. For this Ziggy was in debt to Oliver Blow. Bound to him forever.

Henceforth, perhaps, he would be isolated, insulated from all that was around him, but that would be his force, his healing. He was making a sole and lasting commitment. He would exist only in that realm from now on, where Wendy lived too. The other side of the world. There was nothing else.

'Do you love me?' Oliver asked, his voice tender and vulnerable as never before.

'Yes. In eternity. I adore you.'

'As I worship you. What about here and now?'

'I'm freezing,' Ziggy whimpered. 'Hug me.' Clad in his black leather coat, Oliver wrapped his warm arms tight around Ziggy's trembling body. 'And I'm yours.'

3

LSPETH hesitated as she came across the verandah with the tray, stopping a moment while her eyes adjusted to the bright green grass on which the man had sprawled with the little girl. She could not help sniffing the place with an air of possession: watered lawn, spring flowers, strands of greasy wool floating from barbed wire, sheep dung drying in black bubbles and the perennial unsettled pink dust; she could not help thinking that she and this country belonged to each other. Which was no longer quite true. Cleve rolled over and grinned, wondering whether to get up. Cassie was grappling his shoulders.

The coronial inquiry into Wendy Sunner's death had returned an open verdict, casting doubt on a simple overdose or suicide story. Alfonzo fled the country, leaving Wendy's parents as Cassie's legal guardians. Of the Sunners' two grown-up children, one had brought them grief and the other, Sandy, had married young and had two children of her own. Neither Sandy and her husband nor Isabel and Peter wanted another child to add to their responsibility. Understanding that Elspeth and Andrew Findlay would have no children of their own, Isabel and Peter had been persuaded to let Cassie go to Elspeth, in a private adoption arrangement, while retaining their preferred role as grandparents. As Elspeth stooped to the grass with the tray of tea, Cassie screwed up her face. Cleve chuckled and picked the little girl up, ignoring her squeal, and swung her into Elspeth's arms.

'Nice kid,' he said, scrutinising Cassie's angry red face. He had his pilot's licence now and had flown from Wagga Wagga to Whitepeeper solo at Elspeth's invitation. It was a year since he had gone to the regional Lands Council.

'Is she yours?' he asked.

By asking the question Cleve allowed for the possibility of a magical belief system in which the child could indeed be Elspeth's. She was fiercely custodial.

'She's ours,' Elspeth evaded, meaning herself and Andrew. She might also have been speaking of a more generalised tribe or humanity that the child wriggling on her hip sprang from and entered into. Elspeth smiled delicately, shifting the relationships around. 'She lost her mother – Wendy, my beautiful friend. So I'm going to be her mother now.'

'That right?' Cleve grinned. 'She's strong. You can see she's travelled a long way already.'

Elspeth held the plastic beaker for Cassie to drink. But the child toddled out of reach of her keepers with her own excited purpose.

'I want to give her everything,' said Elspeth.

Cleve looked ironically at the woman. With her clear intelligent face, she was unused to defeat. 'What's that?' he asked.

'You know – I want to make it up to her, for what she's lost.'

'You've taken her away.'

She twitched at his bluntness. 'It's not like that.'

'It's lovely here – this place. But there's not much going on.' He made it sound ghostly. 'She'll need other people. Else you'll spoil her.'

'She's safe here at any rate.'

When she moved to Whitepeeper, Elspeth had believed she could resurrect the place, creating a new world there, balanced and ample. By managing the property well and leading a considered life, she and Andrew could at least justify the income she drew from the family company. Children would grow up there and bring their friends. There would be grandparents and supporters. They had started by refurbishing the homestead, then cleaned up the manager's shack where Worrie and Jenny Goodenough and their kids were installed. They revived the garden, improved the fences and water, reduced the stock and planted trees everywhere. They were experimenting with a cereal crop, using huge machines on land that, being close to where the good earth ran out, had never been ploughed or sown before. Mastermans backed and bankrolled them in all this. When anthropologists and archaeologists started crawling over the property, Elspeth took it as a sign that her vision of a flourishing site at Whitepeeper would come true.

Yet it was slow and hard. The place, remote and solitary, was like an animal that, having been maltreated once, does not learn to trust again. Sly, shifting, resistant country that played jokes of allure and rejection for which a mere idea was not enough. So too the emotional terrain between Elspeth and Andrew that had seemed to hold the promise of watering, of attention, tears and sometime sluggish passion, proved instead to be country where roots took hold precariously.

The more Elspeth was forced to acknowledge her condition, the more her vision of the place became the dream of one good season only, unlikely to survive the drought they faced – even as the experts drove out to Lake Moorna in their four-wheel drives to scratch the same earth like water-diviners. Already, when she stood alone on the verandah at evening and looked beyond the jacarandas, the silky oaks and splendid pines that her grandparents had planted, to the sea-bed of saltbush country where the stock foraged, Elspeth could no longer hold the flighty phantasm of Whitepeeper steady in her mind. It had all changed when she brought Cassie back, the new arrival she had been looking for, and she brooked no resistance in her fight through red tape until Cassie was wholly hers.

'Where's Andrew?' Cleve asked. Cassie was tugging at him.

'He'll be in later,' she said. 'Ralph Kincaid sent me a copy of his research paper on Lake Moorna the other day. They've made him a professor at the National University. Here, have a look.'

Cleve picked up the copy of *Anthropos*. 'He's taken his time.'

'Have you heard of this journal? It comes from Cambridge. The article's not very long – only a few pages, actually, and quite technical. Apparently Ralph had to be very cautious, dotting the i's and crossing the t's, because the results are world-shattering.'

'What's he say?'

'He says the skeletons he found in the sandhills are at least forty thousand years old.'

'We knew that already.'

'He says the skull type is quite different from anything found in this area before.'

'How different?'

'Totally different – from anything found in Australia. Older, far older, and quite different from more recent Aboriginal finds. It might not even be Aboriginal at all, in other words.'

'Depends what you mean by Aboriginal.'

'He says the closest thing to it is Peking Man.'

Cleve laughed at her joke. 'You mean they're Chinese?'

'Aboriginal Chinese of some kind. Maybe. Not the oldest Peking Man, which is pre-human, but a later Peking Man whose original skull was found in the nineteen-thirties, then lost again when the ship carrying it sank on the way to America.'

'You can prove anything with one skeleton.'

'Anything and nothing,' Elspeth agreed. 'But what if there are more they haven't found yet? From the way Kincaid's going on it sounds like they won't be satisfied until they've dug the whole place up.'

'How can they do that? Crazy buggers. Like building the bloody pyramids, only in reverse. Think how many years of erosion it took to expose just the few bits of bone that started this whole business, and that was pure fluke!'

'What should I do about it, Cleve?'

'Your property's become a graveyard. How do you feel about that?'

'The whole country's a graveyard, isn't it? But I don't know if I can just let them come in here any more.'

'How much land have you got here?'

'Ninety-five thousand acres.'

Cleve whistled at the scale of it. 'Then you could afford to lose a bit.'

'Lose it?'

'Give it back.'

'Who to?'

'To the dead people and their families.'

It was Elspeth's turn to laugh. 'Do they still have families after forty thousand years?'

'Those dead belong to the local people.'

'Tell me who they are. In *your* eyes.'

'The people who belong to the land.'

'Yes, but who *are* they? I belong to the land, Cleve. In the sense that it belongs to me. But I don't feel I can claim ownership over those prehistoric bones.'

'You don't *belong* to the land, Elspeth. You're the holder of a crown lease according to white man's law. Your people took the land.'

'My people bought the land off someone else.'

'Well, those people took it, or the people before them. It doesn't matter how far back you go, at the beginning it was stolen. Occupied. Nobody asked permission. It was taken and *nothing* was given in return. It was taken from *my people*.'

'Yes, I know that's how *your people* see it, and I'm sympathetic, of course, but what am I supposed to do about it? A lot of water under the bridge, Cleve. Am I guilty?'

'Since you ask – yes, you are.'

'That's the Aboriginal side of you speaking.'

'Your privilege is ill-gotten gains in anyone's terms.'

'If I *could* just give my privilege back, maybe I would. But that privilege – as you call it – is *me*. I can't just give myself away.'

'You could give this land away. It's a graveyard. What you want it for anyway?' Then Cleve gave a bright smile, pleased at his cheeky logic.

'If I gave it away, who would I give it *to*? I have to give it to someone. Is there a right person to give it to – to make restitution?'

'Is it Kincaid, you mean?'

'No way! He's just using the land for his own purposes, as all of us have done.' Cassie had crawled away from Cleve and clambered into Elspeth's arms where she lay dozing off. Elspeth looked hard into Cleve's friendly eyes. 'Tell me what to do, Cleve. I need your advice.'

He wondered at her plain and simple sense of purpose. He understood the lines she drew around herself, and admired her for that. She was offering him an alliance. Once before, at the Walls of China, she might have offered herself, but had held back. He knew the structure she was imposing on their relationship: she the land-holder, he the Aborigine on the receiving end of patronage. But it could not be like that, not really. On the basis of the relics that had been found at Lake Moorna already, his people could reclaim the land.

Old men and barefoot girls who spent their evenings on the riverbank watching handlines tugged by the current, hauling in carp, or sometimes a cod. Chubby-faced black man hoping for a ride into town from the dump where the government had allocated him a home. Worried woman on a park bench in town waiting for her man to come out of hospital. For all of them, identified as his people, Cleve must fight, using the cultural significance of the land as his weapon. The anthropologists and archaeologists and geomor-phologists and linguists, all their research, was little more than a means to that end: Survival By Any Means Possible.

For friendship's sake he gave Elspeth the only piece of advice that mattered. 'It's not something you can have power of decision over. You're dealing with something that is much bigger than you think.'

'I want this place to be good,' she said in a reply that was at once whimsical and desperate. Cleve could not see what sort of a solution she was proposing. 'I want to give back the bones to whoever they belong to – and keep the land. I want something good to come out of this for all of us. It's not just an accident that those bones have been found here. There has to be a meaning in it. I want to have a role in whatever happens.'

The yellow windsock was stirring limply in the still afternoon. The weather was fine and there were a couple of hours of daylight to go.

Cleve put on his flight gear.

Elspeth kissed him goodbye. He climbed into the plane and went through the checks. 'Wave bye-bye,' she told Cassie, waving her hand as she held her up. The plane ran, then lifted. Cleve waved from the cockpit. Every time he was airborne it thrilled him.

Andrew was working in the back paddock. Whistling, he watched Cleve go. He had worried about the property, blaming Elspeth for her openhandedness. The university wanted exclusive and unlimited access to Whitepeeper for excavation and research. Sooner or later the Aboriginal bureaucrats would want to get involved too. Outsiders poking around meant trouble. Elspeth was a conserver by nature – of art, culture, history – and Andrew considered it his duty to encourage her in that.

'No one but us has any rights at this stage,' protested Elspeth. 'It's entirely up to us.'

'But perhaps not in the long run, sweet,' Andrew said.

'We're in charge. It's up to us to manage the situation properly. We have to put a value on what we've got and stick to it.'

Andrew recognised this patrician tone of Elspeth's. 'What do you think we should do?' he asked meekly.

'You're getting attached to Cassie, aren't you, Andy?'

'When she doesn't bellow in my face.'

Elspeth smirked. 'Protect the site. Deny them access.'

'They'll be down on you like a ton of bricks. You can't lock up the most important archaeological find in this country.'

'What difference can a few more years make? Those bones have been there since the year dot.'

Elspeth put on her grand air. She could not help herself. The prehistoric bones, thought Andrew wryly, offered scope for a new kind of husbandry.

~

Sir Perceval went into rehearsal to open in the spring. The show was to be the big event of the London season. Ziggy wrote all this to Alex, chronicling what was happening to him. He also wrote, more circumspectly, to Herbert Horsfall.

As a man of the theatre himself, Herbert was less easily impressed. Not that he doubted Ziggy's talent. But he was sceptical about talent's chances in a wicked world. Herbert believed it was more important to do work you could be proud of than to achieve success in the public eye. He congratulated Ziggy on getting such a plum West End role, but reserved judgement until he could see the final product. Ziggy had not told Herbert the whole strange story of his relationship with composer-librettist Oliver Blow, but Herbert could guess from the uneasy excitement of the communication that Ziggy was closer to the pinnacle than he had ever dreamed of being: the gaze fixed from afar on a sun-capped peak that drew him forward, the outsider's sustaining dream. Ziggy was almost there, inside it, in the real working world of it, yet always conscious, when the wax started to sweat, that it might all melt and dump him in the sea.

Horsfall wrote to Ziggy from Melbourne where he was trying to raise support for a grand project of his own – a musical based on the life, triumph and cruel decline of Australia's most famous Aboriginal artist, Albert Namatjira. People's eyes rolled when the project was mentioned. *Namatjira: the Death*, they quipped. It was a mammoth pioneer undertaking that Horsfall was developing with a young people's theatre company on money from cash-strapped government agencies and private sponsors – a story, not of death, he replied to his critics, but of life; a story of survival and resurrection. Horsfall never despaired. Every day brought him some small thing to keep his hopes alive. He imagined himself as one of those nineteenth-century explorers of the Australian continent on a quixotic quest for the inland sea. Only on the stage he would actually find it.

Alex's reply to Ziggy was an equally long letter about the drama of the election campaign. What it came down to this time was the election of five lower-house seats in the apple-shaped island state of Tasmania, former severest penal colony of Van Diemen's Land, known for the produce of its cosy green farms and no less for its so-called wilderness country of wild rivers and human emptiness. The southern island, divided in itself as well as divided from the mainland, was in a state of decline as the national economy looked north to the sun and to Asian markets. Should the island sell itself off, log its forests, dam its rivers, give away its hydroelectric power, flush other people's waste into its waters? Or should it preserve itself, putting a value for posterity on the very attributes that seemed to be most disadvantageous, its pristine air and water, its natural forests, its biodiversity, its future as a remote treasure garden at the bottom of the world?

To impose a policy of strenuous environmental protection, vetoing development in line with community feelings, risked treading on the toes of the independent-minded people of the island. To compensate, a deal must be done. If they were to be asked to forego progress in the usual sense, they could not be expected to pay for the losses themselves. If they were to preserve themselves for the sake of the world, then the world must pay. More precisely, the big siblings on the mainland must pay for their little sister state – and pay they would, according to the policy package Alex Mack put together for John Lewin to articulate. Tasmania could be green, if the nation put a value on its greenness. Tasmanians, with their crucial five seats, would make the decision themselves, and their independence would be uncompromised. Voters in the marginal green-thinking mortgage belt across the country, concerned for a world that was becoming unfit for their families to grow up in, would buy this compact and be swayed to the support of the party. This was the message hammered home by Lewin, Shadow Minister for Resources and the Environment, who had become a member of the House of Representatives after a convenient by-election and whose arm had been successfully twisted to make him take over the job of leader of a desperate party only weeks before election day.

Well, it worked, Alex wrote to Ziggy. Thanks to the sublime rhetoric that he masterminded for party and leader in the campaign to save the wild rivers of south-western Tasmania, symbol of saving the planet for a better future for humanity, not only did all the Tasmanian seats go green for the party at the election, but through-out the country the party waltzed into power. Anointed with that green oil, John Lewin became Prime Minister.

In the administrative reshuffle that followed, Alex became head of the Department of Resources and Environment, renamed the Department of the National Estate. After a decent interval the vic-torious Lewin relinquished that portfolio, tossing the political hot potato to Valerie O'Rourke. So Valerie became Alex's Minister. Minister for the National Estate, and his boss. When he was horny, or lonely, he slept with other Canberra women – but not with Valerie now.

Alex Mack had earned his spurs. For one so young he was in a position of exceptional power. He had shinned up the slippery pole and, as he sat there now, he could not help smiling at the destiny that had smiled on him.

I suppose you're never coming back, mate. It would be good to see you again, he added carefully to end the letter. *Love, Alex.*

~

Sir Perceval opened at Drury Lane in the late northern spring of that year. There were ten days of previews, then the opening night. The production closed three weeks later. It was an almighty flop. Even while tentative audiences kept coming, morbidly curious to see if the poisonous reviews were true, the backers pulled out their money to cut their huge losses. If no one ever lost a dollar by underestimating the public, in the old show business adage, no one was ever wrong-footed either by overestimating the bile of London's opinion-formers. The critics convicted Oliver Blow of hubris. Here was a showman, a maker of spectacles, a writer of theme music, attempting to cross over into high art, into epic, into opera for God's sake, expecting his same vast lucrative mass audience to follow him.

'The swine don't know how *vulgar* their ideas of *high art* are,' groaned Oliver with tears in his eyes, wounded to the quick when the response from the press was all thumbs-down.

'You don't need them,' said Ziggy, comforting Oliver in vain. 'They can't touch you!'

The reviews for Ziggy Vincaitis were polite. He was not the target. The critics said he stuck out like a black swan among domestic fowl. But neither did it do him much good.

Taste had changed. People needed a happy ending. They had to believe that triumph was still possible. They had to believe that if an individual made an effort a positive outcome could be achieved. Gone were the days of tragedy. Gone was the time when human beings might achieve self-knowledge in being humbled before the mighty gods, the implacable forces of an order stronger than themselves and enigmatically indifferent. That was Oliver Blow's real mistake. *Sir Perceval* was no tragedy, of course – it was triumphalist too, but in quite the wrong way. It was a story of inner victory in an invisible realm where few could follow. There was no love between the characters, no boy gets girl, and nothing to show for the happy outcome.

~

Jane was in retreat from the unreality and indulgence of an art world that increasingly irked her. Most art was meaningless, she knew, vanity and commercial folly. But the impulse to make art was not meaningless. A bubble of acclaim had awaited her return to Sydney from New York. Her showings were glamorous affairs. She had her own studio at Bondi. But she knew she must prepare for a slower rhythm of achievement when the bubble burst. She had risen, she was recognised – the caravan would move on.

'I always knew you were a masochist,' said Cynthia when Jane told her she was taking on some work at Long Bay Prison as an art therapist. She needed to get SoHo out of her system. By tutoring a few maximum security inmates in how to channel their urge for self-expression, she might connect with the deeper sources of her own art as well as fine-tuning her politics at a time when the fashion was for art to become more directly political. Since she did not see how her lush, sensuous, symbolic style could comply with a highly theorised political inflection, Jane had decided to preserve her purity and imaginative strength and become political in practice instead. The ultimate and basic power relation between people, she thought, was the power of one to turn the key on the life of another.

But there was no sense of confinement on the road to White-peeper. The flat straight strip of orange dirt barely undulated, in long shallow breaths, through the saltbush and light scrub country. For the trip she carried rolls of paper, sketching pads, pencils, crayons, charcoal and the black pen she always used. She took a pile of reading matter and bush gear for any situation. The independence of travelling alone suited her. She conceded now that she would live her life on her own, which made her art matter all the more. It also made her few enduring relationships matter. Reaching her destination, she crossed the stock grid to the yard in excitement and the mongrel pup came yapping to greet her, followed by Elspeth and Andrew and a valiantly toddling Cassie, who fought off the pup. Jane kissed and hugged them all. Elspeth was like a sister to her, and she was auntie and godmother to Cassie, daughter of her best friend, and would inscribe her presence on the child's life, joining her to the world of women, sharing her with Elspeth as far as she could.

She stayed for five days, spending long hours preoccupied with her work, long hours in rambling conversation with Elspeth, Cassie playing around them, making up a third as Wendy had done when they were girls. Jane felt she needed to talk through all their lives before the patterns ahead could be imagined.

'Maybe there is no pattern,' suggested Elspeth.

Andrew, for his part in the visit, was a gentleman and drove Jane around the property showing her the sights. They took hours to drive over the enormous place on the rough winding tracks, opening and closing gates, stopping to notice roos, emus, birds, stumpy-tail lizards, stopping to identify trees and flowering shrubs. Then Jane felt confident going out by herself with her paper and colours. She made marks and wrote words, ending in question marks. She did not draw. Bluebush? Rose-madder? Ellipse? Eclipse? Infinity? She furrowed her brow. The windswept place disordered the thoughts in her mind. The more she wanted to find something there, the more she understood there was nothing to find. That was its meaning. Varying slightly, yet without breaking into the features of even the simplest narrative, the country went on for miles.

The dry sunken bed of Lake Moorna, when at last she reached it, was the dominant feature only because it was even more minimal than the surrounding plain. The huge circle, covered with native grasses and wildflowers, had a pastel glow. On the far eastern side the creamy hillocks that formed the foreshore of the ancient lake gave a mild elevation, with the irony of a grandiose name from elsewhere, the Walls of China. She sought the top of the low sand lunette as a vantage point, her eye needing a position and a view if she was to make a picture out of it. Yet she found almost nothing there, scarcely even shadow from the blazing sun overhead. It was about as far from Renaissance perspective as could be imagined, and even further from Romantic elevation, let alone the Sublime. The negation of landscape as conceived in the pictorial tradition: no alps, no crags, no ruined towers, no nestling hamlets; in that lay its teasing eloquence.

Jane was filled with praise for the poor mad artist who had early grasped this truth – Ludwig Becker, German naturalist and draftsman who died out there a hundred years ago. In minute attentiveness he drew the rats and shells of that domain, on human scale, and the abstract splendour of the whole, gibber plain and falling star, on a contrary scale of endless horizontal and fleeting vertical. At the mercy of a rigid egotistical commander and an obtuse vainglorious managing committee who regarded his art as more useless than his camel-handling skills, he was allowed to die out there. Good riddance to the eccentric outsider who prided himself on his birdcalls and his German songs. Yet he had *seen*, and left behind the record of that quickened serenity of his mind. Jane had studied his watercolours and drawings, not to repeat him, but to remind herself that there were images buried within the ground she stood on. It was as if the spirits that haunted the place were invisible and mute, keeping their secrets in order to drive her crazy. The marks she made on paper, the scrawled words, became more and more chaotic. She wanted an art of radical iconoclasm and negation of meaning, beyond abstraction, beyond minimalism, yet also of presence and sensuous plenitude; she struggled with these intimations, putting pigment to paper intermittently, rescuing single notes from the place. Then at the end of each session she threw down her implements in frustration and returned to the homestead for food and wine and talk.

She began to understand that life there was a trade-off. Tracks, bores and long straight fences to contain stock were proprietorial markings on the mind-crazing unchartedness of the country, as if the occupiers would use the place as they could, for their own purposes, and ask no further questions. The tea on the verandah, the roses in the garden, the endless talk of markets, water, drought, the preoccupation with inheritance and passing it on: exchanges made in the heat of a determination to stay with the place and make it work.

Jane asked Elspeth what she was heir to and Elspeth explained that she felt a sense of responsibility to her ancestors who had worked the land. She did not presume to judge them. Why should *she* cross-examine them? That was history. She acknowledged a legacy of greed and dissatisfaction; her mother Barb, in all her rootless questing, had never found the sense of attachment she craved. Barb was dead from bowel cancer now. It had been mercifully quick, but how Elspeth missed her. Barb had been tenacious in her attachment to life. It was such attachment that Elspeth had tried to create at Whitepeeper. Her mother had understood that. Yet she was not so silly as to want attachment to material things. Had she not once almost given away her house to the orange people, to the Divine Leader's sect? Had she not allowed herself to be rescued from an attachment to Italy and Giugi Bono, who would have loved her? Barb had always been able to hook into her. Not so Angus, her father. And were not her attachments to Andrew, to Whitepeeper, even to Cassie, all coolly conscious? Could that attachment lift away, Jane asked. Did Elspeth see that she was not free, having the weight of her fortune and no choice in the burden of inheritance, in which there was little honour or truth?

'Who will you pass it on to?' asked Jane.

Elspeth looked embarrassed. 'I suppose it will be Cassie's one day.'

'Don't you find that ironical? You keep it in the family in order to give it to the child of two people who have nothing to do with any of it. A junkie and a sleazy Maltese drug dealer.'

Elspeth looked angry. 'Why does that matter? It's my choice. I can make the lineage whatever I want.'

'You're proving your willpower.'

'Wendy almost came here once,' said Elspeth. 'Do you remember that riverboat excursion we went on at school with Joke and Mrs Schumann?'

'That wasn't *here*, was it?'

'It's not far from another part of the property, on the far southern boundary. The river's there.'

'You're joking, Elspeth. I had no idea this was the same place.'

'We chugged up the river from Renmark on that boat. Remember? Wendy worked on her suntan the whole way. She was reading *L'Etranger*.'

'You remember all of it.'

'Then she got the hots for Robbie Masterman. I've still got one of your sketches from that trip. A crow in the sunset over the red cliffs.'

'Oh Jesus. Then this is the place where we found the chaps digging up the Aboriginal graves.'

'Within coo-ee,' said Elspeth.

'Alex was there, wasn't he?'

'He was too. And Johnny, your brother, and all the Mastermans.'

'Whatever happened to those bones? Do you think they could have been forty-thousand years old too?'

'I doubt that they ever got to the Museum,' Elspeth said. 'That headmaster pretended they were ancient bones to justify digging them up, then he dismissed them as recent bones when it came to knowing what to do with them. Do you remember that horrible pink-faced man, so full of himself?'

'Didn't Alex have a skull he kept in a shoebox?' asked Jane. 'His mother threw it out and he was devastated. He never wanted people to know about that. This place is more amazing than I thought,' said Jane. 'No wonder I don't know how to deal with it in my work.'

'Do you understand why I feel attached to it?'

Jane scrutinised Elspeth. Lean and lined, she had gone on to another part of her life's cycle, where she was already a conduit for passing things from one generation to the next. Jane shuddered a little. She was worried for Cassie. Despite the efficient and loving way Cassie was handled, there was a lack of present life about Elspeth somehow. 'I hope you don't turn into one of those skeletons too,' said Jane strangely.

'We all will eventually,' replied Elspeth.

'*Eventually*,' repeated Jane. 'But not yet. Isn't the oldest skeleton out there a cremated young woman?'

'Moorna Woman.'

'How are you and Andrew getting on?' Jane tried to soften the conversation by turning to intimate matters. 'He's like a cringing dog around you. The moment you're not around he starts singing.'

'Like in the shower?'

'He's a sweet bloke. I like him. But I would never have picked him for you. That's all.'

'Oh?' Elspeth was affronted. 'What you're saying, Jane, is that I should get up and take Cassie and walk off this place, and leave Andrew and all the rest of it behind. Is that the message?'

'You're capable of that. If Wendy had done likewise, it would have saved her life.'

Elspeth's clear eyes peered across the land. She brushed the hair back from her forehead, irritated at what Jane proposed for her – Jane who fed off everyone else and gave back what? Jane was a gypsy whom other people would always grant an existence. In return she told people what to do with their lives, making it seem easy. That was being an artist. What Elspeth saw out there, in lieu of Jane's gypsy picture, was a trek through space without end.

'I know,' she said.

4

WHEN he received Elspeth Findlay's polite handwritten letter, Professor Kincaid could not but blame human nature for the gutlessness of its desire for knowledge. Elspeth had exercised her power by insisting that any request for access to the property should come to her in writing for prior consideration. She would no longer guarantee approval. Kincaid saw it as a typical, petty obstruction. He took the whole world of knowledge for his domain. As a socialist, he believed that the common good outweighed individual property rights. As an archaeologist, he was utopian in reverse. His work dealt with other worlds. Present-day arrangements ought not interfere.

'Those people don't even own the land,' he spluttered to the Secretary of the Department of the National Estate down the phone, when he called to make an appointment to discuss the matter. 'It's leasehold. They've got a ninety-nine year lease. It's still crown land. They've got no business standing in our way.'

But Kincaid did not mention names, having learned in Australia, where everyone seemed to know everyone else, that it was better that way.

The office was on the top floor of a new building on the southern shore of Lake Burley Griffin. The view swept in a westward arc from the determined symmetry of the war memorial across the water over low blue hills to the steel elevations of the construction site for the new parliament house that would perhaps be completed in time for the bicentenary of the nation in 1988. The Department of the National Estate took in history, political process and the land, remade according to people's visions. Land and water, in symbolic harmony in the capital, were antagonists elsewhere in the story of Australia. Water – or the lack of it: Alex Mack smiled. Kincaid was coming to discuss Lake Moorna. A lake that mattered because it was not a lake. A lake without water for perhaps fifteen millennia. Lake immemorial.

Ralph Kincaid was known for his shrewd common touch. He had a twinkling wit and did not sulk when he lost a battle, as long as he won the war: the best lobbyist for archaeological heritage in the country. When he started out, there had been no market for archaeology: no artifacts of gold and precious stones, no tomb hordes, no rare vessels. He had redefined archaeology in Australia as the sites and fieldwork that told stories, promised intellectual discoveries, revised history. Archaeology had always evoked wonder at the grandeur of humanity's achievements beyond the stretch of finite lives. Its real treasure was not gold or silver, but time itself, Kincaid argued, making palpable Australia's claim to be the oldest continent. There was a continuity between land and people that stretched further back than anywhere else. And the latest arrivals in Australia, immigrants all, wove themselves into the story as excavators and articulators. As proposed by this clever man, Australian prehistory was an essential nation-forming discipline. Governments and administrators gratefully took note.

Mack was clever too – and young, Kincaid was reminded, when he walked, unfazed, into the lofty office.

'Good to see you, Ralph,' said Alex, coming out from behind the large table to shake the older man's hand. His hair was smooth and wavy and he had on a new shiny suit. What he lacked in experience, he made up in clear imaging of how the future must break with the past. He knew the old world was wrong. To right it he saw no alternative but to change everything. That was his job.

The Professor, a short man with a moonish face, wore the tweed jacket and timeless trousers of academic costume and had plastered down his thinning hair.

'Farsighted of our new masters to put you into this job,' Kincaid began, reminding the Departmental Head which one of them was the new boy. 'We need people like you.'

'Thanks for your confidence. The truth is we need people like yourself.'

'There aren't many mad enough to give a lifetime to Australian archaeology as I've done. Digging in the sands of time! Well, maybe we're getting somewhere at last. The ripples are still going round the world about these finds at Lake Moorna. They make us the earliest recorded site of human civilisation.'

Alex squinted. His long nose hung down sniffing. 'Is "civilisation" the right word, Professor?'

'The ochring of the skin. The cremation procedures. It makes us the first known place where death had meaning. That implies something about life in turn. Death was ceremonious. It was part of a story. Life did not just simply stop, it transposed, changed gear, modulated key, however you like to put it. There was an understanding, shared by the community, of something that came after. Those people were not animals or mute dispensable units. They were part of the process of creating a pattern in their existence. In that essential participatory sense, they were citizens, so I allow them to be called civilisation, continuous with our own.'

'Right,' nodded Alex, excited to follow the direction of the Professor's argument.

'It makes them of immeasurable importance,' declared Kincaid professorially. 'I propose that their site be listed on the National Estate forthwith and that we institute procedures for a world heritage listing.'

'Can we do that?'

'What could possibly have a stronger claim? It's easy enough to argue, Alex, if the political will is there.'

'What are the implications?'

'A listing will place certain obligations on the leaseholders in that area.'

'You said on the phone they're denying access.'

'Well, they would benefit from some guidance. I think they really don't know what to do.'

'I see.'

'What would Valerie's position be?' Kincaid queried.

Alex paused warily. He looked at the Professor, wondering what complications lay concealed behind this nice idea. Then he let his anxiety go. He was interested in what would work. 'The Minister would probably welcome something of this kind. It would be a chance for us to develop the gazetting mechanism, apart from anything else. I'll have a word with her.'

'If you think it would help, Alex, I'd be more than happy to do a lunch.'

'The case would need to be supported by a body of fully substantiated scientific opinion,' Alex cautioned.

'Of course. That's straightforward enough. I've prepared some notes.'

From his old leather briefcase Kincaid drew out a file, checked its contents and passed it across the desk.

'Thanks,' beamed Alex. 'Something constructive at last. Something more interesting than the usual grinding disputes between greenies and the exploiters of the land.'

The Professor nodded, his head bobbing repeatedly, as he got out of the chair to end the interview. He believed in conserving his tremendous energy. A little went a long way.

After seeing the man to the door, Alex paused to notice a rowboat zipping across the lake. In a moment's contemplation of something outside and particular, he could balance himself for the next step forward. Like a tightrope walker. Not unlike a lone oarsman. If he stopped to reflect too long, however, he would lose the flow. He could not afford to go back over things too much. This highly developed technique, the ability to clear his head by focusing on a fly's buzz, or a tree's gusting, or the sweating nape of the person in front, for a mere instant, before bowing his own head to the yoke again, had been achieved when, as a student, he was a successful examination candidate. In his position of Secretary of the Department, he created spaces for people to operate in, tracks on which they could be carried toward destinations that were always far enough off to be shifted if necessary.

Adept with language, he understood administration as a matter of words. To conceptualise, specify, grade, blur, bend, simplify, persuade, enforce and applaud. Having a command of words himself, he had never bothered to resolve the relationship between words and the world through a philosophy of language. People's needs, material production, life and death: he might worry about these things, but he had never worked them out finally, since language was sufficient of itself to all intents and purposes. Language was a zone of mastery he need not step beyond. Formulation, presentation, word of mouth, the media, oratory, the vote. Politics was language too. Creative politics meant inventing things. Once invented, they would be there forever. Then it was over to the numbers people.

He turned from the window and put Kincaid's file to one side, having decided what to do. He left the building and walked across the grass to Valerie O'Rourke's ministerial suite in the old parliament house. Every day parliament was sitting, he took this walk as Department Secretary to brief his Minister. He liked the serried pines and large standard rosebushes in circular plantings in the park – a pleasing pattern successfully imposed, a model he could imagine extending to Australia as a whole. As head of the department that managed both the natural and human environments, he worked with a process of taking imaginary blueprints and making them real. That was how he would present the proposed National Estate listing of Lake Moorna to Valerie O'Rourke, as a way of taking nothing and making it a place on the world map.

Nothing.

He had driven across those plains so many times, east–west, west–east, when his main concern had been to avoid hitting a roo or his car breaking down. A long dull tunnel through emptiness, the road was good for relaxing the mind. He had not a clue himself what was out there. Once the Minister agreed, he would put one of his top assistant secretaries on the Lake Moorna proposal to work Kincaid's documents up into point-form policy that would create a heritage site out there. A national park, created from nothing. A place where people would come to visit a landscape. Multidimensional setting for human leisure. Pleasure. Mental cultivation. A park could happen anywhere within the government's power to decide.

With this big picture in mind, Alex Mack went up the steps of the gloomy parliamentary building, already on the way to becoming a museum, and proceeded down the long corridor, doors open, doors shut, to the Office of the Minister for the National Estate.

It was the house's early dinner break. Valerie was dressed in a green linen suit with power shoulders, stiff hennaed hair and a touch of gold on her ears and neck. Although she despised Thatcher's politics, she had not been immune to the image of the British Prime Minister.

Valerie was tired after another day in the stuffy chamber of men. She looked with amusement at Alex as she fell into a chair and took the white wine he poured her. As one of Prime Minister Lewin's inner circle, she was always in the limelight these days, and on the spot.

'Balls for brains,' she said, cursing one of her colleagues. 'He's forcing me to make all the running. I don't know where he gets his stuff from. It's totally inadequate. I'm expected to gild the lily. Cheers. They think that Environment includes everything. Animals, women, children – in that order – nature, culture, agriculture. Dogs in space.'

'It's an expanding portfolio,' replied Alex, 'I'm sorry to say. It's one of the few things people care about enough to define for themselves.'

'Everything but the money to pay for it all. Jesus Maria,' said Valerie, flicking through the folder of ministerials that offered answers to the questions likely to be asked that session. 'It's looking a bit tokenistic.'

'Community-based,' replied Alex, interpreting for her. 'It's okay. We're responding to specific local needs and initiatives.'

'Small is beautiful?'

'Small is cheap.'

'I don't just want a whole string of good works as if I'm some sort of new-fashioned Country Women's Association. Well, that's what it's starting to look like, isn't it? We need a big ticket item, Alex. A pioneering piece of legislation, something for future generations. The Tasmanian stuff belongs to the last election. We need a new start.'

'What went wrong with Tasmania was the way the Commonwealth had to steamroller the State government. State rights and the compensation issue. That's what took the shine off.'

'Whatever we do next time, it has to be with a co-operative state government.'

Alex and Valerie were cosy together. They could make sense of the contradictions and paradoxes, failings and downright unpleasantness in each other. Since they had ruled out becoming lovers again, despite an easy affection between them, they were able to operate in an intimate alliance, substituting for sex a highly stoked passion for power. As minister, Valerie O'Rourke had the role of carrying the values of her constituency – progressive egalitarian educated women and the men who shared their outlook – forward into a tougher political environment. Her vocation consisted of tireless struggle and compromise, preparing for another generation to take the baton. Alex was different, serving ideas not people. Adviser-administrator and representative-legislator, they were two sides of a coin, and although the pragmatic and worldly terms they talked in might have sounded ugly to an eavesdropper, they believed they were making a good society, Valerie doing so in support of human nature, and Alex in spite of it.

'How would you like a world heritage listing in the backblocks of New South Wales?' asked Alex. 'In an area where there are no conflicts with logging or hydroelectricity or sandmining or any other use? In an area of marginal forgotten country that is of supreme interest to palaeontologists and archaeologists and nobody else? There's a place in the far west of the state where some human bones have been found in a dried-up lakebed that have been dated back *forty thousand fucking years*. There's a proposal from the university people to list it on the National Estate. The first world heritage listing in outback Australia.'

'Would anyone actually want to go there?' Valerie asked.

Alex gave a naughty chuckle. 'That doesn't really matter. If it's a world heritage site, the idea is not to have visitors. You can always just close it off.'

'It's in New South Wales, you said. We can work with them, can't we?' Valerie smiled instructively back at Alex, like a schoolteacher. 'That's important.'

'I gather the site is quite spectacular in itself. Ancient sandhills, local fauna and flora, vast flat plains, miles and miles of empty space.'

'Great place for a holiday,' snickered Valerie. 'We could go there for a naughty weekend. Where is it exactly?'

She had a map of Australia framed on the wall of her office. Wineglass in hand, Alex joined her in front of it. Together they stared at the familiar coastline and cities and state borders, straight but for the River Murray that divided Victoria from New South Wales, and the apple of Tasmania off the bottom. There were a few country centres then all the large areas of empty space, unmarked on the map. Somewhere near the border of New South Wales, Victoria and South Australia Alex's finger circled in the air.

'Somewhere here,' he said cautiously.

Valerie snorted. 'There's *nothing* there.'

'That's right,' he replied. 'But there will be. Thanks to you.'

Valerie frowned at Alex, tightening her political instincts. 'Is it really a good idea?'

'It's an important idea, Valerie. It embodies a vision of Australia as an ancient land for all humanity, for all time. Australia the land of good custodianship and good management of our assets. That is our world role – Australia as world park. We need forceful symbols – high-profile National Estate and world heritage sites – to make that point. Don't you love the idea of a major archaeological site in a country that has no Stonehenge, no Parthenon, no pyramids? By making a vanished site of human settlement into world heritage, we're making an important statement. The land becomes its own monument. It's beautiful, Val.'

Valerie was delighted by the impassioned glint in Alex's eyes as he argued the case. 'Are they still finding things out there?'

'They hope to. The first finds happened by accident. Some geezer in a small plane. Who knows what else is there?'

'The first find – what was it?'

'The bones of a woman, cremated.'

'A woman?'

'A young woman called Moorna. Moorna Woman. She started all this.'

'You're kidding. That's nice, isn't it? An appropriate touch.' Valerie's conviction was growing.

'Will the Prime Minister support this?' Alex asked her.

'Oh yes,' she said, 'John'll have to.'

'The land will need to be acquired,' continued Alex, 'as a gift to the Australian people.'

'That will cost,' hummed Valerie.

'If we gazette first, place it on the heritage list so that any other land use will be restricted, that should drop the land value. It's lease-hold, you see, all through New South Wales. Crown land to start with. Under those circumstances I imagine the leaseholders would be happy to get out with a gold watch and a handshake.'

'They've had a good run,' Valerie guffawed. 'All that empty space on the map and nothing to show for it.'

'Wool,' Alex reminded her, 'and a few failed experiments with wheat.'

'They put all their eggs in one basket. The world market for one or two commodities. Monoculture,'Valerie sneered. She had taken on the idea. She glowed when she had a new campaign to embark on.

Mack's Department worked in close consultation with Kincaid and his colleagues to put together the Lake Moorna National Estate and World Heritage Listing submission. A search was done through federal, state and local council registers to compile all existing knowledge relating to the site. Geomorphological analysis was made from aerial photography. Species lists were produced. Past usages were accounted for and a historical register of occupancy, subdivision and transfer of leaseholds was produced. The central argument for heritage status, backed by the standing of the scientists involved and the will of the Australian government, was Lake Moorna as a dynamic index of geological, anthropological, historic and biosphere-related factors of change on a human and supra-human scale.

In a very short time the listing had taken place. Legislation was prepared to enshrine the compliance of all levels of Australian government with world heritage guidelines. The boundaries of a new Lake Moorna National Park within the world heritage area were drawn up, to be announced on World Environment Day by Minister O'Rourke. Once the decision was made public, a plan of management for the site would be drafted in consultation with all those on the ground.

It was only a few days before the press release went out that Alex caught sight of a reference to Masterman Holdings in the list of properties to be affected by the decision. He rang the assistant secretary in charge who found the file and quickly returned her boss's call. When she read out the name 'Whitepeeper', Alex stopped the woman in her tracks.

'Yes, that's the central leaseholding,' the assistant secretary replied. 'That's the station with Lake Moorna actually on it. It's to become the main body of the new national park.'

'Have you spoken to the leaseholders?'

'Not directly at this stage. The plan is to go with the public announcement first, right?'

'Right,' sighed Alex wearily. 'Thanks.' He hung up the phone and, staring across his desk at his view of the real, if artificial lake, gave a manic laugh and scratched at the skin that seemed to tighten round his neck. Wasn't Whitepeeper Elspeth Gillingham's place? Mastermans deserved to have their land appropriated. But not where Elspeth lived. He must speak to her before it was too late. But it was too late already. Without realising it, he had turned her home into a national park, compromising its value, taking it out from under her. How would she react, when she heard that, by law, it could no longer be used for existing purposes? Nor even perhaps for private occupancy: the details remained to be worked out. Alex saw how Kincaid had carefully avoided any further consultation with the leaseholders after they gave him his first cool rebuff. Names were not even mentioned. Alex blamed himself for not looking at the map more closely, not making the connection. Big picture stuff only. The devil was in the detail. His throat tensed. Too late now. The press release would be in the papers in the morning.

It was his mother's face he saw when he put his head in his hands. Clarice's natural wish that he should marry Elspeth Gillingham, daughter of her best friend Barb, who was a Masterman, had always irked him. Elspeth was all right, but he never wanted to marry her or her property; and now here he was lifting their land from them. Was it subconscious revenge? He wished – or did he? – that he had the chance to convince Elspeth of the importance of the world heritage listing first, so as at least not to appear sneaky.

He got home to his townhouse and, digging his dog-eared private address book out of a drawer, found Elspeth's country number. That was always how he thought about her. Elspeth in the country. He had never really known where she was. Just the name Whitepeeper. 'Elspeth? It's Alex Mack here. Yes, out of the blue. I know. How are you?'

'Oh, we're fine, thanks. Cassie's settled down now. I think she's happy here. She's certainly made a difference.'

'Oh – Cassie? Wendy's –'

'Yes, she's twenty months now.'

'How wonderful. I'd forgotten you had her with you. What does she look like?'

'She looks like her mum,' said Elspeth with gentle restraint. 'Just as beautiful.' People who had known Wendy were hard for Elspeth to deal with, and with Alex there had always been friction and sensitivity. They had always challenged each other.

'I'm calling from Canberra,' he said.

'You're something big there now, aren't you? I heard. Well done.'

He laughed at her belittling of his achievement. 'It's to do with my work that I'm ringing, I'm afraid.'

'Is it because of the bones?' she asked at once.

'So you know? Partly. That's right. Only the bones are in Canberra now, at the university.' He told her that an area of country including Whitepeeper was to be gazetted as national park under a world heritage listing.

'Just like that?' she queried ironically. 'Who said they could take the bones away anyway?'

'It's been a long process to arrive at the proposal. I had no idea you were involved.'

'Proposal?'

'That's all it is officially at this stage, although it has actually gone further than that. You weren't contacted, I suppose, because it's crown land. The government is entitled to change the terms of the lease when the lease expires.'

'They've probably been talking to Masterman Holdings,' Elspeth said.

'Who's that?'

'Well, Brice Masterman. He's the current chairman.'

'That must be who's been spoken to. None of the details are public until the Minister makes her speech in a couple of days.'

'I never understand how bureaucracy works. What have you got to do with it, Alex? Why are *you* ringing me?'

'Oh, I'm ringing informally. I'm the head of the Department of the National Estate that's doing it.'

'And you didn't know? Really? You used to be good at geography.'

'Back in primary school,' he countered.

Elspeth felt an uncontrollable mixture of anger and amusement. 'Are we going to be paid for it, or is this highway robbery?'

'I'm sorry, Elspeth,' he whispered. 'There will be proper consultation once the announcement is made.'

'I told you, it's not my decision. You'll have to talk to Cousin Brice. But I doubt that he'll be very amenable. You know how people like him feel about government intervention. Have you ever been out here, Alex?'

'I must have driven past on the road from Adelaide to Canberra.'

'That's miles away!' she hooted. 'Look, what worries me is who said they could take *the bones* away in the first place. Shouldn't you be worrying about that?'

'That was before my time.'

'Cassie loves it here. I mightn't care much otherwise, but for her sake I do care, actually.'

A calculation stopped her asking Alex about Cleve Gordon. If she, as the occupier, had only just been spoken to, it was unlikely that the Aboriginal people whose bones might be lying there, far more recent than forty thousand years, had crossed the horizon of the Department's mind.

'This is the work of academics?' she asked instead, accusing.

'In a way. It's part of a redefinition of Australia in the eyes of the world.'

'I wish I could see you, Alex. What do you look like now? You sound the same. After all this time. It's funny.'

'I haven't changed,' he said.

'Come and see us, Alex. Come and see the place for yourself. Before this goes too far.'

'I'm sure we'll be in touch again.'

When Elspeth returned to the dinner table with the news, her husband Andrew fell to his habitual cursing of governments and cityfolk. Then he looked at it from a different angle.

'We could buy our own place somewhere,' he said optimistically. 'There must be some money in this for us.'

'Yes, we could,' Elspeth doubted.

Masterman Holdings received a letter from the government advising that the property known as Whitepeeper was listed for gazetting as a national park in the new Lake Moorna World Heritage Area. The Commonwealth of Australia wished to acquire the land for a negotiated price at the leaseholder's convenience. The original ninety-nine year lease would not in any event be renewable when it expired in five years' time.

Brice Masterman was blustering about the letter when Elspeth saw him in Adelaide. He was suspicious when she said she had heard about it in a phone call from Alex Mack. Masterman was trying to remember the Macks' kid, one of his son Robbie's friends. He could picture a scrawny figure on the beach the morning Clarice Mack drowned, but without a face, and that was years ago although it seemed like yesterday.

Since Cleve's visit, Elspeth had been brooding. Whitepeeper was keeping her somewhere she perhaps should not stay. They got so little out of their farming. Wool – and wheat, Andrew's innovation, one year in three a good crop. Yes, she loved it when the shearing shed filled with sheep and shearers and rouseabouts, a galleon afloat in the paddock with a full crew, and a good cheque when the clip was done. But it was so little compared with the age and beauty of the land – the middens and burial sites and things undiscovered nor yet understood.

She asked Cousin Brice what it would cost to give the place away. What kind of gap in the business would it make, she meant, without considering how it could be given or to whom.

Masterman would have preferred to have the discussion with Andrew, but Elspeth had confided none of this to her husband. It would only make him uneasy, when he could not see himself anywhere else, even while he had come to wonder whether Whitepeeper was just another of Elspeth's settings or masks. But before any of that could be considered, Elspeth needed to get a feel for Brice's reaction.

'Don't be an idiot, El,' he said. 'The place is worth a packet. Ninety-five thousand acres of dry-land farming potential. It's the size of a small country. It's a top asset. Our livelihood depends on it.'

That bullied his young cousin into silence. 'Another drought won't do much for our livelihood,' she retorted at last.

Masterman waved the letter in her face and asked if it was some scheme of hers to allow her to cash in on Whitepeeper. 'It's not yours to give away – or sell,' he snorted. 'It's a directors' decision.'

'Looks like it's theirs to buy, though.'

'I'd like to see how they negotiate a price.' As chairman of Masterman Holdings, the weathered farmer could be attracted by a bird in the hand.

'It could work to our advantage, couldn't it?'

'Depends how bad they want it. What about the improvements? The homestead, the sheds, the manager's house, the fencing? They're not much good in a bloody national park.'

'They would become part of it.'

'You too, living there on show, like the drover's wife?'

'I would have to be relocated,' said Elspeth.

'We shouldn't let it happen.' Masterman rubbed his neck. 'They shouldn't be allowed to get away with this. You better talk to your friend Alex before it goes any further. It's better if you do, isn't it?'

Elspeth smiled. In the end her cousin was all bluff and bluster. He was unhappy once he got off his own place and had to deal with any female other than his wife Rosie. He was a rubber stamp. But it had gone too far already. Elspeth read about the

Minister's speech in the paper where the declaration of the Lake Moorna World Heritage Area was hailed as a major advance in centralised stewardship of sensitive environmental and heritage sites. The government was congratulated on its foresight and initiative.

Masterman Holdings' lawyer advised that the company was powerless to overturn the government's decision not to renew the lease when it expired in five years. The opportunity was now, while there was a political commitment to consult on the site management plan. Having gone public, the government was obliged to buy out the leaseholder as soon as convenient. That gave Mastermans leverage.

But Elspeth did not want Alex to have another victory. Ever since he was a kid, he had been getting away with things. She remembered him boasting about looking into the eclipse of the sun without going blind. She remembered him daring to eat dirt and not getting ill. He would probably get away with it now, reaping big rewards for himself and his Minister and the government. She hated the way he could just do that by producing documents from an office in Canberra. Something in Elspeth wanted to obstruct the transaction.

~

The bronze Mustang churned up dust on the road out to Whitepeeper, bumping over the stock grids without regard. The dogs were barking like crazy. The manager's wife went over to investigate. Alfonzo Vella, in his beige cotton suit, straw hat and sunglasses, disarmed her immediately, explaining he was on his way to Sydney with his sister and brother-in-law for a holiday. They were old friends of Elspeth's from Adelaide, he said. Jenny Goodenough knew that Elspeth had some weird friends and, since this fellow was well-spoken and dapper, she did not question. She invited them into her kitchen for a cup of tea and said only that her husband Worrie was out on the block with

Andrew. She said nothing about Elspeth's being away in Adelaide.

The visitors drank their tea quickly and went outside to wait. Alfonzo and Tony, his brother-in-law, made themselves at home in the wicker chairs on the verandah. Leila, Alfonzo's sister, checked the backdoor of the homestead and, finding it unlocked, walked inside. If caught, she would say she was looking for the toilet. She found the child's room filled with stuffed toys and hung with mobiles, all ruffs and ribbons, neat and unslept-in. But the broderie anglais curtains were drawn and there was no child.

Leila looked through the other shadowy rooms, noting the silver and the cedar, pursing her lips at the portrait of a man, a pin-up with his crown jewels on show, that hung in the guest bedroom. The wrong type for the woman's husband. Then she came out into the heat and said that the kid was not there.

'Where is she?' whined Alfonzo. 'I want to see her room.'

The gloss had gone off Alfonzo Vella in his year on the run. Using an alternative passport, he had checked himself into the spiritual community at Goa for six months until the police were off his trail. They satisfied themselves by arresting a couple of receivers and some drug users they caught in the act. The rest went underground. Since he re-entered the country Alfonzo had been living with his parents behind the neat white portico of their anonymous house in the Adelaide suburbs. He put in long, ascetic hours of meditation in order to void himself of negative feelings about Wendy, making that whole interlude of his life a veil of illusion, a robe of false desire burned away to dust and ashes by spiritual awareness. Yet there was a process of retribution still to be carried out. He needed to save his rightful daughter from these people who thought they could get away with everything because of their class and money.

When he came to Cassie's room Alfonzo burst into tears of anger. Leila heard him and came running inside to calm him. He picked up a photo of Cassie and showed it to his sister as proof. She had his skin and eyes.

'She's beautiful,' said Leila, tisking at the monstrosity of a little girl being kept from her own father.

Then Tony, unnerved at keeping guard in this empty place, came in to see what was happening. 'It's no place for a kid,' confirmed Tony. 'It's like a ghost house out here.'

Alfonzo put the photo in his suit pocket, lit a cigarette and went and found a crystal ashtray in the living room. He held the match, watching the flame, until it burnt his fingertips. He did not hear Andrew Findlay come in until there were already footsteps inside the house. Jennie Goodenough had warned Andrew, but he was taken aback to find that the visitors had made themselves at home. He did not recognise the flash man sitting in the chintz armchair, the dark, well-groomed woman or the strong, wary man who stood by the French doors.

'Have you been waiting long?' apologised Andrew shyly.

'Well, we didn't have an appointment,' joked Alfonzo, introducing himself by his Christian name. 'If that's what you mean.'

'Cassie's not here, I'm afraid.'

'Oh yeah? Where is she then?'

'With my wife in Adelaide.'

Alfonzo twitched uncomfortably. If his timing was that bad, then the karma was bad too. He spoke less smoothly, in the manner he used for getting to the bottom of things with his couriers. 'Then I hope you won't mind if we wait for a while. Just in case.'

Andrew frowned. 'What for?'

'What do you think?'

Leila, worked up, spoke out loudly. 'This isn't that kid's rightful home. No one can say it is.'

'That's okay, Leila,' said Alfonzo softly, fortified by his sister's display of loyalty.

'That poor kid's mother was no good. Cassie's only hope is to be with her own people in a good family home with love and a bit of discipline —'

'Hush,' said Alfonzo, cutting off Leila's aria. Then he turned to Andrew. 'We only want to talk.'

'I should point out that you are trespassing on this property and that, as far as I know, you have no legal rights over Cassandra whatsoever. You're lucky to be walking around a free man today.'

Tony began to flex his builder's muscles.

'Would you like me to let the police know you're here? If not, then kindly be on your way.'

'She's my kid, man,' said Alfonzo. 'She'll never be yours. Don't fool yourselves about that. Why don't you have a kid of your own instead of stealing someone else's?'

'You know where the door is,' Andrew said, leaving no room for negotiation. For the briefest moment he sided with the man in his impotent hatred. While Alfonzo lit a match for another cigarette, Andrew went out into the hallway to open the front door. He got his rifle from the hall cupboard and cocked it. When he came back, Alfonzo was holding the newspaper he had lit. It was like a flaming parrot in his hand. Then he hurled it across the room. It landed on the basket of dry gumleaves by the fireplace, which started to crackle.

'Are you crazy?' cried Andrew. 'Get out of here!'

Tony calmly walked over and kicked the basket across the floor, burning, where the flames would reach under the skirts of the sofa.

'Don't you understand English?' said Andrew as he put the rifle to his shoulder and pulled the trigger. There was a loud crack and the bullet burned through the floorboards at Alfonzo's feet.

Leila screamed. Andrew reloaded the rifle and held it up, chestheight, as the visitors ran from the house. Andrew followed them outside. By this time Worrie and Jenny Goodenough had come out running to see what was happening. As the Mustang drove off, they saw Andrew fire a shot into the air. Then he yelled at them to get the hose as he rushed back inside to beat the fire out with the Persian rug.

He debated with himself before calling the police. He knew the local police would pick the man up and pin a charge on him. But Andrew's rage was against Elspeth. He had taught them his own lesson. Whitepeeper came out of it with no more damage than a burned wood basket, a ruined sofa cover and a bullet hole through the floor – to remember Andrew Findlay by. Instead of calling the police, he phoned Elspeth.

~

Cassie squealed with delight each time Grandpa Sunner, on his hands and knees, popped his head out from behind the armchair. If he waited too long, she would run and get him. But if he timed his absence and his reappearance right, she would shriek in ecstasy. Isabel Sunner looked across at Angus Gillingham and shook her head with content, as if to say that her husband and Cassie were both kids alike, despite Peter's silver hair. His hair had changed colour overnight when Wendy died. Their old friend Angus was drinking his third cup of strong tea and stuffing himself on Isabel's melting moments, like a boy too. He was trying to keep up with the roaring football match on television, but his attention was taken by Cassie.

'They've got such energy,' sighed Isabel. 'This one has.' Cassie was wide-eyed and determined, a performer for her grandparents – all three of them. When Peter stopped playing with her, she ran and threw herself between Angus's legs, causing his tea to slop into the saucer.

'Careful,' he boomed as he caught her, gauging her height and weight with his doctor's hands out of habit. 'There's nothing wrong with our Cassie.'

'Barb would have loved her,' sighed Isabel with her residual smile.

'Not Barb,' Angus replied. 'Barb thought that children should be seen and not heard. That's how we brought Elspeth up. Of course that's all gone out the window these days.'

Peter Sunner had a big box of the famous chocolate-coated apricot cubes for Angus. Although his factory had been taken over, the Sunner brand name had stayed and the new owners allowed him to buy any Sunner product at a discount.

'For Elspeth to take back with her. The best chocolates in the world.'

'Yes, I better be going.' Angus had stopped being aware of how the hours passed. 'Thank you, Peter. You really shouldn't.'

Cassie grabbed at the box. Peter eagerly took the chocolates back from Angus and opened them so the little girl could have one. All the Sunner family had grown up on chocolates and Peter didn't see anything wrong with that. But once Cassie had stuffed one in her mouth, she wanted another. The doctor in Angus Gillingham took the box back and closed it. Then he bundled the protesting child out to the car.

Elspeth had left Cassie to stay the night with Wendy's parents while she stayed with her father who was still knocking around by himself in the old two-storeyed house. But after twenty-four hours apart, Elspeth ached to see Cassie again, and Angus was proud to deliver her safely back. Elspeth took the child from her father's arms. 'Did you have a lovely time, sweetheart, with all your grand-parents? Aren't you lucky!'

Keeping the rooms of the old family home as they were, in case the children needed them, was the first of her father's excuses for not moving. The amount of work the house and garden required was another, since he had time on his hands. But he had left the pool cover on all through the last summer and when autumn came it filled with slimy leaves and Elspeth was disappointed for Cassie's sake.

'I want to swim, grandpa,' Cassie said.

'If *you* promise to come and see me again when the weather warms up, then *I* promise to get the pool ready,' Angus replied.

He had passed his medical practice on to a younger man. His cellar was another of his excuses. Having grown up in a wine family, he knew wine as he knew the ins and outs of his patients, over forty years, and had cellared the best. Where would it go if he moved into a smaller place? So Elspeth started the sorting and pack-ing for him. And she went through her mother's wardrobe. That was one thing Angus would never get round to. There was so much of Barb's stuff to dispose of.

'Dad,' she asked over dinner that evening, 'the land at Whitepeeper? How much of it do we have to keep?'

'Bloody politicians and bloody boongs,' he said. 'What a bloody awful combination.' He poured out the rest of the good Barossa shiraz. 'Your mother never worried about disposing of assets when she needed to. The important thing is to make the right decisions. Straight, honest, real decisions.' He was alluding to Elspeth's tendency to make fantasy decisions. 'In the end you're responsible for yourself. No one else is. That's what I've understood since your mother died. I wasn't ready for being on my own.'

'Well, you haven't made many decisions,' Elspeth taunted.

'I'm in no hurry. For you it's a bit different. People respect you for what you decide, as long as you stick to it.'

Elspeth knew her father was giving her a bit of a lecture, as forcefully as he dared. She always resisted when he told her what to do. When she was a child he had always anticipated health problems and blamed his children for bringing his medical expertise under scrutiny when they got sick.

'People will judge you for the decisions you make. You have to think about that. I mean Cassie. Whatever decisions you make, that child will judge you. You have to be ready for that and try to get it right.'

'She's the only one I'm thinking about,' Elspeth replied.

'I know, Elspeth, and you've already made some huge decisions on her behalf. When she grows up she will judge you even more severely than most children judge their parents.'

Elspeth sipped her wine in silence, absorbing what her father was telling her – his doctor's analysis of the human condition. In doing her best for Cassie, she had not thought that the child herself might turn it round against her.

'Don't look so worried,' Angus grinned. 'There's nothing much you can do about it, except be prepared to stand by what you decide. Operate on a human scale. That's what being a doctor taught me.' He held up the half-full glass of red wine. 'That's why I like this stuff. It's a tonic. It has body and proportion. It has human scale, like our own bodies, that have their span of life, give or take a few years, some better than others.' Even as they spoke his relationship with his wilful grown-up daughter was as it had never been before. Stronger than he was, she was listening thirstily to what he had to say. 'There are always the same basic elements to work with, but within that you are free to make it how you like. According to your own lights. Then there's the taste test. When it's had time to breathe. You have to learn how to know the wine that's in the bottle. The great ones are no more than an extraordinary variation on a theme.'

'It looks like Andrew and I have come to the end of the road, Dad. That's what he was ringing about earlier. I'm relieved for myself,' Elspeth said, gazing at her father. 'I don't know how Cassie will take it. Is that what you meant, Dad?'

Angus Gillingham drained the glass and went Ah! 'I suppose it is,' he concluded.

DANIEL III

D ANNY looked forward most to the weekly visit of his art therapist to whom he would show the work he had done during the week. Jane would sit and make marks on paper beside him. She was a funny one, Danny reckoned, smiling and laughing and tossing her hair all the time, with opinions about everything. He didn't know enough to contradict or agree, but he turned on the charm, made a joke or two, told her she was great. She had nothing else in her life, no kids, no bloke, not much of a job. Their art sessions together did her as much good as they did him, he could tell.

First he made a sketch in charcoal and crayon. Then he drew it again in faint pencil and painted it in watercolour. Last he attempted the version in oils. Either he rubbed out his mistakes or coloured them over and tried again or he destroyed the attempt that had gone wrong, no matter how near it came to completion. Sometimes he worked through a bungle by repainting so that no one would know. Because he was such a careful worker, oils suited him. He would work brushstroke by brushstroke, making the painting surface something to be proud of. Again and again he returned to the same ideas: the gates, the winding road to the summit, the hills across the plain, the church against the blue sky, the snaking tree, the cross. He was compelled to tell a story of the spirit that had driven him into the only corner left him. It was crime and punishment he dealt in. He had killed his sister's man and the family judged his action to be as wrong as if he had killed his own brother. He had done the deed to do right by the family; to do right by the family again he must accept and live out their judgement of his deed. He was cast out from the family and it was only by taking the punishment for his action on himself that he could make amends and be accepted back. Sometimes his cellmate heard him crying out in the night and gleaned a fragment of the intense private drama Danny was going through, as if a ray of light shone out through a fracture of bone. But no one really knew the hell of Danny's guilt.

Walls and locked doors and gates were his world. Meant to be of finite duration, his confinement had been infinite so far, not for doing wrong – just for being. That was nothing special. There was no more telling when it would end than when the world would end. The judgement he took to heart and set out to atone for was that his family had turned against him in the trial. That was all, and being aware of his daily rights as a prisoner: moving in and out of solitary; in and out of the psychiatric observation unit; seeing the medical staff; participating in sport and art therapy.

His family was an inward matter. He felt their will from within. The will of that drunken old man on the dump. On the back porch of a cream brick gubby house in the sun with his drinking mates, and dogs chasing sticks thrown among the scattered old car bodies, his father was still a force. If nothing else, he could lay a moral imperative on his son. It was his will and it must be done. The son must be punished. The son must make a sacrifice. The first crime must be paid. Danny worked it out stroke by stroke in his paintings, until he got it perfect. He must take the crimes of humanity on himself, he must suffer them, he must redeem them. He was Jesus,

Son of God. So he cried out in the night. His cellmate had never heard him crying out like that. Danny was on his own.

Paranoid delusion and hallucinations were added to the diagnostic list on Daniel Gordon's file.

He was a man of few words, which Jane liked, being talkative herself. He was dedicated to the task at hand. She preferred to make up her own mind about a person without reading the files. He had dragged the disposable plastic razor across his wrist. You couldn't do much but scratch yourself that way. His right wrist was covered with sticking plaster by the time Jane saw it. His painting hand. Perhaps he had been driven to a frenzy of self-wounding in frustration at not being able to paint the meaning inside himself. It was a feeling she could understand. To want to paint the world – inner or outer world didn't matter – and be unable to do so because of your own deficiencies, the technical limitations that came with this longing in the first place, was a source of gnawing despair.

Jane understood this in her own way. Two years after the crest of triumph in New York, Cynthia Temple, who could sell anything, could no longer sell Jane's work. The tide had gone out. The art world said Jane Woodruff had lost it. If she ever really had it. The wheel had turned. Flailing about in panic, like a ray left on the beach when the water recedes, Jane questioned what she was doing. She did not think she was doing anything different from when success had come easily. Maybe she had gone stale, or started to repeat herself. Or maybe contemporary art wanted something else. She was confused as to where to go with it, whether to flow with what the times demanded or to resist, move against the current, stick to her guns, be herself as an artist. Then her work would not sell and how would she live? Go back to teaching. She felt herself fading, vanishing, as eyes turned away from her. She would soon be invisible. Dead.

A professional crisis had drawn her into her work in the jail. She was prepared to work with people, but would take no nonsense. She needed to return to the beginnings of art, as far from the vain, judgemental surfaces and angles of the art world as possible.

Her visit to Elspeth and Lake Moorna had been decisive. The notes she made out there, the squiggly loose marks on paper, the annotations of colour, were the beginnings of a redirection. She was fighting to lift off layers of artistic self-consciousness, and looking at Danny's raw painful diligent work she saw that her problems as an artist were the palest reflection of his struggle to give expression to the only thing that could save him: his own meaning in the world. When he was disgusted by his efforts, when he screwed up an offending sketch and flung it into the bin, she understood the depth of his defiant repulsion at the shit in himself that was polluting his vision. Humanity's shit. The Christian sin and guilt and heavenly purity and love that Danny's people had bartered their old spooky world for.

'Oh yeah?' Danny said when Jane told him that bones had been found out at Lake Moorna that were forty thousand years old.

He knew the area, the river and the riverland, the orange orchards and vineyards by the river, near where he had lived as a kid, where his father had worked. Where the irrigation stopped, the mallee started. You could go off wandering through the scrub. Further off the country opened out into sparsely wooded low hills and flat plains and erratic sandhills in the middle of nowhere. It had frightened him to go out there as a kid. There was a dead lake and, beyond that, a real lake where a tide rose and fell, home to pelican, black swan, cormorant and duck, and across the lake the dead trees started, rising from pale, wind-ruffled water like a host of black spears. That water was enough to slake the thirst of all the people buried there in their thousands.

That was where Jane had been, somewhere out there. She said that Lake Moorna dried up in prehistory, thousands of years ago. 'Further on,' he disputed, 'there's plenty of water. Yeah, that's my country. From the river west and north as far as you can walk.'

Jane told Danny to put his childhood memories into his painting. He said the winding road up the Hill of Calvary could be a winding river through the dry country.

'Or a shining snake,' he said, smiling. 'It can be anything you like.' He only wanted to paint the brown church with a cross on top, on the green hilltop against a blue sky. He wanted to paint the road leading to the distant hills. He wanted to paint the three timber crosses on the hilltop at the end of the winding road that started from the grand iron gates between two pillars of stone. He wanted to paint God's face in the sun up in the sky.

There was his Mum, bless her, Mary, who brought up all the kids with only one arm. There was old Joe. He had a colour photo of Joe in his red beanie. There was his big sister Rhonda, and Lorna and Grace. And his poor brother Arthur. Then he discovered he had a twin brother no one ever told him about either, and another little girl who was taken. He had always known there was someone else out there walking near him, hidden from sight, on another path.

'Where are they?' asked Jane.

'My brother's working for our people. He's a bureaucrat.'

'Why doesn't he come and see you?'

'The lady comes and sees us. Paula. She pops in with her guitar and we do country and western. I get my guitar and we play really good together. *Fy-yah!*' He sang, and gave a clap. '*I'm on fy-yah!*'

'Paula Morgan's the Aboriginal women's officer. That's her job. Why doesn't your brother come and see you?'

'He's busy. He's keeping an eye on me.'

'What's his name?'

'Cleve.'

'Gordon?'

'Same as me. Like I'm Daniel Gordon.'

'I knew a Cleve Gordon once, he was Aboriginal,' she said. 'In Adelaide.'

'That'll be him. There's not another one that I know of.'

'Really? If he's your brother, why hasn't he done anything to help you?' Jane was angry.

'We're different, but,' said Danny. 'It pains him like it pains me. He was taken away when he was only a baby. I got away that day. I was a teenager nearly when I got picked up. There's nothing he can do about me in here. He's not my keeper.' Danny smiled. He had his pride. Whatever was between him and his brother was not strangers' business.

'He could do *something*,' persisted Jane lamely. Elspeth had mentioned that Cleve Gordon was a bigwig in the black bureaucracy.

'Maybe when I get out I'll go find him.'

But Cleve was not family of Danny's heart and mind, the family who had turned their backs because he had sinned. His near ones and dear ones. Cleve had not betrayed him, nor had he betrayed Cleve. His brother was not the one who denied him. It was his loving sister Rhonda. She was the one who refused him forgiveness.

·PART FOUR·

·INLAND SEA·

1

C LEVE Gordon sought advice from the Aboriginal Legal Service before going to the Minister for Aboriginal Advancement. The Minister was a young West Australian from the Left faction who was glad to put a dent in the smooth consensual politics played by Valerie O'Rourke and her cabinet cronies. Not that Cleve came face to face with the Minister. It was enough to point out to his friends in the Land Council that the traditional owners of Lake Moorna had not been consulted about the world heritage listing and that sensitive material had been taken without permission to a university laboratory, just like in the old days, when skulls were collected so evolutionists could measure the cranium. The Minister's office would do the rest, welcoming an issue that pushed the junior portfolio into the public eye.

When advice came through supporting a land claim, Cleve got in his car and drove to Canberra.

He drove from the business centre across the bridge to the parliamentary triangle, parked and walked to the national art gallery which was filled with a jumble of art from all over the place. It was what visitors wanted to see. Then he walked to the immense glass palace that was the High Court and marvelled how long that grand institution had taken to think about justice for Aboriginal Australia. Then he went on to the national library and browsed in the souvenir shop where he found a postcard of an Aboriginal man posing with a cricket bat. Nannultera, a young cricketer of the Natives' Training Institution, Adelaide 1854. A hundred years before his own time. Cleve, who had grown up not quite white, understood every nuance of white ignorance, fantasy, delusion and fear even better than he understood the history of his own people. His head scrambled when he thought about the dispossession and genocide, as a matter of policy, of a people who had fought back for survival, recognition and, one day, reclamation. Sovereignty. He thought of his twin brother still imprisoned behind those same bars. No wonder his brother was in a mess. But Cleve believed that one day Danny would be free too. Notwithstanding his crime, for which he must be forgiven, Danny would have his life one day.

Cleve walked through the rose garden to the Tent Embassy that still stood in protest across the road from the old parliament house – a tent, a fire to cook a meal on, a rusty drum for rubbish, as in any outback town, and the Aboriginal flag flying from the flagpole, red, black and yellow against the grey Canberra sky. The Tent Embassy stood where it had gone up in the early defiant days of the Land Rights movement, facing off the grand entranceway that swept into the white wedding-cake building, as a mocking envoy for all those who refused to disappear.

Rugged up, the woman who tended the Tent Embassy was sipping coffee from a polystyrene cup. She had come up from the South Coast. 'Cripes, the cold gets right through to your bones,' she said. The capital was part of her region. She offered the brother a coffee. It was embassy protocol.

'Right on,' Cleve said, by way of farewell, as he crossed the road to the parliament house that he had read and heard about since primary school. To avoid a body search he turned away before he reached the top of the steps. The only way forward was to find your own line, your own understanding, and ignore the impressive portals to left and right. That might mean circling back about as far as you could go.

He told the librarian at the Aboriginal Archives that he was interested in the movement of people out west, across the New South Wales and South Australian border. He had done a lot of talking to people out there and wanted to find out more. His people came from there; he had ended up in Adelaide himself. When he suggested he could start with a map of the different mobs – the nations – the librarian laughed. She said all the maps were wrong. She pulled out a map that gave land boundaries to different language groups, all disputed now, she said. There was dispute about what constituted a language and contestation of the idea of boundary lines. Why did a language-world need to be converted into exclusive territory defined by lines on a map? That was the concept behind the twin evils of territorialism and property the Europeans had introduced. The old people had roamed far and wide, speaking many languages, with one area or group shading into another, so that despite different languages the people ended up intermeshing as one complex society, open, changing, their allegiances always up for negotiation. You could say who belonged to a place. You could never say who did not.

The librarian's instruction made sense, so Cleve asked her the first of the two particular questions he wanted to pursue.

'I'm interested in Lake Moorna,' he said.

'Oh yeah?'

'It's out west there. An old dry lake where they found some ancient human skeletons.'

'Forty thousand years old,' said the librarian. 'I know what you're on about.' She walked over to a worktable on the other side of the open stacks. 'We've been commissioned to do a report on the linguistic evidence surrounding Lake Moorna. It's for the Department of the National Estate,' she said, blinking proudly with intellectual fearlessness.

'What is the linguistic evidence?' asked Cleve.

The librarian put her hands on the pile of books and papers on the worktable. 'Place names mostly. Dry creek beds. Watersoaks. Some objects possibly connected with the area, transported to museums with a name attached from the place of collection. Words that get corrupted into other words. Like Moorna itself. No one knows where the name comes from. Maybe it was the name of the first station holder's wife or mother, misspelt, Aboriginalised. Who knows by what sort of speaker? If it was an Aboriginal word, it might be a transcription of something like *muwana*. The doubled "u" vowel –' she pressed down on the work table with all her weight, '– "moo" as in cow. *Muwana* written down as Moorna. Can you hear that?'

'*Muwana*,' tried Cleve. 'What does it mean?'

'I'd be guessing. It's lost its language. Yes,' she said, 'Whitepeeper's another one. The name of the property surrounding Lake Moorna. We believe it's a corruption of Watpipa. The name was written down by a German who couldn't spell. It probably means "Old Man" in one of the Darling River languages.'

'Whitepeeper? Elspeth and Andrew's place?'

'Is that who lives there now?' asked the librarian. 'It's an old Masterman property. They used to run all that land out there. Big pastoralists.' She blinked again.

'You can tell me then,' Cleve said. 'Who are the people whose language was spoken at Lake Moorna in the old time?'

Releasing her weight from the books and papers, the librarian sucked in through her teeth. 'That's the problem. There's a missing language. Going by the linguistic evidence, you have to postulate a lost language for that area with no speakers left.'

'What does that mean?'

'It means that the people who lived there once have moved on.' She had sorrow in her voice. 'Vanished. It could have happened as recently as the 1930s.'

'There must be someone left.'

'They were dispersed. They wandered. They married into other groups. They stopped speaking their language. They forgot where they came from.' She was talking brightly. 'They died. It's another part of the tragedy.'

Cleve shook his head. 'What happens then?'

'In other areas where one lot dies out the neighbours take over as custodians. That has happened in many parts of Australia. One nation absorbs a disappearing nation's space and culture. The community is what matters.'

'Then who are the neighbours at Lake Moorna?' asked Cleve, eagerly pursuing this approach.

The woman sealed her lips and her dark eyes went liquid. She looked pious. 'It's not for me to say.' She held her palms open to him. 'It's for the stakeholders to decide.'

'The stakeholders? Who are they?'

This time she did not blink. She gave Cleve a clear, direct gaze. 'All of us.'

The librarian had answered his first question. His second question would wait. He had requested files on his missing sister Pauline through all the state records without success. If she were still alive but her name had been changed, she would be impossible to trace unless Cleve could reconstruct from the archives every detail of what might have happened to her. Then he might find her. His brother Daniel had been found by accident. Pauline, Cleve could not help but hope, might be found by hard work. Records were incomplete, slapdash, falsified to cover tracks. Even the Aboriginal Archives could not help. A person could live a life and leave no trace. But if he could only understand from the archives what *might* have happened, then, Cleve believed, he would find out what actually had.

People often asked to meet Alex Mack for a drink, wanting something. But Cleve Gordon's call, so casual and peremptory, worried him. If there was something important to discuss, why had he waited until he lobbed into town to ring for an appointment? Alex had not seen Cleve Gordon since they left school. There had been that school debate, and the trouble over the bones Alex brought home from the dig. From the Aboriginal gravesite the school had taken him to when he was a silly kid. A naive show-off kid. What was the teacher's name – the bone-piper? Mr Benjamin, that was it. Whatever became of him, poor bloke, the master who wanted to show Alex what was under his kilt? Didn't someone say Benjie had been caught exposing himself to a boy in a public toilet and been lynched?

Alex had been aware that Cleve Gordon was a DAA officer out west. Had that come from Elspeth? A young turk then, he remembered throwing the weight of the Department of the Prime Minister behind Cleve's efforts to squash a corrupt local mayor. He had enjoyed testing the effect of a few bland lines on letterhead and a few phone calls from Canberra. Always in a good cause. But small things could blow up in your face, those slight twistings of the rules, that slightly excessive pressure, never forgotten by those who were its victims and always remembered by its beneficiaries as knowledge of your soft underbelly to be used against you when the time came. That was probably why Gordon was ringing him. But there was something strange – sly – about it.

Elspeth had been to see him recently too. He took her to an expensive Canberra restaurant filled with politicians and journalists locked in gossip and intrigue who nodded to Alex as if he were the Archbishop. Elspeth's poise adapted quickly to the frazzled, roaring scene, about as far from the home paddock as you could get. She wanted to know what say Mastermans would have over the Whitepeeper land if it was turned into a national park. A national park was a national park, Alex explained. It belonged to the people. Former occupiers had no say in how such land was run. It would be managed by Parks and Wildlife. Mastermans were only lease-holders and they would be bought out of their lease.

'At a negotiated price,' said Elspeth.

'At a negotiated price,' repeated Alex, and they nodded in agreement.

The question was what that negotiation would involve. Elspeth did not want a purely financial negotiation. 'What's to stop us running sheep on part of the land?' she asked. 'What's to stop us staying on in the old homestead even if the place is a park? The park needs a ranger, doesn't it?'

Her intensity made Alex recall that she had joined a sect once. He saw that look of fanatical commitment in her eyes. 'Someone with qualifications in park management,' he laughed. 'What you're saying is that you wish to be consulted about the management plan,' he summarised. 'That will make you more accommodating about the price.'

Elspeth laughed back, in a different, discordant key.

As he signed the expense-account slip for their lunch, realising how little leeway there was, Alex concluded, 'The Commonwealth is committed to acquiring the land. I'm confident the process can be amicable all round.'

Outside in the carpark, in the silvery daylight, he reassured himself that a level of cooperation was possible with Elspeth as the conduit to Masterman Holdings. 'It's great having you on board. What an extraordinary connection it is,' he said positively. Then he asked Elspeth once again if she understood the exceptional importance of the site.

Her reply alarmed him. 'I understand its importance for Aboriginal culture. I really don't understand its importance to you, Alex.'

He must be friendly and allow a space. Why had he not suggested dinner at home instead of a meeting in the bar? That was an exercise in distance and control. No trust. But there was no way to make contact and rearrange the meeting.

He signed all the documents his secretary had prepared for him and walked out of the Department early to go via the supermarket, pick up a few things and drop them off at his flat, so there would be food and drink if he brought Cleve home later.

About all Alex did at home was eat breakfast, read newspapers and sleep – by himself. He figured he spent as much time in the bathroom of his flat as in any other room. It was a bad way of life.

Only the importance of what he did kept him going, making decisions as every day great breakers rolled in and every day he rode them. There was no one in the country who would not take his call.

It was dark at twenty to six. He ran inside the supermarket, not bothering to take a trolley. The supermarket shone brighter and more colourful than ever. He would make mango chicken, served with rice and creamed spinach with nutmeg. Dips first. Pâté. Hummus. Nuts. Icecream and berries afterwards. He dashed around gathering those few items in his arms. Chardonnay. Beer. What if Cleve did not drink? What if he was vegetarian? Mushrooms. Alex ran around hunting, knowing he must not be so much as one minute late for the rendezvous at the bar. That he must be early, in fact.

Suddenly his way down the supermarket aisle was blocked. A woman's huge trolley, with just a few items in it, sprawled in the way. She had a child with her.

Alex worked with such tight, strained timing that his impatience was always ready to flare. He was losing his cool. The woman and the child, a dark-haired little boy, were unaware of him, or deliberately ignoring him, as he tried to squeeze past. The child was helping the woman choose a packet of breakfast cereal. She was coaxing him to have Weetbix. He wanted Froot Loops. What was bad for you against what was supposed to be good.

'Excuse me,' muttered Alex, turning sideways and trying not to unsettle the pile of groceries in his arms and the plastic bags hanging from his fingers as he edged by.

There was something ungracious enough in his tone, distant yet urgent, for the woman to look up from her crouching position by the breakfast food shelf and stare the man in the eye. She had short-cropped spiky dark hair and white, slightly freckled skin. Her face was skinny; she wore small rimless glasses.

Alex noticed – it was the detail he registered first – that she had a floppy black felt hat hanging from one hand. She wore black jeans and a crimson roll-neck under a green woollen jacket. The boy gazed at him, with wide hazel eyes, sensing something. The woman saw a tall thin man in a shiny suit, with grey already combed through his wavy hair. There was a sharp, almost annoyed percipience on his face, which reached towards her. His long nose quivered as he looked at her, not daring to ask.

'Hallo Alex,' she said, flatly but surely. She had no doubt it was him. 'It's Josie.'

'I know,' he replied, thrown by the fact that she had spoken first. 'I wasn't certain. I didn't like to – I knew you were someone I – recognised.'

'This is my little boy, Isaac,' she said with a proud smile. 'Say hallo to Alex.'

The boy was four years old. He did not have his mother's pale skin. His skin was the colour of honey. He had thick dark hair and round hazel eyes with long lashes. He stood like his mother, slim, lopsided and gaunt.

'He's great,' said Alex, not knowing what else to say.

'It's been a long time,' Josie murmured, as if warning Alex not to ask any questions.

But he could not help wondering. 'What are you doing here?'

'We've been living down the South Coast,' she explained. 'I'm doing my degree part-time. There's a course this semester so we've come up to town. I'm a student after all these years.' She laughed at herself. 'Isaac's starting a new pre-school, aren't you, mate?'

'It's great to see you,' said Alex. 'Unbelievable to run into you like this.' He knew his reaction was inadequate, but he needed time to react adequately and there was no time. He fell on his hurry as an excuse. 'I'm just running in and out,' he apologised. 'We must get together. Catch up.'

'If you like.'

'Where are you staying?'

'We're staying with friends at the moment in the government flats.'

'I'll give you my number. Work and home. Ring me. Please.' He wrote the telephone numbers on a blank forward page of his personal diary, ripped out the page and gave it to her. He would worry about December the twenty-fifth when it came around. He hoped she would notice.

'Thanks.' She peered at the torn little page. Christmas Day.

'Sorry, I've got to fly.'

'See you later,' she said serenely, almost uninterestedly. She put the Froot Loops back on the shelf and bent to Isaac to continue their argument about breakfast cereals. She still did not move the supermarket trolley out of the way.

The bar was packed with men and women in suits when Cleve came in. It was reminiscent of the old swill, when the pubs stopped serving liquor at six o'clock; only nowadays the swilling started at six when the offices closed. He wove through the noisy crowd, looking around, waiting to be recognised – a handsome, well-built man with a thick neck and chubby face, in jeans and a patterned ski jumper under a blousing cotton jacket. He broke into a smile as the man got down from the bar stool and came to greet him.

'You're keeping well?' asked Alex as they shook hands.

'I've put on a bit of condition,' Cleve joked. He saw the flash silk tie round Alex's neck, and the disarrayed boyish manner that Alex had not outgrown.

Alex ushered Cleve to the single vacant stool at the bar, standing himself as he bought the first round. 'What's it to be? Beer? Now, how long is it?'

'Must be ten years,' said Cleve.

'Can't be.'

'At least ten. Twelve. More. We're not kids any more. Cheers.'

'Cheers, Cleve. Good to catch up.'

They stayed at the bar, going through the awkwardness of filling in their lives. As they presented it to each other, their lives had run almost in parallel. They had done their time at university and begun their public service careers at the point of convenient first entry. He strongly identified as Aboriginal now, Cleve told Alex, but that was not the whole story.

'It's your choice,' suggested Alex.

'It's not a choice. There's no choice about it,' Cleve retorted. He was privileged, though. He had luck, if you saw it that way, to be fostered out through the Catholic system. Luck to survive as an Aborigine. The rest was a personal life he had not handled well. He had climbed the ladder, like Alex. In the Aboriginal bureaucracy he was considered a role model now. People looked up to him and that made him feel good. But when he was alone he was as lonely as a little scholarship kid at St Joeys and he had still never come round to deciding whether the whitefella God was for him or against him. Cleve grinned.

'He's not for or against anyone,' offered Alex sympathetically. 'That's the problem. It's how you make it, isn't it? Shall we go?'

Work had displaced his own personal life too, Alex thought as he led the way through the carpark. His work was his life, but unlike Cleve he was not doing it for anyone else. He was doing it for his own principles, if you liked to see it that way. His most sophisticated relationships were the intricate entanglements he enjoyed with his two mentors, Valerie O'Rourke and the Prime Minister.

The crisp air was revivifying after the stuffy, raucous bar. 'I appreciated your intervention that time, by the way. You've probably forgotten. Your help came just at the right time for the folk out in Nulla and for me.' That was all Cleve said as they arrived at Alex's flat. He did not tell Alex what he thought of achievable outcomes, of making politicians look good, of covering your arse and corralling the public to your agenda. He did not say that politics was an ignoble process to be exploited for noble ends.

'You still drink this stuff?' Cleve laughed in recognition of the cloudy Adelaide beer that Alex poured out for him.

'Nothing else,' said Alex.

'You lost your mum, didn't you? Your dad still around?'

'He's over in Adelaide. Here's home now,' said Alex. He shrugged, realising how little the impersonal flat looked like a home. 'As much as anywhere. You're not married? No kids?'

'Nup,' said Cleve. 'I'm okay. You get on with the cooking. I want to watch the television news.'

When Alex brought the mango chicken to the table, Cleve came and sat opposite him, ready to talk again. 'You remember that bit of a brawl we had the time of the debating competition? It's been a long time, mate.'

Alex giggled. 'That's right. You remember that too? "Beauty is in the Eye of the Beholder".'

'Everything is,' said Cleve as he ate. 'That's what I reckon now. Good tucker. What happened to your mate? Ziggy. Do you still see him?'

'He's a famous actor.'

'I wondered if it was the same fella. I read something about him.' He swallowed slowly and looked across at Alex. 'You took me home and showed me your collection of Aboriginal bones. I got the willies.' Cleve was chuckling. 'Whatever happened to them?'

'My mum took them away.' Alex hesitated, then went on. 'Took them to the tip.'

'Bugger me,' said Cleve, 'and no one had a clue what they were. You know where they come from? That's Marawara land, just down from Rufus River. They could be as old as the Lake Moorna bones.'

'Lake Moorna?'

'Sure,' said Cleve, 'the bones they found on Elspeth Gillingham's place. Your bones could have been as old as them.'

'Probably not,' resisted Alex.

'Well, we'll never know,' conceded Cleve. 'They should never've been taken away like that by you kids. It's a bloody disgrace.'

'It couldn't happen these days,' added Alex. 'Things have changed.'

'Yeah,' Cleve chuckled. 'It's not nineteen-sixty-something any-more. We're talking the 1980s.' Cleve leaned forward. 'But that's just it. It *can* still happen. It does. It *has* happened. The Lake Moorna bones – Moorna Woman and Moorna Man – that's what I wanted to talk to you about. We want them back.'

Alex sat back in his chair and looked nervously at Cleve. 'You know a lot about it. Is that why you've blown in?'

'Elspeth says you're behind all this. Elspeth. Your pal from schooldays.'

'I know who Elspeth is. She came and saw me the other day. She didn't mention she was seeing you.'

'She's not *seeing* me, if that's what you mean.'

'No, of course that's not what I meant.'

'The bones are on her place, or they were before they were taken away. There's a whole lot of other things there too. Important things for my people.'

'It's not Elspeth's land, though. That's the problem. It's crown land, leased to her family company.' Alex gave Cleve an intense stare. 'The old Emperor of the Bush never did your people much good, did he?'

Cleve was getting argumentative. 'He was paternalistic but he looked after the old people. He appreciated them. I wouldn't be ashamed to have a bit of Masterman blood in my veins.'

'Have you?'

'Like I said earlier, I don't know exactly where I come from. Not what happened before my parents. I could be any bloody thing.'

'It won't be a leaseholding for much longer, anyway,' said Alex. 'The government's getting it back. Elspeth's selling out.'

'You're right about one thing. It's not Elspeth's land. Listen to me, Alex. It's *our* land. We want it back.'

'Who's we?'

'My people. The people out there.'

'That's bullshit. There aren't any of *your* people at Lake Moorna.'

'There aren't at this moment, but there used to be, didn't there, before they were got rid of. You have to acknowledge what happened.'

Alex got up from the table. 'Do you smoke? I've got some here somewhere.'

'I didn't think you were a smoker.'

Alex pulled the cigarette packet from a drawer. 'Help yourself.' Then he went through to the kitchen to hull and wash the strawberries. 'Whoever they were, they can't be *your* people,' he called back from the kitchen.

'What would you know? The custodians of that place are the people down the road,' called Cleve, echoing the ideas he had heard that afternoon at the Aboriginal Archives. 'Your own experts will tell you that much. They're more my people than your people. On that we surely see eye to eye.'

Alex brought the big bowls of icecream, strewn with sugared strawberries, to the table and sat down to face Cleve. He felt the strong determination of the man who was resting back opposite him, deep in his chair with his arms folded, quietly waiting.

'You said you didn't know who your people were,' suggested Alex gently, his mind ticking over.

'I know enough,' said Cleve, leaning forward to pick up his spoon. He dug into the icecream. 'I know who I'm acting for. If they accept me, it's good enough for me. We're going to put up a land claim as soon as the government has lifted that land off Elspeth.'

'Why wait for that? You could buy it off her yourselves,' suggested Alex, leaping to a bureaucratic solution. 'You've got enough money in the land fund.'

'Why waste our money?' guffawed Cleve. 'We've got piss-all. Anyway, the place is already gazetted as a park. Without consultation. You've made a booboo, man.'

Alex lit up a cigarette. He saw the force of everything Cleve said. He had taken Ralph Kincaid at face value in setting out what should be taken into account about Aboriginal interests in the site. But Kincaid's concern was with forty thousand years ago and only with himself in the present. He wanted preservation and access. He wanted pastoral interests denied in favour of heritage and scientific values. He, even he, had overlooked the claims of potential traditional owners. In their zeal to create a world heritage area in their own backyard, Alex, and then Valerie O'Rourke, and then the Prime Minister, had bought Kincaid's line.

'They're working up the management plan for Lake Moorna at the moment,' Alex threw into the discussion, almost absentmindedly. 'Your people will be consulted as fully as possible over that.'

'It's an important place for our people. It's a valuable asset. But we've had enough of consultation. We want the land back.'

They finished off the icecream like two hungry boys.

'Why are you doing this, Cleve?'

Cleve bared his teeth and threw back his head for a raw, open-mouthed bout of laughter, possessed, like a spirit released. 'Me? What can *I* do? What power have *I* got, Mr Smarty Alex?'

Alex stood up and backed away from the table. 'Are you doing this to get at me?' Then Alex laughed too. 'Do you hate me?' He could not believe what he was saying. 'You bastard.' Then he calmed down. 'I support your entitlements. In theory. But if you do get the park back, what are you going to do with it?'

'What's your Parks and Wildlife going to do with it? Lock it up? Let a few scientists dig it up and take it away? Put the sheep off and let it become infested with rabbits and feral goats? Who is going to want to visit it? There's nothing there!'

'You're contradicting yourself, aren't you? You just said it was a valuable asset.'

'If Moorna Woman and Moorna Man go back there, and our people are there, we can make something of it. Otherwise it's nothing but a graveyard that's been robbed and pillaged. Once it comes back into our hands, then we can talk about forty thousand years on our own land. Always was, always will be. Get it? That's important.'

Alex scratched his head. 'You would have to abide by environmental and heritage values. That's legislated.'

'No strings attached. No one can tell us what to do with our land. If we want to open a convention centre or build an amusement park or grow cotton with chemicals, that's our bloody business.'

'That flies in the face of all our wilderness thinking,' snapped Alex.

'Who says it's wilderness?' said Cleve, getting stroppy at Alex's resistance. 'It's our country.'

'I sympathise with your objectives, but the wider community is not ready to hand over the national parks to the Aborigines. Not yet. There would be no political support for such a move. You'll fail, Gordon. It will only damage your cause. You have to go slow on these things.'

'Where has going slow ever got us?' said Cleve with defiance. 'I come here as a friend to tell you. Our Minister's ready to support us. We've got legal advice. Your Valerie will be rolled if she tries to stop us.'

'The Minister will stop it all right. If a claim goes up it will undermine our whole environmental approach. We have our treaty obligations. I'm sorry, but to give it to the Aborigines, it's like washing your hands of it. That's how people think.'

'You shouldn't have said that, matey. What I'm talking about is a very important thing.'

It had taken Alex until this stage in the evening to remove his tie. He was getting hot. He paced over towards Cleve and said, 'You always were an impressive debater but *I'm* telling *you* as a friend you won't win this one. You can't. The Minister won't take a defeat. She'll look like an idiot if a land claim goes up. Save your strength. It can be different next time.'

'Someone will look like an idiot,' Cleve murmured. 'Elspeth's on our side.'

Alex was about to say that it was not a question of sides when he paused. Suddenly he saw the power of an allegiance between the old pastoralists in the person of a refined young woman who was sacrificing her home and the Aboriginal people who were reclaiming their land out of respect for the spirits of the dead – both ranged against a Minister in Canberra. He saw as his worst nightmare how the media would play it to damage Valerie O'Rourke.

'But Elspeth wants to sell, as far as I know,' said Alex.

'She wants to sell to the government, so the government can give it to us.'

'The bitch. What are you and Elspeth trying to prove?'

'This is politics, Alex. This is your game.'

An uncontrollable fury could come over Alex in meetings, when he started to fidget, or to bury himself in the agenda papers, anything to prevent his tongue lashing out with its own pointed energy, leaving little unscathed, including himself. The amorphous destructive capacity he worked to suppress beneath an artifice of competent consensual confidence was always ready to spill through to the surface like toxic black oil. It was a trait, he suspected as he grew older, that he had inherited from his mother. In the form of subterranean despair it had destroyed her in the end.

'You want to brawl like when we were kids, Cleve, is that it? We're big boys now. Grown men.'

'Don't take it so personally. This is a great opportunity for our people.'

'For you.'

Cleve nodded, saying nothing. The time had come for him to leave. The atmosphere was becoming unpleasant and he was satisfied in leaving Alex to consider where to move next.

Alex asked Cleve if he had read the documents Professor Kincaid had prepared on Moorna Woman and Moorna Man.

'I haven't gone into it in detail. Forty thousand years – it's a long time ago.'

'His report is strictly confidential. Between you and me, as old friends, eh? But I'll tell you this. The skull structure of those two people is unlike that of other later finds in this country. It's not just slightly different. It is radically different. You could say that they are no relation of any present-day Aboriginal people.'

Alex watched Cleve's face for the significance of his trump card to register.

Cleve slowly lowered his eyelids to show his boredom. 'Oh, that stuff,' he said at last. 'That's a cheap trick.'

Alex started to bluster. 'Don't you get it? How can you argue for forty thousand years' occupation of the land if the people forty thousand years ago were someone completely different? Another race. Anything could have happened between now and then.'

Cleve looked at Alex, who was squirming with aggressive excitement, and yawned. 'That's right. Anything.'

'If you people lodge a land claim and it turns out that you were occupying someone else's land, that you have not been here from the beginning but probably drove the original people out, now that won't look too good.'

Cleve smiled. 'Like you say, a lot could have happened in forty thousand years. You can make up a lot of theories on the basis of two skeletons. Who came first, who came after, in the great river of time. We'll never know. The number of years doesn't matter. Twenty, forty, sixty thousand.' Cleve's face was strong and angry, as it had been when he was a boy, as he stared into Alex's eyes. 'What's wrong with good old time immemorial?'

Alex was white with barely contained rage. 'Are you interested in truth or lies?' he demanded of Cleve.

'That's what I say, brother. We would all be better off if those bones were put back in the ground where they belong and never disturbed again.'

'A cover-up?'

'You're a funny man, Mack. Well, I'll be getting along. Great to see you again, mate. Thanks for a great night.'

Swaying a little, Cleve walked out the front door of the flat into the clouded Canberra night, leaving Alex to the washing up. He would find a cheap motel. Or he could warm the car up and sleep on the backseat.

Light spilled in a long yellow rectangle onto the concrete porch, reaching the carpark, where Cleve was turning the engine over. Alex stood like a stick figure in the doorway, like a wobbling figure on stilts, waving the dishmop and calling for Cleve to wait. He was drunk. He ran over to the car in his light shirt and clawed at the door until Cleve opened it to him.

'What's up?'

'You remember Josie? Josie Ryan from Adelaide? You know.' Alex was raving. He had to communicate the wild strange news, stranger than everything else that had happened during this strange evening, news that seemed to come from a different zone. 'She knew you.' Cleve could barely follow what Alex was saying. 'Josie's in Canberra. She's here. I saw her in the supermarket on the way home. I meant to tell you before, but we –'

Cleve would not allow himself to display the knot of his own emotion in front of this man – this man who brought the news. But he was sure that Alex, even in his drunkenness, sensed the sudden tension in him. Cleve had forgotten about Josie because there was nothing else he could do. He had been placed on the other side of a wall of silence, a barrier of unknowing, from her. There had been no word from her, no sign or information since she had left the town on the bus that dusty morning five years ago. She had never wanted him in her life.

'Where is she?' asked Cleve flatly, ambushed by her name.

'I don't know,' cried Alex. 'She wouldn't tell me. She's staying with friends in the government flats. I thought you might even know something.'

'How would I bloody know?' Cleve blurted.

Alex was shivering in his thin shirt. His head was spinning with the blast of cold. 'She had her boy with him,' he added disconnectedly. 'A beautiful little kid.'

Cleve stared at Alex, who was dishevelled and red-eyed, like an overwrought child himself. Straining to look Cleve in the eye, Alex slumped against the car. Cleve frowned and bit out the words as if warning Alex to keep back. 'No, I don't know anything about where she went. How would I know?'

'I don't know, mate. I don't know. Just wanted to ask. Thought I'd try you out.'

Alex slammed the car door with the weight of his body. There was no point saying anything more. Cleve revved the engine. Alex waved the dishmop like a wand, almost losing his balance as he twirled round in the carpark. Cleve paid no attention. Alex waved, shouting goodbye, as Cleve's car growled slowly away, creating clouds in the darkness with its exhaust.

2

YOU knew where you were with someone who had failed. No matter how they climbed back up, their feet of clay had been exposed. Humbled, they had done their time. For his West End flop, which was not *his* failure anyway, Ziggy Vincaitis earned scorn but also a degree of fascinated pity. As he had always done in performance, he took people's sorrows – *their* failures – on himself. Herbert Horsfall had been right to twist his arm and bring him back home for the white man's part in *Namatjira: the Musical*. No matter that Australia's top two black performers would play the parts of Albert and his sweetheart Rubina, Ziggy Vincaitis's name was what it took to garner enthusiasm for the project.

Herbert installed Ziggy as an associate of the Youth Theatre Company in Melbourne that was producing the show. Mr and Mrs Vincaitis moved into the same street in South Yarra as their prodigal son. Karolis Vincaitis had a bad heart. Vida, elegant and miserable, continued her acid commentary on life. Ziggy could look after his parents with no more success than they looked after him. He spent his money on imported clothes, rejuvenation cream, books, music and cafes. He missed the hard discipline of theatre work, so great in what it could, rarely, achieve. Enshrined between Alban Berg and Brahms, alongside John Blow, Henry Purcell's contemporary and a distant relative, were all the recordings of Oliver Blow. It was enough to know the lineage, back and back . . . Ziggy carried it forward and passed it on to the precocious young actors.

Oliver had not believed that Ziggy would leave. He could not believe that there was anywhere else. As far as he was concerned, brutal, bloody London was the one and only centre. Europe. The mountain-top. The far cold north. For him there were no alternatives and he resented Ziggy's having another space. He told Ziggy it would be temporary. The colonial with anything to offer always came back full-circle to the Motherland. Ziggy was deviating – a refugee still. Oliver had never loved anyone as he loved Ziggy and could not bear to lose him. At this stage of his life, when he would never love again, here was the dearest beloved, the chosen of his knights, slipping through his fingers like golden light.

To Bath they had gone in this valedictory mood, town of healing sulphur waters and old golden pleasures, where twilight came early as they walked the splendid streets of bygone business and leisure, golden stones stained and worn, lines of buildings embodying on a human scale the classical ideal of a perfected cosmos, city of the golden mean, where the body set the scale and the self-delighting mind could be satisfied. Oliver, who was ill, had immersed himself in a scungy commercial spa. But Ziggy, watching as his bulky friend delicately lowered himself, refused to join in. Oliver wore his black hat and long leather coat as he guided Ziggy. He said the very gods of life would abandon the young man if he turned his back on them.

In the evening they went to the old Regency theatre to see a performance of *Don Giovanni* in a production that recreated a bare-boards eighteenth-century style in that warm intimate acoustic. When Mozart's fiery Don was dragged down to hell, icy cold wrapping the hot amorous man in its dark eternal embrace, Ziggy felt a chill run down his own spine. The supersubtle strings were feverish

and amused. The Don's courageous cry of protest at human fate –
in vain! – was his – and Oliver's.

'Bravo!' Oliver howled at the end.

Afterwards, in the restaurant, he drank to their separation. Ziggy
was going into the cold dark infinite spaces. He was taking himself
off to the end of the earth. Taking himself off. Severing the flow of
life. Oliver bowed his head into the soup and wept. 'Look, sorry,' he
apologised, patting his eyes with the white damask napkin. 'I'm all
stirred up. It's as if the stone statue had invited *me* to supper. Why
do you have to go play this part in a bloody Aboriginal musical of
all things? Some crummy bit of theatre-in-education. What ever
happened to Chekhov and Strindberg and all that? Shakespeare?
What are you doing to yourself, my Siegfried?' It was as if Oliver's
vein had been cut.

'It calls me,' Ziggy replied. 'I don't expect you to understand.'

'It calls you up the garden path. I order you not to go.'

'But I need your permission, Oliver,' pleaded Ziggy dutifully.

Oliver was ill and must put a brave front on it. He faced the cold
lonely spaces too. In that he was an iron-clad Yorkshireman. For all
his love he would not claim Ziggy for his deathwatch, nor had he
said anything to his friend about his illness. They were moving into
new, separate orbits of unknowing. It was as uncertain as it was possible to be.

'Go! Go!' shouted Oliver at the top of his huge voice to the
consternation of the other diners in the sedate, muffled, best French
restaurant in Bath. Then he trembled in his low falsetto: 'Remember
me!'

Back in frictional, suspicious Melbourne, Ziggy did remember
Oliver Blow. He remembered Oliver's warning that he was deviat-
ing from the path up the mountain-top. Up the garden path instead.
Up shit creek without a paddle.

Ziggy remembered when the phone call came in the middle of
the night to say that Oliver had succumbed to pneumonia. Alone,

refusing medication, he was dead. Only a few days before they had been talking across the great space that divided them, and Oliver sounded cheery. He had dedicated his last-completed work, his *Cantata of the Black Bear*, to Ziggy Vincaitis. 'There's only me and Bach now. He's inexhaustible. I'm in ecstasy.'

'Marvellous, marvellous,' he croaked ironically when Ziggy told him they had started rehearsing *Namatjira: the Musical*, 'marvellous. Absurd. Go forward, Captain Stardust. Till we meet again. Remember. Perceval! I'm so proud of you. Oh!'

Click.

The show was a hit. Houses were good. The tour was up and running. Ziggy was earning some real money again. The musical introduced a version of Albert Namatjira's story to a new generation. Namatjira was born on the mission station at Hermannsburg in the red land of Centralia at a time when the white people, the Christians, had brought a new day to the Western Aranda. His parents came from the desert for his birth and baptised the child Albert. When he was a youth, the old men took him back into the desert to be initiated. His totem was the carpet snake. He fell in love with a woman of the wrong country named Rubina. The old men tried to stop them. The Christians tried to stop them. Long years Albert and Rubina had to stay out bush. Drought and scurvy took their children. Their people were slaughtered. The sacred sites had their secrets stolen. Then the art teacher came from the south, a whitefella named Rex. That was Ziggy's part. 'How much do you get for a painting?' Albert asked Rex. 'I can do the same.'

He hardly needed teaching. Mimicking the European way of painting, he painted his own country with his own meaning: a freak, a genius, an in-between, the most famous Aborigine there ever was. He got a dog tag, a permit making him an honorary citizen, like all the white people. He was taken to Canberra to meet the new Queen. He could buy drink – but he was not allowed to share it with his people. He was sentenced to hard labour for selling drink to a mate. The next year he was dead, cut down, crucified, his success flung back in his face – the tragic wanderer between two worlds. Yet his work and his spirit lived on. Like the morning-star, he pointed the way to his people. Wherever the musical played, his story brought tears to the audience's eyes and a warm feeling that it was possible to move on from the shame of the past.

Ziggy was glad to be out of Melbourne and on the road. He was a star again. He was loved.

Welcome a new Australia
Follow the morning-star!

So went the rousing finale in which Albert, Rubina and Rex led the company.

When Ziggy bowed low, clasping hands with Albert and Rubina for the curtain call, the roaring applause blew his head off.

So the tour rolled on to Canberra. The day the show bumped in, Ziggy enjoyed speaking to Alex's secretary on the phone about the tickets he would leave at the box office. She called Alex Mr Mack. He was so important now.

Moves had been made on an Aboriginal land claim to the Lake Moorna site. The Department of the National Estate had advised that it would oppose any claim. The Minister did not want her world heritage listing taken away. The media got wind of a storm brewing between Valerie O'Rourke and the Minister for Aboriginal Advancement, and the Prime Minister had called for an explanation.

It was Alex's line that a national park belonged to everyone. There was enough resentment out there already towards the preferential treatment the Aborigines were getting. Did they want a backlash? Softly softly. The gazetting of the area was a decision about protecting an environment of scientific importance to all humanity. Its management was ultimately the world's responsibility, held in custody by the Australian government. It was not the property of one group. The young fox goes out on thin ice and gets into trouble. That was what the *I Ching* had told Alex all those years ago, when René Baum had read the throw of the sticks for him. An old fox would have stayed on the bank. Alex knew he was in danger but he could not go back. The situation made him feel sick.

When Alex walked into the dressing room after the show, Ziggy could see in a flash that his old friend was troubled. Brash and kitsch, the show had rubbed salt in Alex's wound. Ziggy's performance made the hairs on the back of his neck stand on end. Alex looked wearily important, yet he was smiling, his eyes twinkling to see his old friend. His shoulders sloped inside his cashmere jacket. His chest was flat. His face was lean and blotchy. His greying hair sat on his head like a mat. All this Ziggy took in at a glance, who, by contrast, looked beautiful, but exhausted. He exuded satisfaction and glee at the joke of being able to toss off a brilliant performance and then sit backstage in a dressing-gown and receive his oldest friend in the world.

'What did you think?'

'Positive thinking,' Alex laughed. 'Congratulations.'

Ziggy uncorked the cheap champagne. Bunches of flowers, doubled by their reflection in the mirror, crowded around the make-up table. Ziggy's robe fell open just enough for Alex to glimpse the raised scar that ran between his nipples.

Alex refrained from commenting.

'You see that?' asked Ziggy. 'It was my initiation. Done by a bear's claw.'

Alex's eyes sparkled. 'You've come a long way, Zig.'

They were demolishing a *quattro stagioni* pizza along with little bottles of spirits and mixers from the mini-bar in the featureless serviced apartment that Ziggy had been given for the Canberra run.

'Who would have thought we would meet up again in this plastic nowhere place,' laughed Ziggy, 'There's not even a car going by outside. I always thought we had something more refined in store for us. *Follow the morning-star!* Indeed.'

Alex raised an eyebrow. 'Summer pudding on a chamomile lawn? You would have had all that.'

'Melbourne's giving me the shits. Time to move on again, I'm afraid.'

'Already. You've only just moved there.'

'When this tour is over, I plan to retire.'

'Retire? At your age? You're not much older than I am. You can't retire at thirty, can you?'

'For a while, anyway. My first retirement. Like Melba's, the first of many. I need a rest. I need my own world around me. It's time for a big change and I need to prepare myself.'

'For what?'

'For whatever will be the stage after this. I need to care for myself better.'

Ziggy turned up the heat from the fan as he crossed to the rubbish bin and crumpled the greasy pizza box.

'You look wonderful,' insisted Alex. Ziggy's skin was golden-pink, firm and shiny.

'I know. That will change soon enough.' He flicked open the heavy insulating curtains and pressed his nose against the cold glass. It was black outside in the silent suburb and fog was thickening. 'Wendy's gone. That upset me. It changed a lot for me, not being able to know that she was still here. I still don't accept it. Not really.'

'People walk away,' Alex said, after the silence.

'Like your mum.'

'Mm.'

Ziggy could still plug straight into Alex's thoughts. 'And Elspeth's got Wendy's kid. How did Alfonzo stand for that? He's so macho. This won't be the end of it. Migrant families. They never let you go. My parents are the same. Their greatest horror is that I'll go over to the other side and turn into a bloody Australian.'

'You are an Australian.'

'*Prakeikti australai!*' Mouthing Lithuanian abuse, Ziggy gave a hard sharp hyena's laugh. 'You don't find me attractive any more, I suppose, do you?' he asked, turning his profile to the light as his mother used to do. 'Remember the time you covered my arm with chocolate and licked it all off? Like I was a chocolate bear? I think that was probably the most exciting experience of my whole life. Other things notwithstanding.'

'Don't say that.' Alex was listening for the tone beneath Ziggy's disconnected remarks. He could not make it out. 'Can you afford to retire?'

'I don't mean literally retire. Withdraw. That thing I did in London, *Sir Perceval*, was a turkey. A real ginormous lemon. But Oliver Blow's music was good. Really good. Now that he's dead, the recording has started selling like hot cakes. It's huge. Cult. Isn't that absurd? Dear Oliver. The original cast recording, before the show was pulled – it's my voice. Oliver gave it to me in his will. All the royalties come to me, forever and ever. I suppose he never forgave himself for the ordeal he put me through, by making me star in his flop. He thought it was the humiliation that made me leave. That I would still be working in the West End otherwise.'

'He must have known the music was good. If he gave it to you.'

'That's where he went wrong. He became a victim of his own pride. He was creating taste, not following it. Go out and buy one. It's an astonishing work.'

'Contribute to your retirement fund!'

'That's right, my dear. The time has come for the house on the clifftop overlooking the ocean that I have always dreamed of.'

'*He who has no house now will never build one.* Rilke. I never knew you dreamed of anything like that.'

'That's right. Will you visit me?'

'It's such a waste of your talent to withdraw. You were sensational tonight.'

'I'm not needed anywhere, Alex. There's only the inner need. The time has come to cultivate my own garden. I need to live in peace.'

'Then I'll come and disturb you.'

'Please. I don't want to be alone, but I can only live by myself.' Ziggy rattled through the mini-bar to see what was left, now that the whisky and vodka were gone. 'Is there anyone in your life, Alex?' he called out, turning suddenly, offering the brandy or the gin. 'I saw the empty seat beside you. That old white-haired woman came down and took it after interval.'

How could Alex explain to Ziggy that he might have bumped into Josie Ryan even on the way to the show, even as the bell rang? How could he explain that he had kept the spare ticket for her even though she had never contacted him? He looked her up in the telephone directory. He rang the university and pulled rank but the officer would only give out a post office address. He did not even know what name Josie went by. The kid must have a father. Mrs Jo Something-or-other. She could be anything. But he desperately wanted to see her and it hurt that she had not tried to reach him. He was trivialised by her indifference and yearned for her all the more in her inaccessibility, as if she were the key, as if he could explain himself only to her as she would explain herself to him. That, only that, was what he wanted from her. After work he lurked at the supermarket where he had seen her, like a teenage kid. Departmental Secretary in love. But he had never fallen out of love with Josie. 'I haven't had time the way things have been going for me. I couldn't subject anyone else to the way I live.'

'Then what do you do for kicks?' insisted Ziggy. 'You haven't told me anything.'

Alex was embarrassed about admitting his addiction to his work. He had kept himself open that way. Availability, promise, perpetual ambivalence and unfulfilment were the lifeblood of power relations at the top. Yet he shuddered, thinking of the Prime Minister's call about Lake Moorna, that unmistakable tone, in John Lewin's voice, of affection turning edgy.

'Do you see Jane?' Ziggy asked, fishing.

'That was then. Have *you* caught up with her?'

'I saw her new show in Sydney. Strong work. Exquisite work. Inspired by a prehistoric lake somewhere out near where Elspeth Gillingham's living now.' Alex nodded impatiently. He did not want to hear of anyone else inspired by Lake Moorna. 'The critics slaughtered it. Jane's having a hard time these days. Her work in the prison is about the only thing keeping her going. Oh yes, she's working with a guy at Long Bay – do you remember that Aboriginal boy at St Joeys in Adelaide? Cleve? One of the guys Jane's working with is his twin brother!'

Alex moaned. Not Jane too. He felt surrounded, assailed on all sides – as if the noose was tightening around his neck. 'The weird thing,' said Alex, 'is the way people from my past keep cropping up. It's like there's all this unfinished business. It's like a lasso.'

'You mean me?'

'Jane. Cleve Gordon. It's like we're knotted together in a tangle of roots. It's not meant to work like that. I can't work like that. I need to operate on a clear and open surface. I want things to move forward freely, unencumbered by the past. In the clear light of day. Do you understand what I'm saying, Ziggy? I don't want the subterranean world. It's all death and destruction.'

'Just look out there. So still and black. We're in the subterranean world already.' Ziggy cocked an eyebrow and mixed new drinks for them – Bundaberg rum and Coke this time. Then he sat down opposite Alex, formally, as if he were a counsellor. 'Go on, Alex, this is important. What are you denying in yourself? The dark is part of life. It's the source of all life. What are you frightened of?' Alex was suddenly aware that Ziggy had flown in from somewhere else. He had dropped down in Canberra after so many years on a visitation for Alex's sake and effortlessly their words had taken them to the brink of Ziggy's purpose. 'Did you ever get over your mum's dying? The way she turned her back on the light. You're never going to let yourself do that, are you?' Ziggy had command of an extraordinary range of facial gestures. He brought down one eyebrow and raised the other interrogatively.

'There's a curse on me,' said Alex in a dead calm voice.

'What sort of curse?'

Alex stared, then hung his head. 'As if I'm not living my own life.'

'Whose life are you living then? You always were ordained – for something.'

'Yes, but it was not done by me. It's like I'm on a map, on someone else's grid.'

'You're blessed, Alex. You always were.'

'There's something blocking the blessing. That's what I mean by a curse. It's like someone else's will acting inside my body.'

'Sounds like sorcery to me.'

'It's like this whole country – if we could only break that grip, the whole place could be different. I would be different. I'd be brave and strong. I would be able to see clearly.'

'You must exorcise it before it kills you. It's up to you. We can't both die, darling. Someone has to live.' Ziggy went to Alex and put his arms around him. The warmth of their bodies slowly softened the resistance of bones. 'Sleep with me,' whispered Ziggy.

Alex shook his head. 'No.' He kissed his friend on the cheek. 'Not this time.' He stood up and, standing, held Ziggy in a tight embrace, burying his head in Ziggy's shoulder. There were tears in Alex's eyes. 'You're a saint.' Then he gave Ziggy a playful thump on the back. 'A lousy old saint. Well, we'll see what happens.'

'Do you want to see the show again? *Namatjira?*'

'Do I have to?'

'*Welcome a new Australia, Follow the morning-star!*' Ziggy sang in parody. 'No, I just want you to come and see me in my retirement.' Then Ziggy's eyes bored into him. 'Only if you go into the dark will you come out into the light. The past is the future. Once you find the desired act to make it so. To lift the veil. To see to the other side. You know what I'm talking about, baby?'

3

Not only had the city changed in the ten years that René Baum had been away, so had the population metamorphosed from floating, self-absorbed students into spouses and parents, property owners and professorial material, senior advisers, opinion formers and local celebrities. He read about his old buddy Alex Mack in the local newspaper and surprised him with a telephone call. They met at a sandwich bar where public servants bought their lunch, the most neutral of places. Alex wore the shiny suit and tie of a departmental head, René was in blue jeans and an indigo-dyed jacket with Chinese buttons. They took their sandwiches, buns and juice to a bench in the sunshine and sat side by side like kids in the playground, grinning in disbelief.

René could only laugh at Alex's seniority and importance. He took Australia less seriously than ever if it was in the hands of people like his young friend. It must surely be a ship of fools, an operetta regime. How different from the gerontocratic Chinese administration! René was neither in awe nor envious, but he found it marvellously funny. That refreshed Alex, who did not have to justify himself or protect his flank for a change. He laughed in return at René's political change. The Maoism of yesteryear had proved to be chameleon's colouring. But they both agreed that they had not sold out, only moved on. When René gave his casual commentary on Chinese politics and thought, Alex was amazed by the depth of insight revealed. It was René Baum, on that sunny public bench, who was the first person Alex heard present the simple scenario that saw China developing into a major economic power and Australia inevitably loosening its ties to Europe and America and turning towards Asia.

'What are the main implications of that for us?' Alex asked.

'You have a country of more than a billion people barely able to feed itself, and you have a country of less than twenty million people with land to spare. The main implication is the movement of people. Who is our land for? Is it for ourselves because we happen to be here already – in my case, the son of Jewish refugees from Germany – or is it for humanity as a whole? In which case, what is our duty to humanity? Is it to make the country some sort of protected space, or is it to let more people in? Who is humanity? Humanity is the Chinese.'

Alex frowned. 'You're joking.'

'From their point of view they are normative humanity. Of course. The oldest continuous culture, the most people. Whatever we do for humanity, we will be doing for them, or at least in line with their values.'

'That's too neat, isn't it?'

'It's the reality if we're talking about a world in which China dominates.'

'That's not possible, is it?' asked Alex, worried now. His responsibilities towards the National Estate seemed hugely magnified all of a sudden.

René grinned. 'That's what I'm saying. It's inevitable. The problem for me is where I am going to be.'

'You could be on either side.'

'Right.'

'What does Australia mean to you then?'

'From a Chinese perspective it means nothing. It scarcely exists. A bit of ballast on the map.'

'Yet they want to come here.'

'They're not coming to any place that exists. They're creating a better life for themselves. They're seeking a better world. Colonising new lands.'

Alex looked at his watch. 'I've got a meeting. Let's do this again. I want to hear more.'

Black-eyed, black-haired René Baum had spent ten years in the Chinese world, sharing the people's transformation of their root-bound society. His Mandarin was so good that he could pass for a native as long as he remained invisible. If he was seen, he was assumed to be from Central Asia or a mixed-blood hybrid left over from one of China's border expansions. René's friends and sympathies were Chinese; his mind – as far as he could make it – had become Chinese; and there was also the repudiation. He had maintained a darkly analytical perspective on things, never letting himself become, as a foreigner, entirely trustworthy. Loyalty, he decided, was a vice. But he would never finally betray the thing to which he had given himself so completely. When political campaigns broke out he followed the purges of his restive friends and comrades, experiencing the calibrations of fear manipulated by the black monster of the Chinese state-system, until he eventually became *persona non grata*. He only wanted to go further in towards the Chinese essence. The greatest Chinese, he considered, were not emperors and generals, but the creative spirits who were detached from the movements of their time and linked to each other across centuries. Thus he traversed the ways of Chinese history, interpreting it and taking it forward. Holy mountains, mighty buddhas, imperial tombs, revolutionary sites, layer upon layer. To roam was to work. To slurp noodles or drink tea with a Chinese companion was to study. That was René's youth, and when at last he was forced to return penniless to Australia, he felt like Rip Van Winkle.

He lived, back in Canberra, in a university room. By day he went to the library to replenish himself on Chinese periodicals, knowing it would be dark again by the time he came out. At night he roamed the empty Canberra streets with his Chinese friends, their jackets flapping in the cold wind as they went for hamburgers and chips from a lonely cart. They raved till dawn about what had really happened under Mao and what was really happening under Deng, imagining that one day their words would be heeded. By dawn they had forgotten they were in an outpost of a foreign land while great Chinese history, the only history that mattered, marched implacably on.

There was a woman among the Chinese graduate students who was rumoured to be connected to one of the highest-ranking figures in the Chinese Communist Party. Her name was Xiao Jing. She was writing a doctoral thesis in Developmental Economics on the world grain trade. Her first major, at an elite Chinese university, had been in English literature. She had a firm, soft-spoken manner and her round face beamed with satisfaction when she had the opportunity to display her knowledge. She had an insider's understanding of Chinese politics and an astute, ironic sensitivity to character. For that reason she liked René. She could not help admiring the complexity of mind that had taken him so far into China. She was a Chinese princess.

René could never quite prove that her father was the head of the secret police, but it might explain her melancholy silence about herself. The other students in Canberra were wary of her although she went out of her way to help them. She argued against the Western belief that economic prosperity would bring China democracy. Xiao Jing knew that whoever delivered wealth would be enthroned on high, not toppled. She used René as a sounding-board. She swore in front of him and didn't care what he thought. He understood China better than if he had been born Chinese. He understood *her*. She teased him about his Chinese girlfriends. She was fascinated by his magical empathy. How else could he have learned so much? He knew she was flirting with him and imagined with greedy eyes what she offered: a way through the doors of the Forbidden City into the maze of supreme central power, the enclave of the rulers, the highest circle of the most powerful people on earth.

At Chinese New Year René and Xiao Jing gathered with the other Chinese students to make dumplings together. One chopped the herbs, one kneaded the dough, one rolled it out, one cut the rounds and two or three formed the neat crescent-moon-shaped packets for steaming. Enthusiastic eating followed, the dumplings dipped in brown vinegar and washed down with spirits. Talk was kept small and joking. Everyone had a role and a reward. The elevated presence of the princess and her foreign friend notwithstanding, all belonged to one group, and when the party ended, heads spinning, bellies full, all could roll into deep long sleep. For René it was as much family, as much home, as he thought he would ever know. It was his world, even if it seemed to have no relation to the world around him.

The garden of the university staff club became the setting of choice for René's free-ranging, portentous lunchtimes with Alex, their plates piled high with salads and bread. Then Alex twisted René's arm to take part in a departmental working group on immigration. Population was a fundamental issue for the custodianship of Australia's National Estate. What population was optimal to sustain existing resources? What obligation was there to the world's refugees, many of whom were pressing southwards from Indo-China, continuing time-honoured paths of Chinese migration? Environmentalists argued that the continent was overpopulated already and that the environment was being degraded as a result. Economists argued that high migration was good for competitiveness and productivity. Sociologists argued that migrant labour was cheap and lawless, taking jobs from the decent citizens who were there first. Humanitarians argued that Australia had a moral responsibility towards the dislocated victims of ideological wars and the inequities of an unbalanced world. Alex asked René to hypothesise a Chinese perspective.

René was quite capable of putting a White Australia line, on pragmatic, not racist grounds. Australia's best chance, he might have argued, was to close its doors, police its borders and create a fat green secret garden that would be the envy of anyone who got an inkling of it. But that would be to resist the flow and pressure of history and humanity building up against those fortress walls and one day toppling them. It would be better to try now to absorb the outside energies, better to allow the seeds of ancient civilisations to shoot again in new soil. René believed that new people must flow into Australia, making of the white or European or British interlude little more than a valiant holding operation that would be swept up and washed away by the incoming flood. He welcomed the transformation of which he was already a part, seeing that the movement was forward and that nothing could be preserved except what the mind carried. His vision would have been apocalyptic except that he saw Australia as nothingness to start with. He felt no loss, only anticipation.

It was the role of administrators to manage this flux, René argued to the working group. The function of immigration policy was to make the transition smooth. National Estate did not exist in order to be preserved. National Estate was the thing that had yet to be formed. Such radical ideas startled and titillated Alex, who argued vociferously against them. As René put it with sharp succinctness, China's environment would soon be made uninhabitable by overpopulation and depletion of resources. If Australia created a good environment, why should it not attract people from elsewhere? Statistically most of those people would be Chinese. Whose birthright was the earth anyway?

Xiao Jing did not entirely approve when she heard that René was advising the Australian government. It was a dubious role for someone who knew so much about China. A dangerous role. He would draw attention to himself with the Chinese authorities. 'You'll end up as Ambassador,' she joked. Still, he could be used. It would have suited her better, personally, if he had remained a wandering scholar, a bookworm disengaged from the world. For the larger purpose, however, René might help by having the power to influence political processes. Xiao Jing certainly did not agree with mass migration of the Chinese. She thought entry should be managed strictly on the equivalent of a caste basis. The Chinese workers who were needed as labourers to grow vegetables, wheat and rice, to raise sheep, shear and scour wool for weaving into textiles in China's great mills, dig minerals from the ground, by hand if necessary, should be brought out in a controlled way under command of officials. Xiao Jing's own caste would benefit from the proceeds and lead a fine life in Australia. As people of higher quality, Xiao Jing and her kind would introduce a necessary element of Chinese culture to order and refine the raw local pluralism.

4

J OSIE and Isaac walked barefoot under the roadside trees. The
road stopped at the dunes where a path led over the sand to the
beach. Their house was in the third row back. It was an unused
weekender on a bare block of land that Josie had rented since she
came to live in the small community on the South Coast of New
South Wales. It had storage space underneath and wooden stairs up
to the deck and the front door. Every weekday she took the school
bus into town with her son, who had started school now, and in the
afternoon – she finished work early – they took the school bus back
together through the farmland and forest. There were a few other
kids, children of local builders, carpenters and plumbers, who lived
in the place, but the community was mostly retired people, elderly
couples or widows who had come there to walk in the bush and on
the beach and tend their gardens. The presence of the old people
explained the brilliant patches of lawn and the violent colour introduced into the soft grey of native seaside vegetation – the purple
dahlias and orange asters and yellow roses, the golden cypress and
blue cedar. Her own yard was cropped kikuyu grass, a couple of big

gums, and a spiky tuft of blackboy. Behind her house the bush began. Parrots came flying in from the swampland at dawn, splashing colours brighter than any garden flowers. At dusk the wallabies came in and fed on people's lawns.

The beach was like a garden too. Soft, white, steeply inclined, with a rocky lowland at one end and a high headland grown thickly with ferns, palms and creepers at the other end where the cliff dropped in spectacular columns and the surf pounded against rock, rumbling like a pipe organ. The sand in between was sparsely littered with weed and driftwood and shells, and the water changed through a spectrum from grey to green and blue, from sleepy to stormy. It was the place Josie had given Isaac to play in every day of his uncluttered life. Just the two of them.

When she took the bus to Adelaide five years before, she was still uncertain of the decision she would make. She went home to her mother's house, not far from the railway crossing on the wrong side of the parklands, and sat on the porch looking at the pruned crepe myrtle in the neat front garden where nothing had changed, except her grandmother was in her grave. Audrey Ryan sat at the little table next to her daughter on the porch in the late afternoon with a big brown beer bottle and the racing guide creased in front of her, canny when it came to horses, if not men. She had hugged and cursed and cried when Josie came back. The fantasy of being immaculate, the high holy calling, lily-white Josie Ryan under the hat, out of the sun – no more.

'Ah well, you take after me,' keened Audrey, puffing up with her prodigal daughter in her arms. It was not what Josie wanted to hear. But the virgin was off her pedestal now and willing to face it out in front of anyone. With her mother's help, Josie let her vows go and kept the child. Nursing the baby from the front porch, she could see the spire of the school chapel up the hill where the baby's father had passed those troubled years. She named him Isaac, the child God spared from sacrifice.

Audrey looked after the baby when Josie went to work part-time as an English-language teacher to boat people from Vietnam and Cambodia. Josie was learning to walk through the secular world. She wanted to push her mind until there was nowhere beyond its reach. She wanted to move, to journey, to grow and change herself. It was not good enough to stay in her mother's house. When her application for mature-age entry to university was accepted, she started looking for work and a living situation that would enable her and Isaac to survive on the single mother's bene-fit. When a job came up as a teacher of literacy at a centre on the South Coast, two hours from Canberra, she decided to take it. She wanted to study Philosophy, Linguistics, Anthropology and Prehistory at the national university. Her mother would still be drinking beer and working out her bets on the porch when she was a hundred, Josie knew. But Audrey could travel by long-distance bus from time to time, rocking across the plains, and look after Isaac on the beach. Her squawking voice and flashing wit would add extra colour to the coastal gardens when she came to visit, while Josie would have time to read her books.

Josie could keep to an argument. The politics of things inter-ested her, the real world, its material conditions, the force of people and their massed wills, in which the faith of individuals still played a part. Her belief in the power of the spirit grew into a committed interest in how the institutions, customs and old scarring prejudices of the material world could be radically altered in the name of equity, justice and human opportunity.

One afternoon she stopped at the public telephone box by the beach and rang Alex Mack. Clouds were sailing across a blue sky in the salt breeze off the sea. She had deliberately left him no way to trace her. After so many years it was up to her to initiate whatever might happen between them. Barefoot, in her old faded black jeans and sleeveless T-shirt, her hair cropped, earrings dangling – and Isaac beside her, his sleek swarthy legs frosted in sand – she stopped, put the coins in and rang him. She pictured him, high and mighty, sharp and sorrowful. He interrupted his meeting to take the call.

~

The chilli prawn soup in the Vietnamese restaurant near the university made them laugh and sweat and drink. They had gone quickly from prickly reticence to an equally impersonal, but more entertaining talkativeness, maintaining the barrier, denying the excitement between them. Always in the right place at the right time, Alex had run through his life sticking to the surfaces of things without reckoning up the cost. His cheeky willingness to stare into the eclipsed sun was what Josie knew of him. Across the table she looked and felt that side of him concealed and obscured. Her own life had proved so much more daring: single-minded and uncompromised. She had come east to make a new start as a single working mother and an older student. She worked with various support groups on the coast, who gave her support in return. She tried to channel her anger into constructive efforts to help people take charge of their own lives. As Alex saw it, she had lost none of the shining idealism that had been such an attractive oddity when she was a child. If she had redefined God in her own terms, at least He had not abandoned her.

Josie grinned scornfully at Alex's argument that unless you first had power, you could achieve no constructive change. She saw only the obstruction of white hierarchical male power. But she did not judge Alex. She knew that the world she wanted was even less likely to come about than the world he imagined. Therefore she concentrated on living her own life without compromise as far as possible. Alex felt rebuked by her sparky spirit.

She had always liked him. He was thoughtful. He was diligent. He was original. He wanted to know about the course she was taking. She told him about the town out west where she had worked, about the kids she had taught there. Where there had been total utter blindness, she wanted people to see. She was taking Professor Kincaid's course. Alex asked if Kincaid ever mentioned a place called Lake Moorna. She shook her head. But Professor Kincaid had used a date of forty thousand years as the indicator of the age of Aboriginal civilisation in Australia.

Alex should not have been so indiscreet as to talk about his work, but he had to share what was preying on him and he felt he could say anything to her. The Prime Minister had sided with the Minister for Aboriginal Advancement against Valerie O'Rourke, who had been rolled in cabinet. The matter had been wrested from the control of National Estate and Valerie blamed Alex. She should never have gone along with the idea of turning a bit of old desert into a national park. Accordingly she dumped him.

Alex had been asked by the Prime Minister if he would consider moving to head the Department of Immigration. It was the poisoned chalice, and he temporised.

Josie did her best to follow the byzantine ins and outs: she understood the underlying pattern. It was how things were. God's mysterious work. If Alex had suffered a fall from grace, she trusted it would be his salvation one day. She laughed out loud.

'I didn't tell you one thing,' she said. 'The relationship I had out west – the father of my son – he's Aboriginal.'

Alex remembered the kid. 'I didn't know. I wasn't sure.'

'Yes,' said Josie affirmatively. 'He doesn't know.'

'Who doesn't know?'

'The bloke doesn't know. The father. I've kept out of his way.'

'Won't he take responsibility?'

'I never wanted to ask that of him. He had enough on his plate.' Josie looked hard into Alex's glistening eyes. He was eager for her to go on. 'I'll tell you something,' she said, feeling her desire to speak pulling her, like a current flowing back through the years. 'You remember Cleve Gordon?'

Alex folded his arms over his head to block his ears. 'You're not going to tell me Cleve Gordon's the father of your child,' Alex groaned. 'He's the one who's behind *all* this. He's part of what *I'm* up against with Lake Moorna. He's everywhere.'

The old smile came over Josie Ryan's lips at Alex's distress – superior, blessed, amused. She reached for his hand across the table. 'How can he be your enemy? Unless *you* are *his* enemy? It takes two. If you're trying to stop something that must happen, Alex, then you've erred in your judgement. Let it go.'

~

428 ~

On his first free weekend he drove out of Canberra telling no one where he was going, not even the Minister's office. He felt loose, hurtling through the darkness, and on an edge, as if he might lose his step and go into free fall. The road dropped precipitously, cut from mountainside in the winding tracks of the pioneers, through forest to the sea. On the car radio a reporter was giving a speculative version of Valerie O'Rourke's difficulties over the Lake Moorna World Heritage Site. The gloating tone of the journalist hinted at scandal and incompetence. It sounded like a leak. He drove faster to put it behind him. For the last stretch the road was totally dark and his was the only car. He put down the window and could smell the sea, hear its roar. He made a wrong turn and drove to a dead end and, obeying Josie's instructions, approached the house whose lights were blazing out through open curtains. Isaac ran out onto the deck and said not a word. 'Hallo Isaac,' Alex said, and the kid ran inside. Then Josie came out and welcomed him, laughing to see him in a jacket and tie.

He drank red wine, picking at food, and stalked the room. His talk and agitation were an intrusion into the quiet homely evening. Isaac was excited, asking questions to draw attention to himself, complaining that he was hungry. Josie tried to give him his food first, but Isaac protested, and when the food came he rejected it. She was trying to converse with Alex, but in the end there were tears from the boy. By the time she finished settling Isaac, the dinner was overcooked, and she slumped down in the living room chair with a hectic laugh.

'He's not usually like this. He'll be better in the morning.'

'I wouldn't have come if I thought it was going to cause trouble.'

She wondered how long it would be before Alex relaxed. To keep him off other subjects, she told him about the issue that was dividing the small local community. Each house depended on rainwater from its own tank. It was a high rainfall area and there was usually no problem. Sometimes at the end of a long dry summer, people's water might get low and the gardens might suffer. Recently there had been a move by the council to pipe in mains water. This would increase the rates and the rents and open the community to development, attracting people who would not accept the limitations of rainwater and who, with the prospect of unlimited mains water at any price, could realise more ostentatious ambitions for their house or garden or business. 'Who needs it?' Josie shrugged crossly. She was in the opposition.

'You're against progress. You're a Luddite.'

'A rainwater tank is good enough for me. If they want mains water, they should stay in the suburbs. It has split the community. The council is determined and they're winning over the gardeners with horror stories about their dahlias drying up in a drought. Who needs dahlias?'

'Sounds familiar,' said Alex. He began to laugh. 'We should be able to mastermind a strategy to ensure that you win.'

'Are you serious?'

'It's politics. It's *not* serious. That's the whole point.'

Josie looked at Alex sharply. 'Don't you want me to take you seriously?'

'Not ever,' he said. 'That's the wonderful thing.' She frowned. 'You look tired,' he said. 'Go to bed. I'll wash up. Then I might walk down and look at the beach. I'm all revved up after the drive. Just show me where to sleep and I'll see you in the morning.'

They made up a bed for him in the living room, then she said goodnight. But she did not sleep. Isaac slept with his door open and a hall light on. She listened to his breathing. She listened to Alex clatter the plates and drain the dirty water. She heard him open the door and go out onto the deck and down the steps. Free, lost, unsettled person. It was dark out there. She lay waiting, following him to the beach in her mind, waiting for the sound of his steps returning up the stairs. Alex Mack. She remembered him with a green snake coming out of his mouth. After all these years.

Isaac was up early and into bed with his mother, bringing all his books. Alex got up and put the kettle on. He took a cup of tea in to Josie then took his own tea out onto the deck. The parrots were twittering. Josie sent Isaac out to keep Alex company. The boy set himself up at the far end of the deck with his books and building blocks. He asked Alex what he could build. Alex put down his tea and got onto his knees beside the boy and started to build a service station. He broke the rules, using the wrong windows and doors, and Isaac corrected him.

The boy was tall for his age and slightly chubby, a healthy child with thick dark floppy basin-cut hair, freckles on his face and smooth dusty-coloured skin. His hazel eyes were still encrusted with sleep. He had Josie's neck and mouth. Alex looked for Cleve Gordon and could see him in the boy's eyes and build. But the boy was his own person, bossy about his building blocks as slowly he accommodated the stranger into his own subtle play of determination and feeling.

Alex enjoyed working with Isaac, building the model service station in bright arrangements of red, white, yellow and blue. He cherished the boy's vitality, envying Josie her closeness to his daily growth and struggle, admitting to himself that he felt almost fatherly. Then he searched round for another word. It was a longing that he and the boy should be friends. He wondered about the opportunism of children's affection. The relationship would always be mediated by Josie, the mother. Then one day the boy would be a grown man.

After breakfast the three of them went down to the beach. Borne by currents from the South Pole, the water was icy and the sea, restless and moody beneath a clear sky, erupted in foam. They walked for miles that day, not noticing the distance. Alex piggy-backed Isaac when the boy complained of tiredness. Then it became a joke. Alex was tireder than the boy.

Josie was looking ahead to Isaac's later schooling and her own work when she finished her degree. She would like to go on to a Masters or a PhD, but did not see how she could continue working to earn enough money to put Isaac through school at the same time. She wanted to stay living on the coast; it was less expensive than the city, and safer and healthier for a kid – a peaceful wholesome life, that was her priority, but not at the expense of developing herself.

Canberra buzzed like a mosquito in Alex's mind. He tried to brush it away, but once Josie got him talking he could not stop. He wanted to put the Lake Moorna business to rest, so that it would not annoy him further, but he felt aggrieved. He had been betrayed by the actors in it who were supposed to be his friends. Where he should have been part of a triumphant outcome for Lake Moorna, he had dug in.

It was not personal, Josie said. Alex would only make himself irrelevant if he tried to impose an administrative arrangement that prevented power being put back into people's hands. He should not blame Cleve. Would Alex destroy himself, staying on and getting battered in one dogfight after another, until he lost respect all round? She wondered.

They reached the headland and climbed to the top, tunnelling between ferns and palms and lanky stands of slender temperate rainforest trees through which the choppy sea was visible as a spangled backdrop. Houses nestled in bushland had views far out to sea, at the highest point, north through east to pale hazy south. Below was a sheltered, creamy cove.

Those who lived there were secretive and proud. It was only the death of a retired history professor that had released the old loved house of worn timber and louvred glass onto the market: the house that Ziggy Vincaitis had bought from the family in a private sale.

Still on tour with *Namatjira: the Musical*, Ziggy was exhausted and thought only of retirement and a chance to recuperate. He had heard about the house from Herbert Horsfall, who was a friend of the late historian, and flew down from Brisbane on a Sunday when there was no performance in order to inspect it. He agreed at once with Herbert's assessment that the house, engulfed in ferns and creepers, had perfect music. It was indeed the house on the mountain that Ziggy had been looking for. The historian's niece showed him through and he did the deal on the spot, committing all the money he had banked from *Namatjira* and the accumulated royalties from *Sir Perceval*. No.3 Endeavour Drive. A curving dirt track named to commemorate Captain Cook's ship that had probed this mysterious shore in wonder.

Josie found the overgrown number and led the way down the stone steps through huge fern fronds that joined hands over the path. In the enclosed garden wild shrubs grew impervious to the salty air, and mosses glowed from the shadows.

'Wow!' cried Isaac, as a pair of scarlet and sky rosellas lifted from a birdbath.

Bamboo blinds covered the closed glass louvres. The house, guarded with potplants, overgrown with rushes and knobbly bulbs, was all shut up among the trees. The timbers creaked as the intruders' feet clattered over the planks of the deck. Through slits in the bamboo they peered at the rosy wood and red walls of the dark interior. Removalists' cartons labelled Z. Vincaitis stood in a row.

Creeping around, peering through, then turning away, pleased with the scouting, Isaac was the first to catch sight of the shining blue light through the trees. He ran forward. 'Look, you can see the island.'

Below the brow of the headland was the fast-moving channel that cut off the island, like a lost child. Fishermen would go out in their dinghies to clamber over its seaward rocks and falling veils of surf, and thousands of birds nested there on its humped back.

'What's Ziggy going to do here?' asked Josie.

'Live out his life,' stated Alex.

She shrieked. 'Lucky him! Eh, Ize? Lucky him.'

'You remember him, don't you?'

'I remember his red hair – like floss. He carried on like he was the little prince, Isaac. The funniest thing I ever saw. You always kept him secret, Alex. You told me his mother was a witch. You said if I ever went to their shop you would give me a Chinese burn. As if he was really weird. So I never got to know him. The famous Ziggy Vincaitis.'

A stillness had settled over them, translating into ease and good humour, by the time dinner came round at the end of that day. Alex went on building with Isaac. Then Isaac was in bed, the dinner things were cleared away, the dishes washed. Josie and Alex sat on the couch with glasses of wine in their hands. Only the light from the hallway was on, to prevent Isaac being scared. They talked in low, slow voices. Alex was drowsy from the walk and the sea air. He nestled close to Josie, who now felt more comfortable with him in her house.

'Isaac's an interesting kid. I don't understand why you don't let Cleve know about him.'

'When I'm ready,' she replied. 'When Isaac's ready.'

'When will that be? Doesn't he ask? I can help you arrange it.'

'I don't need that. Thanks. I suppose I don't want to upset the equilibrium right now. It has taken me a long time to get to this point.'

'You have to do it sooner or later. Are you frightened?'

'What, that Cleve might take the boy? He can't do that.' She was like rock in her certainties.

'He can be a father to the boy.'

She nodded. 'He should be. It can never be proved, you know. Nothing like that can ever be proved.'

'It's a matter of what will help Isaac for later in his life, surely.'

'I didn't have a father,' she said. 'That's why I turned to God. God did all right.'

They were resting warmly against each other. 'Are you sleepy?' murmured Alex.

'Go and clean your teeth,' she said.

'Josie, I can't believe I'm here.'

'Go on.' She gave him a shove. When he returned from the bathroom, she was standing in the doorway to her room. 'Well, goodnight, Alex. Sleep tight,' she said.

He came over to her, put his hands on her hips and kissed her lightly on the mouth. 'I don't know what you want to do,' he said. Then he hugged her. 'Josie!'

But she did not respond. Feeling his desire, she gently eased herself free. 'Leave the light on for Isaac,' she said, turning away into her bedroom. 'Don't forget.'

He reached toward her. 'Wait, Josie. Please. Love.'

'Don't say that, Alex. It's too early. We're not ready. So good-night.' Then she shut the bedroom door. Ever since she was a girl she had been saying to him that he must make himself worthy of her, that he must drop down through the surface layer of their interaction to a deeper relation, that he must let go of everything that confined him within himself, before they would be ready to be together. But how could he make that happen, he wondered.

DANIEL IV

I T was hot and muggy in the jail. You could almost feel the yachts out on the blue water, the bodies cavorting in the waves at the beach, the end-of-year parties all around the city, while inside Long Bay men wasted themselves in darkness. Danny had stopped his normal exercising. His eyes were red. The new medication affected his concentration, making him veer from listlessness to aggression. He had been sent over to the special observation unit after a further episode of self-mutilation. He had scraped his left wrist this time, with the blade of the disposable plastic razor, and had spent the night moaning and headbutting the cell wall.

Different people had different responsibilities towards a prisoner like him. There were the warders, on shift round the clock; there were the ordinary medical officers and the psychiatric staff, duty nurses and counsellors, visiting therapists, and higher up, those who made the decisions on a prisoner's progress and future. Each person's defined power and jurisdiction was reflected in the complex interrelationship of files that were separated so that no one saw them all at any one time. Notes that originated in one place could be moved to another, leaving no trace. It was easy, and no one's particular fault, for a prisoner's overall circumstances to be ignored. That was the system.

Danny's record of medication did not refer to his personal history file, nor did his psychiatric file refer to his Aboriginal background, so it took weeks to have the new medication queried. The response came just before Christmas, pending the arrival of a new psychiatric doctor after the holiday break. He was abruptly taken off the medication.

Jane had brought him a Christmas present. The art book that contained colour reproductions of work by her favourite artist, Pierre Bonnard. She wanted Danny to see Bonnard's colours. She wanted him to see the Frenchman's interiors and still life. She wanted Bonnard to offer a new departure to Danny in painting that had no story or cause but was all colour and sensation. Moments drenched in plenitude. She believed he could manage that now.

Danny took the book warily, smiling, giggling almost, on the brink of tears. He opened it and turned its glossy pages. Beauty and colour presented themselves – here and now, but for him far away, over there, back then. He admired the sheen of the paper. He could not see anything else there, or, if he could see, it was not for him. Slowly he closed the book and thanked Jane, saying he would look at it later. He told Jane he wanted to cut his hands off.

She said she often felt like that too.

He laughed. 'Yeah,' he said, 'I don't like what my hands do. I don't like what I see.'

'We should try a new style,' she suggested.

Danny was painting a large canvas, a metre square, for Christmas. Jane looked at its strange picture plane, flat, tilting away. The picture showed Danny's usual mountain, a huge brown form against a bright blue sky, and on top of the mountain the grand building with towers, windows and doors. It could have been a school in the olden time, or an asylum, or a prison. When Jane asked what it was, Danny said it was Heaven, surrounded with a fence but with its iron gates flung open. From this Heaven a wide green path ran down the hill, snaking right and left, and on the path were three black children, a girl in a party dress and two boys in bright red and blue uniforms, all three hurtling down the path. Here Danny's perspective trick came into effect. It looked as if the children were flying through the gates of Heaven into the eyes of the viewer. At the bottom of the picture the path spread out into a green landscape dotted with childish trees – green balls on black sticks – that edged a blue horizontal band of water that was the river, flowing right to left with a single black swan on it. Among the trees on the bank stood a man and a woman, a sheep, a cow, a dog and a kangaroo. The man and woman were black and wore hats, and between them was an empty space.

The imaginary scene that Danny had devised was inspired by the Nativity story, but here there was no manger and no Christ-child, just animals standing around a bare patch of ground between an old man and an old woman, whose lost children were coming running back to them from captivity in the sky.

The eye was drawn to the empty space between the two old people. Jane wondered aloud whether the spot should be accentuated in some way.

'What can I put in there?' Danny asked her.

She shook her head. 'I can't tell you.'

'A cross?' he asked fearfully, sarcastically. 'X marks the spot.'

'It needs something,' she said, not getting him.

'Then it will be done.'

They were given orangeade to drink in the art room for the festive season. Jane told Danny she was driving out west to stay with her friend Elspeth and her little godchild Cassie for Christmas, to do some work out there. It was Danny's country. She told him that according to her friend the government was giving the land out there back to the Aboriginal people, all round Lake Moorna, and it was thanks to the efforts of Danny's brother, Cleve Gordon.

'He's not my brother.'

'I thought he was your twin.'

'They don't want to know me.'

'That's why I'm telling you this, Danny, because you are part of it. You must be. You'll get something out of it too.'

Danny looked at the woman with sorrowful eyes, seeing and unseeing. His face, unshaven for days, was grey and bloodless. The space between his eyes was crossed with a frown. He was a good-looking man, not yet thirty years old. He could still be forgiven for what he had done, but it all seemed so far away and unlikely. He could not see through to the other side of hope. All he could feel was guilt and the burden of uncompleted punishment.

'He's done it for himself,' said Danny, 'so he can be one of us. I'm different. I've always been with our people even when I've been locked away. You see that, don't you? I've got a different part to play. He's not the saviour. I am.'

Jane could not understand Danny's meaning and did not want to antagonise him by appearing dismissive or obtuse.

'Do you want to send Cleve a message?' she asked.

'He knows I'm in here. He always knows that. It's like you're always missing the other one. That's why he can never rest till he brings all of us back together. He needs my spirit before he can do that. This picture – he can have that when it's done. You give it him from me when it's done.'

Jane felt unhappy about leaving Danny when the session came to an end. Although he seemed philosophical about spending another Christmas inside, as he had spent most of them, she was worried about the deeper than usual agitation, disturbed by words that she knew she had failed to interpret. She made a note in the work book that it would be a good idea if one of the nurses had another look at Danny and called in outside help if necessary, since the new psychiatric officer was not starting until the new year. The nurses were busy preparing for the Christmas party and were not looking for extra work. There was nothing that could not wait until after Christmas, including Daniel Gordon, they said in response to Jane's note.

Danny took his new picture back with him to the special observation unit where there was a large table he could work at, shared with other prisoners. He left the painting lying there when it was time to go back to his cell. The summer's night was humid, and he would not sleep. He paced his solitary cell until after dark, and after midnight he began jumping up and down off his bed, muttering to himself, letting the voices in his mind ooze out through his mouth. He had requested a sleeping pill from the night warder earlier in the evening, but his regime of medication was subject to monitoring, and the night warder had no authority to give him anything. Unable to sleep, Danny felt his reserves of control draining away. All his energy went into his sense of misery. He was alone, sentenced by a society that declared him unable to cope unless he was locked up, and condemned by his family to this eternal punishment until he wasted away to nothing and was dead and no more. He circled that narrow space between the walls wondering what he could do to save himself.

The prison chaplain had been on his rounds at suppertime dispensing gifts of dried fruit and Christian books for those who liked to read. Those who did not read might get a cassette tape of Jesus giving the Sermon on the Mount. Danny had always played up to the prison chaplain, getting cigarettes off him. The chaplain was a funny old bloke and his visits were an amusing part of institutional life. He was like some crazy old relative who took Danny back to his adolescent years, the smarmy protective side of his institutionalisation that had gradually rendered him unfit for life outside. The chaplain was another one of the type that included the principal of the Boys' Home who had dobbed Danny in on account of his drawing of Matron Campbell. Danny understood all that now, how Matron Campbell had led him on, yearning for the affection denied her by her travelling psychiatrist husband who, sensing the current of desire, had struck back, making the principal recommend Danny's removal to a place of greater brutality. Danny laughed as he was reminded of it by the chaplain, who was the same sort of holy pretender.

The chaplain gave him a Walkman for Christmas, and in the small hours, in the silent cell, Danny played the tape over and over, repeating the funny commanding words of Jesus talking. *If thy right eye offend thee, pluck it out, and cast it from thee: for it is profitable for thee that one of thy members should perish, and not that thy whole body should be cast into hell. And if thy right hand offend thee, cut it off, and cast it from thee: for it is profitable for thee that one of thy members should perish, and not that thy whole body should be cast into hell* . . .

As he lay on the bed, exhausted, he dreamed that he walked away, invisible, shining, a skeleton of light. He walked through darkness, through bones and knives, slapping hands, growling jaws, enraged eyes. He walked through monsters. He walked through the fire, unscathed like his namesake. He walked through besuited, befrocked, respectable, jeering, condemning humanity and tears streamed from his eyes like fountains of light, washing away his heaviness until he was so light that he could fly into the dawn. He had the painting to work on. The weight of it hung on him.

The next afternoon he put himself to it, grinding on until the picture was almost finished. He peopled it with uncles and aunts and brothers and sisters, even Mrs Fleyer who had been good to him in her guesthouse, and his mate Matt who had already drunk himself to death, and Paula Morgan who used to visit with her guitar, and even Jane the art therapist sitting at the side of the picture on a stool, painting another one for herself. He left it to dry when the time came for the Christmas Eve party with the nursing staff. The prison choir sung carols and they all joined in *Away in a manger, No crib for a bed* and afterwards they were allowed an hour of dancing to heavy metal, but not in pairs. There were not enough women to go round, and the blokes felt silly dancing with each other. Danny could recite the words of Jesus in the Sermon on the Mount from his head now without needing to hear the tape.

Next day there was ham at breakfast and the staff were bad-tempered, despite triple time. The work room was hung with garlands of silver and gold tinsel and chains of coloured crêpe paper. Danny did not respond to greetings of Merry Christmas. He was deep inside his own head, communing with his family, his sister Rhonda, the angel who had gone to court against him, for his own good, to teach him the law, and his old father, toothless and drunk, taking them kids round the country with him, self-reliant and dignified Joe, unable to save his son from the world, and Arthur his brother the day they were nabbed riding those fancy bikes round and round in circles in the dirt under the trees. He thought of flying out over the river on a rope as a kid, all the people cheering, holding on as long as you could until you let go and dive-bombed the flowing water. He thought of his mother, one-armed Mary, and the care and love she had for him and for all of them without end or thanks until the day she died. He saw them all there with him. What was around him in the work room, the tinsel and the bars and the stainless steel, he didn't see at all. He had closed his outer eye. He bent low over the painting. He had the brush in his hand, a fine slender brush that he dipped in the sticky black paint and held tight as he inscribed a precise circle in the space at the bottom of the painting, between the old man and the old woman who were the parents. His gaze was concentrated on the work, the place, the black circle he drew. But he was not seeing the surface of the painting. The circle was an eye-hole that took him through to the other side where he could see with his inner eye, all his family and all his life, in beauty. His life was no longer an unending line to nowhere, it was a circle, and the circle was a seed. *Mil* in the old language. He could remember that too. The word clicked on his tongue, his mother's word, as if one of the old people was taking over his throat.

When he finished the exact and glistening circle, Danny sat up and closed his eyes. When he opened them again he saw the painting. Clumsy and heavy and crude. Everything packed in. It was finished. All it needed now was the address of his message. Still with the slender black brush he began to do the letters. Danny never wrote. He hated writing. It was a child's skew lettering that he left.

FOR CLEVE, ME TWIN BRO.

With the brush in his hand, nestled parallel to his forearm like a splint, its end black and shining, Danny got up from the work table and headed for the toilet cubicles. There was no one around. He went inside a cubicle and shut the door behind him. The door could not be locked. He got down on his knees, wedged between the door and the stainless steel bowl, and stared ahead at the concrete wall. He had the brush in his hand, reversed, so the long slender handle was pointing towards him. He raised his arm. Both his eyes were open wide, and his right arm was poised. Then with all his strength he rammed the brush handle into his right eye. With an almighty scream, he slumped forward. The officers came running and, unable to push open the cubicle door, started kicking at the hinges. Danny's body was jammed between the toilet bowl and the door, and blood was running out from underneath. As the men kicked from outside, Danny was shoved forward. The paintbrush rammed deeper into his eye. When they got to him, they found only the head of the brush, glistening black and blood-red, protruding a centimetre from the eyeball. The handle had penetrated Danny's brain.

The siren threaded like a needle through the Christmas Day traffic. He was in a coma by the time the ambulance reached the hospital.

When the people on duty at the prison looked through the files to see who should be contacted, they whistled in alarm. The only family member they could find who had an up-to-date contact address was a brother at the Aboriginal Lands Council in Wagga Wagga. They did not like the look of that. Besides, it was Christmas. How could they get a message through? The doctor pronounced that the case might last some days, but the man would not recover. Might as well turn him off now. The prison officers cursed their luck. It was a death in custody for which they would be called to account, just because they happened to work overtime on Christmas Day, just doing their job. A message went through to Cleve Gordon. He was unlikely to get it until the day after Boxing Day, when business resumed.

Cleve walked outside, away from the homestead towards the flat pink land. He smelled the pungent dusty air. It smelled of rain. His head was spinning a little. His face burned from the drink that had accompanied the huge Christmas meal. He sniffed the air of the empty land. Then he staggered across the dirt, as if a body of wind had knocked him. The sensation made him look up, and momentarily he lost his balance and with it the knowledge of where he was. High to west, he saw the tower of stormclouds that would fall on the needing land as rain, dark colossus split by lightning, the bones of an arm reaching for him. When that rain fell, all could mourn. Until then loss would shadow the victory.

A ceremony was to take place at Lake Moorna a few days after Christmas, a time when it would attract no notice. Andrew Findlay had gone. He was in Adelaide with his family, where there was a solid set of loyalties. Elspeth stayed with Cassie to witness the ceremony. The bones of Moorna Woman and Moorna Man were to be returned to the site and solemnly reburied in the sand of the Walls of China. They were to be spared the gaze of further strangers.

The event signified the return of the land. Elspeth wanted to see it done properly. Masterman Holdings had agreed to the government's price for the buy-out of their leaseholding, including a premium for the manager's shack, which would be used to accommodate a park warden. Part of the property would become national park. Mastermans would lease back eighty thousand acres for dryland farming that complied with the land use criteria of the world heritage listing. Mastermans would retain use of the old Whitepeeper homestead. Ownership of the land was to be vested in the Aboriginal Lands Council in trust for the traditional occupiers.

Cleve Gordon argued from his office in Wagga Wagga that it was people like himself Lake Moorna belonged to, people from the area whose background was all mixed up, it belonged to all of them. Since the last people had been moved off in the 1920s, everyone who travelled across that area felt a custodial relationship with it on behalf of those who were no longer there. It was a victory for Cleve. His people would get some money at last.

Three days before Christmas he rang to find a time to visit Elspeth. She was moved by the way he had changed, more than anyone else she knew, into a maker of history. She was honoured by his friendship. To share Christmas with him seemed the very best way to celebrate. He would fly the plane out from Wagga Wagga on Christmas Eve. Jane had promised Elspeth that she would come out to Whitepeeper too. She wanted to do some more drawings out west. She was pleased with what she had done at Lake Moorna, although the work had not sold well. When Elspeth told her that the return of the bones was happening, she drove the seven hundred kilometres non-stop from Sydney.

Then on Boxing Day someone in Cleve's office in Wagga Wagga rang through to Whitepeeper with the news. Elspeth was in the room when he took the call. She saw his shoulders fall and his voice deepen. She had picked up the phone herself and heard the frenzy in the caller's voice. 'What is it?' she asked.

'Something's happened in Sydney. My brother's in hospital. I have to go.' He was staring through her.

'The brother in Long Bay?'

'He tried to kill himself. With a paintbrush. He took out his own eye. Poor fella.'

Cleve stood there showing no emotion. Elspeth went to him and put her arms around him and held him.

'When did it happen?'

'Yesterday. They couldn't find me. Because I was here!' He did not cry. He stood like a mountain of earth. It was as if he should never have been there, rejoicing with the wrong people at the wrong time. 'I'm going,' he said.

'Will he live?'

'I'll fly to Wagga, refuel and go through to Bankstown. I can be in Sydney tonight.'

'You're in no fit state to go all that way alone.'

'I'll pick up a mate in Wagga Wagga.'

'I don't want anything to happen to *you*.'

'I'm sorry,' Cleve said, breaking away from her.

'Will you be back? For the ceremony?' she reminded him. 'Cleve, you must. You have to be there when those bones are buried. It's vital. It has more to do with you than any of us.'

'I'll make it if I can. Otherwise you'll just have to wait for me to get back.'

'We'll wait,' she said steadily.

'No,' cried Jane when Elspeth passed on the news. 'No, I only saw him a few days ago. He was doing okay. He was going to make it.' Then she was weeping. 'You poor guy! I knew something was wrong. Why didn't someone help him? It's vile. It's all vile.' When she calmed down, she remembered. 'That painting was so important to him. That's why. It was the last one.'

For Elspeth the news of Danny was like a demon appearing in the way.

Cleve reached the hospital in Sydney. Late in the evening of a public holiday, the place had a grim air. No one wanted to be there when the car accident victims were brought in. Life, blundering on somehow. And he was too late. Danny had died and his body had been moved to the hospital morgue where Cleve was asked to go and identify it.

Danny lay there, a violet colour, cleaned up, immobile. He looked far younger and leaner than Cleve. He was a good-looking man still, even in death. But they had never been identical. Cleve put out a hand and gripped the damp shoulders. He did not care how horrible it felt. He inserted his fingers between the fingers of Danny's hand. The left eye was smoothly shut. The right eye was a wound, stitched up. Choking, Cleve kissed his brother's head, his lost brother, his twin, his darker, more vulnerable self – the soul who paid the price in suffering for the two of them, freed now from prison and earth. Known and not loved, loved and never known, Danny had given up his life, the one thing he had left with which to make amends.

The morgue attendant stood respectfully back with a clipboard, confirming the identification. It was cold in there.

The life was Cleve's now. Cleve understood that. He took it from Danny as a trust from that time forth.

Running shoes, jeans, a Walkman, a tape of the Gospel According to Saint Matthew, a book on Pierre Bonnard, and a bundle of old letters, pages almost falling apart, from Rhonda and Arthur and other people connected to him, a meagre bundle for so many years – all were listed when Cleve went next day to sign for Danny's things. Then there was the stack of pictures leaning against the wall.

'You can take these off our hands,' the woman said. 'Prison property, done with prison materials, but we've got nowhere to store them. They'll only be destroyed.'

The paintings were face down. Cleve pulled the top one back.

'Careful, that one's still a bit sticky,' she warned him.

Slowly Cleve let his eyes rove over the surface of the painting, absorbing its fierce colours and strange child's images. Then he noticed the inscription. At first it seemed broken off. Then he realised it was complete. FOR CLEVE ME TWIN BRO.

He hung his head with shame and only wanted to get out of the administrative officer's sight. He signed the documents she put in front of him and she allowed him to bundle the stuff up into his arms.

Before he left he heard himself speaking in anger and disbelief at the woman. 'Why didn't you get anyone to help him? Why did you wait so long – for this to happen? We'll want to know. We'll want to know why and we'll want justice done. Why didn't you contact anyone? All this bloody paperwork! All these bloody files. We'll want a full inquiry. Why didn't you people even *try* to help him? Because he was never even another human being to you. He was only a problem to get rid of. That's why. My poor bloody brother was just about the last creature left on earth you had to lord it over. You're in trouble. I'm telling you.'

PART FIVE · THE MORNING-STAR ·

1

ELSPETH woke to the apostle birds, nosy squawking creatures with puffed-up ruffs and rakish topknots, hopping on the verandah and bouncing against the screen door of her bedroom. They demanded to know why she was not up with the sun, cheeky birds that would walk into the house and take crumbs of Christmas cake from under the table. Cassie was still uneasy about them. It took a display of anger to make them fly away. In the heat of the day they fought with the resident sparrows and swallows in the old shearing shed, whirling and cracking their beaks like frenzied bats.

The shed, one of the glories of Whitepeeper, predated Masterman occupancy. It floated above the dusty paddock, as a memory of dreams and repeated cycles, of fortune's wheel and the Chinese labourers who had hauled its Murray pine over bush tracks from the river, when despair at the cheating earth drove them inland from the goldfields, their God of Wealth no less capricious than anyone else's. The peculiar craft of the great shearing shed was their testimonial. Where a Chinese worker was crushed by the weight of logs dragged over his body by the bullock team, a ghost still returns. One among many at Whitepeeper.

For years the wool shorn on the slatted floor of that ship of a shearing shed was carried by bullock team back to the river, where it travelled to port to be loaded on to seagoing vessels, back to England for milling into cloth that would go out again to the Empire, a journey from one corner of the world to another. The Emperor of the Bush had fitted into that system within living memory. Wool and beef from the largest pastoral holdings in the world had gone everywhere, until he became a ghost too, a legend talked about for the audacity of his achievement and the negligence of his methods, who took from the land in good years and abandoned it in bad, who shared his blanket with the natives at night.

Cleve was in Elspeth's thoughts as she crossed into consciousness from the secrecy of dreams. She wanted to comfort him as she wanted to bring him flying back. She remembered that back garden in Adelaide, the kids' birthday party, where they had been playing cricket, and Cleve was bowling and she threw him the ball, the first time they ever spoke. Cleve had wanted her to take him seriously, but it made her nervous. There was too much of a gulf between them. She remembered the inoculation scars up and down his arm. As wanting him became a real possibility, she grew more nervous still. She would not risk taking advantage of him. But then the slow unbending had started to occur, with Cleve's persistence, his hard work, his triumph. She rolled over in the bed and stretched. In the space beside her curled another presence, the body of a sleeping man, who was also a dead man, Cleve's twin, invisible now as the smoke rose and dispersed from the crematorium incinerator in shimmering heat and air, another ghost. Still it was dangerous, still it must be resisted, because what could she give? She felt as light and airy as this barely stirring summer morning, as if she had nothing to give him at all.

Like a bird herself, responsive at last to the impatient pattering of the apostle birds' feet on the old timbers of the verandah, Elspeth got out of bed. The rest of the house was quiet. A heavy summer rain had fallen like strokes of the lash over the parched land, leaving bright cloudless sky and the country freshened and revived, the soil flesh-pink, the vegetation pert and shiny in a tingling pot-pourri of washed air, settled earth, pungent leafage and sharp sweet flowers. Animals were restless – kangaroos, sheep and cattle, magpies and parrots, ants, beetles, locusts, butterflies. When she opened the French doors to the verandah, Elspeth heard a murmur of voices where another set of doors was open. The house carried sound with the resonance of an old cello. She heard the words but could not understand them, as if they had been changed into a foreign language. Jane and Cassie were whispering to each other. It was Cassie's great joke and joy to climb into the bed while Auntie Jane was still sleeping and wake her up and make her tell stories. And Jane, prizing the chance of Cassie's presence, laughingly obliged and never got enough sleep.

The other guests were sleeping in the shearers' quarters. They had driven in convoy from Canberra the previous day, all the way through the winding hills and across the western plains. Kincaid was at the wheel of the university's black Range Rover. In the back of the black tank travelled two sealed pinewood boxes which contained the remains of Moorna Woman and Moorna Man. Duly cleaned, examined, photographed, scraped, carbon-dated, X-rayed and labelled, they were covered by grey army-disposal blankets as protection from the heat and prying gazes at truck-stops along the way. The boxes might have been two small coffins custom-made in the lab. Every now and again Ralph leaned over and felt the wood beneath the woollen blankets, as if to reassure the contents that they mattered, that they were at the heart of this journey. His children, who had stayed with his wife in Canberra, might have whined from the backseat, 'Are we there yet, Dad?' But unlike his own and the other kids in the backs of family cars on the road that day, Moorna Woman and Moorna Man were silent and patient, journeying home.

~

Following Kincaid down the strip of tar that ran due west across the dry plains was a car with Alex Mack at the wheel and Josie Ryan beside him in the passenger seat. Alex had been nominated to represent the Minister for the National Estate at the ceremony, hanging on to his position until the end of the year. It was Valerie O'Rourke's parting joke. The road was familiar. He had started driving it years ago in a powder-blue old Jaguar that held the road better than his present commonwealth government sedan. Ziggy was in the back with Isaac fidgetting beside him. Josie had twisted Ziggy's arm to make him come along for the ride. For Alex's sake. Ziggy stared out the window with the same appalled astonishment at the emptiness and endlessness of the country as on that first trip, when he had sat in the back squeezed against Alex and Jane and Wendy sat in the front.

'At least this car's got suspension,' Ziggy said, 'and airconditioning. Do you remember how hot it was that time? But look out there. It's absolutely godforsaken.'

Ziggy's cartons had been unpacked, his books and records and tapes lined up on the red timber shelves, his pictures and posters hung on the walls of his new house. Every day he climbed down the headland to the little sandy cove and played in the picture-book surf like a child. At night he slept soundly, lulled by the crashing rhythmic monotone of the sea, and in the morning he sang, extending his lungs to produce great bellowing passages of sound. Or he just sat staring at the light behind the trees. He had never felt better.

His parents had come for Christmas in the new house. His mother had brought back the little bear. At the time she told him she had tossed it into the fire to punish him, but it had been hoarded in a box of his childhood things with his parents' lumber all these years. He could still remember when the black wooden bear had seemed taller than he was.

His parents were proud of him for being visible, while they remained unseen and unheard. But they would never know the long backwards journey Ziggy had made in order to be able to bounce around on the open sunny deck of his own house on the headland – bare-skinned and tanned – with salt water dripping from his mane. His mother had torn that little black bear from his arms in the last refugee camp, wanting nothing more to do with men who gave gifts. Not Vittorio, who had arranged for the toy to be given to her boy, nor Siegfried, the first one, the German officer who was Ziggy's namesake. The boy had sat there holding the bear, taunting her, possessing his mother's secret, and she had snatched the bear back from him before he grew strong in the hidden knowledge of sacrifice and enslavement.

Ziggy put the bear on the shelf. It sat upright on its hind legs with a shocked, silly look on its wooden face. The past was over, or transformed as they carried it with them over the threshold into the present, after more than a quarter of the century.

Ziggy stood on the overgrown step at the top of the steep path and waved his parents goodbye. Then he scrambled down to the beach for a swim. Certain things need not be spoken of again. Betrayal, revenge and violation had vanished into the glare of light. He came back to the house and, shaking his head, hopped on one foot, his head on one side, to get the water out of his ears. He was glad he was going to dinner at Josie and Isaac's house that night.

The first thing Josie had done after Ziggy moved in was to make him sign the rainwater-only petition. If she could achieve nothing else, she could stop the neighbourhood being ruined by greed. Ziggy laughed at Josie for being as cross and fanatical in her way as his Lithuanian parents were in theirs.

Isaac pestered Alex to build fancy castles and forts out of building blocks until it became a joke between them. There were better things to do together, like building real castles and forts of sand on the beach, or going into Isaac's room where the games they played behind the closed door were secret from the boy's mother. When it suited him, Isaac was quite happy to form an alliance with Alex against Josie. The rest of the time Josie wanted to be given a hearing herself. Understanding that Alex wanted no secrets, she made even his most solemn privacies burst like bubbles. She saw right through him, but she preferred to talk things out – as if finding words made the weight of things shareable.

Alex had been broken by his bureaucratic crucifixion. Too many people were envious of his rise for the brakes to be put on when his slide commenced. Not that he was down and out yet, as designate head of the Department of Immigration for the coming year. But even that promised appointment would fall through if he had lost the favour of the Prime Minister. The details never mattered: it happened in wordless scorn and murmuring. There were rumours now of a move against Prime Minister Lewin, and the numbers might be there for Valerie O'Rourke to get up. That was what Reg Rufus said. If the white-anting of Prime Minister Lewin went unchecked. And then who could say where Alex might be?

'You judge people so harshly,' Josie said to him. Her expectations were lower than Alex's. She would sing hallelujahs when the mains water proposal was stopped. Whereas Alex, with the highest expectations, had been corroded faster than his experience had tempered him. 'You don't trust anyone, do you?'

'I trust you.'

'How do I know? Sometimes you seem to be just performing very effectively as a person and yet your way of reading the world around you so skilfully is really a kind of *skin* that's trapping you. Like a body-stocking. A suit of armour. You're not really reading the world at all because you can't actually touch it. Or let it touch you. Don't you ever feel that?'

In reply he stroked her freckled forearm.

'I don't know,' he said. He liked the way Josie, with her tough trust in humanity, had come along to save him. He realised it was what he had always wanted from her.

'You like Ziggy because he's an actor.'

'He's a spirit too.'

'Yes, well he's special. What I mean is, I would like you to let what is inside of you out, let it flow out and let other stuff flow in, let *other people* flow into you. I believe you are brave enough for that, Alex. Otherwise what is the point?'

'You have Isaac. You have someone who is already part of you.'

'I could have you too.'

'Will you let me in?'

Josie smiled and took his hand. 'You're staying in my house, aren't you?'

'I love being here – with you,' he said, sounding like a sly bureaucrat. 'You're the one who is holding back. I am being as honest as I know how. What else can I do?'

She resisted him. She forbade the fulfilment that he imagined. Once again she closed her bedroom door. He lay on the couch. He had found the little orange poetry book in which he had slipped, years before, the only two letters she had ever written to him. She had felt at least that need to communicate the early milestones of her life – markers of the wrong road.

'Don't. You embarrass me,' she exclaimed when he produced the specimens of neat writing on paper, folded in four and discoloured now. 'Why did you keep them?'

He had marked the place: . . . *oh, why* have *to be human, and, shunning Destiny, / long for Destiny?* . . .

Josie did not tell him she had already been to the Lake Moorna he talked so much about, once before, pregnant with Isaac at the time. That was her double secret. She had to think carefully through the implications of going back there. It was not only on her own behalf but also for Isaac's sake. What Alex proposed was like a dream to assemble the different stages of her life at one place and time for a reckoning to be made. Above all it was Cleve. Cleve would be there. Was it fair on Cleve for her to front up as part of Alex's entourage, with the child whom he never had a chance to acknowledge? Was it fair on Isaac? It was for the boy's sake, out of love, that Alex wanted Isaac to come along, and Josie with him – to give the boy back that other part of himself. Was it fair on her? Was it fair on any of them?

'Will you do it for me?' Alex begged her. 'Only for me.'

'Why do we have to?' She insisted on knowing.

'I can't explain why. It's necessary. We have to forget who we were and see who we are. We're not strangers, none of us. Yet we are.'

Josie gave Alex her peculiar sharp sideways stare. She shuddered. He was right.

~

'It's those two people,' Alex explained to Isaac, 'who are the real cause of our journey. They are the ones who have brought us all here.'

Isaac's eyes widened. It was scary to think of the bones rattling round in boxes in the back of the black vehicle in front. What if the lid came off? What if those ancient bones got out?

Under a cloudless sky and a bright moon, as dusk fell, they saw the land change. Grey kangaroos stared at the headlights, then turned and fled. The young ones, confused, bounded down the road in the path of the oncoming cars. Then the mothers panicked and sprang back across the beams of light. The last dusty stretch was difficult, before the lit windows of the homestead appeared in the darkness, like yellow eyes in a skull.

'It's fucking amazing,' shrieked Jane, her arm in Ziggy's to greet him. 'We're *all* here.'

'Well, almost all of us,' said Elspeth, turning vaguely to the woman and child standing to one side in the shadow, who were welcome too. The light from the verandah spilled in a circle between the cars. She waited for Alex to speak.

'Well, you know Josie.' Alex smiled, surprised. 'Josie Ryan? You remember her, don't you, Elspeth? And this is Isaac, her little boy.' Alex put his arm round Isaac's shoulders and brought him forward to present him to the intrigued grown-up faces.

'G'day – Elspeth. Jane,' said Josie brashly.

Elspeth had last seen Josie Ryan as some sort of nun in Nulla, that country town she disliked so much. 'Josie. Of course. You look great.' The transformation to this cropped, wiry woman was extreme.

'You really didn't recognise me,' Josie laughed. 'I suppose I should be grateful.'

When what Elspeth was wondering – was frowning over – was whether people were capable of change at all. Was *she*? What was the thing that remained, changeless through time? Was there anything?

Jane stepped forward and clasped Josie's hand between her own two hands, somewhere between formal distance and an embrace. Josie had never been a friend. Then she kissed Alex evasively, not meeting his eyes.

The death in custody of Daniel Gordon had warranted a tiny paragraph in the newspaper in the midst of cricket, yacht races, tennis championships and record temperatures. The gruesome detail of the paintbrush stuck in the dead man's eye connected his death to her, Jane felt. She was cheated of her hope for Danny, which was also faith in art and a vestige of hope for herself.

Then Cassie swayed across the grass with a saucy gait, her wispy golden hair like straw and her face tilted upward. It was Wendy they saw.

'This is Cassie,' said Jane. 'Say hallo to Isaac, sweetheart. A little boy has come to visit us.'

'Cat got your tongue, Ize,' asked Josie.

Cassie ran over to Isaac and looked at him with a demanding face. The boy gave out a gravelly laugh of delight.

'Come on,' said Cassie, who was older and taller than Isaac.

'Go on, Isaac,' said Alex.

The smell of smoke and old beer, piss and grease, dry timber and lead paint, and the shearers and their sheep, lingered in the shearers' quarters where the visitors were to sleep. Each person had a cell of a room with a single iron-frame bed made up with a prickly blanket and worn sheets. There was a little window, covered with rusty wire-mesh, and a door that opened straight on to the dirt. There was a communal washroom at the end of the row. Elspeth put a towel on each bed for them. They laughed at her matronly manner. Meanwhile, Elspeth explained, the manager's house had been prepared for another group of visitors.

A group of senior Chinese officials was in Australia to inspect sheep-farming properties. It was Xiao Jing who set up the visit through the Australian Department of Foreign Affairs. Her friend René Baum was hired by the Department to be the interpreter and guide for the delegation. Apart from the Deputy-Minister of Agriculture, Mr Yang, there was the Director of the Textile Bureau, Mr Yao, who said that this was the thirty-fifth foreign country he had visited in an official capacity, an arid-area expert called Mrs Guan, and two younger bureaucrats who had been assigned to study sheep breeding and sheep shearing respectively. Then there was Chalky, the Australian driver, a Vietnam veteran, who was on overtime during the holiday period.

As a developmental economist, Xiao Jing grasped the complementarity between Australian wool production and the Chinese textile industry. If the Chinese could source Australian wool for their cloth mills directly, cutting out the middleman, not only would profits increase, but Australia would be tied to China as once the colony had been tied to Great Britain. That had geopolitical advantages, Xiao Jing understood. Through her high-ranking father, she was able to have sufficient funds earmarked for the purchase of large-scale Australian sheepfarms by the Chinese government. To invest money overseas, out of reach, went against the grain of Chinese conservatism, but Xiao Jing was a moderniser. Land was land, she argued to her father. Fertile land was fertile land. If the Australians could not make it work, then the Chinese had a claim on it.

Grazing properties where the old leaseholds were designated for return to Aboriginal ownership were top of the list. If there was any trouble getting the local pastoralists to lease the land back from the new Aboriginal owners to run sheep, let the Chinese have it. To the

Department of Foreign Affairs in Canberra, the arrangement had a certain appropriateness. The Chinese and the blacks had always been brothers.

René had done his homework by calling Alex at National Estate, and Alex encouraged René to put Whitepeeper on the itinerary. The famous property out west, whose leasehold was running out, boasted an ancient line of sandhills that homesick Chinese labourers had named the Walls of China. All over the world the Chinese thought of home, commented Deputy-Minister Yang, moved and curious when René told him. When they lay down on warm hazy autumn nights, their bellies growling, those Chinese brothers of another time had gazed at the red wall of sand rising across the illusory lake by the light of the eighth moon and had named their vision for the glory of their fractured Empire. It was Chinese compatriots who had cleared much of that country out there, René added for the benefit of Deputy Minister Yang as Chalky drove the minibus west. According to Xiao Jing, whose national pride was pricked by this story, it was only right that China should take over this land again.

The Chinese had *not* been invited to attend the ceremony, Elspeth explained carefully to Professor Kincaid, who lodged an objection when he heard that a diplomatic delegation would be spending the same night in the empty manager's dwelling. Elspeth believed in being hospitable to foreigners. But the tour of inspection, a formality only, would come nowhere near Lake Moorna.

The more pressing matter concerned the two crates in the back of the Range Rover. After a brief consultation with Alex, as senior government representative, it was decided that the most respectful approach would be to leave the bones where they were, sleeping under a blanket. It would be Kincaid's responsibility to see they did not walk.

At the long polished cedar table in the dining room they ate the roast hogget Andrew had killed before he left, served with homemade mint sauce. Elspeth brought out the best red wine and let the guests make free with it.

'We can't finally say who they are, or what they are,' speculated the professor in response to Jane's quizzing about the bones. 'They are humans, same as us, but from two human skulls it is possible to erect almost any theory. The people who lived here all that time ago inhabited a different world. There was fresh water in the lake and herbage on the shores. Seafood in abundance. Maybe in winter there was snow on the surrounding hills. They were different people, in that sense, and the long story of their connection with us – or rather with the later Aborigines who occupied their place – must be a bit of a blank. They may even have been brought here from somewhere else for reburial, even then, but I can't think why?'

'Isn't that what you're doing all over again?' interjected Jane.

'I find it more plausible to think that they might have started from here,' Kincaid replied, ignoring her implication.

'Started?' asked Ziggy.

'In their long evolution into the form of the later people.'

'That's an unprecedented shift, isn't it, Ralph?' said Alex, keeping Kincaid honest. 'A quantum leap in evolutionary time.'

'But not impossible,' insisted the professor.

'Is anything impossible?' asked Elspeth.

'I'm talking scientifically. They might have started from here in their long journey outwards to other places where similar bone structures have been found. Present-day Ethiopia. Northern China.'

'This could have been the first place then?' demanded Jane.

'*Could*,' the professor emphasised dubiously.

'The first place?' echoed Alex. He raised his eyebrows at Josie who was seated opposite him.

'Then they should be called Eve and Adam,' Josie quipped. 'I'll check the kids. I'm about ready to hit the sack.'

The boards creaked. It was not just Alex who was restless. The place was restless too. Smeared in insect repellent, he listened for the mosquito whine around his head. The door was open to the cooling air. Snuffling and snoring came from the other rooms, he did not know whose, and he could hear the coughing of sheep and the plangent cry of an owl, that became the note of the piper. He was transported back to the shearers' quarters where he had slept as a boy that time, that place on the river, on the school trip, where they had cracked the baked earth with water and dug for bones in the name of adventure and dominance. The pibroch was drifting through the night. In the name of desecration, as if to expel the ghosts. The piper in his skirt with his hot desire. The desire of all of them to ravish. It had been his initiation into a manhood that wielded the knife, cutting light from dark and death from life. He felt that denial in his own groin as he thought about it. The connectedness of life and the ancient contraries that made human experience whole – denied. Ziggy saw that denial in him and had tried to save him. It was what Josie saw too, he guessed. He was his mother's son but he must dive back under, turn in a somersault, conserve his strength and head for shore. He must open his eyes without being afraid. If he had burned out his child's eyes by staring at the black moon blotting out the blazing sun, then he must learn to see around his blindness until his sight healed and grew back. Was he – were any of them – more than they had been as children? Mature now, adults with the world in their hands? The skin of sky through the open door was feeling the first bare light of the new day. Drawn to the doorway, he got up and stood there registering the chill. He peered up at the last of the night. The brightest star was the one left to make the crossing into day, the night's last dazzling gift, the morning-star, brighter in its promise than the whole wide creep of morning itself.

2

ISAAC stood in the yard and looked up. He heard a buzzing in the sky but he could see nothing. Then a dark, glinting speck appeared. Josie came out to watch with him. She took her son's hand in hers and shaded her eyes with her other hand. The drone grew louder as the plane approached until it dominated the expanse of sky and country. Elspeth was running to the airstrip. Cassie ran after her, and Isaac yanked at his mother's hand. For a moment Josie would not let go. Then she released him. Cleve's green plane came down like a clumsy bird, lining up with the ground and rocking from side to side in the cross-breeze, churning up dust until it thumped down, bounced and steadied. Isaac waved, goggle-eyed. It was thrilling to have this great green bird churning along the pink ground towards the wind-sock. When the plane reached its position, the solo man turned off the engine and made his concluding checks as the whirring disks of the propellers slowed and the blades became visible.

Cassie yelped. She and Elspeth ran forward, as Cleve climbed out onto the wing. He jumped down and strode across, grinning, tired, and stopped in front of Elspeth. She kissed him on the cheek. He drew breath, in a moment's renewal, reaching down and brushing Cassie's hair. Elspeth was relieved to have him back.

'Everyone's here,' she said. She put her arm through his, longing to comfort him, as they walked the remaining distance across the dirt. 'How was the funeral?'

'A few stragglers came along. That's all. I have to go back and collect his ashes.'

Isaac wanted to run forward, but Josie tugged him back. She waited. Cleve grinned with his usual shy curiosity towards strangers. He did not think he knew these people. It was the familiarity of the child that affected him first, making him look again at the woman in her red sleeveless dress with big white polka dots, from which her legs and upper arms emerged like milk. Then with a shudder he loosened himself from Elspeth's arm, pulled his jacket around his shoulders and strode forward without faltering although he could have dropped down dead. His head buzzed, filled with a whirring insect noise. He walked, aware of the boy waiting with an eager look on his face. The boy, standing there, brought him to a trembling elation as he stopped in front of Josie. 'Who's this?' he asked.

'Hallo Cleve,' she said, slow and calm. 'Yes. This is Isaac. My son.'

The boy twisted with a nervous smile at the pilot, who stared at him so inquisitively.

'Your son?'

'Will you take me up in your plane?' Isaac smirked.

'You heard me,' said Josie, blinking.

'*Your* son,' Cleve repeated. With Cassie beside her, Elspeth was coming over. Cleve looked from Josie to Elspeth and demanded angrily, 'Where did they come from? Did they just fall down out of the sky?'

'That's you, mate,' said Josie with amusement. 'You're the one who's just dropped out of the sky!' But he was storming towards the house, was not ready for any more talk. He knew from that fierce, challenging reproach in the kid's eyes – the opening that would draw him in for the rest of his life. From Josie's courage – he should have known.

Jane was in the kitchen making coffee. The noise of the plane's landing drowned out her conversation with Alex. The business of the day was beginning. She had been probing his relationship with Josie and he was quite forthcoming. He was in love with Josie, Alex said, as he always had been.

Jane raised her eyebrows. 'You never said anything before. What about me?' she asked as the plane's roar subsided. 'So this is it?'

'Except that she's still testing me and, strangely enough, I don't mind. It's giving me time to get to know Isaac.'

'Yes, she's got the boy. Do you know who the father is?'

'He doesn't see the father. It doesn't matter.'

'It does matter,' said Jane, peering at him to see if he was telling her the whole truth.

'It's up to Josie.' He changed the subject. 'Are you looking forward to today? I'm not.'

'I want to paint,' Jane said. 'I can't stop thinking about Danny Gordon. About his pain. Jesus, it's terrible. What's Ziggy doing?'

'Still asleep, I imagine.'

'Actors' hours. Better wake him up or the professor will be on his back. He's rearing to go.'

The two crates were lined with durable plastic and thin sheeting of incorruptible lead. Kincaid had done everything in his power to make the contents immune from decomposition, once the crates were buried again beneath the earth of Lake Moorna. Since the bones had lasted so long already, it was a responsible precaution to ensure their continued survival. Consider it a form of safekeeping. The secret measures he had taken would allow him to revisit the bones when the need arose. There was a pact of secrecy, in any case, among them all on this blazing hot day, a day that would only get hotter the longer they delayed.

They were still hanging around the homestead at midday waiting for the Aboriginal elders to arrive. Three old women, representing three nations adjacent to Lake Moorna, had agreed to act as the traditional custodians. Paula Morgan, who had moved in as the Aboriginal liaison officer in Wentworth, was up before dawn driving the four-wheel drive around the women's far-flung homes to collect them, starting with Auntie Betty Poole from Nulla, then Mona Riley from Wilga, and Dorothy Ah Kin from inland. Paula Morgan, in a turquoise track-suit and a cowboy hat, liked her work and was proud to be delivering the women, who looked beautiful in their bright summer dresses and white cardigans. Auntie Betty wore a felt hat with a feather in it. Mona wore a yellow, red and black crochet beanie. Dorothy wore a straw hat with everlasting daisies. It was their prerogative as guests of honour to arrive late. Then Mona and Dorothy needed to use the bathroom. Elspeth showed them where it was and got cold drinks from the fridge.

Auntie Betty laughed to see Cleve. He was an important man now, but still she called him 'Son', demanding respect in return. 'What you furrowing your brow for, son?' she asked him.

Paula Morgan was about Cleve's age. Auntie Betty called her 'Sis'. Not that Auntie Betty knew Paula any better than Cleve did, since they lived in different towns. All the way on the drive Paula had sung her favourite soppy ballads and the elders loved it. She had a lovely singing voice and played good guitar. She knew all the country songs. Paula had run away and lived in the city for a while, where she had a couple of kids. Then her marriage broke up and she got involved in Aboriginal affairs. She had worked in the prisons, before she finally decided to return to the country.

'Paula's been on the go since sun-up. What have you got us out here for, son?' Auntie Betty asked Cleve, knowing full well.

'You elders are the witnesses. It's important,' he said. 'Things were taken from this place that should never have been taken.

Belonging to our people. No one asked our permission. Today they're being brought back.'

'I'll be a witness all right,' promised Auntie Betty. 'But I won't go near them dead things. Like I told you before, them's bad luck. I got enough troubles of my own without them.'

'Go on!' Cleve swished the flies away from his face. 'Well, maybe your luck's starting to improve.'

'What are you talking about?' scowled Auntie Betty. 'Too bloody late.'

Elspeth went in the first vehicle out to the site, taking Cleve with her. He was cranky. Elspeth watched warily, waiting for an almighty fury to erupt.

'I don't know whether we can go ahead with this ceremony,' Cleve said. 'We have to discuss what sort of ceremony it is with the elders first. They've come all this way, haven't they?'

Elspeth was apprehensive. All that brouhaha would come later. This ceremony was supposed to be a simple private forerunner, the more meaningful for that. An intimate act involving only a few people.

'It's not your right to say what happens,' Cleve insisted.

'I know that. But the job has to be done. Ralph would have buried them in secret if we let him. At least there's a few people to keep an eye on him. This is what you wanted to happen, isn't it? You explain it to the elders.'

'The elders understand more than you do. They're sharp as tacks.'

The Range Rover followed. Jane and Cassie were squeezed in beside Ralph with the crates. The elders followed close behind, bumping over the track. Paula had the windows down and dust filled the car. *Ring of Fire*, she was singing. She had Moorna Woman on her mind, cremated all that time ago. Alex, Josie, Isaac and Ziggy were in the last car, in everyone else's dust, bringing the picks and shovels to dig the pits for the crates. The country was flat in every direction except for the shimmer of sandhills that formed their destination – unwelcoming country, so open and untroubled that it pushed the spirit to expand. Or suspended the mind, as the snake froze in its tracks, acting dead, while the cars swept by. Strange, soft, smoky-looking country, bounded only where vision itself broke apart into shining, floating bands.

Ralph Kincaid had indicated on a detailed map where the remains should be relocated. It was impossible to pinpoint the places where the bones had come from originally. The wind had blown, the sand had slipped and the ropes and pegs were all gone, as if the terrain had moved. And bones, of dead animals, lay scattered over the surface. It was at last Elspeth who turned the first clod. People had become argumentative about where they should dig. Then each person took a turn at the digging in a ritual of inclusion. Only the old women held back. Auntie Betty kept her gaze averted from what was going on. Under a stunted tree she found a scrap of broken shade and sat down on the sand with the other women to wait.

Sweat ran from under hatbands, heads started to spin. Soft loose sand ran back into the pits as fast as it was dug out. Then Kincaid gave the signal and they brought the crates across. He and Elspeth carried the crate that contained Moorna Woman.

'I can manage,' Elspeth insisted when Ziggy came to help.

'She must weigh a ton!' he said.

Cleve and Alex brought the second box, what was left of Moorna Man. There was an awkward expectancy that someone should say something, a prayer or a blessing, or some sort of funeral words to give meaning to what was happening.

'What we're doing is an act of preserving our National Estate,' tried Alex unconvincingly.

'These things are going back where they belong,' declared Cleve.

'They should never have been taken away in the first place,' Elspeth added jarringly.

'What we are doing,' intervened Professor Kincaid in his most solemn voice, 'is re-establishing the integrity of this most important site.'

'Have you done it yet?' called out Mona Riley. The others waited anxiously.

Then Isaac yelled. 'Look!' With an outstretched arm and finger he was pointing across the plain. 'Someone's coming.' A cloud of dust was rolling out of the distance in their direction. It took a long time, as they stared, to become clear. Beetling down the straight road towards them across the dry sunken lakebed was a vehicle. A yellow minibus.

'It's the Chinese!' gasped Elspeth.

'Oh no!' exclaimed Alex.

'What Chinese?' asked Cleve. Elspeth had neglected to tell him.

'There was no one left at the house,' figured Elspeth, 'so they must have just set out by themselves.'

'Quick,' ordered Kincaid.

In clumsy haste they transferred the crates to the graves they had dug. The clean new boxes lay neither flat nor quite straight but there was no time for niceties as the pink sand was shovelled in on top, falling with a disturbing hollowness on the resounding cavity of wood. It was as if the bones were knocking back in protest as the sand trickled down the sides and engulfed the crates, that hollow knocking sound standing in for speech. Those without tools scooped up sand with their hands and flung it on top of the exposed timber. No one stopped to ask why it was imperative to have the crates out of sight and properly buried, the job thoroughly done, without a trace remaining, before the intruders reached the spot. There was mutual understanding that the task was to disguise what they were doing. Everything must be covered up before the uninvited guests arrived.

'Who asked *them*?' Cleve blustered. 'Where's my shotgun?'

Elspeth was almost relieved that his anger had somewhere else to go.

The minibus stopped near the other vehicles at the foot of the sandhill where the work was going on.

'The place is starting to look like a carpark,' said Ziggy.

Then the Chinese climbed out, wearing sunhats and dark glasses, cameras at the ready.

'That's what they call the Walls of China,' Xiao Jing was telling the delegation in Mandarin.

René Baum, sent ahead as an advance guard, walked across to the group at work on the slope. 'Hallo,' he called into the open space, without much enthusiasm.

'*René!*' Alex yelled back in a jeering voice. 'Fancy that! I wondered whether you'd turn up.'

The others stared in astonishment at this man who wore baggy blue jeans, a blue cotton Mao shirt, black cloth shoes, a cap and dark glasses. René picked Elspeth as the host and addressed her with sincere apologies. They had got lost on the road. They had arrived late. Finding the homestead deserted, they had set out to explore the property, despairing of finding a living soul. Then Chalky, their driver, had seen movement in the distance and they drove over.

The delegation sauntered after René, complaining about the heat. The airconditioning in the minibus had broken down. Deputy-Minister Yang asked Xiao Jing if they had arrived at a goldfield and whether these people gathered around patches of freshly turned sand in the middle of nowhere were prospecting for gold. The Chinese group began to talk excitedly among themselves. René, fixing on Alex as senior government representative, struggled to introduce the delegation leader.

'Aren't you hot?' inquired Elspeth graciously.

The Chinese men wore suits and ties; Mrs Guan wore a suit but no tie. Only Xiao Jing, in shorts and a T-shirt, was dressed for the occasion. Elspeth offered cool drinks all round. The Deputy-Minister frowned when René explained that they were on Elspeth's land, all ninety-five thousand acres of it. Then Professor Kincaid stepped forward and informed them that Australian civilisation was forty thousand years old at the place they were standing on. But the Chinese were not particularly interested. They knew that at five thousand years theirs was the most ancient continuous culture in existence. The rest was before time. They were in Australia for wool and were unwilling to be distracted. Deputy-Minister Yang asked where the sheep were. Then Paula ushered the three old black women over from under the trees to shake hands with the delegation by way of formal greeting.

'These are the new sovereign owners of the land,' translated René. The Deputy-Minister giggled. He had heard of the Aborigines and was surprised to see them wearing party dress.

'Welcome to our country,' said Auntie Betty.

Xiao Jing returned a patronising smile. She understood lineage.

By now the heat was having a deleterious effect on everyone. The Chinese arrival had disrupted the rhythm of the ceremony, turning it to farce, but that proved something of a relief. René, with some inkling of the situation, was taken aside by Alex and told to say nothing about what was going on. Xiao Jing's sharp, embarrassing questions were left hanging in the air. The whole curious business hung suspended in the heat-haze as, with an air of levity approaching hysteria, they finally made their way back to their respective vehicles.

Only Alex lingered, smoothing the sand with his hands to protect the day's work from burrowing animals. Walking in a circle on the surface of the earth above where the ancient skulls had been returned to their rest, he wished for a sign. But there was only the feeling he had that Joe Skull of years ago was at last back in the ground, back in the dark earth, after all the damage done. It was a gesture of amends, nothing more, but it was perhaps real enough for Joe Skull to understand. Distant heir of Moorna Woman and Moorna Man. The belonger of Lake Moorna. He had come all this way for that.

'Hurry up, Alex,' called Josie.

Dazzled, he looked around him, as if he were seeing the place truly at last. The past in the present, dark behind the light, and the prospect of a further light beyond that darkness. Himself. This continent.

Josie called to him again, an edge in her voice. 'We're going, Alex! You'll get sunstroke if you stay out there.'

He glided over the light crusty sand, breaking into a run, his footprints barely registering. Isaac and Ziggy were inside the car, impatient for the cooling to start. Josie stood by the open door, waiting for him. She put her hand out to take his, in reassurance, her face screwed up and freckled in the sunlight.

'Where's your hat?' he asked with a smile.

Elspeth organised a barbecue in the old shearing shed to feed everybody. Cleve sat at the other end of the shed with the Aboriginal women, in the warm, woolly-smelling shade. His refusal to help get the lunch ready was an act of separatism that would make Elspeth and the others uncomfortable, he knew. That was *their* problem. They would never know how to bridge the divide unless he showed them. He was looking at Paula. There was something about his look that she did not like. She turned her back and wandered over to where Alex and Jane were grilling huge quantities of meat to see if she could help. Ziggy was in charge of making the salad.

'Hey, you peel the carrots,' Ziggy yelled to Paula.

'What do you sing?' she asked back.

'Everything,' he boasted. 'Want to do something together?'

'You're on,' Paula said. 'The guitar's in the truck.'

Then Isaac came running up to say he was starving and needed something to eat. Paula winked to Ziggy that the deal was off. She took Isaac over to where Jane was turning the meat, took the barbecue fork out of Jane's hand and skewered a sausage. Then she pinched it off with her fingers.

'Careful,' said Jane.

'Sorry,' replied Paula, handing back the fork. Isaac reached for the sausage. 'In a minute, boy. It's hot.' She took him by the hand and led him off to the far end of the shearing shed where Cleve was sitting with the elders. Sunlight cutting through the cracks, making thin stripes of light that swarmed with dust, marked shifting territories on the floorboards. The cavernous space was mysterious and exciting to the boy. 'This your kid?' Paula casually asked Cleve as she blew on the sausage and gave it to Isaac.

Cleve looked up as if he didn't know what she was talking about. He had drunk a couple of beers and his eyes were swimming.

'Yeah, I suppose he is. You're my boy, aren't you, mate?' The boy stood his ground, waiting patiently for the man's answer. Paula pushed the kid forward to test what Cleve would do. 'Don't be scared,' Cleve said. Isaac walked forward and Cleve put his arms out. 'Your old man won't hurt you, fella.'

Then Isaac was lost for breath as Cleve grabbed the boy.

'Are you my dad?'

'You bet.'

'Spitting image,' agreed Auntie Betty.

Josie was watching from the other end of the shearing shed. Her attention had been caught when Paula led Isaac away, but she drew back. Cleve knew she was watching. He looked up and met the woman's gaze across the great gloomy space with a look so intent that it made the child turn to see what was in the man's eyes.

'Mum!' called Isaac. 'Mum, come over here.'

Josie stepped slowly forward into the circle around Cleve. 'Now you know,' she said.

'He's great,' replied Cleve. 'He's a real credit to you.' He was filled with joy.

'He takes after you in so many ways,' she said, almost complaining.

'He'll have a better life than mine, but. Won't you, boy?'

'I'm sorry, Cleve. I didn't let you know. I just couldn't.'

'What's done is done,' said Cleve, brushing her words away. 'It's a bloody miracle.'

Auntie Betty threw back her arms and clapped them down around Josie, her bosom rumbling with laughter. 'All this time, girlie. You're a dark one.'

Then a door opened in the side of the shed, a banner of sky, and Ziggy's voice boomed to the back stalls. 'Come and get it!'

The Chinese ate and drank the most heartily, although they protested that they were unaccustomed to sheep meat. Deputy-Minister Yang had developed a taste for Australian beer and couldn't get enough of it. Mr Yao kept him company. His face flushed, the Deputy-Minister became vocal with ideas for the future. He ordered René to start negotiating with the Aboriginal women to buy their land from them, if it was theirs now and no longer the property of the lady with long hair. When René translated the message, Auntie Betty took immediate offence. She rose to her newly won proprietorship and said, 'Tell them it's not for sale.'

Deputy-Minister Yang took the old woman's refusal as a challenge. In consultation with Mr Yao and Xiao Jing, he started to bargain. A leasing arrangement subsidised by the Australian government in the name of aid was a deal not to miss. He did not want to stop at Lake Moorna National Park, he wanted the whole of Whitepeeper, all ninety-five thousand acres, on which he could envisage tens of thousands of sheep being run by a hardy gang of shepherds imported from the grasslands of western China. Mrs Guan and the two junior Chinese ridiculed the idea. Who would want to live in this featureless place?

Then it was Deputy-Minister Yang's turn to be offended. Alex explained to Xiao Jing that the land was already tied up. The first leasing option went to the existing managers of the property, Masterman Holdings, represented by Elspeth. The Chinese would still have to talk to her about any possibility of negotiating a sub-lease. Since China was a major market for Mastermans' wool, it was unlikely they would help the Chinese become wool-producing rivals. Xiao Jing passed on Alex's comments in heated Chinese to Deputy-Minister Yang, who became redder in the face, interpreting this attitude as discrimination and contrary to Australia's free trade principles.

Then René stood up and accused the Chinese delegation of wilful misunderstanding. He refused to assist in any discussion aimed at lessening the benefit the Aboriginal people would derive from the return of their land. He spoke as a patriotic Australian, one of the masses, knowing how that stance would enrage the Chinese, who persisted in seeing Comrade Bao as one of them.

Cleve told René to shut up. Whatever deals the traditional landowners made with their land was their business. It was their right to respond to offers. It was up to them to decide whether they wanted Chinese tenants. They had the right to veto Masterman Holdings.

In officious Mandarin Mr Yao warned that, as the delegation's assigned interpreter, René was under Deputy-Minister Yang's authority and was obliged to obey instructions. René retorted that he was in the pay of the Australian government and reminded the Chinese that they were guests in *his* country. The Chinese delegation was under Citizen René's control if they wanted to get technical about it. They must submit to his advice.

Australians did not know what was good for them, insisted Deputy-Minister Yang, talking business pure and simple. The Aborigines had no civilisation worthy of the name and were as lazy and useless as their white colonialist masters. The land would be wasted unless it was taken out of all their hands. What was the meaning of friendship between Australia and China, the Deputy-Minister wanted to know, if it did not mean letting the Chinese people share some of Australia's empty space?

René could tell from the look on Xiao Jing's face that she could not help agreeing with the Deputy-Minister, who was her father's crony after all. She could see a bright future for herself managing the whole growing investment from Sydney while enjoying that city's enviable lifestyle.

'With due respect,' Ralph Kincaid interjected, 'I think you ought to know that one of the closer relatives of the two ancient human skeletons that belong to the Lake Moorna site is your Peking Man. It may well be that he originated here.'

When this was translated, the Chinese laughed in chorus.

'Not *Sinanthropus Pekinensis*,' Kincaid said loudly. 'That's erectus. The gracile *Homo sapiens* skull at Zhoukoudian that came a bit later.'

'Forty thousand years,' said René. 'Did you hear that? People have been here longer than your civilisation has even existed. Without question. You must respect that.'

'Forty thousand years,' Mrs Guan repeated in English, laughing still. 'Really? Impossible!'

'If they are really Chinese,' indicated Mr Yao, the cosmopolitan member of the delegation, 'then we are right to make them part of China.'

'But they are *not* Chinese,' said Alex. 'You could never say that.'

'Then why is the place called the Walls of China?' asked Xiao Jing.

'The Walls of China were only a dream to those poor exiled workers,' Elspeth went on, trying to be helpful.

'Maybe the bones are their bones,' suggested Xiao Jing.

'Those bones could conceivably belong to the original civilisation of *Homo sapiens sapiens*,' pronounced the Professor. 'It could be the mother site. The Garden of Eden.'

Kincaid's lay-down misére was a surreal idea in view of the dry unvarying lakebed and the desiccated, grotesque hills of sand they had seen earlier.

'Do you believe that humanity emerged only in one place?' Josie asked.

'It's a fairytale,' said Jane. 'If you believe that, you'll believe anything.'

'Yeah,' shouted Paula, supporting Jane's gutsy approach.

'It's no harder than believing that people popped up all over the place at the same time like mushrooms, is it?' argued Alex.

'In the beginning God created Heaven and Earth,' intoned Auntie Betty.

'What about our Dreaming, Auntie?' threw in Paula.

'However it happened, there's only one humanity,' said Josie conclusively.

Then Cleve, with wavering conviction in his voice, croaked, 'It begins here. It still does. You can believe in it if you want to. Some of us have no choice. This place has always been the beginning and the ending.'

How else could he explain his feeling that this country, separate from time immemorial, unique in all its forms, was connected in barely known ways with other continents and other worlds, as if here history was joined in one creation with all that lay beyond?

René Baum had never felt so brave as in sticking up for his own place and time, putting it out of reach of the Chinese. He got his anthology of Tang dynasty poetry and went off to find a shady spot in which to savour the time when China had been the apogee of world civilisation. He had drunk nothing at lunch and his mind was lucid. He was satisfied that he had played his part in a revolution.

The Chinese group retired to the manager's house for a nap.

Alex, drowsy in the heat, crawled back to his cot in the shearers' quarters. He lay with the door open and the air singing. He heard Josie go inside her room and close the door. He was restless and wanted to communicate with her, but no sound came from her room. If she was sleeping, he only wanted to look at her. He knocked lightly on the wall.

'Come in,' she said softly.

He closed the door behind him when he went in and sat down beside her, laying a hand gently on her skin. She put her arms around him and kissed him. How easy it was. Looking longingly into his eyes, she said she loved him. He replied adoringly, 'Oh Josie.'

'Stay with me,' she said, squeezing his hand.

It was what Alex wanted to do – to stay with Josie and her son and make their lives part of his. Even his work would be different, if he stayed on, now he understood what was in his charge. He could turn around the Department of Immigration's old frontier mentality, with a moral conception of what he held in custody, not only for these people – for a space and a time – but for creative humankind in all its disarray everywhere.

On the other side of the wall Ziggy lay in a heavy afternoon doze. Through the flimsy timbers he heard the groaning of the bed springs, the slapping of skin, the breathing and moaning as Josie and Alex's love-making communicated its pulse to him and made him horny, made him smile, made him want to live in the flow of essence that carried him along, bobbing on top of a fountain, a single gushing source.

No one could be bothered about what Ralph Kincaid was up to when he returned to the site at the Walls of China to take more precise measurements of the location of the twin crates. It was just too hot. Jane said he would become delirious out there anyway. Delirium would throw all his measurements into disarray.

The other empty bed in the shearers' quarters that afternoon was Isaac's. Cleve honoured his promise. What else were fathers for? The little aircraft trundled down the corrugated dirt airstrip and lifted into the air without warning and Isaac's stomach lifted too. They rose higher and higher, and although there were no strings to hold them up, the boy felt secure beside his pilot-father. Strapped into his seat, he listened to Cleve's commentary through the headphones as the plane circled out over the dead lake and followed the lunette of sand, the Walls of China, which looked from the air like a long pink muscle exposed above the earth. Each pink cone of sand, each gully, each bushy mound, was clear and close, and patterns emerged that were invisible from the ground, tracks and circles, rings of pink, orange, fawn and white, midden sites and buried fence lines marked by rotten posts; formations repeated as one dry lake pan after another was revealed, scattered in a chain to northwards, across the length of the world heritage area.

Then the plane banked and turned. They were heading in the direction of the river that ran not far from the southern boundary of the property, where there was a real lake, fringed with luminous sand and swaying groves of willow and bamboo and native pine. 'The inland sea,' Cleve said into the microphone.

The water's surface reflected like mother-of-pearl as Isaac peered down at the plane's little black shadow, not much more than an eagle's, crossing the water.

Completing the circle of flight back to the homestead they hit the ground with a bump. When the plane came to a halt, Isaac heaved with disbelief. 'I can fly!'

'You can fly, man,' confirmed Cleve, giving the boy a cuddle. 'You can fly any time you want!'

Isaac ran to tell his mother, banging straight in through the closed door.

'I went up in the plane,' he cried. It scarcely stopped his excitement to see his mother and Alex lying bare together on the bed.

'I know,' she said. 'I could hear the engine roaring. Was it great, darling?'

'We didn't crash.'

Josie laughed. 'Were you scared?'

'I trusted him,' replied the boy solemnly. Isaac would never forget. His father was a pilot. His father had wings.

Jane looked up at Cleve through her dark glasses. She was lying on a banana chair in the shade of the verandah. 'Women all over you,' she quipped.

He ducked his head as he passed, annoyed by her comment. 'Too right.'

'Elspeth's inside,' Jane called after him. 'Go and talk to her. You haven't had a kind word for her all day.'

Elspeth lay in her bedroom, exhausted from the exertions of the day – and from the emotion of it all. She lay with her head on a puffed-up white pillow on the dark double bed. The shutters were closed. The pillow was damp where she had been crying. Her long hair sprayed out around her face. She stared at the ceiling as she listened. She had left the door to the hallway ajar in case . . . but she did not want to be disturbed. She was surrounded by people, invited and uninvited, to celebrate an occasion that was intended as a reunion of sorts as well as a last farewell and had not worked out at all as she imagined. Even her own understanding of the celebration had become confused. It was farewell to her old life and old arrangements in which she was a representative of her family, her class, a line of ancestors who were greedy, oppressive ghosts. She was the one who had toppled their world. Not for the sake of destruction, but to conserve even more important things. She had not expected to feel so alone, with almost no one who understood what this day meant to her. Only Jane had any idea and Jane looked from outside, the artist, sceptical of the sensation of outflowing that Elspeth had hoped to experience. She missed her mother, who knew these conflicts of old, and wished her father had not broken his promise to be there. It terrified her as she lay on the bed that the answer might rest with Cleve, who had behaved so badly to her that day, sulkily turning away, with too much confusion in himself for it ever to be clear. Alex had brought Josie Ryan with Cleve's child deliberately to stir things up. The boy's eyes darted, the way Cleve's did, connecting one thing with another. Cleve had talked of Josie with only a kind of sorrowing sympathy, then he was gone. He had never said a word. What right did she have to expect him to be honest with her? She was happy, now he had his son, but where did that leave her? The low buzz of his plane had drilled at her head. He was the pillar on which everything rested now.

With a warning knock, Cleve walked into the room.

'Are you all right, Elspeth?'

'Just tell me,' she said with urgency. 'Be honest with me. He's yours, isn't he? That little boy.'

'I never dreamed he existed. I'll be a lucky man if I can watch him grow up. I didn't think it mattered.'

'Everything matters, Cleve. Why didn't you keep in touch with her?'

'She wouldn't let me. She ran away.'

'It must have been hard for her.'

'She didn't want anything from me.'

'A kid needs a father.'

'It's Alex who did this to get at us,' Cleve stammered.

Elspeth screwed up her face and shook her head. 'He did it because he wants Josie for himself.'

She ran her fingers over the bare flesh of his upper arm, where he sat, bent over, beside her on the bed. 'I've wanted to touch these marks ever since I was a girl.'

'It tickles. Gives me the creeps. Don't ever look down on me,' he warned. She counted the five wide inoculation rings.

'Don't you ever come to hate me either,' she retorted. 'Will you? This is yours now. All of it.'

It was as if they were binding each other with promises.

'I think I'm wanted outside,' he said. He went out into the hall-way. Paula was bustling through to the kitchen.

'Ah-ha,' she nodded at him cheekily. 'There you are.'

'Where are your women?' he asked her.

'They're yarning in the living room. Time to take them home.'

Cleve followed her. 'Paula, wait a sec. I've been meaning to ask you. Where do you come from?'

'I've been all over the place.'

'I mean – originally?'

She was the same swarthy colour as Cleve. She thought of her-self as a bitsa. A bit of everything. 'I spent a bit of time in the city. Grew up there. Then I came back up the country. I don't know. This is my area now,' she added firmly.

'Down around the river, you mean?'

'Nah, I'm not from the river. Other way. Up round Moree's where my people were. Further north. The dry country. That's what they tell me.'

The three elders were sitting comfortably in the big armchairs in the living room, gossiping and giggling, each with a gilt cup and saucer from Elspeth's china cabinet in her lap. They had been drinking tea there for hours through all the goings-on with no one taking any notice of them.

'Been up in that plane of yours, eh?' smirked Auntie Betty when Cleve came in.

The women grinned at him.

'Cleve's been asking which mob I belong to,' Paula told them with a lilt in her voice.

'Our mob,' declared Dorothy Ah Kin.

'Our mob too,' chimed in Mona Riley.

'Paula's a good name,' said Cleve. 'So's Pauline.'

'I used to be Pauline. I hated that name. Changed it meself, to Paula.'

Cleve hesitated before he spoke. 'I've been looking for a Pauline.'

She tossed her head at him. 'Well, I'm not Pauline. I'm Paula. Paula Morgan,' she insisted.

Cleve stuck out his lower lip. 'Where does Morgan come from? Is it your married name?'

'Now that's a long story. I didn't want to keep my married name, and I didn't want to go back to the name I had before that, which was Boon, because I never knew where it come from, so I took the name of my auntie up in Moree, which is Morgan. So I'm Paula Morgan.'

Cleve did not know how far to push it. 'But you could be some-one different.'

'Not as far as I'm concerned. I'm Paula Morgan and I come from up around Moree. So I'm not the person you're looking for, okay?'

'Maybe you'll do anyway,' he said to her.

Paula was putting the women's things into bags. 'What do you mean?'

'Maybe you could be my sister.'

Paula laughed. 'No, I don't think so. Yeah, I could be your sister, but no thanks, mate. I don't need anything like that. I'm not inter-ested. You know what I mean? I know who I am. Look, I've got to deliver these ladies home.'

'Don't you get it?' asked Cleve, casting his gaze around the com-modious, overfurnished living-room, the armchairs with their chintz cushions to match the new sofa cover that replaced the old one destroyed by fire. 'They *are* at home. This is theirs now. It's ours. It's yours.'

'Whoever I am?' asked Paula.

'It's up to you who you say you are.' Cleve wasn't letting go.

'In time,' said Auntie Betty, heaving herself from the soft depths of the armchair on to two shaky legs. The cushions gave a sigh. 'We'll come back another day, eh girls? When the accommodation suits us better.'

Cleve sat on the verandah surveying the land as the shadows lengthened. Its colours softened at the end of the day and its contours became sharper. Detail of sparse scrubby trees and low blue-grey spiky grass jumped out at him. He watched an eaglehawk fight for territory with a crow round the stump of an old peppercorn by the bore in the corner of the home paddock. The eaglehawk was showier, more ungainly, kindlier than the crow. Feathers ruffled, he made a noisy flap. The crow, sleek, bright of eye, sharp of beak, quicker and more ruthless, would win.

It was only yesterday that he had flown from Bankstown airport, after bearing his brother's coffin from the hearse. In never really knowing Danny, he had failed him. All he could do now was remember and work so that the denial of an ordinary human life to Danny was not inflicted on any more of their people. He needed time to feel the weight of the great act of restitution that must be made, its justice and rightness and irreversibility. What further gains would be achieved were up to the likes of him.

The Chinese delegation wanted to go to the Chinese restaurant at the club in Wentworth. It was two hours' drive away. They were interested in the poker machines at the casino on the riverbank there. They were adamant that they could not eat another meal of Australian mutton or their health would suffer. They were constipated already. They wanted chicken, fish and rice.

It was the night of the full moon and Elspeth said the lunette would be magical by moonlight. René had told Xiao Jing he refused to go and eat with the delegation. Deputy-Minister Yang came to see René where he was reading under a tree, suggesting that perhaps there was some misunderstanding. Comrade Bao had been a friend of China, he understood the Chinese people, he was practically Chinese, insinuated Yang. As delegation leader, the Deputy-Minister insisted that René leave this primitive place and accompany them for dinner. But René had refused outright. They were kidding themselves if they thought they would get edible Chinese tucker at the club in Wentworth.

He said that Chalky was quite capable of driving them there and bringing them back safely anyway. They would not get lost and since Xiao Jing was going along to help there would be no problems of language or culture. But Chalky had consumed more beer at lunchtime than anyone else and had fallen in a drunken heap. René shrugged his shoulders. He was exhilarated by his new-found non-cooperation. He did not care who disciplined him later for displaying a bad attitude. He was a free man, an Australian, a larrikin at heart.

Deputy-Minister Yang retreated in a huff and sent Director Yao and Mrs Guan to wag fingers at René. But he remained obdurate. If Chalky couldn't drive, it was up to one of the Chinese. Then Xiao Jing came to plead with him. René hinted that she should stay to enjoy the full moon with him as it rose over one of the most ancient places of the earth. Her shining eyes were irresistible. But Xiao Jing said it was her duty to accompany Deputy-Minister Yang, on whom her future depended. She criticised René for not coming to her rescue. Becoming coquettish, she ran her fingernails over his neck, wheedling him to come. She said she would never forgive him if he refused.

'It would be much more romantic if just the two of us stayed back,' René responded. 'We would have the full moon and the manager's place all to ourselves. It's the opportunity of a lifetime.' He was as stubborn as a mule.

The other Chinese were determined not to lose face at the abandonment of protocol. The junior bureaucrat, destined to learn the art of sheep shearing, tried to rouse Chalky from his stupor. Deputy-Minister Yang announced that they were leaving and not coming back. He ordered all their things to be loaded into the minibus. When he went looking for someone to farewell, he found

Cleve in his reverie on the verandah, who barely noticed what the Chinese man was trying to say. The negotiations would continue, Deputy-Minister Yang promised. Later, later. But neither thank you nor goodbye was said when René came over to help out.

'That's it for now,' René translated for Deputy-Minister Yang. Cleve just grunted.

Xiao Jing shook hands with René in a rather formal goodbye. When he went to kiss her, she ducked. If he would not do her bidding in a simple matter of accompanying the delegation to a Chinese restaurant, he could never be trusted with secret innermost affairs between nations. He would never pass the Chinese Ministry of State Security or her powerful father's other tests. An uncouth, uncompliant, clever Australian, Comrade Bao was no use to the Chinese people – no good to anyone, including himself. Like a cut snake, he was best left alone.

Director Yao warned René that a report on his insubordination would be sent to the foreign ministries of both countries and relevant measures would be taken. Then Deputy-Minister Yang made his exit in the high dudgeon of an insulted general from a Peking opera, careering down the road in the yellow minibus, with Xiao Jing at the wheel. René stood alone in the yard and waved. At the end of the dusty road indigestible celestial food and diabolical gambling machines awaited them. Groggy Chalky had sworn in terror at the vision of a gook who tried to rouse him, then lapsed into deeper stupor. They left him stretched out under the shearing shed. Xiao Jing patted her brow with a tissue as the minibus rocked from side to side. René wondered if they would ever make it. He had let them down. He had betrayed them. Or had they betrayed him?

Xiao Jing had never let on that she could drive. They did not come classier than her in China, or anywhere else in his experience. He felt more than a twinge of regret at letting her go. His world might not have been much revolutionised, but he was changed and he wanted to share it. He wanted to roll in the dirt and rejoice, as if he were suddenly back in his parents' yard in

Bellevue Hill and could roll himself up into a ball in the fragrance of wild fennel.

He skipped off to confess to Alex that the Chinese delegation had done a bunk. He would take full responsibility for any diplomatic incident that resulted from the deep offence given to Deputy-Minister Yang. But he could not stop laughing wickedly. He was free to view the full moon rising above those illusory walls of sand or he was nothing.

~

As the sun went lower in the sky, the sand dunes were accentuated by elongated shadows, the red end of the spectrum intensified and the westward face of the lunette was transformed into hundreds of sharp little peaks as the wrinkled skin of earth seemed to loosen and tremble like milk about to boil. In that rosy light the colours of things became impossible to fix. Sculptures could be elephant-grey, warm cream or butter. They could glow rose-pink as the whole embankment responded to the sun's last ardent rays. The rumpled surface could be immodest drapery about to be plucked away and burned. Beneath might be ice. As the sky glowed, the first chill could be felt, cold air mimicking the wind's patterns of cascading water, water frozen in motion, runnels of sand shot through with icy glass. It was through a fantasy landscape they walked as, turning from white to orange, the sun made the hillside tumuli gather close like a chorus of warriors on an opera stage, or the ghosts of all the dead who might be buried beneath those dunes, rising up in flowing veils of sand, smeared with the red ochre that gave meaning to their consumption by fire and their dispersal as ash in the bitter wind.

They walked among these forms in silent perplexity, as Elspeth led on to the highest point from where to watch the plunging descent of the sun into the extremity of the stretching plain. To turn away was to miss a spectacular transience, brass-green along the horizon line, the sky violet behind and the sand flesh-pink. The horizontal rays of the sun braided the whole low plain with a line of tinsel that crept just ahead of the deep hunting shadow. As it hit the earth, that dying ball was squeezed into a fat thumb of fiery jelly with a pointed star at its core. Then the sun became a flat white door into the tunnel of infinity. The horizon flashed green. The sun was a frill of rose, gone into blackness. The breeze picked up. The spiky trees sprouting from the armpits of the place began to moan. The sky turned a deeper violet, with no sign of any moon, and the sandhills were flat, grey and indecipherable.

Ziggy struggled to light a match in the breeze. René found a steep fall of sand and could not resist rolling down a surface that looked as smooth as silk. He rolled himself up into a ball and somer-saulted forward, head first, tumbling in a parabola until he was quite dizzy. When he was at last at rest, he slowly opened his eyes to see where he was. The world was skew-whiff. The sand had its light, the sky was dark. Then he latched on to a star, the only star in the sky, to take his bearing. He shook the sand out of his hair and sniffed. There was a bush in bloom somewhere near him. It was sweet and pungent at once, filling the air around him. It was the wild fennel that had grown beyond the garden wall. He was imagining things. It could not possibly be the same. It was some other thing. Wild mint or wild sage. He stayed there, curled on the sand, inhaling that perfumed air, afraid of how disconsolate he would be when the moment vanished.

Alex was wondering about his experience of the sundown, about how it might differ from that of others, not only the people he was with but all the other people who had occupied the place through time, whoever they were. The sky had been different once, the land had been different. Over time it had been unimaginably, inconceivably different, and people had been different too. Knowledge itself had been different. Yet those other experiences were also connected with his and he could only begin to know them through being, in a puzzling sense, one of their heirs, squat-ting on their shoulders, the one who was in their place, his con-sciousness registering it as theirs had, bearing forward traces of dreams and nightmares that were somewhere the same. If the first people had been here, then he was the latest in their line, brought to this place by the long, chaotic processes of humanity through time, as the man sitting next to him on the peak of sand, Cleve, had also come here. What they made of it was what it was, and what it would become, for a time, until the next ones came along. In the moment the sun set, the sandhills became transparent, turning to pink glass, for the briefest moment, when everyone was looking away, before they vanished again into grey compacted sand.

'It's good that we put those bones back,' said Alex in a low voice. 'The place feels much better.'

'What was that?' asked Cleve, in a trance.

'Can I ask you something?' Alex went on. 'Josie and I are going to stay together. If it's all right with you?'

'What's it got to do with me?'

'I'll have charge of your son. Can you trust me with that?' But there was no reply. 'You'll have your own job to do,' Alex continued. 'Can we work something out?'

'It depends,' came Cleve's reply. Then the wind picked up, resuscitating the moaning of the trees, amplifying it.

'You put a curse on me once, long ago, when we were kids,' said Alex. 'You remember that?'

'I haven't forgotten.'

'Is it over now? Is that gone?'

Cleve grinned at Alex's plea. 'You put the curse on yourself. That's what you people have always done. You people reckon that our people are a cursed and tragic people. That's your problem. Your doing. Always has been. You're the accursed ones. We're okay. We've had a bloody shocking time of it, but we're okay. We're surviving. It's simple. What our people want has always been simple. Give it to us and there'll be no curse.'

'What *do* you want?' Alex asked.

'Most of our people would be happy to get a bit of land that no one can take away from them. With a proper house on it. A job. A healthy kid or three. Nice shoes for the kids to wear. That would be a start.'

'Then this is a start,' said Alex.

'Lake Moorna? It's out in the middle of nowhere, mate. Yeah, it's a start. If no one tells us what to do with it.'

'Look!' called Elspeth. She stood and hollered into the darkness. Sitting on her lone peak a little distance away, she had rotated through one hundred and eighty degrees to be ready for the moonrise. 'The moon!' Then she walked over to sit with Cleve and Alex.

The others came trudging up the sand in response to her summons. They settled in a line on their vantage-point to hold vigil. The spot they were watching was diametrically opposite where the sun had gone down, as if a balance had come into operation.

The moon oozed over the horizon to form a hesitant pearl ball that silvered the sky in its vicinity. Then it just floated off, lifting through the air on its voyage. For a time it seemed to approach, returning like the lost lover of legend, but with rising it diminished, growing as remote and airy as a freed balloon. Ziggy burst into tears over the beauty of this gift from the darkness. Sitting with the others, he felt quite alone. He did not take their presence into account. It was for him that all this was happening, just him, in this place that was his.

Alex strove to see what quivered within the moon. There was the resemblance of a skull, grown over with new flesh, as if the skull was re-forming into a head on this journey through the sky. Then the moon winked at him, open and shut, like the click of a shutter. He turned to Josie who was looking back at him, as if she had seen what he had seen. Then she asked her son what he saw in the moon. Isaac would not say. So Jane asked Cassie. And she would not say either.

'That's it,' said Elspeth, leaning over to Cleve and hauling him to his feet. 'Let's go.'

Cleve charged down the sandhill with Elspeth's hand tight in his.

'Who-ah!' she cried, with no control of where her feet were landing until he stopped and she was wrapped around him.

He spoke in her ear. 'It's not all mine. It's ours. We've got to have a go at it together. Is that what you want me to say?'

Elspeth's eyes glowed at his in the darkness. She loved him.

'The full moon of the twelfth month and the last day of the year,' said René, standing and stretching. 'We better be on our way.'

'Only if we can come back later,' pleaded Jane. She already had her eye on seeing the morning-star come out and dawn appearing. The lunette of sand was as if watered by the moonlight. 'Tell me what you see in the moon,' she demanded of Isaac and Cassie, taking the two children by the hand as they walked down the hill. *Tell me what you see!*

But the children, who knew what they saw and would remember all their lives, were keeping the secret.

AUTHOR'S NOTE

This novel would not exist in its present form without the work, inspiration and help of many people. I wish to thank all those people who generously provided information or made comments on the text and everyone involved with the editing and publication of the book. *The Custodians* is a work of imagination and as its author I am responsible for the fictional reinterpretation given to details and other suggestions drawn from primary reference material. The novel takes place against a background of historical events and I gratefully acknowledge the following sources which readers may wish to consult further: above all, the *Report of the Royal Commission into Aboriginal Deaths in Custody*, in particular the *Regional Report of Inquiry in New South Wales, Victoria and Tasmania* and the *Report of the Inquiry into the Death of Malcolm Charles Smith*, both by Commissioner the Honourable J. H. Wootten, AC, QC (Australian Government Publishing Service, Canberra 1991) and the related documentary *Who Killed Malcolm Smith?* (Film Australia, 1992); also 'Coming up out of the nhaalya: reminiscences of the life of Eliza Kennedy' by Eliza Kennedy and Tamsin Donaldson,

Aboriginal History, vol. 6, no.1, 1982; *A History of the Aboriginal People of the Willandra Lakes region* by Jeanette Hope, Tamsin Donaldson and Luise Hercus, Australian Institute for Aboriginal and Torres Strait Islander Studies, Canberra, 1986 (unpublished report to the Department of Environment and Planning, New South Wales); Gillian Cowlishaw, *Black, White or Brindle* (Cambridge University Press, 1988); *The Lost Children*, edited by Coral Edwards and Peter Read (Doubleday, Sydney, 1989); and 'The Sixties', by Lyall Munro, in *Republica 2*, edited by George Papaellinas (Angus & Robertson, Sydney, 1995).

Tom Ljonga, in the epigraph, is quoted from T. G. H. Strehlow's *Journals*, Book I, 24 May 1932, as cited by Philip Jones in 'Namatjira: Traveller between two worlds', *The Heritage of Namatjira*, edited by Jane Hardy, J.V.S. Megaw and M. Ruth Megaw (William Heinemann Australia, Melbourne, 1992). Lines from *Duino Elegies* by Rainer Maria Rilke, translated by J.B.Leishman are quoted by kind permission of the Estate of J.B.Leishman and Chatto & Windus.

Nicholas Jose
Sydney, 1997

DATE DUE